LOST MEMORIES

"We don't know how you got here, Ms. LaPorte. You walked into Emergency and collapsed. Did someone bring you? Did you drive yourself?"

Gemma moved her head slowly from side to side and felt a twinge of pain. "I don't remember."

Will paused, regarding her with dark, liquid eyes. She could sense his strength and knew he was good at his job. A tracker. Someone who never gave up. Someone dogged and relentless. She shivered involuntarily as he said, "You don't remember the circumstances that brought you here."

"No."

"What's your last memory?"

Gemma thought about it a minute. "I was looking out the window and thinking we were drowning in rain. It was a downpour. The dirt was like concrete and the water was pouring over it in sheets."

The deputy was silent for so long that Gemma felt her anxiety rise. She sensed that he was deliberating on an answer.

"What?" she asked.

"It hasn't rained for three days . . ."

Books by Nancy Bush

CANDY APPLE RED

ELECTRIC BLUE

ULTRAVIOLET

UNSEEN

Published by Kensington Publishing Corporation

NANCY BUSH

ZEBRA BOOKS
KENSINGTON PUBLISHING CORP.
http://www.kensingtonbooks.com

ZEBRA BOOKS are published by

Kensington Publishing Corp.
850 Third Avenue
New York, NY 10022

All Kensington titles, imprints, and distributed lines are available at special quantity discounts for bulk purchases for sales promotion, premiums, fund-raising, educational, or institutional use.

Special book excerpts or customized printings can also be created to fit specific needs. For details, write or phone the office of the Kensington Special Sales Manager: Attn. Special Sales Department. Kensington Publishing Corp., 850 Third Avenue, New York, NY 10022. Phone: 1-800-221-2647.

ISBN-13: 978-1-4201-0340-3
ISBN-10: 1-4201-0340-7

First Zebra Books Mass-Market Printing: April 2009

10 9 8 7 6 5 4 3 2 1

Printed in the United States of America

Prologue

A yellow moon rose over the line of fir trees, so close and huge that it seemed like an artist's distorted vision, not the real thing. He watched it climb slowly upward through dispassionate eyes. It sent an uneven strip of light across the field behind his two-room home and glimmered in the pond that was ruffled by a light wind.

As if in response to the moon's appearance, a light switched on in the main house across the field. Equally yellow. An evil color. A witch's color. He was glad the house was so far away, wished it even farther.

For a moment he saw her standing in the field, dark, near-black hair flowing around her shoulders. She wore her witch's garb and she stared back at him, her eyes black pits, her mouth curved.

"C'mere, boy," she said, and he wanted to go, but she was looking beyond him. She wasn't beckoning him. She'd never asked for him.

Still, she stripped off her clothes and melted into the pond. A moment of shadowy reflection and then just moonlight.

She was a witch. She had to die. And he was the hunter.

He gazed hard at the moon, now glowing a ghostly blue-white, shed of its earthly restraints, higher in the sky, smaller, more intense. He closed his eyes and saw its afterimage on the inside of his eyelids.

Witches had to die. He'd already sent two back to the hell they'd sprung from. But there were more. And some of them were filled with an evil so intense it was like they burned from the inside out.

He'd found the one who'd stolen from him. He'd been on a search for her, but she'd eluded him until last night. In a moment of pure coincidence, he'd seen her walking across the street. Wearing her witch's garb, hair flying behind her and tangling in the wind that swooped down, bitterly cold for such a mild autumn.

He'd followed her and it had been a mistake because he'd gotten too close. She'd sensed him. She gazed hard at him and he turned sharply away, afraid she'd recognize him. But then she'd been the one to run away, out the door as if Satan were at her heels. And she'd put herself out of his reach, but it wouldn't be for long because now he knew where she haunted. Now he knew where to find her. Soon, he would strip her bare, crush her naked body with his, thrust himself into her again and again as she howled and scratched and screamed.

Then he would throw back his head and roar because he was the hunter. A wolf. Hunting his prey.

Jaw tense, he threw another look at the moon, now a

white, hard dot in a black sky. The natives called it a hunter moon. The full moon seen in the month of October.

October . . .

The witch's month.

He was the wolf. And it was time to hunt the witch.

Chapter One

She wished him dead.

She knew about him. Witnessed the way his gaze ran lustfully over some preteen girl. Saw how his eyes glued to her athletic limbs and small breasts, how his lips parted and his cock grew hard.

But wishing wasn't enough. It almost was, but it wasn't quite. Sometimes wishing needed a little push. So, she waited for him to go to an unlucky place, the kind of place where bad things happened. Deaths. Accidents. Poisonous secrets. She knew about those places better than anyone because bad things had happened to her at an unlucky place a long time ago, and she'd spent many formative years getting payback for those bad things.

She waited with her jaw set. She was good at action, not patience. But today it had all come together, his unlucky place had materialized: a soccer field, with lots of tweens, their limbs flashing in nylon shorts and jerseys. She herself was very lucky and when people asked her name, which wasn't often because she avoided encounters with strangers as a rule, she told them, "Lucky," and they generally oohed and aahed and said what a great name it was.

People were stupid, as a rule.

The soccer fields were full of young bodies. A jamboree was taking place: kids of varying ages playing half-hour games and then moving on to another field to challenge another team. The boys were playing on the north-side fields, over by the water tower. The girls were closer in, on the hard-packed dirt of the south-side fields—fields that looked as if they'd been forgotten by the parks department. Fields good enough for girls, not for boys.

Her lip curled. Figures, she thought. She wasn't a man-hater, but she had definite thoughts about certain members of the male sex. She was responsible for the deaths of several of their gender and didn't regret any of them.

She waited in her stolen car. Well, not stolen exactly. *Appropriated* for a specific purpose. She'd learned a few things during the twenty-seven years she'd been on the planet. She knew how to take care of herself. She could accurately fire a gun up to twenty yards. Well, fairly accurately. And she could break into and steal older-model vehicles—the only kind she would drive because she distrusted air bags. Those things could kill you. She knew a guy who would dismantle them for her, which was a good thing, because it was getting harder and harder to find vintage cars available for her purposes, although she currently had a ready supply from Carl's Automotive and Car Rental. Hunk O'Junks. That's how they were advertised by the amateurish spray-painted sign posted off Highway 26, about fifteen miles east of Seaside, Oregon. Hunk O'Junks. Yessirree. They could be rented for $19.99 a day, but Lucky didn't bother with that. A sorry line of tired-looking vehicles they were, too, but they served the purpose. No one noticed when they were gone. No one commented when they were returned.

Cars were a simple matter to hot-wire. And she was adept

at using a flat bar to slide down the inside of the window and pop the lock. It was then child's play to dig under the dash, yank the wires, spark the ignition and drive away.

But the Hunk O'Junks were perfect in one more aspect: the owner left the keys under the mat. In the early hours of this morning she'd simply helped herself to the one farthest from the flickering vapor light at the corner of the automotive garage and driven away. The horny mechanic and sometime car thief who'd shown her the ropes and introduced her to Carl's Automotive had been as unfaithful as a rutting bull. She'd used him as a means to an end and they'd almost parted friends. But he'd pushed it, had actually attempted to rape her. Lucky had been down that road before and nobody was going to try *that* again and live. She'd grabbed a nearby table lamp's electrical cord and wrapped it around his neck. He'd been bullish enough to scarcely notice, so involved was he in spreading her thighs and jamming himself into her. She'd pulled the cord taut with all her strength, with all the rage of injustice she'd nursed from years of abuse. He passed out and she held on. It hadn't been his face she was envisioning; it was someone else's. Someone faint in her memory, yet dark and looming. Twenty minutes later she'd surfaced slowly, as if awakening from a long illness, her fingers numb, her mind clearing. She didn't have much faith that anyone would believe her about the attempted rape, so she gathered up the lamp and its cord from the dirty and sparse living room he called home, wiped down everything she'd touched, and left someone else to find his body. She'd made the mistake of entering his home after this, their last car-thieving lesson, because she'd begun to think they were friends.

She hadn't made that mistake since.

Now, she slouched behind the wheel of her current Hunk O'Junk, her gaze centered on a light brown van parked near the jamboree parking lot exit. This maybe wasn't the best venue for what she'd planned, but it could be worse. And it was where he trolled. *And* it had that unlucky feel she could almost taste. Edward Letton wasn't aware that he was being followed. Didn't know she'd found him out, that she'd tailed his van through parks and malls and schools, the environs of little girls.

Lucky had originally picked up on Letton by a means she didn't fully understand herself. They'd crossed paths in a small clothing store in Seaside, a place that specialized in beach togs and gear. She'd brushed past him and read his desire as if he'd suddenly whispered his intentions in her ear, making her skin crawl. Glancing back, she saw the way his gaze centered on a young girl who was trying hard to display her breast buds as the real deal, the tiny buttons pushed up by an underwire bra, the girl thrusting them forward, her back arched like a bow. She was around eleven. Gawky. Unformed and unsure. She both hung by her mother for protection, and stepped away from her scornfully, as if she couldn't bear the idea that Mom was so old and completely uncool.

Letton stared and stared. He was so hungry Lucky felt his lust like a living thing. It filled her senses as if he were secreting pheromones. Made her ill. So, she started following him. That day she tailed him a good fifty miles, all the way back to Hillsboro and the untidy green-gray house where he lived with his adoring, mentally-suspect wife. Not the brightest jewel on the necklace, her. Letton was some kind of middle-grade manager at a machine-parts company. Lucky had watched him from the parking lot of his workplace and followed him around, in and out of restaurants, to an all-you-can-eat place where she seated herself in the booth in front of him, her back to his. Even though he was with a co-worker she sensed he'd unerringly watched the girl in the T-shirt serving soup whose chest was so flat she could have been a child.

He didn't drive the van to work. It was parked in his garage, and Lucky didn't know about it at first. Neither did his dimwit wife. His garage was his domain. He drove a Honda

Accord to work, new enough to be reliable, old enough to be forgettable. She knew those kinds of cars well.

And then she realized he used the van when he went trolling. Nobody had to tell her what he was planning. She knew that hunger. That build-up. That need. She'd been on the receiving end of it and it hadn't been pretty.

He had almost grabbed a girl at the mall, but she was with friends and hard to snatch. Lucky had watched him, her gloved hands tensing on the wheel of her appropriated car, but he'd passed up the chance, though he'd climbed from his van and paced around it, watching with distress as his victim and friends meandered across the parking lot, ponytails flouncing, out of his reach.

But here he was, a scant week-and-a-half later. Saturday morning. Cruising past soccer fields was one of his favorite pastimes. She'd parked today's Hunk O'Junk, an early '90s model, half a block down from his house, dozing a bit as she'd risen before dawn. When he backed the van out of the drive, she let it disappear around a corner before she started to follow. He didn't try any tricky moves on the way to the fields. He drove straight to the jamboree. Once there, he circled around, parking at the end spot near the girls' fields, nose out. It was early, so Lucky parked her sedan across from him, a couple of slots down, and let him see her as she locked the vehicle and strolled across the road toward a strip mall with a coffee shop, its door open to the cool morning air. She wanted him to think she was just another soccer mom, biding time before the games, going to buy a latte or mocha.

As soon as she was across the street, she circled the east building of the strip mall and settled behind a row of arborvitae directly across from the jamboree parking lot. Hidden behind the trees, she put a pair of binoculars to her eyes, watching Letton through the foliage.

More cars arrived. Teams of boys and girls. Letton watched and waited as the girls banded into teams, running in their uniforms, blurs of red, green, yellow, and blue, young legs flashing in heavy shin guards and cleated shoes.

She had never played soccer herself. That had not been the kind of childhood she'd experienced. Mostly she'd plotted and dreamed of escape. Sometimes she had thought of murder.

Now she waited until another crush of people arrived—more vans spilling kids and equipment onto the pavement—then hurried back, blending in with the other moms, sliding into her silver car. Letton was too enthralled by the bounty of adolescent flesh to even notice her. She was pretty sure he was jacking off in the driver's seat.

The teams began to gather in groups, readying for play. Every group was a tight, wiggling pack, like a hive of bees on the move.

And then a young girl, ponytail bobbing, broke free, running across the fields toward the parking lot, her gait stuttering a bit as her cleats hit the pavement. What worked on grass didn't offer the same kind of purchase on asphalt. She was clomping toward the portable bathrooms, passing directly in front of Edward Letton's van. He called to her. Lucky had rolled her own window down and now she turned on the engine and slipped the car into gear, foot light on the brake.

"Hey, you're with the Hornets, right?" Letton called to the girl, climbing from his seat. He was obviously quoting from the back of their jerseys, which displayed their teams' names in block letters. He left the door ajar for a quick getaway. She could hear the thrum of excitement in his voice as he headed toward the side door of the van, sliding it open. His pants were still unzipped.

"Yeah?" the girl said warily.

"I've got those extra balls your coach wanted. Let me get 'em. Maybe you could take some back."

"I'm going to the bathroom."

But Letton was already reaching into the van. The girl

hesitated. A soccer ball rolled out and started heading toward her. She automatically went after it, the movement drawing her closer to the van. She picked it up and said, "I can't take it now, I'll come back for it," reaching toward him, intending to hand it to him. He didn't make a move to meet her, just waited for her to approach.

Don't go, Lucky thought, foot off the brake. *Stay back.*

The girl hesitated. Lucky could practically feel when she made the decision that Letton was "with" their team.

Before the girl could take another step forward Lucky smashed her foot down on the accelerator and jammed the horn with her fist. The car leapt forward like a runner at the gate. The girl jumped back, startled. Edward Letton forgot himself and lurched for the girl, but she'd automatically moved out of range of the silver car shooting down on them, running for the safety of the soccer fields. Letton glanced up darkly, his plan foiled, glaring murderously at Lucky. His mouth open to . . . what? Berate her for unsafe driving? He looked mad enough to kill.

She slammed into him at thirty and climbing. Threw him skyward. Threw herself forward. The steering wheel jumped from her hands. The sedan's grill grazed the back bumper of the van. Someone screamed. She grabbed the wheel hard, turning, both arms straining, sensing calamity. Then she spun past the van, tires squealing. Letton's flying body thunked off the roof of her car and bounced onto the asphalt, an acrobat without a net. He lay still.

In her rearview mirror Lucky stared hard at Letton's body. She drove away with controlled speed, slowing through a tangle of neighborhoods, weaving her way, heart slamming hot and fast in her chest, zigzagging toward Highway 26. She had to get this car out of the area and fast.

It was only when she was safely away, heading west, keeping up with fast-moving traffic, that she saw the blood on her steering wheel.

A glance in the rearview. Her face was covered with blood. The impact had smacked her face into the steering wheel. Her left eye was closing. She hadn't even noticed.

There was Windex in the back. Rags. Bleach. She would wipe up the evidence, clean herself and the car. All she had to do now was keep the growing pain and swelling under control. Her vision blurred.

She had to get to an off road near Carl's Automotive, one of the myriads of turn-outs on this winding highway through the Coast Range. Later tonight she would sneak the car back onto the weed-choked gravel lot and hope that the front grill, lights, and body weren't too damaged. The vehicle needed to stay undiscovered at the Hunk O'Junks lot for a long time.

She swiped at the blood running down her forehead, blinding her.

Not good. Not good at all.

But she was lucky. She would get away with it. She would . . .

She just hoped to hell she'd killed him.

Chapter Two

Surfacing from a yawning pit of blackness, her eyes adjusted to an unfamiliar room: cream vertical blinds, cream walls, television on a shelf bolted high on the wall, blankets covering what must be her feet, wood veneer footboard.

A hospital room.

Her heart clutched. She thought of surgery. Pain. Inside her head was a long, silent scream.

Automatically, her hand flew up and touched the bandage wrapped around her head. One eye was covered. She didn't know why, but it wasn't the first time she'd blacked out. Far from it. But this time she'd hurt herself, maybe badly. What had happened?

She had a terrible moment of not knowing who she was.

Then she remembered.

I'm lucky, she thought, memory slipping back to her, amorphous, hard to grasp, but at least it was there. At least *some* of it was there.

And she was angry. Hot fury sang through her veins,

though she couldn't immediately identify the source of her rage. But someone had to pay. She knew that.

A nurse was adjusting a monitor that was spitting out paper in a long, running stream. Red squiggles wove over the paper's lined grid. Her heartbeat. Respiration, maybe? She closed her eye and pretended to be sleeping. She wasn't ready for the inquisition, yet. Wasn't ready to find out the whys and wherefores of how she'd come to be at this hospital.

She heard the squeak of the nurse's crepe soles head toward the door. A soft whoosh of air, barely discernible, said the silent door had been opened. Not hearing it close, she carefully lifted her eyelid. As suspected, the wheelchair-wide door was ajar. Anyone could push inside and stare at her, which consumed her with worry. She had to stay awake.

The last vestiges of what seemed to be a dream tugged at her consciousness and she fought to hang on to the remnants but they were slippery and insubstantial, spider threads. She was left merely with the sensation that she was heading for a showdown, some distant and unwelcome Armageddon that was going to shatter and rearrange her world. Maybe not for the better.

But then she always felt that. Always awoke with that low-grade dread which followed the gaps in her memory. Maybe someday she would wake up and not know who she was at all. Maybe her memory would be gone for good.

What would happen then?

The door swung in noiselessly and a man in a light-tan uniform entered the room. He was with the county sheriff's department and, seeing her looking at him, he said, "Hello, ma'am. I'm Detective Will Tanninger with the Winslow County Sheriff's Department."

She nodded, eyeing him carefully. He was in his mid-thirties with dark brown hair and serious eyes, but she could see the striations at their edges, from squinting them in either laughter or against the sun. "Where am I?"

"Laurelton General Hospital. You've been admitted as a Jane Doe. Could you tell us your name?"

He was steely polite. Alarm bells rang. What had she done? It took her a long moment to come up with her name. "Gemma LaPorte." She hesitated, almost afraid to ask. "Are you here to see me?"

"We don't know how you got here, Ms. LaPorte. You walked into the ER and collapsed."

Her hand fluttered to her head once again. "Oh . . . ?"

"Did someone bring you? Did you drive yourself?"

Gemma moved her head slowly from side to side and she felt a twinge of pain. "I don't remember."

Will paused, regarding her with dark, liquid eyes. She could sense his strength and knew he was good at his job. A tracker. Someone who never gave up. Someone dogged and relentless. She shivered involuntarily as he said, "You don't remember the circumstances that brought you here?"

"No."

"What's your last memory?"

Gemma thought about it a minute. "I was making myself breakfast at home. Oatmeal and cinnamon. I was looking out the window and thinking we were drowning in rain. It was a downpour. The dirt was like concrete and the water was pouring over it in sheets."

The deputy was silent for so long that Gemma felt her anxiety rise. She sensed that he was deliberating on an answer.

"What?" she asked.

"It hasn't rained for three days."

Will Tanninger regarded the woman with the scared green eye and stark white bandage with a healthy sense of skepticism. Her skin had paled at his words. He understood about trauma-induced amnesia. More often than not, serious accident victims couldn't remember the events that led to their hospital stay. But they usually lost a few hours, not days. In Gemma LaPorte's case, he couldn't tell if this was a ploy or the truth. The half of her face he could see was swollen and bruised, blue and purple shadings of color already traveling from her injured side to the other. Even so, he could tell she was rather extraordinary looking. Smooth, prominent cheekbones and a finely sculpted nose beneath a hazel-colored eye that glinted green when hit by the hard morning light coming through a twelve-inch gap in the hospital drapes.

According to the staff, her injuries weren't as severe as they looked. Concussion. Bruising. Her face had run into something—something that could very likely be a steering wheel. Was she the woman who had purposely run down Edward Letton yesterday morning? Had she sustained those injuries in the crash? She didn't really look much like the woman described by Carol Pellter, the young soccer player who'd narrowly missed being mowed down by the hit-and-run driver (that was Pellter with two l's, Carol had informed him seriously when she saw him writing her name down incorrectly). She also said it "scared the shit out of me, to quote my father," and said Father looked decidedly uncomfortable when those words shot from his daughter's young mouth. Carol, however, was decidedly happy to be able to use the language. Her description of the driver was fairly generic: older woman, wearing a baseball cap. Upon questioning both Carol and her parents, Carol's father made it clear that "older" to Carol meant anyone over sixteen. Will had taken Carol to the sheriff's offices to meet their one and only sketch artist, a talented amateur not on the county payroll. The artist had tried to draw a picture based on Carol's description. In the end Will had put the woman anywhere from her mid-twenties to her late thirties.

But the reason Will was here now, with this mystery woman, was that she'd shown up at the hospital with a head injury consistent with one caused by an automobile accident—a ramming automobile accident. She fell loosely inside the right age bracket, and she had the right length of brown hair, and timing-wise, her injuries could have occurred yesterday morning.

But Will was reluctant to ask her directly about the hit-and-run. He didn't want to feed her information until he was ready. He was hoping she'd trip up and tell him something herself. Maybe something she wanted him to know. Was desperate for him to know. Such as that Edward Letton, who was languishing in this same hospital with multiple fractures—the most serious a crushing head injury that had required emergency surgery to stop the bleeding in his brain—had been driving a van equipped with ropes, chains, handcuffs, and items of well . . . torture. Dog-eared pages of crude child pornography were tucked inside the vehicle's pockets. The workshop of a predator about to strike.

Carol Pellter was damn lucky Gemma LaPorte, or whoever, had thwarted Letton from his sadistic purpose. If the man had grabbed the girl . . . Will's mind clamped shut. No need to go there.

But *was* the driver Gemma LaPorte? If so, he would have no choice but to charge her with attempted murder at the worst, reckless driving at the least. According to Carol she'd run down Letton intentionally, but though the deed must have been in full view of the fields, with all the noise and attention diverting the players and bystanders, no one saw much of anything except a silver car driving a little faster than it should, the tires squealing a bit. That silver car had not been found.

So, was it intentional? Will was inclined to believe so. Carol was pretty sure of herself. And her parents, scared that Carol had nearly been run down, had been all about finding that driver and throwing the book at her. Until they'd looked through the open door of the van and seen what Will saw.

Before that viewing they'd been instrumental in dialing 911 and getting an ambulance for Letton; they'd probably helped save him from dying at the site. It wasn't until Will and another deputy were on the scene that anyone really looked inside Letton's van. Then the Pellters stood silent and sober, possibly regretting their good Samaritan actions. When Carol wanted to see what was inside, they'd pulled her away, Carol all the while protesting that it was unfair, and that she heard her mom say, "oh, God," and her dad say, "shit," like they were both really, really scared, so she, Carol Pellter, deserved to know what was in that van!

Mom and Dad Pellter ignored her, staring at Will hollow-eyed, holding onto the whirling dervish that was their daughter in a protective grip that finally seemed to penetrate the spirited girl's annoyance and she stopped fighting them and grew quiet.

Letton's van had been impounded.

Now Gemma LaPorte was looking at him, her eye more hazel than green as the line of exterior light had shifted to illuminate the bruises on her forehead. "What's the date today?" she asked.

"October seventh."

"Three days," she repeated.

A heavyset nurse entered the room, caught Gemma's expression and turned officiously to Will. Before she could berate him for upsetting her patient, he nodded at her. "I'll check back with you later," he told Gemma, then headed into the hallway.

The nurse said to Gemma, "You look like you could use some more pain medication."

Gemma was staring after Will. She *felt* like she could use some more pain medication, but she didn't dare. She needed to keep her wits about her.

"Administration will be calling for your billing information," the nurse added with a slight grimace. The duties and functions of a hospital were well-known.

Hospitals . . . pain . . . she had experienced a terrible moment when she saw a plastic mask descending over her face and smelled the scent of some drug.

"Do you know why that deputy came to see me?" she asked shakily. "He didn't really say."

Nurse Penny had seen a lot of patients in her forty years on the job. She prided herself as a good judge of character. Had only been fooled by someone once, and that was the bastard she eventually married and divorced. She hoped he rotted in hell somewhere.

She could certainly feel this patient's reluctance and fear, but there was no sense of maliciousness or criminality emanating from her. She knew what that felt like. She'd been cajoled and lied to by an assortment of bamboozlers over the years and she'd seen right through them. No. This girl just seemed scared. Maybe angry. She'd muttered some vile things in her sleep, but Nurse Penny believed she was a good person at heart. "There was a hit-and-run. A man was seriously injured. They're looking for the vehicle that ran him down, and the driver was described as a young woman about your age."

Gemma felt cold. She absorbed the news silently. The nurse frowned, not liking the sense that the girl felt guilt. Could she have been wrong about her?

Gemma kept her silence as the nurse bustled around the room. She closed her eyes and pretended to sleep, not fooling Nurse Penny for a minute. Eventually, though, the nurse had to return to other duties and she left the room, pausing for a moment to look at the girl in the bed. She shook her head and left, a faint disturbance of air marking her passage.

The room fell quiet except for the soft whirs and clicks of the monitor.

Gemma opened her eye cautiously. She was alone. Lifting her arm, she examined the IV running into the skin above her wrist, felt the pressure of the cuff surrounding her upper arm. She began peeling off the tape that held the IV in place.

The sun skidded behind a cloud, plunging the October afternoon into early darkness, but the wolf welcomed the veil of shadow. He stood next to the bus stop bench, lifted his head and smelled the thick fall air, heavy with pent-up rain. He was glad for the clouds. He was a hunter and he preferred darkness.

A young couple sat on the bench, fighting over whether they had time to stop by her parents' after visiting his father, who was recovering from hip surgery. The wolf was as remote to them as a distant star. He could have been invisible for all they noticed. Like the people living in the big house, he wasn't worth noticing. He was insignificant. Unnoticeable. Maybe a little dull.

He pushed thoughts of them aside and concentrated on the woman inside the hospital. He'd followed her through all the strange turns that had brought her here. He was furious with her. She'd taken something from him. He needed to take her down, have her in his control. The need was near killing him. He could practically see her spread-eagled on the floor before him. He saw her squirming as he visualized unzipping his jeans and releasing his cock, then jamming it inside her again, and again, and again, as she threw back her head and thrashed and screamed. He knew she wanted him as much as he wanted her, but like the witch of his youth, she was teasing, taunting, pretending. Ignoring him.

He was going to wrap his hands around her neck and squeeze and squeeze while she bucked beneath him. She'd killed his brother. It was her fault. All witches were alike. They had to be burned. Burned . . .

Feeling his hands clutched in fists, he unwound them. The pressure in his head hurt. He had to get himself cool. Hold back. Wait . . .

Hunters needed to be patient. Wolves needed to be patient.

Pressing the fingers of his left hand to his forehead, he rubbed hard. He was afraid he would be noticed by the young couple but their words were growing more and more heated. They couldn't see past their own stupid problems.

He closed his eyes. A tremor ran through him. The pounding in his head felt like a growing beat throughout his whole body. Oh, how he wanted her. The witch. He was going to make her pay for what she'd done. He was going to mount her over and over again and then he was going to burn her. That's what it took to destroy a true witch. Burning. Sending them back to hell. Their birthplace. He'd killed before but she . . . she was the one he hated most. He'd almost lost her, but then had found her again.

The bus came and the couple climbed on board. He moved away, shading his face in the afternoon shadows, his hair covered by a watchcap, his shoulders hunched. On the side of the hospital where the laurel bushes grew high, he crouched into a corner. Several younger nurses walked toward their cars. He watched them in their pastel green pants and tunics, their crepe-soled shoes, pretending to be so clean. So tidy.

But it was all a lie.

He stared and stared.

They were all like *her.* Soulless. Seductive. Raging inside with Satan's fire.

One of the nurses unlocked a champagne-colored Honda three cars down from his. For a moment he saw her ringed by a fiery areola. A witch. Not as powerful as the one who lay in the hospital; no one was, any longer. Not since that first mother-witch. But this one was a witch, nonetheless, hiding herself in her clean clothes when he could smell the rotted flesh underneath.

The stench filled his head and he turned and walked quickly to his own car. He would follow her. Find her. Cut her down. Make her shriek and beg.

Hunger transformed his face into an urgent mask of desire.

He was the wolf again.

And wolves killed witches.

Chapter Three

Will stepped out of Gemma's room, then stopped in the hall outside and looked back through the still open, handicap-sized doorway. In his line of vision was a chair, the end of the bed and the window drapes. He couldn't quite see the hump of Gemma LaPorte's feet, nor was there anything he could view that gave a hint of who she was and why she'd ended up at Laurelton General.

Someone wasn't playing straight with him. Gemma LaPorte wasn't playing straight with him.

"Officer?" a young nurse asked him, and he turned to give her his attention. "Um, Billy's waiting for you in the ER? The EMT who saw her come in? Nurse Penny told me to make sure you knew."

"Thanks."

Will headed toward the stairway. Laurelton General was stair-stepped down the north face of a bluff, its levels ranging from two below street level with windows that only faced north, to three above. Will pressed the down button to take him from four to three, which was street level, then he walked briskly down a wide hallway that angled toward the south end and the ER.

The place was quiet at five p.m., but he doubted it would be for long. It was early October under a full moon. The old superstition about behavior changes at the time of a full moon seemed to hold true. Bad behavior, and just plain odd behavior, prevailed. If anything weird was going to happen, it most certainly did beneath a full moon, and teenagers especially seemed to be affected, at least in Will's experience. They drove too fast and drank and smoked things they shouldn't, not giving a damn what the adults thought.

Live fast and die young.

Will's brother had lived by that credo . . . and died by it as well. Sophomore year, home from college for Thanksgiving, and a wild, drunken party at a friend's parents' house had resulted in Dylan's jumping off the roof into the pool. His leap to the water had fallen short, landing him on the cement apron surrounding the pool.

A year younger, Will had been dinking around through his freshman year when Dylan's death occurred. It had stunned him hard and eventually helped turn his interest to first law, then criminology. Barely out of school, Will had taken a position with the Winslow County Sheriff's Department as little more than a gofer. He'd meant for it to be short term. He'd had bigger plans. Law school. A master's program. Something far away from his widowed mother, whose grip on reality loosened after Dylan's death. But Will hadn't been able to leave either her or Laurelton. Years went by, and he ended up staying way longer than he would have ever credited.

He also ended up in a relationship with Dylan's ex-girlfriend, Shari, which was detrimental to both of them. It only took six months for Will to realize it was a huge mistake; it took eight years to convince Shari of the same. To this day she sometimes showed up unexpectedly at his small, ranch-style house on the outskirts of Laurelton, to throw a scene and collapse into racking sobs. Neither Shari nor his mother had moved past Dylan's death. For years, Will had unknowingly enabled their behavior. These days, he avoided Shari at all costs, and his mom's descent into dementia had necessitated hiring a live-in caretaker for her. In some ways it felt to Will like he was slowly waking from a long sleep. He liked his job but he was itching to move on.

He needed something to happen. Something.

His cell buzzed and he glanced at the LCD: Barb Gillette, his partner, a transfer from Clackamas County. Will grimaced as he answered. She had a thing for him. He knew it; she didn't try to hide it. And yes, they'd even spent a few nights out together, though not recently. It was a fine balance for Will as he wanted to keep their working relationship on an even keel, while Barb constantly fought to take it to another level.

It was all probably going to come to a head. Some ugly, future, unavoidable scene. Ah, well.

"Tanninger," he answered shortly.

"Hey, handsome. What's the verdict? She the mad pedophile-rammer?"

"Maybe."

"Don't tell me. She stares at you with big doe eyes and swears she's innocent."

He grunted.

"Seriously, do you think she did it?" Barb asked.

"Too early to tell. Definitely a lot of signs point to that direction, but she doesn't remember the accident."

"Convenient."

Will thought about Gemma LaPorte and wondered. There was a lot more going on with her than she was letting him see. He finished his call with Barb, clicked off, then pulled a small notebook from his pocket. Flipping it open, he entered the gray-and-green-striped ER waiting room, with its club chairs backed against the walls and nestled in front of the windows to the parking lot. Billy Mendes was the EMT who had seen Gemma LaPorte walk unaided into the ER area. Will had left word that he wanted to speak to anyone who might have witnessed that inauspicious event and Billy had finally gotten the message and let the hospital know.

"I"m looking for Billy Mendes," Will said to a rather doubtful looking aide holding a clipboard. "He's an EMT who has information for the sheriff's department."

"Oh." She chewed on her lip, furrowed her brow and gazed down at her clipboard. "I don't think he's here."

"I was just told he was waiting for me."

"Really? Huh . . ." She glanced behind her to an officious-looking woman in hospital garb. "Lorraine, is Billy still here?"

"He left."

"Um . . . there's a policeman . . . er . . . sheriff's guy here for him . . . ?"

Lorraine looked up. Her hair was dyed black and her lipstick was orange. She looked like every nightmare school-nurse depicted in film and television. "Well, he left. He's got a job, you know. Crash at the four corners. Bicycler involved." She sniffed, as if they were all just asking to be run down by motorists.

"Uh . . . okay . . ." The girl gave Will a look from the top of her eyes. "Do you wanna wait?"

"I'll be back."

Will fought back his annoyance. He'd been trying to connect with Mendes for several days, but they'd been unable to meet for one reason or another. A multiple-car accident was certainly a good enough reason. Will was just anxious to get some solid information on the woman in 434 who may, or may not, be some kind of killing avenger.

He retraced his steps, taking the stairs toward her room. Passing by it, he hazarded a glance inside but the lights were dimmed. He imagined she was sleeping.

He headed on toward the end of the hall, took another flight of stairs to the top floor, then walked the hallway directly above Gemma's room. Outside the bank of windows facing north was a wall of black cloud. Rain was about to return and deluge them after a few days' respite. Maybe it would finally penetrate the packed earth that was hard as stone, a result of a parched summer and dry early fall.

He came to a closed door with an empty chair outside. Ralph Smithson had been sent over by the sheriff's department to guard Edward Letton, but he apparently wasn't taking his job seriously, which was no surprise. Will knew the guy well and was sure Smithson felt playing babysitter wasn't up to his level of expertise. Smithson was big and loud and could complain like it was an Olympic sport. He would consider keeping watch over Letton to be beneath him, yet he wouldn't be happy with a job that required him to expend any energy either. He was one of those guys that needed to be shit-canned like yesterday, but he toadied up to Sheriff Nunce on a regular basis, so Will was stuck with him for now. And Laurelton General was outside the city limits and therefore the county's problem, so good old Ralph was going to have to suck it up and play bodyguard.

Except he was missing in action from his post.

Silently cursing the man, Will placed a palm against the light oak door and pushed, taking a few quiet steps inside the room. Letton lay beneath the glow of a light attached to the headboard of his bed. His right leg had been broken in three places and he was skinned up like he'd been scraped over a cheese grater. But it was the injury to his skull that had placed him in a coma. Smithson probably figured there was no way the guy was leaving this place on his own power and had decided to check out the lunchroom. Nevertheless, Will didn't plan on leaving till the guard returned.

Seven minutes later Ralph came hustling down the hall carrying a tray. He'd raided both the cafeteria and some vending machines, as he balanced a heaping helping of some kind of stroganoff with mystery meat, and several bright, plastic bags of Fritos, Doritos, and other Lay's and Ruffles products.

He jerked as if caught in a nefarious act upon seeing Will. "What're you doing here?"

"Looking for you," Will said mildly. "What's the status on our patient?"

Ralph hesitated, quickly reviewing his options. Will could practically read the questions running behind his bullish forehead: Should I play it safe? Be contrite? Come up with an excuse? Should I bluff my way out? In the end he regarded Will balefully, choosing to go on the attack. "Do I look like a doctor?" he sneered. "The fucker ain't no patient. He's a fucking pedophile."

"I'd ask you where you've been but it would be a redundant question."

"Yeah?" Ralph's jaw clenched pugnaciously.

"I'd just like you to stick by the door."

"That's what I'm doin', Kemosabe."

"I want Letton to wake up and explain about that gear in his van." Will carefully tucked his annoyance behind a stoic facade.

"He's a sick fucker," Ralph said, ripping open a bag of Fritos and stuffing a fistful into his mouth. "Hope he dies. Not that I'd do anything to help him along, but if he made a run for it, I'd drop him, man."

"He's not going to be running anywhere," Will pointed out.

"He's going straight to hell, that's where. You tell that girl in room 434 she did the world a favor. Almost, anyway. If this fucker lives . . ." He shook his head and reached in the bag for another hammy fistful.

Will left him to his food and retraced his steps toward the ER. At Gemma's room, he gave up all pretense of disinterest and peeked inside.

There was no one in the bed.

No one in the room.

Climbing out of bed had been all fine and good, but the dizziness that overwhelmed Gemma made her realize she wasn't going to be able to hightail it to freedom with any real speed. She was injured, and her body wasn't eager to move.

"Damn," she whispered, swaying as she headed toward the bifold closet doors which, when opened, revealed a small, built-in chest of drawers and little else.

She found her clothes in a plastic bag in the top drawer of the chest. They were identified by the number 434 written on the bag in black felt pen. Gemma pulled the items out carefully and gazed in a kind of awe at the blood-soaked T-shirt and ripped jeans. The fabric over one thigh was sliced as if by a knife and Gemma looked down at the thin, superficial wound that ran down her corresponding leg.

Another wave of wooziness grabbed her and she stumbled back to the bed, her clothes squeezed inside her fists. Her head throbbed. It took a lot longer than it should have to remove her hospital nightgown, and when she was undressed her eyes automatically moved to her left hip, where the hipbone did not flare out in the same way as it did on her right. An old injury, with a scar that was shaped somewhat like a dagger. She tried to remember what had happened there but her mind shied away. She sensed she knew, or almost knew, but her mind was locked down.

There was no underwear. No panties. No bra.

Girding her loins, she stuck one leg through the blood-spattered jeans and felt a wave of nausea that almost made her throw up. She slid the other leg inside with more care. When she'd gotten the pants on, she zipped them up and buttoned them, then paused a moment, gathering strength. A rip ran down one leg from thigh to just below the knee. She had more of a mental struggle with herself than a physical one as she dragged the T-shirt over her bandaged head. Dressed, she cautiously moved to the bathroom and, propping herself up against the sink, examined her reflection in the mirror. Her breath whooshed out in a rush of distaste. She turned away from the staring eye and bruised skin and white bandage.

Her insides quivered. God, she looked horrible.

And then she had a flash of the man she'd been chasing. The bastard with his putrid lust for *children.* But she couldn't quite remember. Couldn't quite put it together. She'd wanted to kill him. *That*, she could recall.

It took her long, long minutes to find her shoes: a pair of sneakers, also blood-spattered, and she put them on over her bare feet. There were no socks in evidence anywhere. By the time she'd accomplished these tasks she was exhausted, and with a sort of miserable dawning realized she had no purse. It wasn't anywhere in the room, and for the life of her she could not recall what it even looked like.

Which led her to the next unwelcome discovery: she didn't remember where she lived. She thought hard for a moment, begging her memory to come through, and suddenly it did. She was from Quarry. Quarry, Oregon. And she'd been making herself breakfast . . . some kind of . . . oatmeal? Her heart banged against her chest. She couldn't remember, but she'd just told that detective what she'd eaten. What was it? What was it? Oatmeal and maybe some fruit?

Gemma lifted a shaking hand to her forehead and closed

her eye. Her head throbbed. She shouldn't leave the hospital. She wasn't well enough. But something told her she had to go. Had to.

A memory shot like a streak behind her eyes:

She was looking out the window and chrysanthemums were getting beaten by a killing rain, their spiky orange heads pressed against the packed dirt.

It hasn't rained in three days.

She tried to concentrate hard, yet not tax her brain too much. She'd been eating oatmeal with cinnamon. That was right. That's what she'd told the detective. Slowly bits came back to her . . .

I'm from Quarry, Oregon. My name is Gemma LaPorte. I'm twenty-seven years old. Or maybe twenty-eight? Or am I older? Gemma took several deep breaths and willed herself to relax. *I live . . . on a farm? My parents' farm? My father is a farmer . . . but he's gone now . . . my mother, too. No, wait. My parents had a diner. The PickAxe. No . . . no . . . That's a different place. A bar, mostly. My parents had . . . LuLu's . . . and I waited tables when I was younger.*

Gemma's eyes flew open, though she could still only see out of one. She recalled wearing the LuLu's uniform, a typical old-time diner dress that came in varying colors—hers had been yellow—with pockets and a wide, white collar. Tourists loved LuLu's, as much for the ambiance as the food.

"I inherited the diner," she said aloud. But there appeared to be a block to that thinking. A dark wall. There was something more that she couldn't quite reach.

"My mother worked at the diner."

Your mother was a liar.

Gemma inhaled and glanced around, half expecting to find the source of that comment, but the words had been inside her head. She felt more pain but was determined to work her way through it. Carefully, she shuffled her way to the door. Would she be able to just walk out? Would they let her leave? She knew there was enough bureaucracy and paperwork waiting for her at hospital administration to make a stronger person weep, but she needed her identification, the name of her insurance company, the address of her home before she could settle her bill.

She wasn't even sure she had the money to make that happen.

But she had to get out. She had to . . . find the man she'd been after and finish what she'd started. It was imperative. She could feel a clock ticking inside her head. Time was running short.

What if someone saw her? She looked like she'd barely survived a war. But then this was a hospital. She wouldn't be the only one bandaged and bloody, would she?

And how the hell would she get to Quarry when she had no money? Did she have a car? The good-looking detective had asked how she'd gotten to the hospital. If only she knew. Had she driven herself and left her car in the lot? Even if she had, it was a moot point because she had no keys! And she had no idea what kind of vehicle she drove.

Nor could she come up with the name of a single friend.

Her heart squeezed. What if my name's not Gemma LaPorte? There was something about it that sounded wrong. Like it was an alias. An identity trotted out when she didn't want to give out her real name.

She moved as fast as she dared given her painful head and unsure stomach. She almost slipped right past the stairs, but then saw the sign above the door—an icon of a man in a running position over a jagged line meant to represent the stairs—and chose them with relief as the best way to escape.

She worked her way down the flight with an effort, her head jarring. On the next level down—identified as street level—she hesitated inside the stairwell, afraid to open the door. How long was the hallway between this door and the outside parking lot? How many people around? How many chances for someone to look her way and wonder about the bruise-faced patient with the head bandage?

Cautiously, Gemma pushed the bar on the door and cracked it open, just a bit. In her sliver of sight she could see a carpeted hallway and a row of windows that looked out toward freedom. She didn't know what she'd do when she got there. But she just wanted *out* of the hospital.

There was, however, no exterior door visible, just rows of floor-to-ceiling windows.

Squaring her shoulders, she stepped into the hallway and walked unhurriedly to her left, keeping the windows and parking lot at her right shoulder. Surely there would be an exit soon.

The hallway angled even farther left and Gemma rounded the corner. EMERGENCY was written in bold letters above a sliding-glass interior door and beyond was a large room with chairs, and even farther, another set of glass doors which led to a portico where an ambulance sat and EMTs were standing by, waiting for a call. No way she was going there. Quickly, she turned on her heel and retraced her steps.

"Hey," a male voice called from behind her.

Her pulse leapt. She pretended to be deaf. Maybe they didn't mean her. Maybe—

"Are you leaving the hospital, Ms. LaPorte?" the voice asked calmly.

Gemma looked up reluctantly, gritting her teeth at the familiar tone of the detective's voice. Of course he was still here. Of course he would be the one to discover her. She had to slide her gaze away from his probing stare and taut physique. "I don't have a purse," she said. "My clothes were in the room, but I don't have a purse."

"Did you come by car?"

"I don't remember." Did he think he was going to surprise her into telling him something she didn't know?

"Do you know where you're going?"

"Home. To Quarry."

"By . . . foot?"

"Detective . . . Tanninger," she said, reading his name tag. She couldn't remember his first name. "I need to leave. Whatever this is costing, I can't afford it. I need to find my identification. I need to go home." Her voice quavered a bit and though she didn't feel quite as weak as she sounded, she let him think what he wanted. And yeah, she felt bad and it was a simple matter to show it.

"You look like you could use a wheelchair."

"I know what I look like," she said wryly.

"Have you talked to the doctor about being released?"

She met his eyes again and didn't change expression.

His lips twitched, but despite the lines at the corners of his eyes, Gemma didn't trust that he possessed much of a sense of humor. She hadn't known many people in law enforcement, but those she had—though she could not for the life of her call them up at this moment—had been notoriously lacking in humor and self-awareness. Their officiousness had left her with the vague sense that police officers were not on her side. Better to handle your own battles than call in the cavalry. Bad things lurked beneath the surface of those supposedly sent to serve and protect.

"You should probably be back in your room," he said. "But if you want to go to administration and give over your address, name, and social, I can lead you there."

He was afraid she intended to scam on the bill. That's what he meant. She was outraged, yet wasn't that what she'd planned to do? At least in the interim until she could figure out the missing pieces of her life?

Gemma didn't want to go anywhere with Detective Tanninger. But she sure as hell didn't want to go back to her room, either.

Yet . . . she sensed the weariness that was taking hold of

her, a dark, descending gloom with strong tentacles. There was an urgency inside her. A need to finish some half-forgotten task, but she also had no means to get to that task and no reserve strength to make that happen. She was bound by her own lack of identification and funds, a weary, beaten body, and a sputtering memory that seemed to blink on and off like a traffic light.

"I think I'll go back to my room," she said tremulously.

"All right." He led her toward the bank of elevators and punched the button for the fourth floor.

Gemma didn't say anything more, concentrating solely on moving her quivering legs back toward her room. Will cupped her elbow with one hand and helped steady her. If he had more questions, he kept them to himself as they reached the fourth floor and he guided her into her room. Gemma sat herself heavily down on the bed and took a deep, calming breath.

"Do you feel up to a little more conversation?" the detective asked.

No, Gemma thought. All she wanted to do was lie down and gather her strength again. Actually, all she wanted was to recall how she'd come to be at the hospital. But she didn't want to give Tanninger any reason to make herself seem more interesting. "Fire away." She eased herself against the headboard and pulled her shoes off, dropping them to the floor.

Nurse Penny looked into the room. "What are you doing?" she asked Gemma sharply.

"Trying to escape. But I got caught."

The nurse whipped around to glare at Tanninger, as if it were somehow his fault. She pursed her lips, said she would bring Gemma a new hospital gown, then steamed out of the room as if they had both purposely thwarted her authority.

"Don't you have more pressing cases than a mystery patient?" Gemma asked before Tanninger could speak.

"I was waiting to speak to the EMT who saw you come in two nights ago. We haven't connected yet."

"You said I walked in?"

"And collapsed."

Gemma struggled to remember but her mind was empty. More gaps. "Did you tell me where I came in?"

"To the ER. From the parking lot. I'll know more when I talk with the EMT."

"I want to be there when you talk to him."

"So, you're not planning to disappear again, then, after I leave the room?"

"No."

"I'm not sure that's going to work out—"

Nurse Penny hustled back inside the room and gave Tanninger a look that said *vamoose*. He walked out the door and Gemma got a good look at his strong back, wide shoulders, and narrow hips as he disappeared from view.

"Let me help you put this on, hon," the nurse said, and Gemma let her undress her and tie the gown around her back. "You don't have someone to bring you fresh clothes?" she asked, inclining her head to the T-shirt and jeans.

"It'll be okay. I'll just head home and change. Tomorrow."

"Maybe tomorrow, maybe the next day. Depends on Dr. Avery."

Tomorrow, Gemma thought determinedly. She had to get back to her real life. She had to remember what she'd been doing. What showdown she was heading for. Who, or what, she'd been after.

The nurse looked as if she wanted to take Gemma's clothes with her, but she left them in a neat stack on the chair. Gemma momentarily wondered if she had the strength to put them back on, distasteful as that thought was becoming. But even as she gave up the idea for the moment, Detective Tanninger reentered the room.

They eyed each other for several moments, and then he observed, "If you're too tired, I can come back."

"I'd like to help you. I just don't know if I can."

"Where do you live in Quarry?"

Gemma hesitated. "It's a farmhouse."

"You don't sound too sure."

"It's coming back, but it's not all there yet," she said.

"Take your time."

"A lot of homes in Quarry are farmhouses, though there aren't as many farms anymore. It was my parents' place, Jean and Peter LaPorte, but they're both gone and they left it to me."

"You live there by yourself?"

Did she? Gemma opened her mouth, thought hard, then said slowly, "Yes. . . ."

"You think your memory difficulty is from the concussion?" he asked casually.

"What else?" she responded quickly, her pulse jumping. But she had a moment of remembrance then. A mental snapshot of herself and her mother in the front room of the farmhouse. There was another woman sitting on the edge of her seat, staring hard at Jean LaPorte. Anxious. Waiting. And all around them the cloying, sweet scent of peonies from the magenta bouquet bursting in a vase on the scarred table.

"Your memory lapse seems greater than what I would expect from a concussion," he said. "What's your address?"

"I don't really want to talk anymore." Gemma looked away.

"You can't remember it."

"I've been in some kind of accident, detective. I'm not a hundred per cent. If you have a specific question, ask it. Otherwise I don't think I can help you any further."

He looked at her hard. "Afraid of me finding out that you ran down a man with your car?"

Gemma stared at him in shock. "What?" she asked softly.

"The man's unconscious, upstairs. He's a pedophile, by the looks of what we found in his van."

"In his van . . . ?" she repeated faintly.

"It looks like you ran him down on purpose."

There was no humor in his face now. It was hard and tough and an accusation hung in his dark eyes. Gemma tried to remember. She'd remembered the man's lust. She'd felt it. She'd chased him . . .

Or, had she? It felt like these were someone else's memories. Manufactured. Not real, and not hers!

"No . . . I don't think so," she denied.

"You don't think so."

She didn't respond and Tanninger went on to tersely explain about the man who'd been run down at a soccer field, how he'd been driving a van filled with handcuffs and chains and ropes, how some unidentified woman had aimed her car at him and flipped him into the air, how he'd survived the attack, but just barely. As Gemma listened she understood that the detective had been plying her with questions in order to find out what she knew, if anything, about the attack. He half-believed—maybe even fully believed—that she'd been behind the wheel of the car that had attacked the man, a pedophile.

When he was finished Gemma's head felt like it was going to explode. Is that what she'd done? Is that why she couldn't remember?

"I don't know what you're talking about," she said in a shaking voice that nevertheless rang with conviction.

Tanninger drew a breath, expanding his chest. What did it say about her, Gemma wondered, that even when he was panicking her with his questions, she could notice how tan his skin was, how good he looked in his pressed shirt and dark pants, how strong and able he seemed, like someone she could depend on.

But then she recalled, with almost a ping of remembrance,

that she'd always been attracted to a man in a uniform, no matter whether they had a sense of humor or not.

Outside good old Laurelton General, Inga Selbourne had raced to her Honda compact as soon as she'd gotten off work. She was proud to be a nurse. Proud to wear the uniform. Proud to have a job—a really good job!—at the best, the only, hospital in Winslow County. She'd congratulated herself again as she'd hurriedly unlocked the door and climbed inside, and she'd been congratulating herself all the way home to the little apartment attached to the farmhouse on the outskirts of the town of Laurelton itself.

Or, was it the inskirts of Laurelton? she thought with a grin, as it was on the eastern side of the city, toward Portland.

She'd had one heck of a time getting through nursing school. Whew, those classes had been rough. She'd had to pull all-nighters more often than she cared to admit, and even then if it hadn't been for Jarrod Benningfield and his copy of that anatomy test, she would have been screwed! Jarrod's sister had whizzed through the semester before, and Jarrod had handed Inga the test and the answers and all she'd had to do was pretend to be his girlfriend—the pimple-faced little horror—and oh, yeah, give him a blow job or two, but she'd been through that drill enough times to know that sex was a bargaining chip, nothing more.

Luckily the shortage of nurses made it a slam-bang for her to get a job as soon as she graduated. And she was good at what she did, anyway. Really, really good. There was a hell of a lot more to caring for the sick than acing a few tests, that was for sure. Everyone told her how good she was at her job and it just swelled her with pride. It sure did.

And she'd wanted to be at Laurelton General. It was totally perfect! It wasn't too far away from her apartment, and if she wanted some fun, it was a straight shot into Portland on Highway 26, the Sunset Highway, on that last stretch before Portland city center, and when she needed to go to her job, well, that was a cinch. She was thinking about heading into Portland tonight. Lately she'd been going to that new nightclub in the Pearl that played hot music and served Caribbean martinis. Whew, they were powerful. She'd had to take a taxi home a few times, and she'd gone home with friends a few times, too. Slept with a couple of guys she shouldn't have. Fuck-buddies. She shrugged her small shoulders. What'cha gonna do.

As the wheels of her car ate up the miles, Inga shrugged those thoughts aside. She didn't dwell on past mistakes or less than perfect decision-making. Life was good. She had her own place and her own life. The apartment was small: a studio with a partition. The only honest-to-goodness room was the bathroom. It at least had a real door. But the space was all hers and now, as she drove through the dark toward home, she felt a smile cross her lips despite the sudden rain that was peppering hard against her windshield.

She switched on the wipers. Jesus, what a downpour. You'd think it was the middle of winter.

The couple in the front farmhouse—her landlords—were kind of out of it, but they left her to her own devices. It was a little creepy sometimes because they'd given up farming years earlier and the property was overgrown, with a barn of gray, broken wood, that listed heavily. Beyond the house was a pasture of Scotch broom and weeds with a stand of firs ringing the northern end. Nothing had been taken care of for years.

But her apartment was the best. The absolute best. And cheap!

She hummed to herself as she pulled into the drive that ran alongside the farmhouse, tucking her Honda into the space provided for her at the north end of her apartment. She hurried up her front steps and unlocked the door. Her ears caught the sound of another vehicle pulling into the gravel drive, somewhere behind her on the route she'd just traveled. The farmers? There'd been lights on in the main house and she'd just assumed they were inside. Huh.

She hesitated for a moment, listening. She thought she heard an engine, but the crunch of wheels on gravel was gone. Was someone waiting inside a car around the front of the farmhouse where she couldn't see? Or was it just roadway sounds she'd let enter her mind?

Inga let half a minute pass, then lost interest. She had places to go, people to see, dances to dance, drinks to knock back. Quickly she dropped her purse and coat on the single chair in the main room and tossed her keys on the kitchen counter. She then headed to the bathroom, turned on the shower and stripped off her uniform, letting it pool on the floor.

There was a guy she'd met. Daniel. He was so damn hot, with longish dark hair that brushed over the collar of his shirt, and the most fabulous blue eyes. His physique was lean and taut, just the way she liked it. She'd wanted to moan when they'd slow-danced, his crotch pressed to hers. Whenever she saw him it was like he radiated the word *sex*. She didn't care what it took, they were going to get together tonight. She'd find a way to go home with him. Her shift didn't start tomorrow until eleven, so they had hours to kill making love.

She practically gave herself an orgasm just thinking about him.

She was toweling off when she heard the sound. A slight squeak of a soft-soled shoe. Her heart clutched. Had she locked the door? Had she? She could visualize her keys tossed on the kitchen counter, but she couldn't remember twisting the lock.

She was naked. Carefully, she stepped from the shower and pulled her uniform back over her head. Minutes passed.

Finally her breathing turned to normal. There was no one out there. She was making it up. Living alone did that to her. Every noise sounded alien.

Nevertheless, she grabbed a glass bottle of bath salts, tested its weight, then threw open the bathroom door, letting it bang hard against the wall, bath salts held high, ready to take on any danger.

There was no one there.

But her front door was unlatched and she quickly crossed the three steps to take care of that mistake.

Her fingers were reaching for the lock when the front door suddenly slammed inward, sending her reeling. Inga staggered, her back hitting the opposite wall. A man stood in the aperture, his arms hunched forward, his head thrust toward her, breathing hard.

She shrieked in fright, and then he was upon her, his hot breath in her face, his body big and hard, his hand grabbing hers and twisting her arm in one swift movement so the bath salts fell to the hardwood floor and shattered, little lavender grains of sand flying everywhere.

"Witch," he said, throwing her down so that her head cracked hard on the floor and she saw stars.

"Wait . . . wait . . . I have money . . . please . . ."

He was unbuckling his pants, humping hard against her. Determined. She knew he wasn't hearing her.

"Wait! Please . . . !"

Part of her brain was disengaged. Her hand groped along the floor and landed on a sharp shard of glass. She grabbed it and jabbed forward, gouging the piece into his neck, pulling it out and stabbing again and again for all she was worth. She couldn't let him win. Couldn't!

In surprise he jumped back, clapping a hand to his neck, his eyes wide. He looked kinda crazy to Inga's way of thinking and he threw his head back and howled like a beast. Then he hit her in the face till she was dizzy. She flailed the glass at him again and again until he ripped it from her hand.

She tried to scream but his hands circled her throat. “Burn in hell,” he growled through gritted teeth.

Her fingers scrabbled to loosen his hold but it was no use. His grip was too tight, too hard. Pinpoints of light swirled in front of her eyes. She fought against the darkness but it was no use. The pressure wouldn’t give. Wouldn’t quit. She tugged and tugged at his hands but he was too strong. Her trachea was clamped shut. She couldn’t breathe!

Couldn’t . . . breathe . . .

Oh, God. Please . . .

“Witch,” he spat and then Inga’s world circled and spun into blackness.

Her last thought was a regret that she wouldn’t get to be with Daniel after all.

Chapter Four

Dr. Avery was in his fifties, with silver hair and black eyebrows and a stony expression that would have worried Gemma had she not learned that beneath his cold exterior he was a man who fiercely loved his wife and two sons, one of whom was engaged to be married. She knew he'd been in to see her before but she'd gained mostly impressions about him, about what he thought of her injuries, nothing concrete or substantial.

This visit he'd removed the bandage over her eye, the white of which was half-filled with blood.

"I look gruesome," Gemma said.

The doctor didn't answer, just kept writing vigorously on her chart.

She'd spent a restless night, waking up to shadowy thoughts and images, fading back to sleep, waking again with her heart pounding in fear and a sense that she needed to save someone, falling to unconsciousness once again, back to the fleeting ghosts and skittish memories.

"Am I going to be able to leave today?" she asked a tad belligerently as the doctor just kept on writing.

He didn't look up.

"When's the wedding?" she tried, hoping small talk might get his attention if medicine wouldn't.

"What wedding?"

"Your son's."

His gaze slowly lifted from the chart, which he slid back into its holder at the foot of her bed. "The end of next month."

"So, are you releasing me? I feel incredibly better than yesterday. Even if I'm gruesome."

He gave her a studied look. "You seem to have recovered fairly quickly. Your head injuries aren't as severe . . . as we initially suspected," he said cautiously. "You have some bruising around your chest, probably from the seat belt. You've lost some time, maybe as a result of concussion, although you haven't displayed other symptoms."

"Seat belt . . ." Gemma repeated. "So, it was a car accident?"

"We'll know for sure when you locate your vehicle."

"Then . . . I'm outta here?"

He nodded once, shortly. Gemma had already spoken on the phone to someone from administration and given them information about herself, which though meager, was enough to satisfy them. She knew her own social security number, or at least one that popped into her head, so she'd rattled it off and the woman at the end of the line had typed it into her file. It had to be hers. It wasn't like she would know anyone else's, right?

She was torn between just skedaddling and throwing herself on the hospital administration's mercy, asking for some cold hard cash to find her way home.

The doctor stood for a moment, rocking on his heels, as if he had something else he wanted to say. Gemma waited somewhat impatiently. She'd redressed in her blood-spattered clothes, knowing she was going to burn them the first chance she got. She just wanted to get out of here and find a way back to Quarry. She couldn't recall her address but she had a murky idea of the direction to go.

Maybe if Detective Tanninger were around today, trying to meet with that EMT . . . maybe he'd give her a lift. It was as good a plan as any.

Dr. Avery finally headed toward the door and Gemma swung her legs over the bed. But the doctor hesitated before entering the hallway, gazing back at her thoughtfully. "I haven't told anyone my son's getting married. Didn't want the hospital staff talking about something that might not happen. My son and his fiancée have had a very on-and-off relationship. I don't know how you knew."

"You must have told me earlier. I drifted in and out for a while."

"I wouldn't have," he said positively.

Something feathered along Gemma's skin. A cold whisper of awareness. "Maybe I dreamt it and it just happened to be true."

He gazed at her a long moment, then pushed out the door.

I'm a mind reader.

She rolled that idea around and found she didn't like it much. But it felt . . . real.

Gemma didn't waste any more time. She found her shoes again and after a quick, horrifying look in the mirror—the whole right side of her face was a technicolor mess—she took a deep breath and prepared herself for an uncertain future.

She was in the hallway when an orderly holding a wheelchair stopped short. "Ma'am, you need to take a seat. Hospital policy."

She suspected it was hospital policy to take her to administration for check out, too, but the orderly did not appear to be someone who would take no for an answer so she perched on the wheelchair, wondering wildly if she could make a break for it when he rolled her near an exit.

Mind reader, she thought again, and felt decidedly uncomfortable.

Billy Mendes was lanky and bowlegged, as if he'd just gotten off the ranch. He walked with a kind of cowboy strut as well, though it wasn't an affectation, more like a natural hip swing to get his bowed legs in line.

He came inside the ER and shot a look at Lorraine, the battleaxe nurse with the dyed black hair and orange lips, before crossing the waiting room in a couple of big strides and walking up to Will.

"You the guy lookin' for me?" he asked. "From the sheriff's department?"

"Detective Will Tanninger," Will acknowledged, and the two men shook hands. They moved toward a section of striped chairs near the window where no one else was sitting at the moment.

Mendes kept standing, his hands shoved in his pockets. "You wanna know about the woman who staggered in on Saturday? The one that got out of the silver Camry? I thought the guy who dropped her off was gonna park and come inside and help her, but he never came back. He just drove off and then she just kinda walked from side to side, like she had no balance, y'know? Swaying, like. And then she makes it inside and just crumples to the floor. I came runnin' from the ambulance." He waved in the direction of the portico outside the ER. "We were just gettin' ready to go, but there she was, and I got my ass chewed for that one." He threw a dark look in Lorraine's direction. "But hey, we had an accident victim right here. I thought we should help her first."

"It delayed you from making your call?"

"Not much, it didn't," he asserted. "Thirty seconds? Lorraine started screamin' and I helped the woman to lie down flat. She was out cold by then, but breathin' okay. ER team grabbed her up and Pete and I took off to the accident on Highway 217. One of those nights where everybody smashes up their cars. Couple of fatalities."

"So, you saw a man drop her off in a silver Camry?"

He nodded.

"It was definitely a man?"

"Yeah . . ." He started to sound uncertain.

"Can you remember why you thought so?"

Billy looked puzzled for a moment. "I guess 'cause he was drivin' kinda fast. Not that girls can't, too, but not so much in a hospital parking lot. He kinda screeched in and then she got out, and then he reached over and pulled the door shut and left. I thought it was weird he didn't help her when I saw that she couldn't walk so well. Maybe it was a chick. Since she didn't even try to help her friend? But then I thought he or she or whoever was gonna park the car and come back. I don't know."

"Could the driver have come back after you left in the ambulance?"

"I suppose . . . you can check with Lorraine . . ." He grimaced, letting Will know exactly what he thought of that idea.

"Was there any body damage to the Camry?"

"Uh . . . I was lookin' at the girl, and I just saw the car's rear end, mostly. Don't recall any passenger-side damage. Didn't see the front."

Will grilled him some more and learned Gemma had arrived at the hospital in the early evening, just as it was getting dark. If she were the woman who'd run down Edward Letton, that would mean there had been a lot of hours in between the accident and her appearance at Laurelton General.

There didn't appear to be anything more to learn from Billy, so Will shook his hand and thanked him for the information, then he turned back to the exit. He was out the door and heading to his department vehicle, when he abruptly changed direction and returned to the hospital, making for the bank of elevators. What was it about Gemma LaPorte that kept him wanting to see her again? Was it just this investigation? The fact that she was an enigma that he couldn't quit puzzling over? Was it that he both wanted her to be innocent of hit-and-run, and yet somehow hoped she *was* that avenger? Someone who wanted to rid the world of sick scum no matter what the cost?

That was the kind of thinking that could get him fired, or worse, he knew. That kind of vigilante philosophy that the bad should be punished without benefit of a trial. That murder, in the name of good, was almost okay.

He'd seen it a couple of times in his career. Law enforcement officers who, burned out and frustrated, took their job to that next level. Not waiting for the judicial system to pass its verdict. Deciding to wipe out the offender first and ask forgiveness later.

Only there was no forgiveness. There was prosecution and jail time.

But Will didn't think he had burned out. He didn't truly condone Gemma's behavior. Vigilantism was not to be tolerated at any level. It was just that inwardly—and this Will would never admit to anyone—he applauded her courage and ability to act.

The elevator took him to the fourth floor, and when the doors opened he saw Gemma in a wheelchair, being pushed toward the elevators by an orderly. Simultaneously, another elevator's doors opened. Edward Letton's wife, Mandy, stepped out and glanced over at Will, whom she'd met briefly in Letton's room. Then as both sets of elevator doors closed behind them she turned to Gemma, whose bandage had been removed, leaving the splendor of her bruised face and swollen eye for all to see.

Mandy understood who Gemma was instantly. "You . . ." she said tautly. "What are you doing on my husband's floor?"

Gemma, who'd seemed locked in her own thoughts, looked blankly at Mandy.

"This is the fourth floor," Will told Mandy. "Your husband's on five, but he's not allowed visitors. You know that."

She didn't even register a word. "You're the woman who ran him down."

Gemma's eyes widened.

"Ms. Letton, I'm going to have to ask you to leave," Will said, stepping between Gemma and Mandy Letton, whose gaze had zeroed in on Gemma like twin laser beams.

"I don't know what kind of monster you are," Mandy said with a catch in her voice, "but my husband's barely alive because of you! Were you drinking? On drugs? Or was this some kind of thrill kill! Luckily, you didn't succeed. He's still alive and he's going to make it."

Gemma's gaze turned from Mandy to Will. He could read the questions in her eyes: Why didn't Letton's wife know what Letton had been about to do? Will would have loved to tell her that members of both the Winslow County Sheriff's Department and the Laurelton Police Department—the city where Mandy and Edward Letton lived—had tried to explain about the guard at Edward Letton's door, but Mandy was actively not listening to anything they said that alluded to—or explicitly described—the van and its special chains, cuffs, and restraints.

"You should be the one with the guard outside your door," Mandy declared in a shaking voice.

Gemma's lips tightened. "I'd choose my words carefully if my husband were a predator."

"Wait." Will put up a hand and blocked Mandy's view of Gemma and vice versa.

"You're the one who started those vicious rumors! I should sue you for assault *and* slander!"

"If your husband survives, he's going to jail," Gemma stated certainly. "He earned that all by himself."

"He's going to survive. And you'll be the one going to prison for attempted murder!"

"Ms. Letton, I'm going to escort you downstairs," Will said, turning to Gemma's orderly. "I'll meet you down there," he said, actively blocking Mandy from any further progress toward Gemma.

Gemma was having none of it. She climbed out of the wheelchair and walked the last few steps to the elevator, slamming her palm on the call button of the second elevator. "I'm leaving on my own power. You can tell whoever's in charge of hospital policy, what they can do with that wheelchair."

Mandy Letton tried to get past Will, who kept his body between her and Gemma. He realized he would probably find humor in the situation later on, but in the moment he was aware that, given their own devices, these two women could end up in a physical fight. Stranger things had happened.

Mandy struggled again to get past Will. The orderly tried to convince Gemma to get back in the wheelchair. Gemma's elevator car arrived with a bell-like *ding*. Will watched her get inside and turn to tell the orderly she didn't want him or the wheelchair anywhere near her, then the elevator doors closed.

Mandy Letton pushed Will hard in the center of his back. "Damn you. You're letting her go? She tried to kill my husband!" Hysteria flooded through the anger.

The orderly said in awe, "You just pushed an officer of the law."

Mandy whirled her flash-fury on him. "Shut up. Shut up! Everybody shut up!"

"Ms. Letton, you need to get control of yourself," Will warned. He didn't want to arrest her. Didn't want this scene to become a deep hole and more fuel for the media on the Letton case.

Her mouth quivered and her eyes grew hard. When the second elevator arrived, she turned into it blindly and faced to the back. Will and the orderly joined her. Nobody said a word.

As soon as they hit the street level, Mandy pushed past both Will and the orderly. They watched her hightail it to the parking lot and Will was hot on her heels. If she was looking for Gemma LaPorte, he was going to make sure no physical violence occurred.

Gemma was nowhere in sight and Will was annoyed. He followed Mandy out to her car, a white compact, and waited under a watery sun as the wind threw a shimmer of rain at him.

Then he slowly turned around, searching the lot for a glimpse of a woman with straight brown hair whose movements were cautious with the need to keep pain at bay.

She had no idea how to get home, but she was outside the hospital. In the parking lot in a fitful rain. No purse. No socks. No damn underwear. No funds. No means at all. She couldn't think of the number of a close friend—for that matter she couldn't think of the *name* of a close friend—and her half-baked plan to ask hospital administration to loan her cab fare and add it to her bill, was out the window. She wasn't going back in there for any reason. Any reason at all.

She was free, and she intended to stay that way.

And she was insanely furious at Letton's deluded wife. Insanely furious. The pounding in her head was rage which was aggravating her injuries.

Had she tried to kill the man? She hadn't believed herself capable, but God, she hadn't expected the depth of her revulsion, the extent of her anger. She wanted to throttle that blonde, pillowy bitch. The woman was all curves and boobs and hips and a mouth that just kept yammering.

And she was driven by fear, too. Mandy Letton's threats about Gemma's possible incarceration had been heard, processed and given her more impetus to get . . . the . . . hell . . . out!

But now she was stuck. Standing in the gray, late-morning light, a cold breeze throwing rain at her, cutting through her clothes and making her quake like she was stricken with seizures, she scanned the lot for deliverance. She'd used up all her strength just leaving the building. Now she wanted to collapse on the ground and hug herself to contain the little warmth that had followed her outside.

She heard the footsteps behind her and whipped around, nearly overbalancing herself. She knew before seeing him that Detective Tanninger had followed her. She heard a car turn down the lane, squealing a little as it came too fast, then the detective grabbed her arm and pulled her aside.

Tanninger grated, "Let's not make it your day to die. Come here. I'll drive you wherever you want to go. My car's over there." He actually put an arm around her and guided her toward the department-issue car at the end of the row. She could have cried, the warmth and strength of him felt so good. She sensed dimly that she'd been negotiating life on her own for a long, long time, and the support was welcome yet unfamiliar.

He bundled her inside, grabbing a jacket from the backseat and laying it across her knocking knees. She smelled leather and maybe a hint of aftershave and a whiff of coffee from the forgotten paper cup in the cup holder. He climbed into the driver's side with a squeak of leather. He switched on the ignition, put the vehicle in gear and eased toward the exit.

"Quarry?" he asked.

She nodded.

And that was all they said until they were away from the hospital and down Highway 26 to just outside of the Quarry city limits, some thirty minutes later. Will drove the patrol car through the city's downtown area—basically one street with businesses on either side that petered out and turned into rural farmland at the far end. Gemma gazed out the window as they passed Thompson's Feed & Grain, Century Insurance Co., Pets and More, the Burger Den, and other businesses whose names rippled through her consciousness, familiar and yet it was like she'd entered a parallel universe, everything felt so out of sync. At the west end of the street she saw LuLu's, a one-story rectangle painted green with white trim with a handicap ramp leading to the front door. Her family's diner. Now hers. Across the street and facing a different direction was the PickAxe, Quarry's only tavern and bar. She ran through several remembered moments from each establishment, pictures from her own youth. Yes, she was definitely from this place, although the particulars were still hazy.

"Am I still going the right direction?" Will asked.

"Turn on Beverly Way," Gemma directed. "Go almost to the end. My house is down the lane to the right. The fields back up to the quarry for which the town's named."

"You have acreage?"

"Farmland . . . ranchland . . . my father dabbled in both." She gazed out the window and thought about Peter LaPorte.

She could scarcely visualize him. He'd blended in with the surroundings, a quiet man who seemed content to let his wife run the show. Jean LaPorte had been fiery and intense and opinionated. She'd been the one who'd insisted they adopt Gemma.

Adoption . . .

And suddenly Gemma was hit by a memory so sharp she was surprised she wasn't cut and left bleeding. She wasn't even sure the memory was true, or if it had been fed to her so well and so often that she believed it to be real. It didn't matter. It was part of her history either way.

She'd been found on a Washington State ferry when she was five or six years old, alone, shivering, freezing cold. She'd been wearing several layers of clothing—one of them being a leather shift that was reminiscent of Native American dress, specifically from the Chinook Indian tribe. The note pinned to her outer jacket said simply, *I am Gemma. Take care of me.* It was scrawled in a spidery hand, and the law enforcement officials believed she'd been raised by an elderly person from one of the tribes living on the Olympic Peninsula. These tribes were modern-day Native Americans, yet the chemise was very traditional. The authorities believed that Gemma had been deliberately placed on the ferry and abandoned, and though they questioned various groups of people—and also the people on the ferry—all they learned was that a very stooped woman with iron-gray hair in braids, was seen with a girl, maybe Gemma, when they were boarding the ferry. Some felt the elderly woman got off the boat before it sailed. No one was sure. All that was for certain was that Gemma was sitting quietly on a bench when it docked and complaining of a headache.

And in truth she'd had crippling headaches as long as she could remember. The LaPortes, her adoptive parents, had taken her to doctors who prescribed pain medication, and Gemma had taken this medication most of her life.

Now, she lifted a hand to the injured side of her face. Yes, there was pain, but it was the pain from physical force. It was not from something inside her head.

"What?" Will asked, throwing her a look as he turned onto Beverly Way.

"I just remembered something I'd forgotten."

"About the accident?"

"No."

Her adoption had been messy. She had no papers. No record of birth. The process went on for years before she was given proper credentials and therefore a social security number, the one she'd recalled at the hospital. She knew that sometimes she felt like she could almost remember the old woman who'd left her on the ferry. She could smell charred firewood and taste a cornmeal patty of some kind. There were words, too, but they were singsong, like a chant, for her young ears. A nursery tale. Indian lore.

But where did she fit into all that? There was nothing about her that said Native American. Her eyes were greenish/hazel. Her hair was medium brown. Her skin was white and burned like a son of a gun when she spent too much time in the sun. Will Tanninger's was far darker than hers. If any part of her was Native American, then its percentage was small for she sported no latent features.

And why had she been left on the ferry? Why had she been rejected? Was there something about her parentage that had spurned her from their group? Some reason she was tossed out?

Maybe because she possessed extra *unwanted* abilities?

She shivered, then tried to reach back into her consciousness as far as she could. The effort made her head hurt like hell and all she recalled was a plastic hospital mask descending on her face and a sickly, chemical scent. She gagged at the memory.

"You okay?" he asked.

"Fine," she said flatly, thinking now—as she had many other times, she realized—that she was extremely lucky Peter and Jean LaPorte had adopted her. They'd taken care of her, loved her the best way they knew how. Peter had been a tad removed, but it was more because he didn't know how to show affection rather than any aversion to Gemma in particular. Jean had loved her fiercely. Had wanted Gemma to be just like her. Had fashioned her in a way that spoke more of what Jean was made of than anything to do with Gemma herself. Jean bullied, pushed and fought her way through life.

And she'd lied . . . about . . . something . . .

"This turn," Gemma said, surfacing with difficulty. Will eased onto the rutted lane and they drove down an oak-lined drive and then across an open grassy area. Ahead, the two-story, white house with the wraparound porch looked like a prototype for "Early Twentieth Century American Farmhouse." Gemma recalled her father working constantly on the house's upkeep. Now, several years after his death, the neglect was starting to show in the dry rot on the edges of the siding, the missing shingles on the roof, the streak of rust at the edge of the gate latch.

"You having trouble remembering?" Will asked as he pulled to a stop.

Gemma realized he saw much more than was comfortable for her. Her first instinct was to lie. Just like her mother did. That thought caused her to hold her tongue, and she simply said, "It's not likely I'm going to forget my whole life for long."

He walked her to the front door, both of their heads bent against the stiff breeze. She hesitated a moment. "I can get in through the back," she said. They walked across the porch, down a few steps and along a dirt track. The rear porch was basically a couple of long, wide steps, the paint chipped away from use. Gemma reached around the sill of the door but found nothing. She hesitated a moment, willing her brain to think while Tanninger looked on. He shifted position and she heard the rustle of his uniform, the squeak of his shoes. It sounded vaguely sexual to her and for a moment she wondered who the hell she was. Why did she think these thoughts? What of her own history was she not recalling?

And then another memory surfaced. "We moved the key to under the bench," she said, and reached beneath the seat of the back-porch bench, finding the key wedged in a niche between thin slats of wood.

Threading the key in the lock, she murmured, "So this is what Alzheimer's people must feel."

"Memory coming and going?" Tanninger did not follow her inside and Gemma turned back to him.

"Pretty much."

"It's only been a few days since your accident."

"Yeah."

Gemma nodded and worried there was something else, something more, at work here. She wondered whether she was obligated to ask him in, but he took the decision away from her by pressing a card in her hand and telling her to call him if she remembered anything. He glanced at the battered white truck parked near the outbuilding, then said good-bye and headed back around the front of the house to his car.

She hurried through the house to the windows, looking out past the front porch to see him climb into the vehicle, turn it nose-out, and then leave splattered mud as he drove up the gravel drive.

Alone, Gemma slowly turned around and exhaled. She was glad Detective Tanninger was gone so she could think. Absorb. Plan.

She examined the decor in the living room/parlor. Her mother's. Lots of quilts and florals and stuff. She felt suddenly claustrophobic. Jean had been a hoarder. Keeping items way past their pull date, in Gemma's opinion.

"How long ago did you die?" Gemma asked her, her voice hanging in the empty room. It felt to Gemma like eons, and yet she sensed it was within the last few years, like her father. She could remember Peter's death clearly. Could see the casket at Murch's Funeral Home and the smattering of people, small groups that moved through the viewing room and on to the gravesite. Could remember her own sadness and a sense of apprehension that filled her. The apprehension, she realized, was because she'd been left to take care of her mother, who had always had a strong opinion on what Gemma should do with her life: stay in Quarry and help in her mother's business as a psychic.

Her mother the psychic.

Gemma sat down hard on a needlepoint-upholstered footstool.

Charlatan. Flim-flam artist. Crook. Liar. That's what her mother had been. Gemma had left home at eighteen, following after an army man who'd been stationed at Fort Lewis in Washington State. He'd moved all around and she'd followed, but their relationship had dwindled as her headaches and memory loss increased when she'd scornfully thrown away her medication, believing the drugs to be the work of her parents, whom she'd deemed at the time to be self-serving and harmful to her health.

Not completely true. Her boyfriend . . . his name escaped her now. So frustrating! Her boyfriend had been the pernicious one. Eroding her self-esteem. Overpowering her and claiming her sexually. Enjoying a sadistic streak that manifested itself in a myriad of ways that Gemma, too young and inexperienced, had chosen to either ignore or absolve.

But she'd always had an incredibly accurate ability to predict the future. Something her mother had seen early and grasped onto and found a way to make a buck from. Of course, Jean's clientele believed her to be the psychic, but it was Gemma who could suddenly pop up with some future scenario or path the seeker should take. Gemma the underappreciated, and unseen.

The boyfriend . . . was . . . dead . . . She couldn't recall how, but she was pretty sure he was gone. Maybe as a result of the war in Iraq? Somehow that didn't feel right but she felt she was on the right track.

After his death, and a period of bumming around, working at diners and restaurants, Gemma had returned home, and that's when Jean's Psychic Readings had really taken off. Jean had opened shop in this very house, using the first floor bedroom as a kind of office.

Now, Gemma walked to that office and realized someone—herself, she suspected—had completely redone the space. There was no couch, no beaded shades, no knickknacks of moons, stars and other astral images. Instead there was a simple, hand-hewn fir desk—courtesy of Peter LaPorte—and two rather modern club chairs. Beside the desk stood a file cabinet, a lamp with a caramel-colored glass shade, and bookshelves filled with hardbacks. Gemma went directly to the file cabinet, which was locked. Her attention was momentarily drawn to the lamp, which was plugged into a floor socket embedded in the fir planks. Spying the cord, she tugged on it gently, thinking there was a reason it seemed out of place. Maybe she should move the lamp to the other side of the desk.

Before that, though, she wanted to see what was inside the file cabinet, and spent a fruitless twenty minutes searching every drawer and cubbyhole in the office looking for a key. Foiled, Gemma sank into the wooden, swivel desk chair. She was certain the file cabinet held the information she sought: bills, identification papers, bank accounts, all the accoutrements needed to prove one's existence in this day and age.

If she sat still and let her mind go blank, perhaps more memories would come. She'd made it this far.

With that thought, she then considered her medication. Scrambling to her feet, she hurried as fast as she could up the stairs to the second floor and the bedroom at the far end of the hall. Her bedroom. She'd not moved into her parents' room after their deaths, though it was closest to the only upstairs bathroom. She couldn't make herself.

Entering her bedroom she stopped short. The walls were a soft, rose red with white paneled wainscoting. The bed was white. All white. The books stacked neatly in a pile on the white nightstand had to do with tapping into unused parts of the brain. Gemma picked one up carefully and leafed through it. Passages were underlined and she suddenly, sharply remembered placing the pen to the page and making those marks.

There was another book on psychological abnormalities. She picked it up and scanned the bold headings inside: Borderline personalities. Multiple personalities. Sociopaths. Pedophiles . . .

The book slipped from her fingers and fell with a clunk on the fir planks. She picked it up immediately and leafed through it some more. In this one she'd made no notes, apparently, but this is what she'd been reading about. This and accessing inaccessible parts of the brain.

She was becoming more and more convinced that she'd been chasing Edward Letton. Her pulse started a slow, hard, deliberate pounding. She'd run him down, known he was going to hurt someone. A young girl.

And then she heard her own voice inside her head:

Red's your color. It helps you learn things, know things.

The medication keeps you from having the headaches but it interferes with your ability. Red helps you access the inaccessible . . .

Gemma gazed wild-eyed around the room. She could almost feel her mind expand and she forcefully shut it down, terrified of what might enter into it. Hurriedly, she raced to the bathroom, found the pills, shook some into her palm and swallowed them dry.

The rain had ruined his plans.

His head pounded. Rage beat at his temples. He'd meant to burn the witch at her home but couldn't and now the other one was gone. Gone from the hospital.

But he knew where she haunted. He knew he would find her scent again.

Now he looked over the fields behind his house. Far across, in the dying light, he could see the fir trees sway. He stepped outside and stood in the feel of the wind. There was no moon tonight. It was hidden by the clouds.

He needed the rain to stop. He needed dry weather to feed the flames.

Across the field, lights switched on in the main house. Fury licked through him. They were spying on him, feeding information about his family to everyone who would listen.

Quickly, he stepped around the side of the house to the carport where his brother's truck stood. The carport roof sagged in the middle, nearly touching the GemTop which sat over the truck's bed.

He could smell her.

Over the evil scent of the witch was the putrid odor of death.

His hand automatically clapped to his neck and the bandage he'd laid over the vicious wounds she'd inflicted. He'd had hell to pay at work over that one. "Hey, retard, you cut yerself shavin'?" Rich Lachey had said when he'd stopped in at work.

Wolf had been in a hurry. The body was under his GemTop so he'd parked the truck at the end of the lot. He hadn't had time to do more than change clothes and slap a bandage over the jagged wounds on his neck before he showed up to tell Seth it was gonna be awhile before he could get to that engine.

But he'd run into Rich instead. He'd wanted to smack the grin from his face. His hands clenched in preparation. He wasn't slow, he was careful. But everyone, especially the witch-mother, had underestimated him.

"The name is Wolf, not retard."

Rich threw back his head and roared with laughter. "Okay, Wolf. Where ya been? Seth wants to know."

"I'll be back next week."

"Next week? Seth ain't gonna like that."

Seth can suck my dick.

Wolf knew his value. He didn't ask for much pay. He didn't ask for anything except the freedom to choose when he was available. His brother had paved the way for him.

Now, opening the GemTop, he looked in at the body. A blanket was tossed over her body, one arm hanging out. He could see his own blood on her fingers and rage filled him anew.

She had to burn.

He wanted to set up a pyre in his own backyard but he knew better . . . he knew better . . .

But the other witch. The one he'd chased. The one who'd escaped the hospital.

He knew where she haunted.

And it was the perfect place to take this one.

He would burn them both.

First this one, then the other.

On her own evil hunting ground, he would find the site for his pyre.

They all had to burn.

Every last witch.

Chapter Five

The Winslow County Sheriff's Department was a one-level, cinder-block structure that wasn't going to win any architectural awards but was more than adequate for the twenty or so personnel who worked there. Sheriff Herbert Nunce occupied a corner office that was filled with untidy, stacked files and fishing paraphernalia. Detective Barbara Gillette shared an office with Will, her desk butted up to his. Her side was obsessively neat while Will's was genially messy. He wasn't a slob, but he couldn't bring himself to have a desk whose surface was uncluttered. His "in" pile always held a couple of pages, and envelopes and notes were tucked to one side of a leather desk pad that was occupied by his coffee mug, some pens and pencils, and a framed picture of himself and Dylan a couple of summers after high school graduation.

Will rarely wore a hat, and as he entered the building he ran his hands through his dark hair, pulling out rainwater. Indian summer had departed as if it were in a hurry to get somewhere else, and they were facing slanting rain, the kind normally reserved for late November and into winter.

The reception desk was behind a wall of glass. Bulletproof glass, ever since one of the crazy meth-heads had come in and threatened with a gun. No more relaxed Mayberry offices after that.

Will waved to Dot, the receptionist, who buzzed open a metal door. Behind it was a utilitarian hallway that led to the offices whose windows were not bulletproof, which only proved that governmental disposition of funds made no real sense and everything was management by crisis only.

The shoulders of Will's uniform were dark with rain and his shoes were soaked through so that he could feel a clamminess in his toes. Barb was seated at her desk, so her back was to the door; Will's desk faced the entry. She swiveled when she heard him enter and her dark eyes gave him the once over.

"Umbrellas not manly enough for you, Tanninger?"

"Didn't have one."

"Wouldn't use it anyway," she observed. "Or a hat."

"Rain's gonna stop today," Jimbo said as he walked by. James Sanchez, lean, mean, and full of swagger, worked Narcotics. His near-black hair was long and scruffy and his uniform was a pair of dirty jeans and a plaid flannel shirt over a black T-shirt. He'd come from Portland on a task force and he'd stayed on. He played by big-city rules. The sheriff didn't quite know what to do with him, but Jimbo could get the job done that others couldn't. No one believed he was attached to the sheriff's department. No one.

Barb ignored him. "You'd rather just get rain running down the back of your neck," she said to Will.

The slant of her look as he rounded his desk was decidedly sexy. Will inwardly sighed. They'd worked together over a year before they'd gone out on their first of two dates, and it had been pleasant and uneventful. Barb was a flirt, but Will hadn't really been interested. Then one night she'd walked into a pub where he sometimes stopped after work to grab a beer and a sandwich, and they'd ended up spending several hours together. He'd gotten the impression she wanted them both to head to her house afterward, and as a means to sidestep the problem, he'd invited her out to dinner the next Friday evening. That had been a mistake. From the frying pan to the fire. Barb had dressed for the occasion in a silky dress that showed off every bump and scoop of her trim body, and she'd swayed in her seat at the restaurant to the soft jazz. She'd wanted to dance but there thankfully was no dance floor. Will had extricated himself from the evening somewhat awkwardly. He'd taken her back to her condo and excused himself after one nightcap. She'd wanted him to kiss her and when it was clear he was uncomfortable with that, she'd gotten mad and snarky. He'd left in a hurry and she'd been pissed at him the whole next month. She had only softened up—at least sort of—after he'd told her he just couldn't go there right now. He hadn't given her a specific reason; there was none, really. He just wasn't all that attracted to her. But he'd treated her fairly, and slowly her fury had turned to a low simmer. Now she teased and verbally jabbed him, a play for attention, but it was better than the anger. Some of the other guys shot him looks of amusement or fake sympathy, but so far there hadn't been any remarks that would have resulted in Barb getting all furious with him again.

"Hey, Burl knows your hit-and-run friend from Quarry," Barb said. "He lives around that area. Gave us a whole rundown on the LaPorte family. Colorful. Very colorful."

Will grunted. His interest was piqued but he didn't want to share that with Barb. She was always fishing, where he was concerned, inordinately interested in how he reacted to any information. And Burlington "Burl" Jernstadt was about the biggest horse's ass Will had run across in law enforcement. He made Ralph Smithson look like a piker. The fact that Burl was retired and had given up his job reluctantly—which translated loosely to leave or be let go—and that Will had been promoted into Burl's job, didn't mean that Burl had given up haunting the department offices. It didn't matter that he'd been a loud, ineffectual, socially inept buffoon who'd screwed up more cases than he'd aided in, and that he'd been lucky to be eased out of the department rather than fired. Burl couldn't stay away. That he resented Will for taking his job went without saying. To date no one had had the gumption to tell him to get out and stay out. Will sensed that day was coming. He half-dreaded, half-welcomed it.

Whatever the case. He really didn't want to talk to Burl. Except that the man knew something about Gemma LaPorte, and Gemma LaPorte was still his number-one guess for the avenger who'd run down Edward Letton.

"Anything on Jean LaPorte's car?" he asked.

"Still no sign of it."

As soon as Will had learned Gemma's name and situation, he'd done a background check on every member of her family. He'd learned a number of things about them, but what had snagged his attention first was that the LaPortes had owned two vehicles: Peter's white Chevy truck—which he'd seen at the house—and Jean's silver Camry, which was apparently MIA. Maybe the guy who'd dropped Gemma off at the hospital had it, or maybe Gemma had crashed it into Edward Letton, or maybe it was parked somewhere on the LaPorte property. Whatever the case, to date it hadn't been found, and Gemma hadn't called to say differently. There was no vehicle in Gemma's own name.

"Burl still around?" Will asked Barb.

"Always. Probably by the coffee machine."

Which was next to the doughnut boxes. "No other silver Camrys with front-end damage discovered?"

"Not in this county. One in Clatsop County but it was a Dodge Durango and the guy who smashed it up is in jail with his second DUI. Dot says your little friend's been calling. Pellter with two l's. Check your voice mail."

Will punched in the numbers of his phone and waited. Carol Pellter, having been saved from assault and probably death at the hands of Letton, had taken her story public, though her parents were clearly uncomfortable with the whole thing. The media had run the girl's story of a really bad man trying to get her into his van, and had taken pictures of the outside of the impounded van. But it had been nearly a week since the event, and since Carol was alive and well, the prurient interest of the news watchers had moved on to events with more salacious pictures and tragic outcomes.

Carol, however, was hanging onto her fifteen minutes of fame with all ten fingers.

"Hi, Detective Tanninger," Carol's recorded voice stated primly. "I want to help in your investigation. I think you might need me. Could you please call me?" She left her number, speaking it clearly in a precise tone, twice.

Will smiled to himself. Looking forward more to talking to Carol than dealing with Burl, he placed a call to the number she'd given him and ended up with Carol's prim voice suggesting he leave a message on her voice mail. He waited for the beep then told her it was Will Tanninger returning her call.

Kids with cell phones. It was the norm rather than the exception.

Barb was pretending not to be avidly listening to his every syllable. Will had to push aside the distraction of her laser-like interest in him with almost physical force. God, things were getting bad.

He got up from his desk. "Where're you going?" Barb asked, swiveling around as he circled toward the door.

"Gonna see Nunce," he said.

"I'm coming with you." She bustled to catch up to him and fell in step beside him in the outer hall.

Will's temper was slow to rile, but Barb had been getting on his nerves for quite a while. He held back a sharp remark with an effort.

Sheriff Herbert Nunce was gray-haired, gray-eyed, tanned and weathered like old leather. He was slim and straight and distracted. He'd gotten the job by being the last man standing: his predecessors had all been promoted or left the sheriff's office. He'd been sheriff for seven years and he'd gradually spent more and more time on the creeks and rivers that ran through the Coast Range, chasing steelhead and salmon and anything with fins. His interest in law enforcement—never strong, Will guessed—had been displaced so thoroughly that it was hard to get him juiced about any investigation, be it robbery/homicide, or narcotics, or anything in between. Will had written a report on Letton's hit-and-run but he would bet Nunce hadn't read it yet. This appeared to be borne out when Nunce greeted him with, "Smithson still sitting outside that hospital room?"

Will nodded. He could've reminded the sheriff that Letton's life could still be in danger, but it wasn't like the sheriff didn't know. Nunce just reached for the one part of the investigation he was familiar with.

Burl had been nowhere in sight when Will and Barb entered the room, but now he snaked in around the doorway, an eavesdropper hoping not to be noticed. Will turned to gaze at him dead on, which caused Jernstadt to fidget.

"Burl, we're having a talk here," Nunce said, almost kindly. Nunce had wanted Burl out as much as the next man, but like everyone else, still tiptoed around the man's feelings. The humorous part was that Nunce didn't want the uninvited talk with Will and Barb much, either, and would probably have come up with an excuse to put it off except it was preferable to interacting with Burl.

"About that pedophile hit-and-run. I know. Did she tell you that I know that family? The LaPortes?" Burl jerked his head toward Barb but his gaze was on Will. "A bunch of loonies. The old man was a pussy. Let his wife run roughshod over him, and she was in a wrangle with the Dunleavys something fierce. I'm from Woodbine, right next to Quarry." He hooked a thumb at his own chest. "I know Kevin Dunleavy. A straight shooter, if I ever saw one. There's a long-standing fight over property rights between the families. The quarry's right between their properties and that crazy psycho Jean was always screaming at Kevin and his brother Rome and the rest of the family. But Jean's a piece of fuckin' work, pardon my French, and she made some threat that Kevin should keep his family close if he wants 'em to survive, y'know what I mean? Thinks she's a psychic, or something, and just goes around predicting shit and acts like it's not her making it up. Like it's real or something."

"Jean LaPorte is deceased," Will broke in when Burl took a breath. "You're saying she was a psychic."

"Pretend psychic. *Pretend.* She didn't know her ass from a fuckin' hole in the ground, pardon my French again, but that didn't stop her. And now her daughter's a killer. Doesn't surprise me in the least."

"We don't know anything yet," Will cut in.

"You're making a ton of assumptions," Barb said at the same time.

Nunce waved them all off. "Burl, let's not get ahead of ourselves."

"I'm giving you background." Burl glared at Will as if it were all his fault. "Haven't you talked to her?"

"It's a police investigation." *And none of your business.*

Burl stared at Will as if he were speaking in tongues. "Sounds like she didn't tell you nothing. That why you let her go home?"

Barb said in a long-suffering tone, "Burl, you know we can't discuss the case with you. If we had enough to arrest anyone for the hit-and-run, we would have done it."

"I could get her to talk," Burl said to Will. "I know the Dunleavys."

"The Dunleavys aren't part of this particular crime." Will felt his jaw tighten despite his efforts to not let Jernstadt get to him. He turned to Nunce. "I've got interviews on tap."

"With who?" Burl demanded.

Will brushed past him, Barb at his heels, and Nunce said to Burl, "Why don't you give me the names of all the Dunleavys."

Torn, Burl hesitated, really wanting to follow Will and Barb. But Nunce looked expectant.

"There aren't that many of 'em."

"Write their names here." Nunce pushed a piece of paper in Burl's direction, distracting him, and Will and Barb completed their escape.

"Jesus," Barb breathed.

"Think Nunce'll ever tell him to get the hell out?" Will passed by his office, glancing back as Barb slowed by the door, looking longingly his way. He didn't invite her along and there was no need for her to join him.

"He'd have to grow bigger balls," she said.

He'd have to grow any balls, Will decided but, as ever, kept his thoughts to himself. Nunce might sometimes be ineffectual, but he was a decent enough human being. Not something that could be said about Burlington Jernstadt. If Will really wanted to get rid of the prick he could go over Nunce's head, but that came with its own can of worms.

He walked past Dot in reception and stepped out into weak sunshine. Looked like Jimbo was right. The rain was ending.

The white Chevrolet pickup was a couple of decades old and rattled like it was filled with ball bearings. Gemma had to manhandle it into gear, but the yank and pull was both familiar and comforting. The truck had been her father's, and it had been sitting outside the large garage with the corrugated metal roof behind the house, as ugly a building as the house was architecturally beautiful. Gemma had found its keys hanging on a hook by the back door—along with keys for the filing cabinet and several locks that she still hadn't identified. Not exactly the tightest security around the old homestead.

She'd holed up inside for nearly a week, familiarizing herself, letting her bruises heal, letting herself heal. In that time she'd read nearly every scrap of paper she could find that had to do with the family's finances, the past year's calendar of events, the information on both her parents' deaths. She'd gone through the filing cabinet and rifled through boxes in the attic until her eyes burned and her head ached, and she'd slept a great deal. The urgency she'd felt at the hospital—the need to apparently right some wrong—had eased to a simmer now that she was home. Maybe it was knowing that Edward Letton was still in the hospital, still in a coma. If he'd awakened and been released, she believed she would have heard it on the news, and at any rate, she just sensed that he was still there and for now, at least, she was going to trust her feelings.

She had not found her purse, nor did she have any recollection about her mother's car, which according to Tanninger, who'd phoned to ostensibly keep her informed, was a silver Camry. That had caused shivers of fear to run up and down her spine. Was that what she'd been driving? If, and when, it turned up would it prove that she'd run down Edward Letton?

But what she had found among the papers was her medical insurance information, and she'd called hospital administration right away, happy that maybe she wasn't going to be made destitute by her stay there. At least that was taken care of.

She'd spent most of the last week dwelling on something

else, though: what her day-to-day life had been like before the accident. She had flashes of being in her mother's office and seeing clients, people who wanted a glimpse into their own futures. But she also remembered working at LuLu's, though those memories weren't as clear. Maybe her time at the diner was further in the past. Whatever the case, she was driving there now. She felt ready to see people again, though she wondered what, if anything, they'd heard about her and the Letton hit-and-run. She really had no idea how much, or how little, of the information tying her to that accident had been obtained by the media.

LuLu's was a nondescript, one-story rectangular building with dark green shingled siding, a transparent attempt to put lipstick on a pig. The empty flower beds on either side of the wooden steps that led to weather-beaten French doors didn't help. Even the green-and-white striped awning above the doors seemed like an afterthought, and maybe not a very good one. But still, seeing the place brought back wave upon wave of memories. She'd loved LuLu's. Had filled those flower boxes with red petunias. Had worked as a waitress here, though she couldn't remember her mother on the premises . . . hmmm . . .

Gemma pulled the truck into the side gravel lot, yanked on the emergency brake, cut the engine, then as it coughed and shook itself to silence, she headed up the four front steps and stepped beneath the awning to avoid the surprisingly hot sun. The rain had vanished after a couple of drenched days, and now the ground was as hard and dry as before.

She twisted open the right French door, as she knew the left was fixed in place, entering immediately into the main dining room. Straight ahead was a counter with stools and behind it she could see the stainless-steel appliances and paraphernalia of the kitchen.

The familiarity of the place soaked in, right to her core, and Gemma inhaled deeply, feeling more solidly connected to herself than she had since waking up in the hospital. LuLu's. Her home away from home.

"Hey, sugar," a female voice called from behind the counter. Gemma looked over and saw a tall, red-haired woman in a beige uniform with a white collar, the front pockets gaping open to reveal notepads and pens. Her large bust was propped up with a sturdy bra and she wore enough eye makeup to open her own department store. She was grinning with delight at Gemma. "You look like hell, honey. Get over here."

"Macie," Gemma said, a rush of pleasure flooding her. Macie was the one who ran the diner. Macie was the one who'd treated Gemma like a daughter when Jean was at a complete loss, never flagging in that role even when she had her own child, Charlotte, now eleven.

And Macie was the one who never rolled her eyes in embarrassment or repressed anger when Gemma's debilitating headaches and memory losses bewildered the young girl.

It all clicked together. The diner was Macie's, not Jean's. The LaPorte family leased the premises to Macie, and had for as long as Gemma could remember. Gemma was now Macie's landlord but she'd spent many happy hours in her youth working as a waitress.

"Good grief, girl, you look like somebody smacked you silly." She regarded Gemma with real concern. "What happened?"

"I was in a car accident."

"Woowee. You okay?"

"My face looks worse than it feels."

Macie cocked her head. "I could show you a thing or two about makeup. Would take care of all them bruises, I do believe. But you ain't never let me take a mascara brush to you yet, so I think I'll just save my breath. Besides, you've got it under control. Another couple of days or so and no one'll be able to tell. Anybody else hurt?"

Gemma thought of Edward Letton. "Not that I know of," she said carefully. "I gotta get down to the DMV. Lost my purse and now I'm driving without my license."

"That'll be the time you get stopped."

"Don't I know it." She glanced around. "Charlotte at school?"

"God, I hope so. That child'll be the death of me if she gets into more trouble."

"What's she done?" Gemma smiled, her mental picture of the skinny, tough girl coming into focus. Charlotte wore her hair in a short bob and the scowl on her face said most adults were idiots.

"Just leaves in the middle of her last class. She's done it four times already. Just walks out. School's only about two miles from the diner, so she takes off and shows up here. Meanwhile, I get calls from the administration." She flapped a hand. "They threaten her with detention and black marks and the whole enchilada, but it doesn't faze her. She told me the teacher's a bore."

Gemma's smile grew. Charlotte was everything she'd ever wanted to be, at her age. She felt bonded to the child as if they were sisters.

That thought brought her stomach a funny wave of discomfort.

If anything should ever happen to Charlotte . . .

"Macie!" an impatient male voice called from across the room. A guy in a plaid workshirt, jeans, and workboots was holding up an empty coffee mug.

"Hold on to your knickers, Captain. I'll be right there." To Gemma, she murmured in an aside, "Still thinks he's the only one in the place." She sauntered toward him, snagging the coffeepot from a plugged-in burner on her way.

Gemma sat at the last booth in the row, which was wedged into an alcove, and ordered a sandwich. Her favorite spot. She'd spent a lot of hours at the diner, either working or seated at this very table, catching a meal in between shifts. This was the epitome of normality. This was the arena of her fondest memories.

"Did you ever find that guy?" Macie asked when she had a spare moment. She set the coffeepot back on the burner and sent Gemma a questioning look.

"Which guy?"

"The one you were chasing? The one you had to stop?"

Gemma stared at Macie as one of the other waitresses, whose name tag read Denise, brought Gemma her turkey on rye. She felt slightly strangled, like she couldn't get her breath. "The accident knocked things out of my head."

"The accident?" Macie gave her a *oh, come on* look. "Since when do you need an excuse for your on/off brain. You know it works better than most." She shot the man she'd called Captain a searing glance. "A case in point . . ."

"What guy did I have to stop?"

"You tell me, girl. All I saw was you getting all worked up and tearing outta the diner lot like you'd seen a ghost. I thought it was that guy sitting in the booth by the door 'cause you waited till his vehicle was outta sight before you ran to your momma's car."

"My momma's car . . ." Gemma repeated, her heart jerking. So, it was true . . .

"Well, it wasn't *your* car, now was it?" Macie declared.

"I guess not."

"Hon, you told me yours was on its last legs, so you sold it. Don't you remember?"

"Kind of," Gemma lied.

"Well, no matter." She shrugged it off. "You said you were just driving your momma's temporarily. It's kind of a wreck, to be perfectly honest. Jean sure didn't know how to take care of things. Sorry, hon, bless her soul, but your momma was kind of in her own world. Best thing she ever did was adopt you. Really about the only truly selfless thing she did, but then we know how that turned out, don't we? What are you gonna do about her business, now? Sally Van Kamp was asking if you were ever gonna call her back."

"Not sure I have her number," Gemma murmured. She felt bombarded with information, yet Macie was only telling her the kind of information she'd craved to learn. Psychic readings. That's the business Macie meant. Sally Van Kamp wanted a psychic reading from Gemma. All of Jean's clients had tenaciously hung in there whether Gemma wanted to tell them their futures or not.

"She said she left it on the machine."

"Oh." There were messages on the house voice mail but Gemma hadn't known how to retrieve them.

And then as soon as that thought crossed her mind, the series of numbers to access them came to her as if they had always been there. Her on-again/off-again brain, according to Macie. This was beginning to feel like normal for Gemma.

I'm a freak. Accept it and move on.

"You gonna come help me out again? I had two high school kids but since school's started they don't have any time to give me. Always want summer jobs, but they whine and whine if they have any social activity at all."

"I'd love to." Gemma seized on the idea. Working at the diner sounded . . . good.

"Yeah? Well, you put yourself together for a couple more days. Get rid of the remnants of that eye." She held Gemma's chin and moved her face from side to side. "Honey, you just bashed yourself good, didn't ya?"

Her caring tone caused a ripple of emotion to run through Gemma's heart, leaving her throat hot. She swallowed hard and said, "I'll come in for an afternoon just to get started again. Will I see Charlotte?"

"Oh, you know she'll be around."

Gemma left her booth and lifted a hand in good-bye, then

hesitated at the door. "When was that? When I chased that guy out?"

Macie lifted a shoulder. "'Bout a week ago, or so."

"You didn't recognize him?"

"Wasn't a regular."

"What did he look like?" Gemma asked.

"Like every other middle-aged man in the world. I kinda thought he was from around here, but I can't remember why. He had a baseball cap on, I think. Or maybe that was the other guy, the one that left right after you did. I don't know. It was the morning crowd and they were all hungry. I wasn't paying all that much attention except that you were kinda wild-eyed."

"I almost remember," Gemma said.

"Almost only counts with horseshoes and hand grenades," Macie responded automatically. One of her favorite expressions.

Gemma smiled faintly. "The guy that left after me. What did he look like?"

"More apish," Macie said after a moment of thought. "Rounded shoulders like he worked out too much."

Gemma was heading out when Macie caught her by the arm. "Have you thought about seeing Doc Rainfield?" she asked.

"What?" Gemma asked.

"If you don't want to, that's perfectly okay, y'know. But that shrink doctor of yours has helped before. He's a nice guy."

Gemma suddenly pictured the older man with the creased, sad face. He was a nice guy. And he had helped her.

"Your momma had her fits with him, but I always thought you and he connected. Do what you want." She lifted her hands in surrender. "Just, if things are bad . . . he might be able to help."

With that she scurried off to deal with another order and Gemma left the diner.

Looking in the mirror, Lucky realized she'd been injured far worse than she'd originally thought. She shrank inside herself at the bonanza of colors: green, purple, brown, that ran down the side of her face and covered one eye. That eye was a problem. Blood had drained into the white part and turned one corner a sickening scarlet, which was slowly fading to magenta-ish pink. She'd had to wait over a week for her face to stop being such a show stopper. She'd waited impatiently, afraid Letton would be released from the hospital before she could take care of him permanently—the bastard had had the nerve to survive!—but apparently she'd hurt him pretty damn bad because he was still languishing there.

Good.

She'd used the time to recover herself. She kinda hurt all over. The seat belt had left a deep bruise and it was a little tricky to take a deep breath.

But with each tick of the clock she'd grown stronger. And now that she'd purchased actual rose-colored glasses, her magenta-filled eye looked damn near normal. If she went to Letton's room in the early evening, maybe around dinnertime when there was more hustle and bustle and confusion around the hospital, she might not be noticed as much. But she would have to be careful. Find a way to disguise herself.

She cocked her head and considered. One more day? Two?

If Letton were released that would compound her problems. She needed to wrap her hands around the man's throat and choke the life from him. Or smother him with a hospital pillow. There would be sweet irony in having his place of healing turn into his place of death.

Her temple throbbed and she pressed fingers hard against it, as if pushing the pain back inside.

And then she was hit by a wave of something like lust. Not her own. A sample of what Letton had felt when he was eyeing prepubescent girls. It left Lucky feeling sick, spent and bent over, hacking, on the verge of throwing up. Saliva ran from her mouth; the precursor to vomiting. She wiped it away and drew several breaths, straightening with an effort, staring at her reflection in the mirror. This wasn't the first time she'd been able to sense—physically sense—what someone felt. It was a kind of psychic ability she neither understood nor wanted, but it was something she'd been born with and it had sent her on this quest. This mission.

She visualized Letton, saw the hot need in his eyes.

"I'm going to kill you, you bastard," she whispered harshly.

Edward Letton woke with a snort and a gasp. Demons were running around inside his head. They were spinning. Chortling. Poking fingers at him and laughing like hyenas. He was in hell. He was dead. Or dying. Suffocating.

Slowly he opened his eyes. His mouth was slack and desert dry. There was a tube running from his nose. No. Into his nose. Oxygen. He was being given oxygen because he was . . . in a hospital . . . and he could feel pain, though he was oddly dissociated from it. Drugs. Demerol, maybe, or something like it.

What happened?

He couldn't piece it together. It was too much. He'd been at work but that was on Friday. And then there was—

A soccer game.

He drew a quaking breath of fear and tried to look around. Did they know? He'd been in the van. Oh, God. The van.

Fuzziness ruled his head. The damned drugs. He was in a hospital bed but he couldn't remember why. How long had he been out? Had he *said* anything? Did they *know*?

He struggled to move but his body screamed at even the slightest twitch. He was breathing hard, though he'd scarcely done more than squeeze his eyes closed, sucking up the oxygen, in some kind of real mess here.

What had he done? What happened? How had he ended up in a hospital?

Faintly, as if viewing it from a long, long distance, he saw the young girl with the slim legs and blue shorts. She was so beautiful. He wanted to rub against that firm, nubile flesh. But he knew she wouldn't allow it. That's why he'd brought the van.

The van. He'd worked so hard on the van. Long hours, away from Mandy. Hiding out in the garage, listening with active ears in case she should enter the garage uninvited, surprising him. The sweet danger of that had given him almost a constant erection. If she caught him fitting out the van, what would he say? Would she believe him? Would he have to take her as his first victim, just to keep her quiet? He despised her. Her big tits and fat, cellulite-filled ass. But she was a necessary part of the equation. His cover. His loving wife.

But she never came in the garage. Couldn't be torn away from her reality TV shows. That one where a bunch of shrieking women went after the rich guy really turned her on. She about wet her pants when those guys gave the girls roses. If she'd had an ounce of sexuality herself, she might have given herself a rub and tickle, it turned her on so much. Unfortunately, that would never happen. Mandy liked chocolates, and an occasional gift, though he could never afford the diamonds and furs she salivated over. Maybe if he could, she might have tried to at least enjoy their monthly hump and bump, but she pretty much just waited for it to be over. Just closed her eyes and waited while Ed did his thing. One time, by God, she'd started softly snoring. Out cold. That was about the last time he'd been able to even get it up for her.

She was too round.

Too old.

But girls . . . they were beautiful. Lovely, lovely thighs and ankles and flat chests with skin drum-taut, and narrow little wrists.

It was a sickness; he knew that. He didn't care. Ed had waited all his life for something for himself. When was it Eddie's turn, huh? And he wasn't going to wait anymore. He was going to take what he wanted. What he needed. What he deserved!

But . . . what had happened? He was in deep shit, here, he could tell, and there was a murky memory of something bad . . .

Damn drugs. He was sinking under them, but at least that would mean the pain would go away. He was hurt. He needed to heal.

He could see that lovely, lovely girl reaching for the soccer ball . . .

In his dream he reached back.

Lovely . . .

Chapter Six

The interior of the truck reeked. Reeked with her evil odor. Reeked with her death. His eyes watered but he refused to cover his nose and mouth. He wouldn't give the witch the satisfaction.

And she was burning now. Burning. Her sick, filthy flesh melting from her body.

He drove away as fast as he dared. He'd found a place for her. They would discover her and soon. Her scent alone would draw them near, but the fire would pinpoint the location from afar.

He had a long way to go before he was safe. The other witch's haunts were over an hour's journey from his home, closer to two in the summer when vacationers headed to the beach. He didn't know what had brought her to the town of Quarry, but it was where he'd found her, where he intended to find her again.

Quarry.

His lips flattened into a cold smile.

His quarry.

* * *

Carol Pellter really had nothing more to add to her story but she was bent on keeping Will's interest as he sat across from her at the dining table of her parents' house. Her mom looked both weary and annoyed. Now that the danger was past, their daughter's obsession with the event was something she wanted to switch off but just did not know how.

Carol's tale was sounding less and less like a suspected kidnapping and probable sexual assault case, and more and more like an epic fairy tale where Letton was an ogre bent on destroying everything good and hopeful in the world and Carol was a princess/swashbuckler who saved one and all.

Will pretended to listen closely to her description of Letton, which stopped just short of him possessing horns and cloven feet, while trying to direct her tale-telling toward something a little more productive. He'd already concluded that this trip to meet with her was a waste of time, but he liked her and sensed that her need to keep the attention on herself stemmed from loneliness, the kind suffered by children whose busy parents signed their kids up for every athletic event, every academic tournament as a means of overcompensation. She had no brothers or sisters and possessed an imagination that boggled. Will sought to guide her through the events of the morning of her near-abduction in an attempt to draw her back from fantasy.

"Do you remember anything about the silver car?" Will asked, though Carol had been thoroughly questioned a number of times already. Each time her story became a little more exaggerated.

"It came speeding up then BAM! He just went up in the air and landed back on top. Then he bounced off. There was a lot of blood." She'd been squeamish and white-faced the first time she'd told the tale. Now she didn't bat an eye. "He was kinda moving his legs and arms, like he was gonna get up and chase me like a zombie!" She shivered, eyes wide.

Will could see her adding that to her fairy tale. The Princess and the Zombie.

"You said it was silver. What about the wheels?"

"The wheels?"

"What kind of rim did they have? Chrome, shiny? Or, dull, maybe black?"

"They were just wheels. Round."

"Any kind of logo? Name of the kind of car? Like, Ford or Toyota or Jeep?"

"It was just kinda old."

"How did you know that?"

"I know cars," she said, like he was the biggest idiot on earth. "My dad drives a BMW and my mom has a Ford Escape."

"All right. Do you know what kind of old car it was?"

"The kind people don't take care of."

"Meaning . . . it had dents?"

"The color was not good."

"The silver was more gray than—shiny?"

"It was orange."

"Orange?"

"Like on the back. I saw it when she zipped through the lot like a bat outta hell!"

"Where did you see it? The back of the car? Like the trunk?"

"No, the protector bar. It was kinda bent and—"

"Rusty? The bumper was rust-covered?" Will guessed. Carol had said before she thought the car was old, but she'd never said it was orange before.

"Yeah, that's it. Rusty. The bumper was rusty. Does that help?" she asked, keying into Will's sparked interest.

"Maybe. Those are the kinds of things that help when you remember them."

"I'll keep remembering," she assured him. "Maybe I'll remember some more tomorrow. Can you come by?"

"Carol," her mother sighed.

"Mom, I'm helping!" she declared, right back.

"I'm not sure I can stop by again tomorrow, but you can always call me," Will said.

"Okay." She turned her head and peered at him sideways. "You're not just humoring me, are you?"

"Carol!"

"No," Will assured her. The mother turned three shades of scarlet on hearing her daughter mime her and her husband's own words. "You never know when something might help."

Carol shot her mother a *see there* look as Will's cell phone rang. Excusing himself, he stepped onto the Pellters' front porch and punched the talk button. "Tanninger."

"Will, there's a fire out by the Laurelton Airport," Barb told him.

"Uh-huh." He waited. Since the strip of land euphemistically known as the Laurelton Airport was outside the city limits, it was within the Winslow County lines and therefore the sheriff's department's jurisdiction. But fires were the fire department's problem.

Barb enlightened him. "Dead body at the scene. Looks like whoever started the fire was trying to burn the body."

"Homicide?"

"Yep. ME's heading to the scene. But from what I'm getting, that body's been dead awhile. At least a week. Female."

"Someone trying to cover up the crime."

"Most likely."

"Okay, I'm on my way," Will said.

"I'll meet you there."

Gemma opened her mailbox and was relieved to find a new bank card. She'd made the trip to the bank to access her funds, but hadn't yet gone for her driver's license. The thought of a picture in her current bruised state had really squelched her desire to abide by the law. For now, she was driving without it. If she got pulled over, tough. She would just deal with the consequences.

Even though most of her memory had returned—she could recall a lot of her growing up years although specific details were still hazy—she was at a complete loss about her recent past. She didn't remember any part of chasing out of LuLu's after some unidentified man. The only piece that seemed to stick out was eating oatmeal and cinnamon three days before she woke up in the hospital. Anything before that came in fits and starts, but with Macie's explanation of her on-again/off-again brain, Gemma had accepted this annoyance as part of her own weird makeup.

Still, she'd been desperately trying to remember who she'd chased after, out of LuLu's. Was it that pedophile, Letton? Was she the person who had deliberately run him down? Would she do that?

I would if the target were Charlotte.

She thought about that hard. She would kill to save Charlotte.

She smiled faintly as she thought of Macie's daughter. Eleven years old. A truant. Tough as rawhide, with endless energy and a smart mouth. Charlotte was a truth-teller. For reasons she couldn't explain, Gemma could remember nearly everything about her. She identified with Charlotte, who, though her mother loved her dearly, was independent in the way of only-children and loners. She lived with Macie, but she also lived in a wider world. Everyone around Quarry knew Charlotte. She rode her bike all over the place and knew more about the town's gossip than was probably healthy. Like some forgotten memory, Gemma recalled that Charlotte had learned things about people, things she'd then told Jean, who had used them in her predictions. That betrayal had pissed Charlotte off.

If someone like Edward Letton were after Charlotte, Gemma would have no qualms about running the bastard down. She could remember the emotion—the fury—that had consumed her as she banged out of Lulu's that day. She'd followed him to his home . . . no . . . place of work?

"Where's the car?" she asked aloud to the empty room. She'd looked in all the outbuildings on the off-chance it was there, but there was no sign of it.

Tossing the mail on the front table, she extracted her bank card. She was using an older purse that had nothing in it but two tubes of lipstick and a stack of ballpoint pens. She dropped the bank card into it and decided it was time to buy a new wallet.

"And where's my purse? And who dropped me off at the hospital?"

It was extremely frustrating—*extremely* frustrating—that she couldn't recall those facts.

The phone rang and Gemma hesitated before answering. "Hello?"

"It's Sally, Gemma, dear. Thanks for calling me back." Her tone added the word *finally*, though she didn't say it. "When can I have my appointment?"

Sally Van Kamp. Gemma had been forced to return her call, then had been thrilled when the woman's answering machine had clicked on, giving her a chance to bob and weave. She had no interest in giving the woman a reading. None.

"Hello, Sally. I just wanted to let you know that I'm not scheduling any appointments right now," she began regretfully.

"What? You can't be serious. Jean, rest her soul, has been gone for nearly a year, and you've put me off and put me off. Your mother would never have treated me like this!"

"I'm recovering from a—car accident. I just got out of the

hospital," Gemma said tightly. Okay, it was almost a week ago but Sally didn't have to know that.

"Oh." She was momentarily flummoxed. But then she swept on, "I'll bring you over some of my chicken casserole. Just the thing. Perk you right up."

"You don't have to—"

"Oh, my, my, yes, I do! I'll see you this afternoon."

She clicked off and Gemma was left holding the receiver. She didn't want to deal with Sally. She didn't want her time used up. Before she started work at the diner she wanted to finish a few things. Threads left untied.

With that in mind she headed upstairs to her bedroom and the research books with their underlined passages.

The Laurelton airstrip was a narrow line of hard soil, mowed grass, and a Quonset hut terminal, if you could call it that, painted white. Flags snapped in a frisky breeze, and the sun glared down, a fierce, yellow eye.

The smell of burned flesh caught on the breeze as Will climbed from his patrol car and Barb got out of the other side. Burned, putrefying human flesh. Barb wrinkled her nose in distaste as they circled past a state patrol car and the Quonset hut, and headed in the direction of the group of vehicles clustered around the back of the airstrip.

A fire truck stood off to one side and several men and one woman were looking down at a black tarp, presumably the body. Around them was an area of burned field grass. The fire had luckily been extinguished before it could do greater damage.

"ME was on the other side of the county," Barb said. "Don't see him yet."

They approached the group. The state patrolman's name was Evans and he shook Will and Barb's hands. He introduced the other man—gray-faced and looking about to faint—as Freddie Delray, an airplane mechanic, and the woman, middle-aged, heavy-set, and sharp-eyed, as Maggie Longworth, the Laurelton Airport's resident everything. She didn't seem particularly moved by the burned body or the god-awful stench, but Freddie was having a hard time.

"Freddie found the body," Patrolman Evans explained. "Called 911 and I was first available." He pointed to the fire truck where one of the firemen was leaning against the front bumper. His partner was inside the truck, talking on a cell phone. "There wasn't much of a fire. Freddie saw it immediately and ran out with water before it got going. Nothing really to put out."

"Coulda been bad," Barb observed.

"Real bad," Evans agreed.

Will said, "Can we see the body?"

"Okay, but get ready."

Freddie made a squeak of protest and looked away, swallowing hard, but Maggie leaned forward as if dying for another look.

The charred body was of a woman. It had been doused with water, undoubtedly by Freddie, who took the moment now to simply collapse onto the ground and retch up his lunch. The body had been set on fire but there were also two circular dots burned on the chest.

"Cigarette burns?" Barb asked.

"Maybe ritualistic," Will said.

"What the hell does that mean?" Barb asked the question but looked reviled.

Maggie said, "He's sending a message, maybe."

Both Will and Barb looked at her, then at each other, then down at the body again.

"Looks like the fire was a diversion?" Evans guessed.

"From what? He left the body here for us to find." Will

turned to Freddie, whose head hung forward though he was on his feet again. "How long ago did you put this out?"

"An hour. Forty-five minutes? I don't know." He spat onto the dirt.

"She's been dead awhile," Barb observed.

Will leaned forward. "What would you say? A week, maybe?"

"Smells like it," Evans murmured.

Will gazed around the fields, then over to the Quonset hut. There was no activity. The airstrip could have been abandoned and practically was. From where they stood, someone could easily have set the fire, walked back to a waiting vehicle and driven away without being seen by a soul.

"So, he killed her, marked her with a cigarette, kept her hidden for a week then brought her here to burn. He chose this place because there's no one here."

"We're here," Maggie protested.

"There are no windows in this direction."

Maggie frowned at Freddie, as if it were somehow his fault.

Will glanced from the Quonset hut to the fields beyond. They gave way to heavy brush almost immediately from where they stood. It was the far western point of the airstrip. There was nothing for miles and miles behind them but untended brush and scraggly trees, giving way to timber in the far, far distance. "Coulda started a major fire."

"Why draw attention to himself?" Barb asked. "If he'd just buried her, she might not have been found for a while."

Will gazed down at the young woman's body. "I think he likes to burn."

It was three o'clock when Sally rang Gemma's front doorbell. Gemma heard it from the den, where she was lost in thought, having read more passages in her books on borderline personalities, pedophiles, and various and sundry brain sicknesses, until she felt slightly ill. Gemma answered the door still lost in that world, but seeing Sally brought her back to earth with a bang.

Sally Van Kamp, a roundish, middle-aged woman with curly dark hair and an intense attitude, recoiled a bit upon viewing Gemma's face. "Oh, my, my. You really did have an accident, now, didn't you?"

And here she'd been thinking she was starting to look almost normal. "Well, yeah." Belatedly, she invited, "Come on in."

"I made this up special for you, honey." She held out the casserole and the hot pad beneath. Gingerly, Gemma took it from her and headed into the kitchen, Sally at her heels.

"Looks the same," Sally observed.

"I haven't changed much around here since Mom died."

Sally cricked her neck and eyed Gemma thoughtfully. "I never heard you call her Mom before. Sounds funny. You always called her Jean, like she was a stranger." She laughed like it was a big joke.

Gemma let that go by. It *had* felt strange saying Mom. It was a relief to understand her relationship with her mother a little better, and she realized that maybe Sally Van Kamp wasn't the only one who could gain some information out of their upcoming reading.

The reading itself made Gemma a little nervous. She could recall her mother's hocus-pocus ways, but she would never be able to do that. Or, had she already? Sally acted like they'd not had a reading since Jean's death, but maybe that was just Gemma's hope.

"Er, when was the last time we met for a reading?" Gemma asked as they moved to the office and Sally sat in one of the club chairs while Gemma took a seat behind the desk.

"You're kidding. You've been promising me and promising me, just like you have Allie Bolt and Davinia Noack. I thought it was never going to happen, I surely did." She tilted her head again and peered hard at Gemma. "You still suffering from those spells? Jean worried herself sick over you, but she said you had a gift."

Her words brought a sharp recollection back to Gemma: a tête-à-tête between Gemma and her mother. They'd been sitting in the kitchen and Jean was berating her for taking off with "that Dorrell boy." Gemma had just returned from following Nate Dorrell to Fort Lewis, and in those years when Gemma had been away, Jean had been forced to rely on her own psychic ability—read that to mean her wits—to keep her business afloat. It hadn't helped that brokenhearted Gemma had preferred to work at the diner with Macie rather than become her mother's assistant.

"You're selfish," Jean had told her. "These people need our help."

Engulfed in her own pain, Gemma had lashed back, for the first and last time. "I'm not going to help you lie to them. I'm through with all that. I'm going to the diner! Macie's waiting for me."

She'd tried to slam out the door, but Jean held it firm. "Macie, Macie, Macie. That's all I hear. She doesn't care about you! She's got her own little girl. The only one who cares about you is me!"

"Dad cared about me," Gemma snapped back.

"Peter's gone." Jean clamped her lips together. For all her ranting, she'd loved her husband. "We have each other, and that's all that's left."

"I'm not going to swindle people out of hard-earned money."

"Watch your tongue. You have a gift, dear. You know you do. Better than mine," she admitted grudgingly, which wasn't saying much since Jean's psychic ability was the kind sent away for on the back of a matchbook cover. "You know things, Gemmy." Her look was assessing and sly. "Don't you? You know things."

Gemma had wanted to deny it, but she'd seen pieces of the future on enough occasions that arguing the point would only escalate their argument. "Yes."

"And you don't want to use that to do good? I've told them, you know. That you came from those Indians and you're like a witch doctor."

"Shaman," Gemma corrected, then could have kicked herself when Jean said delightedly, "Yes. Shaman! You see? That's what you are."

"I'm not a shaman. I'm not a seer. I'm not even Native American, as far as I can tell. I'm . . . intuitive and empathetic and I can read people, that's all."

"Keep telling yourself that if it helps you sleep."

"I'm not doing the readings."

"I'm not asking you to. I just need to consult with you sometimes, that's all. Margerie Merrill wants to know if her son is in heaven. She's worried his soul didn't cross over. I want you to look into your brain and come up with an answer."

Gemma had stared at her mother in exasperation and affront. "That's not the way it works."

"Well, how does it work, huh? Tell me that."

There had been no way for Gemma to explain that she simply experienced feelings. A sensation that came off in waves from a person. And it wasn't like whatever she felt had anything to do with any question someone might ask of a deceased loved one. It just came to her. Sometimes.

And besides, Jean knew all that anyway. She was just being querulous, trying to get her way.

Now Gemma suddenly realized that Dr. Avery had not

told her about his son's impending nuptials. She'd simply picked that up by her own internal radar, her mind-reading ability. It had taken her over a week to recover her lost memories, and at the hospital she hadn't known enough about herself at that point to realize what she was doing. But while her face and body healed, she began remembering, maybe not completely, but enough that she understood herself a lot better now than directly after the accident.

But to her mother that day, she'd said, "It's like radio signals. I pick up what's being sent out. I can't send something back. Your friends can't ask me questions and expect answers from their deceased loved ones."

"Gemma, don't be dense. I can do that part. I just want you to say something nice about them. If you pick up a radio signal, let me know. More authentic."

"What if I don't get anything?"

"Just *try.*"

"Gemma!"

Sally Van Kamp's voice brought her back to the present with a jolt and Gemma started as if stung.

"Where did you go, girl?" Sally asked.

"Nowhere."

Sally's small eyes were suspicious. "You having a vision of some kind?"

"I was thinking about you," Gemma lied, "and it took me away."

"I want to know about my Jerry. He's not doing so well since he got back from Iraq. He and Bonnie are always fighting and I think she's stepping out on him. She was whoring around while he was gone, and she's still at it. They may not be married but Jerry thinks of Bonnie as his wife. He wants a family."

Gemma gazed at the red chrysanthemum she'd plucked

from a grouping around the front porch and put it in a vase on her desk. Its spiky petals reached toward her from a yellow center.

"He has a drug problem," Gemma said.

Sally reared back in horror. "Well, now that's a lie, girl. Those are trumped-up charges. *She's* the addict!" She blinked several times. "Why would you say that? That's not the kind of thing you see."

But it was. Exactly the kind of thing Gemma saw but Jean would never let her tell. The unvarnished truth. And she'd picked up a thread of this particular thought straight out of Sally Van Kamp's pea-brain, so clearly, despite her protests, Sally thought it was true, too.

"There are a lot of unresolved issues between your son and his girlfriend," Gemma said. "The kind of issues that may require professional counseling."

"Like Dr. Rainfield," she sniffed.

"Yes," Gemma told her, unfazed. "Dr. Bernard Rainfield would be a good choice."

"Hah," Sally humphed. "Old enough to be my father, and that's saying something. I wouldn't trust anything that man had to say."

"He's been my doctor for a lot of years," Gemma reminded her mildly.

"That's 'cause of your headaches. My Jerry is fine."

"Well, that's what I see," she said.

"What else do you see?"

Gemma thought a moment and shook her head. "That's it."

"Well, that ain't much, is it?"

Jean LaPorte had always given her clients a panacea of rosy futures and expectations, but Gemma wasn't interested. She hoped Sally and her ilk would stop bothering her. She didn't want this legacy and if Sally got the picture today, that would go a long way to discouraging the lot of them.

Sally's sharp eyes stared at Gemma. When Gemma didn't go any further, Sally finally sensed that their session was over. With great reluctance, she reached for her purse, but Gemma stopped her.

"No payment." She waved her off.

"No payment?" Sally's hand hovered over her purse. She looked happy for a brief moment, then yanked out two twenties and slapped them on Gemma's desk. "You just don't want to help me, do you? Trying to cull out some of us. Well, it won't be me! You take this!" She shoved the money toward her, ignoring Gemma's protests. "I don't care if you see Allie and Davinia, but don't you dare get all high and mighty with me!" With that she sailed out of the room and slammed out of the house.

"Lord," Gemma said to the empty room.

A knock on her front door a few minutes later had her thinking that Sally was back to apologize. Gemma drew a breath, then headed for the door.

But it was someone else on the opposite side: a man about her age with a round head and a mouth that dipped down on one side.

Tim Weatherford. A classmate of Gemma's whose mental slowness had made him the butt of many Quarry High jokes. Tim, whom Gemma had defended when they were young. Tim, who was giant-size and dubbed Little Tim by the whole town. He'd had a crush on Gemma for as long as she could remember and as she'd grown older she'd treated him with careful respect, very aware that he was someone who didn't understand boundaries.

Little Tim, whose mind she could read easily.

Another piece of her past she'd forgotten until now.

"Hi, ya," he said as she opened the door. He was over six feet and hunched forward, his head in front of his body.

"Hey, Tim. How are you?"

"I'm real good. Real good. I'm glad you're back. I want to go to the quarry with you."

"Uh . . ." She turned toward the west for a moment, where the quarry lay, thinking. The quarry the town was named after, was behind her property, bordering both hers and the Dunleavys. There was a ridge above it where enterprising high school kids liked to park and fool around, a makeshift lover's lane. This was what Tim meant. "Tim, I have a boyfriend," she said. "I can't go with you."

"Who, who is he?" His moon face looked crestfallen.

A mental image of Will Tanninger came to her—his dark eyes with their lines of humor, his thick brown hair, the quirk of his lips. "He's a detective. A policeman," she clarified. "I love him very much."

"You said you'd go with me."

"No, I didn't," she reminded gently.

"Can I come in?"

"Not now," she said. "But I'm going to be working at LuLu's, starting next week. Come and visit. Bring your mom."

"I don't want to bring her." He slid a sly look Gemma's way.

"You like Macie's peach cobbler."

"Okay."

"I'll get you a piece next week at LuLu's."

Tim nodded but she could feel him trying to come up with another reason to stay. His brain, however, couldn't hold the thought. When she closed the door, he reluctantly retraced his footsteps, hunching back down the long drive. His mother lived in a house at the edge of town and it was a long walk home, but Tim walked everywhere. He'd never had a father that Gemma knew of, and there were no siblings.

As she watched him become a smaller and smaller figure in her line of vision, she realized she was back in her old life with most of her memories still able to be accessed, some more easily than others.

The urgency she'd felt at the hospital to get on with whatever had been driving her seemed to have taken a backseat. Was it because Letton had been incapacitated? Still in the hospital, as far as she knew? Or, was it something she still didn't understand fully?

"Maybe a little of both," Gemma said aloud, running a hand along the ridge of her cheekbone, still feeling a surprisingly jarring ache from the remnants of her injuries.

Chapter Seven

Gemma was in the kitchen preparing a cheese sandwich—the extent of her groceries being bread, cheese, and a head of iceberg lettuce—when her land line rang, startling her. The phone hadn't rung five times since she'd been home from the hospital. Half expecting it to be Allie Bolt or Davinia Noack, she picked up the receiver on the wall phone and answered with trepidation, "Hello?"

"Ms. LaPorte? It's Detective Tanninger."

Her heart rate zoomed. She wasn't sure what she thought about that. Was he planning on arresting her? Did he have enough evidence? "Yeah?"

"Has your car ever turned up?" he asked.

Her pulse slowed down gradually. Of course. The car. That would be the evidence that would convict her or set her free. It made her hesitate a bit. She'd been anxious to find her mother's vehicle but was almost afraid to learn what she'd done with it.

"Uh, no. Haven't found it yet. I guess you haven't either."

"No."

"Is Edward Letton still alive? I'm assuming he is, since I haven't seen a report of his death."

"He's still alive."

"In the hospital?"

He sidestepped that one. "Have you remembered anything else about what happened to you?"

"No."

"Who dropped you off at the hospital?"

"No."

He was still fishing around, thinking she'd done it. For a wild second she thought about spinning him some alibi that she'd been with Macie all day that day. Macie would cover for her. But another part of her—a less self-preservative side—wanted to take credit for her actions. "I'm having enough trouble just remembering my day-to-day life. I hope you're spending as much time on Letton. Checking out his house. Grilling him. That girl might not have been his first victim."

"We're being very thorough where Mr. Letton is concerned," he assured her.

"And his wife? You got her under lock and key? That woman's certifiable." But then who was she to call the kettle black?

"How's your head?" he asked.

"Less purple and green. Kind of brownish, actually."

"Pain?"

"Some," she admitted. "What are you really after, detective?"

"Would it be all right if I interviewed you again? I've got some more questions."

Bullshit, Gemma thought. There were no more questions. He wanted to run over the same material again, see if her story had changed. And since her story hadn't changed, she said, "I'm starting work at LuLu's next week. You could stop by there."

"LuLu's?"

"The diner in town." She explained how Macie had leased the place from her parents and now was her tenant. "She needs some extra help, so I told her I'd fill in for a while. The peach cobbler alone is worth the trip."

"Okay." He sounded reluctant, but she hadn't given him any other choice.

"See you next week," she said, and pressed the disconnect button on the phone before he could say anything else.

That was two people she'd invited to the restaurant, Tim and Detective Tanninger. Macie should give her a raise, she thought with amusement. Maybe once she knew what her pay rate was, she could ask for an increase. Hah!

Gemma looked out the window and saw the late afternoon shadows creeping across the ground. She felt incredibly tired, the weight of figuring out who she was pressing down on her. Heaving a sigh, she trudged upstairs, walked to her room, slipping onto her bed. Dealing with Detective Tanninger seemed to zap her spirit in ways she didn't completely understand.

For a few minutes she ran over her life as she knew it before the accident. She had two classifications, Before and After the accident. After was pretty clear, but Before was still a jigsaw of memories with missing pieces.

What she knew was:

Before the accident she'd been living quietly at her parents', now her, farm. She'd spent a lot of time bobbing and weaving to avoid giving psychic readings to Jean LaPorte's clients, who were a tenacious bunch, to say the least. Jean herself had been gone about a year. Before Jean's death Gemma had been somewhat complicit in her dealings with those same desperate seekers and had helped her mother tell them fairy tales. She'd also helped Macie out at the diner. Had preferred that job to being her mother's apprentice psychic. Since Jean's death Gemma had been doing . . . what . . . ? That piece was still unclear.

If she thought back a few years earlier, she remembered following Nate to the ends of the earth, from military base to military base, planning, dreaming of, a future that included the two of them.

Nate, however, had ruined that idea many times over. He was a self-described commitment-phobe and had proven it by the series of women he flirted with and slept with. He'd denied he'd ever slept with any of them but Gemma had known. She'd seen it in her mind. She'd made the mistake of describing one of his trysts right down to the color of the girl's shoes and had spooked him enough that he'd forgotten about his own guilt. And he'd accused her of seeing other men. Of being involved with one in particular, though Gemma had vigorously denied it.

Nate's guilt was also superseded by Gemma's weirdness, and the relationship had ended abruptly. They'd been on the east coast and Gemma had gathered together the remains of her self-respect and enough cash to make her way back to Quarry.

How many years ago had that been? Two? Three? Longer? Gemma wasn't entirely sure. Her father had still been alive at the time. He'd welcomed her with open arms and Jean had welcomed her with her own agenda.

Fast forward to now: Gemma alone. Living in her parents' house. Fending off Jean's believers. Chasing after pedophiles and do-badders of every kind . . .

"Gotta get to the diner. Then gotta find a real life," she told her reflection in the hall mirror. The glass was wavy and distorted, an antique her mother had acquired in payment from one of the ladies who had little in the way of real cash. Her distorted image looked back at her, both a good and evil reflection of the same face.

* * *

The guy just was not going to die. He was going to *linger*. And after lingering he might even *get better.* This, Lucky could just not have.

She stuffed her hair under the knit cap and stared at her reflection in the old mirror. A sense of time passing filled her head. Seconds ticking by. She had to kill him. There was no other answer.

She'd dressed in baggy denim jeans; a black nylon jacket that zipped up to her chin; used, men's Nike's; and the earbuds of a few-generations-old iPod pressed into her ears. Foundation covered most of the remaining bruises, and she'd darkened her eyes with mascara and eyeliner and smudged the black color beneath her eyes, giving her the pale, wasted appearance associated with drug addicts. Her hazel eyes stared back at her. If she didn't smile, she looked like someone to avoid.

Not exactly the dress of someone who hoped to fly under the radar, sneak into the hospital and find her way to Edward Letton's room undetected. But one thing she knew was that drawing attention to herself could work in the reverse sometimes. Everyone remembered the clothes and the hardness; no one really remembered the person.

She had a gym bag containing scrubs. If she had to, she would change, but nurses, aides, and hospital personnel knew each other more than people thought. A stranger in scrubs was like a red light, so the only way that would work was if no one who worked with the staff saw her. The scrubs were for the fifth floor only.

It was early evening. Dinnertime. Much later and it got too quiet. Better to have some distractions. Some noise. Maybe even a diversion?

Lucky had to think about that. What she wanted was to sail into Letton's room and end his miserable life. Pulling the plugs wouldn't be enough. Alarms would sound at the nurses' station or somewhere and they would all rally round to save his miserable ass. She would like to smother him with a pillow. Simple and clean. Except that when his body went into distress it would also send off alarms that would alert the staff.

She possessed a handgun. She'd stolen it from her carjacking friend and kept it in the glove box of whatever stolen vehicle was in her possession at the time. But bringing it into a hospital was not going to work. Especially considering her disguise.

She would have to improvise. It would have to be quick. A weapon to smash him over the head with. *Kapow!* One shot.

But could she do it? *Could* she? Following him to the soccer field had been easy. And as soon as he tried to approach his victim, she'd been committed. No problem. She also knew she could defend herself if someone attacked her. She'd certainly wrapped Ezekiel's neck with the lamp cord without a qualm. And then there was that first kill . . .

But to physically attack him while Letton lay sleeping . . . or immobilized with his eyes open . . . unable to defend himself . . . well, she just wasn't as sure. She'd committed violence. She'd been responsible for several deaths, but she'd either been attacked first or had stepped in to save someone who was about to be attacked.

She wanted to think of herself differently. Wanted to be a stone killer. Someone with no conscience and no remorse. Unfortunately, she hadn't evolved to that point yet.

Still . . . Edward Letton had to die.

Lucky drove to the hospital in the rattletrap truck she'd appropriated. She parked halfway down one row, beneath a large maple whose orange leaves were shriveling and falling off. As she climbed out of the truck an amazingly large, red leaf sashayed down on the stiff breeze, landing on her hood.

Lucky stared at it a moment, then dragged herself back to the task at hand.

She grabbed her gym bag from the passenger seat. Looking up, she saw an elderly couple edging toward the front doors. The woman was using a walker, carefully negotiating each step, but the older guy kept his eyes on Lucky. She knew what he was thinking. She looked like a thug. To alleviate his fears, she cocked her head to the imaginary music playing from her iPod and started moving to the beat. Bobbing her head and closing her eyes, she was in the zone. When she opened one eye a slit, he'd turned back to his infirm wife and eased her over the curb and through the sliding glass doors.

Lucky rounded the building and chose a side access door that was still unlocked. After a certain time she suspected they locked everything down but the ER. She wouldn't be around that long. She found the stairs and headed upstairs until she saw the guard outside the room, then headed to a different hallway.

She walked quickly forward, assessing. Restrooms for guests were down the right hallway, marked with a little blue sign that stuck out from the wall about a foot below the ceiling. She boogied her way along as there were people in the halls. They all gave her curious looks and then moved on.

The restrooms were close enough to Letton's room to work, but the guard was outside the door, planted stolidly in a chair. As she dipped inside the restroom the guard's head was turned the other way. She caught sight of the bag of Doritos sticking from his pocket just before his head swiveled back her way, but she was safely inside by then.

And she was alone in the restroom. Good. She headed into a cubicle and stripped and changed into her light blue scrubs. She'd also put cleansing cream in her bag and she rubbed it all over her face, listening for anyone entering, but no one did.

Hurriedly, she stepped from the cubicle and rinsed her face in the sink, scrubbing off the makeup until her face was fresh and pink. Now the bruises were visible, faintly coloring her skin an ugly red-brown shade. She put on her pair of rosy-lensed glasses. In the scrubs she looked wholesome and innocuous. She tried on a smile and was rewarded with a friendly, guileless face. Again, good. She reapplied the foundation over her bruises, then finger-combed her hair until it lay faintly poofy against her scalp, but its straightness was legendary and that wouldn't last long.

The gym bag . . . if she stuffed it in the garbage can the police would find it after Letton's death was discovered. They would learn that the hip-hop dude/girl was a disguise.

There were acoustic tiles overhead. Lucky returned to her cubicle, stood on the seat of the toilet and reached above, sliding a tile out with the tips of her fingers. It took her three tries to toss the bag out of sight, and then an inordinate amount of time to replace the tile. She'd just hopped onto the floor when someone burst into the bathroom, a woman in a hurry, who strong-armed open the cubicle next to Lucky and sat down as if her bladder were about to burst.

Lucky eased out of the cubicle and bathroom, heart skittering. This was where she could not run into trouble, this was where another hospital employee could wonder who she was. Drawing a breath, she sauntered down the hall toward Letton's room. The guard saw her coming and he straightened, looking slightly guilty. She could see he was still chewing on something and trying to disguise it.

"Aw, honey, you jes keep on eatin'." She flapped a hand at him and smiled. "The vending machines are better'n the cafeteria, huh. I know, I know. Though sometimes they kin really put on a nice special. Last week the chipped beef on toast was somethin'."

"Yeah?" The guard hitched up his pants, eyeing her appreciatively. "The meat loaf was good, too."

"Mmmhmm."

"The vending machines are closer, though," he said a bit longingly.

"Don't you got someone to cover for you?"

"Just lunch," he grumbled.

Lucky cruised on by, looking back at him through her glasses. "Want me to pick somethin' up for ya?"

"Nah." He grinned at her as she walked toward the end of the hall. Just before she turned the corner, he said, "Hey."

Bingo. Lucky smiled to herself. She glanced back at him inquiringly.

"You got a minute? The vending machines are close, and if you were here . . . ?"

Lucky pretended to consider. "I gotta coupla minutes, but no more."

"I'm like the wind," he said, and was already gallumphing down the hallway.

Lucky returned to the guard's abandoned post, feeling her blood rushing through her veins. She was alone in the hall. Alone . . .

Carefully she pushed open the door to Letton's room. She moved in quietly, feeling unusually alert, alive. Maybe a pillow was the answer. If she were quick enough. If she had enough time to escape.

She eased into the softly lit room. He lay on the bed, eyes open. Her heart jerked. He was awake!

But then she realized he was not really awake. He was in some kind of altered state. A coma.

She moved to the head of the bed, hovering over him, gazing hard into the bastard's flat stare. He was definitely out.

Her hand reached for the pillow but she hesitated. She wanted to strangle him. Make him pay. Squeeze the life from him. Make him suffer like so many men had made her.

She knew without being told that he was dying.

Edward Letton would not be leaving the hospital, despite Laurelton General's best efforts. He was on his way out of this world. Soon to be gone.

A part of her felt relief that she wouldn't have to kill him. Another part longed to snuff the fucker out.

She left in a controlled hurry, retracing her steps to the women's room. To her consternation someone was in her cubicle. Looking up, she could see the acoustic tile hadn't quite fallen back into place. From her angle she could see the edge of the strap of her bag.

For a brief moment she wondered if she should just chance it. Walk through the hospital lah-di-dah, no one noticing another aide in scrubs. They got away with it all the time on television.

But this was Laurelton General. A small hospital where everybody knew everybody.

Her heart pounded, blood singing through her veins. She hadn't done anything. Letton was still alive. But she sensed a mounting urgency to get away quickly. She turned to the door just as the occupant of her cubicle flushed the toilet. As the woman left the stall Lucky scurried to another, closing the door before she could be seen. She waited, counting seconds, as the woman slowly went through her ablutions and took her time leaving the bathroom. Quickly, Lucky entered her cubicle and climbed onto the toilet. She was reaching upward when she heard the door open again and she sank back into a crouch, heart pounding. The new person went straight to the sink and started washing her hands. She heaved several huge sighs, as if life were wearing her down, then yanked a paper towel free of its holder.

Lucky closed her eyes and waited and waited. Finally, after another few excruciating minutes, the woman left. Quick as a cat, Lucky jumped up, slid back the acoustic tile and jerked on her bag. It tumbled into her arms. She changed rapidly and redressed in her disguise, tucking away the scrubs.

She didn't bother with the makeup, just yanked the knit cap over her hair.

A lot of work for nothing.

Sticking the earplugs in her ears she be-bopped out of the place, head ducked low in her baseball cap. People would remember her, but it wouldn't matter. Once again she'd been lucky.

It was her nature.

"What do you think it means? The cigarette burns?" Barb asked.

She'd asked him the same thing twice a day since they'd found the body. Will gave her his stock answer—a shrug—and glanced at the clock. After six. Time to go home.

"Maybe it's nothing," she mused. "He likes to burn things. Maybe he's just bored."

He got to his feet and headed for his jacket, which was in the back room. Sometimes Barb just liked to hear herself talk. His mind was full of thoughts of the still unidentified dead body they'd found at the airstrip. He was also thinking about Edward Letton and felt as if he should go to the hospital and look in on him.

"Is it something I said?" Barb appeared in the doorway of the staff room. He could feel the negative energy and glanced back to meet her snapping black eyes. Will realized with a sense of inevitability that this was it. The showdown. When he least wanted it. He was going to be forced to address the issue that had been simmering between them. "You've hardly said five words to me the past week," she accused.

"We've talked about our cases." Will started to shrug into his jacket, then changed his mind. It was still unseasonably warm outside.

"That's not what I mean. You've shut me down. You've done it on purpose."

They were alone; everyone else had already left. Barb appeared to have specifically chosen a time when other ears weren't listening. Will supposed he should be grateful for her discretion but he felt both annoyed and half-relieved. He wanted this thing between them to be resolved and over. But the way she was standing in the doorway made it impossible for him to leave without practically pushing her aside.

"Well, go ahead," he said, turning to face her.

"Go ahead?" She tilted her head warily.

"Say what you want to say. You've been working up to this for months."

"I don't know what you mean." She was affronted. He'd preempted her first strike.

"We shouldn't have even tried dating. In our jobs, business and pleasure don't mix."

"Bullshit, Tanninger." Her face turned red.

His temper started a slow simmer. He was stuck in this thing now. He wished he could just leave while she had a tantrum, flung herself around and screamed names at him. Get out of the drama.

But he couldn't.

"What do you want?" he demanded.

"You're not the hero you think you are," she declared. "Just because you don't talk a lot doesn't mean you have anything going on in that prehistoric head of yours. You know that, don't you? That men's brains are more prehistoric than women's? The divider in our brains that splits the left and right hemispheres? It's thinner in women. That's why we can multitask while men are single-minded gorillas. It's a scientific fact."

"All right."

"Oh, thanks for placating me. That works so well."

"It was the only single-minded thought I had."

"Funny. You're a laugh-riot. Ha, ha, ha." Barb strode into the room.

"Stop," he bit out, sounding serious enough that she did just that.

But she recovered fast. "What are you afraid of?"

"This," he admitted, indicating both of them.

"I'm not dying for your attention, y'know," she shot back. "But you could give me some courtesy instead of acting like I'm a piece of furniture."

"What would you like me to do?"

"Oh, don't give me that. I'm not a moron. You don't give a shit about anything, least of all respecting me."

Will couldn't help the groan that escaped his lips. Every perp he'd ever had the pleasure of knowing was all about him *respecting* them. It was a universal code for *I got no defense,* a lowlife's gambit to end the inquisition.

"I respect that you're a good investigator," Will said tautly.

She snorted. "You don't respect me as a woman. You ignore me. You shut me down."

"I'm trying to work with you as a partner."

Her brows lifted. "You think I'm hard to work with?"

"You're spoiling for a fight. It's not going to matter what I say."

"You're making me feel like this is all my fault!" she said in a tight little voice.

"I hardly know what we're talking about anymore."

"Oh, for God's sake, Will." She looked like she was about to cry but she shook her head. "Fine." She lifted her hands as if she were completely done.

"Can we move past this? Be partners?" He gazed at her curiously, wondering if it was even possible.

"That what you want?"

"Yes."

His honesty seemed to finally undo her. She turned around and headed back out of the staff room. Will followed her, hesitating by her desk as she sat down and showed an inordinate amount of interest in a pile of paperwork.

"We need to find out who the burned girl is," he said. "No one's turned in a missing person's report for someone her age in the tri-county area."

"What do you want me to do?" she asked tightly. She didn't look up.

"She'll be missed eventually."

"Are you going home?" she asked as he turned to leave.

"I'm going to stop by the hospital. Check on Letton. And Ralph."

"I'm going to my apartment and I'm going to drink a bottle of wine. I'm off tomorrow."

Will inclined his head and went on his way. He wasn't sure anything had gotten accomplished between him and Barb.

Gemma awoke slowly and viewed the red walls of her bedroom. Her brow furrowed. What time was it? She didn't remember going to bed.

She lifted her head and realized she was wearing sweats. Had she been jogging? Tentatively she smelled the fabric, lifting an arm, but there was no scent of sweat.

You were cold.

That thought came flooding back. She'd felt like she was coming down with something and she'd thrown on the sweats in an effort to warm up. She'd been wearing a short-sleeved shirt earlier and some capris as the weather was still surprisingly warm.

She found the shirt hung on a hanger in her closet and the capris in the wash basket in the laundry room, an annex off the kitchen. She picked up the capris and tested the fabric with her fingers. Outside night had fallen in earnest and through the laundry room window she could see pinpoints of stars in a black sky.

"Edward Letton's dead," she said aloud. "Or dying."

You killed him.

She dropped the capris back in the basket and walked into the kitchen, shaking her head slowly. She didn't believe that. She wasn't responsible for his death. She hadn't run him down.

Gemma struggled to recall and got a blinding headache for her efforts. From what Macie had said she'd run out of the diner, chasing someone, and from what Gemma could figure out, that was the last memory before she woke up in the hospital. And it wasn't even her memory.

She heard something outside and froze. She was suddenly conscious of how lit-up the kitchen was. How she stood in the glare of the light, illuminated. She flicked the switch and was plunged into darkness. Sliding cautiously to the back door she tested it to make sure it was locked. Satisfied, she tiptoed into the living room and across the dark room to the front door. She stood there for long minutes, but silence prevailed. Cruising to the other side of the room, she looked out one of the windows. In the corner of her vision she could see the front porch and the envelope lying on the step.

Her heartbeat skipped. She waited more excruciating minutes, then crossed to the door, snapped it open, scooped up the envelope and relocked the door in less than five seconds. Heart pounding, she stood with her back to the door panels and stared at the white rectangle. It was unaddressed.

Rechecking all the locks, she scurried upstairs, drawing the curtains in her bedroom. Sliding a thumb under the sealed flap, she pulled out a sheet of paper.

In a scrawling hand were five words.

I see into your soul.

The wolf drove into his carport and climbed out of the truck, slamming the door behind him. He walked straight through the house and out to the back yard. He could see the house across the way but its lights were snuffed out. Too late for them. They couldn't stay up past nine.

His eyes fixed on the sliver of moon, he threw back his head and roared, the sound funneling from a primitive core, spiraling upward. He could almost see it rise. Fine wisps of smoke racing upward.

The mother-witch was dead.

The nurse-witch was dead.

He needed to find the one who'd escaped him.

It was only a matter of time.

She had to burn.

They all had to burn.

Chapter Eight

When Will arrived at work the following morning he was greeted with a photo of his burn victim smack dab in the center of his desk. The pretty dark-haired girl was smiling on the exterior deck of a restaurant or bar, flanked by other partiers, and holding a martini high in the air like a salute.

"Inga Selbourne," Barb told him coolly. He had a feeling every conversation with her was going to be cool from now on. "A nurse at Laurelton General. She was renting an apartment behind a farmhouse outside Laurelton. The people who own the property, Pearl and Edgar Gillroy, called Laurelton General looking for her. Apparently Inga was late on the rent. They learned she hadn't been to work in over a week and so called Laurelton PD. Missing persons sent that out and I picked it up this morning."

"Gotta be her," Will agreed. "Good work."

She shrugged. "Paint by the numbers." But he could tell she was pleased with the compliment.

"Have you contacted Laurelton PD?"

"Told 'em she was down in the county morgue. They're

going over her apartment. Sounds like it was the crime scene."

Will nodded.

"You going to the hospital?"

Laurelton General was under the county's jurisdiction and the body had been found outside the Laurelton city limits, so the sheriff's department was as much involved in the homicide as was the Laurelton PD. "I'll call Mac and see what's up," Will said, referring to Sam McNally, a longtime homicide investigator with the Laurelton PD.

Within the hour Will was on his way to Laurelton General. While the grunt work at Inga's apartment was being done by the crime scene team, Will figured he'd gather background on Inga herself.

It was the second time in as many days that he'd made a trip to Laurelton General. After his fight with Barb, he'd headed to the hospital and been somewhat dumbfounded to find Smithson's chair empty again. He'd stepped inside Edward Letton's room and been convinced by his waxy pallor and blank stare that Letton had one foot in the grave already, and another searching for a toehold. He thought it would be a miracle if Letton climbed his way out of that wide-eyed coma and back to the land of the living.

He'd had to tamp down his anger as he waited for Smithson to return to his post. Will wanted to crawl up the man's ass over his lack of a sense of duty, but it seemed like a moot point as it was clear Letton wasn't going to be making a break for it and no one seemed particularly interested in another attempt at rubbing him out.

It was another ten minutes before Smithson had returned, ambling down the corridor, munching on those little horn-shaped snacks and sucking down a super-duper large diet cola. He'd made a stutter step upon spying Will, then kept on coming, his guilt at being caught in the act quickly changing to resentment. "Checking up on me?" he asked.

"Yeah," Will said.

"I was barely gone." He'd jerked his head in the direction of Letton's room. "He's not lookin' too good, anyway."

If he'd liked Smithson better, Will would have agreed and maybe even added that he didn't think the man was going to make it. As it was, he said, "Don't leave unless a nurse is with him."

"I hear Jenkins and Turner have been released from night shift. Why do I have to stay?"

Will hadn't bothered to answer. He was the one fighting to keep a round-the-clock guard on the man. Someone had tried to kill him once. It wasn't a stretch to think she might try again.

Now, he was at the hospital once more, in search of a Nina Cox from administration, the name he'd been given when he'd asked about Inga Selbourne.

As he walked through Laurelton General's front doors, fleetingly he thought of Letton's wife, Mandy. She'd come down hard on Gemma LaPorte, shrieking that she'd tried to kill her husband. But Mandy hadn't been much of a presence around the hospital after those first few days. She was about Gemma's same size and build except much rounder. Was there any chance that she was the one who'd run him down? In Will's experience, disenchanted spouses entertained murderous thoughts. If Mandy Letton had learned of her husband's proclivities—and how could she have not guessed, or at least had some idea?—she could easily have become an avenging angel.

"Detective Tanninger?"

Nina Cox was a middle-aged woman with a good figure and a sharp, assessing eye. She took him in in one glance as she waved him around the administration counter toward a back office. He walked past several desks and rows of file cabinets, then through a door into a windowless room with a utilitarian desk and two uncomfortable-looking chairs.

"Ms. Selbourne was only here for eight months," she said briskly, acting as if Inga's short employment record somehow absolved the hospital of the taint from her death.

"What were her duties?"

"She wanted to be a surgical nurse, but she didn't possess the skills or training. Mostly she worked on the floor. You can talk to Janice on four. Inga reported to her."

"Thanks."

On four . . . Gemma LaPorte's floor.

"Go to the north wing. ICU. She'll be around there somewhere. Janet Cumberland, RN." Nina started to lead him back out, then stopped and, without turning around, said over her shoulder, "I'm sorry she's dead, but Inga didn't really fit with our community at Laurelton General."

"How so?" Will asked.

"She talked too much. Chatty, chatty. Cheery, cheery. Like she'd been appointed the job of keeping up everyone's spirits. It was grating. You always knew when Inga was around because she couldn't shut up."

"Ah."

She gave him a sideways look. "Couldn't shut up about her sex life, either. A sex murder, is my guess. One of her cretin boyfriends."

With that she strode forward, head high, almost stomping. Will followed her, then turned toward the elevators in search of Janet Cumberland, RN.

Gemma thumbed through the local phone book and found Dr. Bernard Rainfield's number. It was probably somewhere in Jean's files as well, but it was simpler to just look him up and give his office a call. Placing the call, however, she learned that connecting with the doctor wasn't going to be as easy as she'd hoped. She reached his answering service, who said if it wasn't an emergency then she could wait for his call.

No, it wasn't an emergency, Gemma assured the bored voice, but after she hung up she wondered if a lie might have been a better idea. She wanted to talk to the doctor soon. Felt almost compelled all of a sudden.

She'd been freaked out by the note on her porch. She'd dropped it and backed across the room as if it were about to sprout horns and cloven feet and come at her with a devil's yawning grin. Instead, it floated to the ground and lay there and as time passed Gemma went from terrified to mildly tense to out-and-out annoyed. *I see into your soul* sounded more like the doings of one of Jean LaPorte's impressionable clientele than some evil killer bent on her destruction.

Gemma had eventually picked up the letter and turned it over in her hands. She sometimes could get a reading off people when she brushed up against them, and though her ability wasn't as effective with inanimate objects, she tried her best to feel the author's intent, to no avail.

When nothing came to her, she took the letter and envelope to her office and laid them on the top of the empty outbox. Jean had left the place exceptionally tidy. Anything worth saving was in its proper file and Gemma's cursory examination of said files had only convinced her that half the town of Quarry was nuts, and all of the neighboring hamlet of Woodbine. If she ever did decide to get into the psychic business she would have enough work to keep her busy seven days a week.

She had a sudden desire to phone Will Tanninger but managed to hold herself back. Instead she spent a half hour musing to herself about the missing gaps in her memory, hoping some cemented memory would jar loose and give her a place to start.

Nothing.

She glanced at her watch. She'd told Macie she would come in for the afternoon shift just to get started, though she wasn't really due at the restaurant till the following week. She'd found her yellow uniform hanging in the closet and now she pulled it out, examining it carefully. It was clean and crisp like she'd just laundered it. She pulled it over her head and found a pair of white sneakers.

Staring at herself in the mirror, she grimaced at the remnants of her injuries. The reddish-brown tint to her skin was still clearly visible. Applying thick makeup to her face, she turned her head from side-to-side. It would do for the moment. By next week, when she started her full shifts, it would hardly be noticeable . . . she hoped.

Will found Janet Cumberland RN at the fourth floor nurses' station, a semicircular hub that claimed the corner of the hallway. One nurse stood behind the bar-height counter, reading from a manila folder with a white and red tab. She slid him a look as he appeared, then snapped the folder shut and stood up straight at the sight of his uniform.

"Can I help you?" she asked.

Her ID read J. Stanzo, RN. She was short, trim, and her hair was scraped into a tight ponytail that made her skin appear to pull back at the eyes. "I'm looking for Janet Cumberland," he told her.

Her eyes slid down the hall and Will automatically turned, but there was no one around except a patient awkwardly moving a wheelchair along. As he watched, a middle-aged woman with short, gray hair came out of the nearest room, guiding the man along with a sure hand. When she was satisfied with his progress she turned toward the nurses' station, her shoes squeaking softly along the shiny linoleum floors.

She had pale blue eyes and she looked at Will askance as Nurse Stanzo said, "He's looking for you."

"Janet Cumberland? Detective Will Tanninger," he said, extending a hand. "Nina Cox suggested I talk to you."

"About Inga." She shook his hand, her gaze fixed on his name tag as if rechecking his identity. "We're all shocked. Murder." She didn't seem to know what to do with that.

Janet was aware that Nurse Stanzo was hanging on their every word, so she moved down the hall and Will fell in step beside her. Halfway to the next corridor, she stopped and turned to him. "I don't know what I can tell you. Inga seemed to enjoy her job. She had a lot of energy and she had a tendency to maybe talk too much about the party scene."

"Any particular party scene?"

"She liked to bar hop in Portland. I got the impression she went to dance and meet—possible boyfriends. She was good-natured."

"Possible boyfriends? She wasn't seeing anyone steadily?"

"Not that I know of. She didn't confide in me a lot. Her closest friend at the hospital was DeeAnna Brush in administration. DeeAnna quit about a month ago."

"Ms. Cox didn't mention her."

Janet made a snorting sound. "She wouldn't. Nina's—competitive. That's why DeeAnna left, according to Inga."

"Competitive in what way?"

"She's the boss. No room for anyone else, I guess."

Will nodded. "Ms. Cox seemed to feel that Inga talked too much."

"Nina doesn't like anyone having fun, and DeeAnna and Inga were all about it. They went out partying together from time to time. Nina's judgmental nature drove DeeAnna to distraction. She's at Good Sam now."

"I'll check with her. Thanks. What were Inga's duties here at the hospital?"

"She was a floor nurse on five."

"Five, not four?"

"Both. But the last few weeks she worked on five."

Will felt a tweak of interest. "We have a guard on five, outside Edward Letton's room."

"Inga was only here a few days while he was here."

"But she had contact with him?"

"Not really. Myself and a couple of other long-timers were the only ones the hospital allowed at first. We've all eased up a bit."

"I'm just trying to get an idea of who might have something against Ms. Selbourne."

Janet shook her head.

Will asked, "Anything else you can think of that might help us locate her killer?"

"Well, this is a bit off-point, maybe . . ."

"Anything," Will said.

"Yesterday I was up on fifth and your guard was missing."

"I know," Will said, silently cursing Ralph Smithson again. The man caused more grief than good.

"But there was a woman in the hallway. In scrubs. But she wasn't part of our nursing staff. I know everyone."

Will almost said, "It's a big hospital," but there was something about Janet Cumberland that kept him quiet, made him believe her. "You think she was visiting Letton?"

"I don't know. She was walking away from me. I just saw the back of her, but since the guard was gone I went into Letton's room and he was the same."

"Wide-eyed coma? I saw him yesterday, too," Will explained to her sharp look.

"I think she may have been in his room. Just a feeling I have. But when I walked down the hall after her, she was gone. Maybe took the stairs. Maybe your man knows something more."

"Thank you," Will said a trifle stiffly. "I'll ask him."

She shrugged. "Probably nothing. And I don't think it had anything to do with Inga. I just wanted to mention it, since you're here."

Will didn't know what to feel as he trudged up the stairs to the fifth floor. Smithson was sitting in his chair, looking as bored as he possibly could without actually nodding off. For once he was sans junk food.

"Do you recognize the nurses that attend Letton?" Will asked without preamble.

"Well, sure. Not much else to do around here."

"Did you see a new one yesterday?"

Ralph's face whitened a bit, then filled with red color as if he were suffering from apoplexy. "I was only gone a few minutes. You were here yourself."

"That's not what I asked."

"I'm sure I've seen her before. It was just the first time she talked to me."

"What did she say?"

Ralph opened and shut his mouth twice before saying, "She was friendly. Just passing by. She didn't have nothing to do with the pedophile."

"Are you sure?"

"Yes." He was belligerent.

"How do you know, since you were gone from your post?"

"Jesus H, man. Jenkins and Turner aren't on graveyard anymore. You're just keeping me here to harass me."

"What did she look like?" Will demanded, fighting his temper with an effort.

Smithson shrugged. "I don't know. Cute. Little glasses." He shaped them with his fingers to indicate narrow lenses, then stopped short, as if caught up by something.

"What?" Will demanded.

"I think she had a bruise, man. Kinda had some makeup over her face but there was something by her temple."

Will's heart clutched and he felt suddenly suffocated. He realized Smithson had never seen Gemma LaPorte. "What color was her hair?"

"Light brown, I guess."

"How tall?"

"Five-seven, maybe. Five-eight?"

"What did she say to you?" Will demanded through his teeth. "Word for word."

Smithson grew silent. He knew he was in trouble. All his whining and posturing wasn't going to cut any ice with Tanninger. Something was up. Something bad. "She didn't go in there. You've seen him. He's just the same."

"What—did—she—say?"

"She talked to me about snack food."

Will stared. "Did she suggest you go get some? That she'd stay and watch over Letton?"

"No. She never was gonna watch over him."

"But she thought you might need a snack?"

The silence between them was oppressive. Will waited nearly half a minute, then he grabbed his cell phone, ignoring hospital policy, and ordered Jenkins back to the post outside Letton's door.

Smithson finally said, "The scumbag's just the same as he was."

"You're relieved of duty," Will stated tautly.

Smithson looked like he was going to argue, then he strode angrily down the hall and slammed through the door to the stairs.

Gemma parked the truck in LuLu's lot and headed into the diner. It was busy, the lunch crowd in full swing. Macie gave her an overwhelmed look as she carried a load of plates on her arm and hurried toward a table. "Can you take a few orders? I'll be with you in a minute. Two booths on the end? Denise is sick again. Probably hung over. It's just . . ." She shook her head and her voice trailed off.

Gemma grabbed one of the notepads Macie kept in a stack just inside the kitchen and went to the first booth, where a red-faced man and his long-suffering wife bawled her out for taking so long. Gemma wished she'd gone to the other booth first, as those people were quiet and seemed to understand, at least at some level, that they were short-staffed.

". . . long we've been waiting?" the man was railing. "I coulda gone in there and made it myself in the time we've been at this table!"

Gemma slid the wife a look. She stared back, a beaten woman. She'd heard this rant before, many times, Gemma guessed.

"Why don't you hire more staff, that's what I wanna know. There're people out there dying for jobs. Put out an ad, for chrissake. Unless you like pissing good people off."

"Harv . . ." the wife protested.

"Well?" he demanded belligerently, switching his fury to her.

"Do you know what you'd like to order?" Gemma asked.

"For the last half hour, missy!"

Gemma held her notebook and pen in front of her. Memories were flooding back. Working at the diner had been both a bane and a relief. Nasty customers were enough to make her want to pull her hair out, but the job had been a means to escape Jean's demands.

The wife gave Gemma her order and the red-faced husband reluctantly did the same. Gemma ripped the slip off the pad and handed it to Macie, who'd overheard enough and was heading back to the kitchen. Gemma then went to the next booth, a family of four, who ordered without extra drama.

She met up with Macie in the kitchen. "Bless you," Macie said. "I was close to a nervous breakdown."

"It comes back quick," Gemma said with a smile.

"Trial by fire. Snarky bastard. I am glad you're here."

"How do I look?"

"Like someone's been beating on you pretty badly and you're trying to cover it up."

"What a relief. I thought people might think I was in some kind of accident."

Macie gave a sharp bark of laughter. "Oh, honey, Charlotte's coming up. I've got to have a word with that child. Can you get this order?" She pointed first to a hamburger and a club sandwich that had just come up, then to a booth along the windows. "The lady in the green pantsuit and the guy with the hairpiece."

She whisked past Gemma. Through the front windows Gemma could see Macie's daughter Charlotte approaching, swinging her backpack like she was about to hurl it into space. Gemma picked up the plates and took them to the table Macie had pointed out. The man with the hairpiece—black atop his own graying mane—asked for a refill on his cola and Gemma took care of that as Macie got sidetracked just as Charlotte burst inside.

Charlotte took one look at Gemma and rushed toward her, her short hair bobbing, a frown taking over her thin face. "Did you catch him?" she demanded.

Gemma was automatically going to ask, "Who?" but then stopped herself as she realized Charlotte must have seen her chase out after her quarry. She hadn't realized Charlotte was at the diner that day.

"You saw me go after him?" Gemma clarified.

"Well yeah-uh," she said, as if Gemma were dense. "You came out the door, dead on his heels. I was still in the parking lot."

"Did he know I was following him?"

"I don't know. Maybe he just thought you were crazy."

"But there was no doubt that I went after him."

"I suppose people coulda thought you were having an attack of some kind. That other guy followed after you. He musta thought you were weird."

Gemma didn't know whether to laugh or cry that Charlotte had been at the diner the morning Gemma had run out of the place. She said urgently, "Charlotte, I'm just filling in for a few hours, helping your mom. Could we talk afterwards? I'm trying to remember things."

"So, now you want me to look out for you?" Charlotte arched a brow.

And Gemma remembered that Charlotte had always wanted to be involved in whatever drama Gemma was living, but Gemma had deemed it too dangerous. Her heart began a slow tattoo. "You recall what I was doing that morning?"

"Sure. You were just drinking coffee. I tried to talk to you, but you were like somewhere else. Intense."

Charlotte's hair and eyes were dark brown. She was rawhide lean and had bruises and scrapes running down her legs, which were in shorts, the result of a reckless outdoor life. She was like a street kid, yet she had a loving mother who was overworked and exasperated by her daughter.

Macie wasn't the only one who loved Charlotte; Gemma wanted to love and protect her with maternal fierceness.

"You okay?" Charlotte asked now.

"Just some memory quirks."

Charlotte snorted her *so what else is new?* and said, "Well, in case you remember about that dude over on Carriage Way? The one I thought was beating his kids? I was wrong. He was beating his wife. Kids just kinda got in the way, but it's all okay now."

"How is it okay?" Gemma said, slightly horrified. Why couldn't she remember *this*?

"He was in some car accident, or something. Anyway, he's gone, so he can't hurt them anymore. Left the family, I think."

"Did I ask you about him?" Gemma groped for understanding. The conversation with Charlotte was quickly spiraling out of control.

Charlotte pressed her lips together, looked around, then confided, "You're always worried I'm going to get in some kind of trouble for knowing too much. Don't you remember? That's why I told you about Robbie's dad. You insisted I let you know first if I thought someone was doing bad things to their kids." She frowned in concentration. "I think that's why you went after the dude that day. You knew something about him. Something bad. Did you ever catch him?"

"I don't think so . . ."

"Huh. Too bad. The way you looked at him . . . I thought he probably deserved to die."

Chapter Nine

Charlotte Brandewyne, eleven years old, cursed with boring, limp hair and a pointy nose and chin, and a flat chest that had *no sign* of breasts, where Hester Martin was like a double-D already, and she had blue eyes with sooty lashes—that's how they described them in those books she'd found in the box in the attic. Anyway, boys just went berserk over those sooty lashes, and though Charlotte wasn't much interested in boys, she sure as hell wanted them to be interested in her.

But she was thin, knock-kneed, and ran like a gallumphing elephant, according to her mother. That was a lie. Her mom just thought that because Charlotte made so much noise. In truth, Charlotte was fast. Speedy. She'd run from many a bad situation, smelling trouble before it found her.

But . . . the only thing pretty about Charlotte was her last name. Brandewyne. And it wasn't even really hers. Her mom's second husband had adopted her when she was two, and though he'd been gone for just years and years, she'd kept his name. Her real dad was something she thought of fleetingly without much interest.

Charlotte had grown up around Quarry and Woodbine. The grade school she attended was for both towns and some neighboring areas that weren't towns at all, just a store, or a signpost stuck out somewhere. Charlotte learned early on that she was good at math and reading but her social skills sucked. They didn't use that word, of course, but hey, it was all the same thing anyway and though she'd never fully understood what social skills were, she'd figured out she didn't have a lot of friends and that bothered the school counselors and teachers.

Her answer to all that was to simply leave school when she got bored with it. She did her homework. She was good at her assignments. Way better than a lot of the kids. Penelope Messerlin was an absolute dope. She also had big breasts—*tits* as Davey Corulo described them—but then Penelope had been held back about a zillion grades, so sure, she was mature.

The one person Charlotte liked the most was Gemma LaPorte. Gemma was always nice to her. Well, at least when she was in her own head. Sometimes she just drifted away and Charlotte was pretty sure there was a name for what she had. She'd watched a bunch of those *Law & Order* shows, which were kind of boring—lots and lots and lots of talk—but they also had some cool stuff once in a while. Dead bodies with those Y-shaped cuts because the doctors had cut them open. Yuk! But cool.

But Gemma was also psychic. She would suddenly turn around and say, "Who did you say you saw today?" and it was really, really weird, because Charlotte would be about to tell her something that happened to her that very *day*. It was creepy. Made Charlotte feel like caterpillars were walking over her skin. But cool, too.

When Charlotte heard that Gemma was coming in to work

this afternoon, she just left school at noontime and walked two miles home. She'd been banished from the use of her bike because her mom thought it gave her too much mobility, so she'd had to resort to walking.

That's how she'd thought the Bereth kids were getting kicked around by their dad, by walking by their place every day. They lived down this long lane; practically everybody did around here, but she'd seen them come screaming out of the house one day, a man yelling threats at them from inside the house. She'd told Gemma, who'd gone into one of her trances. Charlotte had wanted to follow Gemma around and find out what she did when she was like that, but someone—her mom, the school, people who recognized her—was always dragging her away. And then Gemma didn't seem too keen on Charlotte's following her around like a dog.

But now, today, Gemma wanted to talk to her. Seemed to think that she, Charlotte, had some information that could help! Charlotte was as close to a panic as she had ever come. She wanted to have something for Gemma. She wanted Gemma to find her important. The trouble was, she really didn't know much of anything.

Charlotte was seated on a stool near the kitchen, trying really hard not to bite at her nails. Her mother hated the habit but it really helped her brain juices, to gnaw away at her fingers. Hard to explain. Hester Martin called her own mother a ball-buster. Charlotte wasn't quite sure what that meant but she had an idea. Hester said her dad called her mom that, so she did, too. Apparently Hester and her dad just laughed and laughed and it made her mom so mad.

Charlotte didn't feel that way about Macie. Sure, she wished she would just give her some slack. Forget the going to school thing. But the way Hester acted about her mom made Charlotte uneasy. In fact, Charlotte almost wanted to hug her mom after hearing those things, but she stopped herself at the last minute. Mom was just too smart. She would think something was up and bug Charlotte about it until Charlotte would just blurt it all out, which was not cool.

Charlotte was trying to teach herself self-control. But as she sat on the stool, she was in a complete panic about what to tell Gemma. Could she make something up? Some story that would intrigue Gemma? Maybe make her think Charlotte was really, really special?

But Gemma had looked stricken when Charlotte had told her about Mr. Bereth leaving his family. She'd heard he was a really mean guy, though, so it was good he was gone. She didn't think the Bereth kids would care. Or Mrs. Bereth. Charlotte had overheard one of the school counselors telling another one that Mr. Bereth was the reason Robbie was missing a permanent tooth. That's why Charlotte thought he'd been beating on his kids. It was only later, when she saw Robbie at school, that she learned he'd been in the way when his dad and mom had had "words."

Words. Hah. Charlotte had asked if she could see his missing tooth and though he'd initially been pissed, he'd finally pulled back his lower lip and there had been a big hole right in the center, like he was a baby waiting for them to come in. It had made Charlotte kind of sad. Teeth were important. She'd been brushing hers with extra special care ever since.

"Charlotte."

She straightened up as if goosed, nearly gasping. Her mom didn't sneak up on her as a rule. "Uh-huh?"

"This wasn't a half-day of school. Your teacher just called. Wanted to know if you were feeling better after I *picked you up*." Mom looked pissed.

Well . . .

"It's just dumb PE, and I get enough exercise riding my bike. Or walking," Charlotte added with an accusatory tone.

"You have more than just one class in the afternoon."

"Math, and I'm two assignments ahead."

Macie pressed the fingers of one hand to her forehead and closed her eyes. Charlotte braced herself. "Why can't you just go to school and stay there?" her mom asked. She really looked tired.

"Maybe you could home-school me," she said hopefully.

"Oh, Lord."

She whirled back to the job. Charlotte watched her mother and Gemma. She wished they would let her wait tables. She would do a good job. She was gifted. Maybe not in the way Bryce Pendleton's parents said he was gifted. They were always saying that and Bryce was a . . . dickwad. She wasn't quite sure what that meant but she was certain it applied.

With time on her hands, Charlotte pulled out her math book. If she was quick, she could be three or four assignments ahead, maybe five. If she finished the entire workbook what would happen then? They would just have to let her leave fifth grade, wouldn't they?

Barb caught Will on his cell phone as he was leaving the hospital. "Take you all day to do some interviews?" she asked.

"Smithson show up?"

"Yeah. Pissed at you."

"What was his version of what happened?" he asked.

She lowered her voice, probably because she was at her desk. "You're a fucking bastard with control issues and could get violent. Want my version?"

"Shoot."

"He's a whiney bitch with Momma issues and could wet the bed."

Will actually laughed aloud, which pleased Barb and she chuckled quietly. "Are you on your way back?"

"Just got relieved of guard duty. Letton's not long for this world. The doctors called the wife, Mandy."

"Where are you?"

"Taking a late lunch."

"Learn anything about our vic?"

"She was a party girl. I'm going to call Mac and tell him to check Portland clubs. I also have the name of a friend. I don't suppose you've heard what they found at the scene?"

"Not yet. I thought McNally was on the verge of retirement."

"Maybe he can't give it up." Will thought about telling Barb he was on his way to interview Gemma LaPorte, but thought better of it. "I've some things to take care of, so I'll see you later."

"Hurry back, big guy."

Will hung up, glad things seemed to have warmed a little with Barb. She was a big girl. Maybe this would pass. Still, it hadn't seemed prudent to tell her that he was on his way for a tête-à-tête with Gemma LaPorte. Smithson might be a whiney bitch, but he sure as hell saw someone who looked like her.

Will just hoped Ms. LaPorte was at home.

Gemma felt like her head was going to explode. As she picked up the plates in the booth after a party of four, she felt slightly dizzy. Carefully she laid the plates back on the table and took a moment, inhaling several long, deep breaths. She wasn't well. This accident had set her back far more than she'd wanted to believe. The sights, smells, and noise of the diner were nearly overwhelming.

"You okay, miss?" a man at the next booth asked with concern.

Gemma nodded, carefully picked up the plates again, then headed for the kitchen. She dropped them on the counter near the sink, the top one skittering off and clattering atop an already growing pile. Milo, the cook with the Rasta braids, said, "What's your problem, girl?"

"Milo." Macie shot him a look as she entered behind Gemma.

Milo shrugged, unrepentant. "She don't look so hot. That's all I'm saying."

Charlotte slammed her notebook shut and scrambled off her chair in the corner. Seeing the concerned look on her face, Gemma waved her away. "I've been away too long from the noise, I think. Or maybe it's just my on-again/off-again brain."

"Nuh-uh," Macie said. "Not like this. You're white as a sheet and look about to face-plant the linoleum. That's not your brain. You're sick, girl."

"I don't know how much is a result of the accident, and how much of it's me." Gemma sank down on the stool Charlotte had vacated.

"Y'all gonna get outta here?" Milo asked, hands on his hips. He wore a do-rag over his hair and his apron was bright red.

Gemma looked away from him and thought, *He's about to be a father and isn't sure what to think about it.* "Do you know the sex yet?" she asked.

He lifted his brows in an exaggerated, *You're nuts* kind of way.

"Is it going to be a boy or a girl?"

Macie gave Milo a swift look. "Shirl's having a baby?"

"Jesus, my Lord," he muttered and slammed back to the grill, scraping at some nonexistent burned-on gunk as if his life depended on it.

Macie slid Gemma a look. "You go, girl," she said. Then, "Lunch crowd's over. I can finish up. You get yourself right." She headed out to the dining room.

Charlotte was staring at Gemma with a kind of awe. "How do you do that? Can I learn?"

"I don't think so." She smiled wanly. "It's kind of a curse."

"Why can you do it?"

"Just lucky I guess."

"Is your head really hurting?"

Gemma gently rotated her neck. "Better now."

"You're different since the accident."

"Am I? How?"

"I don't know. I'll have to think about it," she said seriously.

Gemma gave her a long look. Whether she knew it or not, Charlotte had information. "What do I do when my brain is 'off'?"

"Stare off into space. Say some kind of spooky stuff, like you just did with Milo. Like you were thinking about something else, really hard, and then you return."

"Do I generally remember what I was thinking about?"

"Yeah, I think so. Like when you came out of the restaurant the last time I saw you? You were just totally on him. You remember that?"

"Sort of." Gemma felt her pulse start to escalate.

Charlotte sensed that Gemma wasn't being entirely truthful, so she related, "I was outside and you just banged out of the door right after this dude. I don't know who he was . . . he was sorta familiar but he looked at me weird. Creepy."

"How, creepy?"

"I don't know, exactly." She thought about it, then shook her head. "But then I saw the one chasing you. He was creepy, too, but different."

"In what way?"

"He was kind of hunched over, like his shoulders were heavy. He was staring at you, like with laser eyes."

"Not the guy I was following?" Gemma clarified. "This was a guy following me?"

"Yeah, he had bushy hair."

"And you're certain he was following me?"

"Well . . . yeah . . . it sure seemed like it . . ." Now Charlotte didn't sound so sure.

"Go back to the first guy. Can you remember why you thought he was creepy?" Gemma knew her questions were coming hard and fast, but she was desperate to learn what she had been doing that day. It didn't sound like she had been following Letton, but maybe . . . ?

"That guy? The first guy? His eyes were kind of—intense. He stared at me like he was stuck on me. Like he was caught in a tractor beam and couldn't look away. He was a psycho for sure. But the second guy—he's like a rock. He just had that look about him."

"Did you see what they drove, either one of them?"

Charlotte screwed up her face, struggling hard. "I think the first guy had a truck. Or maybe it was the second one." She shook her head. "I don't know. I was heading inside. I didn't say anything to you because you were like on a mission. Figured you wouldn't recognize me anyway. You never do when you're like that."

She was so matter-of-fact Gemma hardly knew what to think.

Suddenly, Charlotte said, "I've got it! You're more here now. That's what's different. Like you're really back. I can talk to you. Like now."

"You couldn't before?"

"You really don't remember much, do you?" Charlotte looked concerned.

"I've got big gaps," Gemma admitted.

"Maybe that's from the head trauma. People always forget stuff with head trauma. Takes awhile to get over that and you may never remember stuff that happened right before your car crashed," she warned earnestly. "But maybe the accident put your head on straighter. You seem more . . ." She searched for the right words. "More . . . in the moment! That's what they're always saying. 'Be more in the moment.' You're more in the moment."

Macie returned with a huge plastic tub of dirty dishes. She

dumped them beside the growing pile in the sink. "Where's the damn busboy? First Denise, then Aaron. And the new girl's waiting for a ride from her boyfriend." Macie snorted in disgust.

"Don't you think Gemma's different since the accident?" Charlotte asked her mother. "More in the moment?"

Macie gave her child the kind of scared look mothers sometimes can't hide that says she doesn't know quite what to think of this alien creature she gave birth to. She wrenched her gaze away to look at Gemma. After several tries, where she opened her mouth to speak, then changed her mind, she said, "Maybe more focused. You don't seem as scattered. How's the headache?"

"Better. Really. It just felt like a wave of noise and confusion for a minute."

"Good."

"Macie . . ." Gemma followed her to the dining area. Charlotte tried to trot after them, but Macie said, "Give me and Gemma a minute."

"Fine." Charlotte clomped back to her stool.

"What is it, hon?"

"It feels like I'm missing pieces. Big pieces."

"Mmmhmm. Did you call Dr. Rainfield?"

"I haven't heard back from him yet. I left a message with his answering service."

"Answering service? You *are* missing big pieces. That man's old, honey. He sees people out of his home. Gave up his practice to his son, who moved it to Portland. You can just stop by. He's over on Bellflower. The gray two-bedroom with the rose garden? It's all sticks now but that's that man's pride and joy."

"I remember," Gemma said, with a flood of memory. She could see herself stepping up the sagging front porch steps to have a session with the doctor.

"Don't know if he's a quack or not. Most people think he's okay, and I think he helped you. Got you to write that book."

"Book?"

"Your diary, or whatever? To put down all the times you forgot things, or if you predicted something, like with Milo just there? I don't know. You told me about it."

"Did I?" Gemma asked faintly.

"You need to sit down?"

"No, no. It's just—hard—getting these pieces of my past that are lost."

"You don't remember the book?"

Gemma thought hard, then slowly wagged her head *no*. She sensed the information was inside her somewhere, but the more she struggled to pull it out, the harder it became.

"You'd better go home and take care of yourself. See how you feel. I'd like you here next week, but if you can't make it, just let me know."

"I'll be here. Count on it."

"Well, go now. Shoo." She snapped a towel at Gemma. Gemma glanced at the clock on the wall. Four o'clock. "Don't even think about it," Macie declared. "Get yourself well."

"The day I chased that guy I was just having . . . breakfast?"

"You didn't even get that far. Denise was showing off how she'd hemmed her uniform up, and you looked at her and then that guy . . . and you were gone. Like you made some kind of connection."

Gemma said as if from a far distance, "I sort of remember."

"Yeah?"

"The uniform was red."

"That's right. A prototype. But we kept with pastels. Do

you remember why you went after that guy?" she asked curiously.

He was a pedophile.

The words ran across Gemma's mind though she didn't know where they came from. "What time was it?" she asked.

"Early. Seven a.m. Maybe even six."

Letton was killed in the late morning. Tennish. It could have been him. She could have blasted after him, then made her plans to run him down at the soccer field.

Or, did you follow him to the diner first?

Shaken, Gemma left with a mumbled good-bye. She'd chased a pedophile out of LuLu's on the morning Edward Letton was run down by someone who looked a lot like her. She couldn't reconcile this other side of herself with her own view of who she was. Maybe this was how killers justified their actions? Maybe they just didn't think of themselves as capable?

Suddenly she really wanted to find that book, that diary. Hurrying to her father's truck, she slammed inside and headed for home.

Wolf dreamed of her.

> She came to him with her hair down, a smile lifting the corner of her mouth. Her scent was pine, a fresh mountain flavor. He opened his mouth to taste her and she opened hers, but it was a yawning cavern. He could see straight into her black soul.
>
> His body was consumed with heat. Fire. Molten lava.
>
> His arms reached for her. He held her and she started spitting and screaming. He threw her down.
>
> "Burn. *Burn.*"

She howled and thrashed as he flung himself upon her. He was going to have her. She had no choice. No choice!

Br-r-r-ring.

His eyes flew open. The doorbell. Fury raged through his veins.

Four o'clock in the afternoon. Someone at his door. He hated anyone coming to his domain.

He jumped from the bed and strode to the front door. His dick was still stiff and he had to wait a moment before answering.

He opened the door and there she stood. Clipboard in hand.

"Hi. I just need a signature," she said.

He glanced down at the box on the ground. A throbbing started in his temples.

"That's not for me," he said. He couldn't recognize his own voice.

She tilted her head and examined the address. Her lips parted. "Your house number is 2702?"

"Over there." He threw an arm toward the back of his house. To the fields beyond and to *them.* "Behind me. The farmhouse."

A line formed between her brows. "I'm . . . I was sure . . ." She gave him an apologetic smile. "Never mind."

He didn't say anything and she gazed at him uncertainly as she walked away. He watched her tight butt in the brown shorts. Her calves were clean and strong.

But she smelled rotten. Evil.

Bile rose up his throat.

She was a witch. Another one he needed to burn the rot from, from the inside out. A gift to him from a higher power, the next one he needed to send back to hell.

He watched as she stepped into her truck and drove away. He opened his garage door and climbed into the truck which still smelled faintly of the other witch, along with the ammonia he'd used to scrub out the truck bed.

He could pick up this one's trail after she left the farmhouse.

Chapter Ten

Will felt a slow anger building inside him as he headed toward Gemma's. She'd lied to him. He didn't completely believe her story about not remembering. Something was off. And he was pretty damn sure she'd showed up to finish Letton off but hadn't been able to go through with it. Maybe she'd seen, as he had, that the man wasn't going to make it. Maybe she'd had a change of heart.

Maybe he was hoping against hope that she was innocent, even with all evidence to the contrary.

Growling under his breath, he grabbed his cell phone and punched in the number he had for Sam McNally. In other states it was illegal to use a cell while driving unless you had an ear bud. Probably should be in Oregon, too, Will thought, but in the moment he was glad it wasn't.

"McNally," the detective answered.

"Hey, Mac, it's Will Tanninger. Have you heard anything from the techs yet on Inga Selbourne, the body we found at the airstrip? They find anything at her place?"

"A helluva lot of blood," Mac responded. "It's been sent

out for testing. Might be Inga's or could be the doer's. Somebody stabbed somebody with a piece of glass and I'm betting Inga nailed him. But if so, he's not too worried about DNA. I'm going out to view the body this afternoon."

"I didn't notice any cuts, but the body was burned," Will said.

"If it's him that got cut, he's got some marks on him. Got anything for me?"

Will told him about Inga's affinity for the Portland bar scene. "She has a girlfriend named DeeAnna Brush who worked in administration at Laurelton General. DeeAnna quit and moved over to Good Samaritan."

Mac grunted. "Good, I'll check with her and see where their favorite spots were."

"Keep me informed?"

"Same here."

Will hung up and checked the meter of his anger. Down to a low simmer. Good. He wasn't known for losing his cool but he felt oddly out of balance over the Letton case.

He was practically to Quarry when his cell rang. He looked at Caller ID and read: *Home.* Puzzled, he answered, "Tanninger," though the call had come from his own rented, ranch-style two-bedroom house.

"Will?" an older, female voice warbled.

"Mom?"

"I stopped by to see you, but you weren't here." She sounded scared and Will knew just how she felt.

"You're at my house?" he repeated, his heart clutching. She suffered from dementia, possibly Alzheimer's, and although it had been a slow decline to this point, the disease was definitely winning. It was infuriating, and frustrating, and there was nothing to do about it. "You remembered where the key was?" he asked, half-incredulously.

"Oh, yes. I knocked and knocked and finally had to let myself in," she confirmed. "Where are you?"

Will's urgency to talk with Gemma fueled his frustration. "I'm working, Mom. In the car."

"Are you coming home?"

Wild horses wouldn't be able to keep him away. "I'm on my way. Mom, how did you get there?"

"Uh . . . ?"

"To my house. Did Noreen bring you?" he asked, referring to his mother's caretaker.

"I don't think so . . . maybe . . ."

"Did she drop you off?" he suggested. He'd been trying to take her vehicle away from her for the past six months, but had been singularly unsuccessful. He'd hidden the keys, which she'd found, and he'd disabled the ignition, which she'd called a mechanic to come and fix. The craftiness inside the fog of dementia was mind-boggling. But since Noreen had come to live with her full time, he'd thought the situation was taken care of.

"No . . . my car's gone . . ." she said suddenly. "I think it's in a ditch."

"What ditch?"

"The one by the road," she said, sounding amused, as if she thought he was just the silliest thing.

Alarm bells clanged inside Will's head. He told her again that he was on his way and actually put the siren and lights on as he tore back in the direction of his own house.

Gemma walked up the paint-chipped front steps to Dr. Rainfield's door. She pushed the bell and experienced a kaleidoscope of warm memories: eating cookies and swinging her legs as she sat on a too tall chair; playing memory games with the doctor and beating him hands down; writing copiously in a red leather diary that he kept at his office.

Red leather diary.

She'd come here since she was a child. A young child.

Jean hadn't known what to do with a little girl who retreated into fantasy a great deal of the time and so she'd brought her to the doctor. Dr. Rainfield had played with her, had encouraged her to draw and color and express herself through art. Gemma had loved it. Had flourished. His attentions had almost put her back together again. Almost, but not quite. There were gaps.

Gemma heard the labored steps of the doctor, coming to answer her knock. The door creaked open and gray, bushy eyebrows above sharp, equally gray eyes, stared back at her.

"Well, hello, my dear," he greeted her.

"Hello, Dr. Rainfield. I called your answering service for an appointment, but I thought I'd stop by."

"Oh, yes. I meant to call you." He opened the door wider.

The aroma of canned chili met her as soon as she entered. It was early evening and she'd interrupted his dinner. "I didn't realize you were in the middle of a meal."

He gave a short bark of laughter. "My dear, you're a welcome distraction. How are you?" He gestured to a living room chair and Gemma perched on the end of it.

Settling himself on the sofa, he regarded her carefully. And Gemma, although she'd had no intention of saying anything besides *Where's the red diary?* found herself blurting out the events of the last couple of weeks as she knew them, finishing with, "Could I have run Edward Letton down? I don't think so. Unless I'm two people, like a multiple personality or something," she half-laughed.

He gave her an intense look. "I always thought you were just trying to forget things you didn't want to know and sometimes it took out pieces you wanted to remember, too."

His answer soothed her and a part of her relaxed. "Do you have a red leather diary? The one I wrote in?"

"You mean your journal?"

Gemma nodded, figuring they must be talking about the same thing.

"You took that with you right before you left."

"Before I left?"

"With that boyfriend of yours. You don't remember?"

"When I left with Nate," she said.

He almost smiled. "You're fishing. Let me help. You wrote in the journal during your sessions. Or actually afterward, while you waited for your mother to pick you up. But you didn't want to take it home. You didn't think it would be—safe."

Gemma blinked. "My mother didn't have any boundaries."

"True," he admitted.

"I didn't want her to read my thoughts. I was afraid she'd use them to her advantage."

Rainfield's brows lifted. He didn't say it, but she knew he concurred with her. She saw that he had been a port in the storm for her. Jean LaPorte had loved her but it had been a love full of strings attached. Rainfield had been an objective listener and more of a father to her than her own out-of-his-element father, Peter.

Gemma said suddenly, "She used you. As a kind of baby-sitter, tutor, svengali. But she also resented you for that. She resented Macie, too, for being my friend."

"She just wanted more from you than you could give."

"I ran off with Nate to get away from it all. But then I came back." Gemma gazed at him seriously. "I've always had all these gaps?"

"Little gaps."

"They feel pretty big now."

"You said you were in an auto accident. I'm no expert on head trauma, but it sounds like the problem's been exacerbated by the crash. It'll probably pass. What does your doctor say?"

Gemma didn't answer that Rainfield was the only doctor she was seeing. That her physical injuries hadn't been examined since she left the hospital. But he understood nevertheless and he tsk-tsked her.

"You should see someone."

"I'd like to see you," she responded. "On a regular basis."

"Oh, child, I'm retired. My answering service is more to keep me in touch with old friends and old patients, but it's just for friendship. I don't see anyone anymore. My son's taken over my practice. He has offices in Portland." Rainfield climbed from the chair and Gemma got to her feet as well. He shuffled toward the kitchen, stopping just inside the open door. Out of Gemma's vision, he reached for something, then returned with a card in his hand. "I'll call him and tell him you'll be making an appointment."

Gemma looked down at the card. Dr. Tremaine Rainfield's offices were in downtown Portland. She didn't want to drive to Portland. She didn't want to make the trip, and she didn't want to see someone else. She also still didn't have a driver's license, and she felt she was flirting with disaster every time she got behind the wheel. But she didn't disclose these thoughts, just let him think what he would.

"So, *I* was in possession of the journal last," she said as he walked her to the door.

"I don't think you gave it to Nate."

"Me, neither." Nate Dorrell had turned abusive over time. She recognized that he had simply been an escape route, though at the time she'd convinced herself that her decision to leave Quarry with him had been wrapped up in feelings of everlasting love, joy, and desire.

"Call Tremaine," he said, nodding at the card in her hand. "But you can stop by anytime, if you'd like."

If you need a friend, was what he meant.

Gemma smiled and wished him good-bye. She needed more than a friend. A lot more.

* * *

The patrol car was practically still moving as Will jumped from behind the wheel and ran to his own front door. It was ajar about six inches and he had a moment of dread before he heard his mom tunelessly humming from somewhere inside.

He found her in the kitchen. She'd discovered a bag of store-bought cookies from God-knew-when from the cupboard he used as a pantry, and was happily munching away. He hoped she didn't break a tooth.

"Hi, Mom. I don't see your car," he said. "You said it's in a ditch?"

"I'm not supposed to drive." She raised her brows and gave him a look that said he was a naughty boy for denying her.

Dementia sufferers had little or no logic and reasoning. Nevertheless, Will tried to remind her of their earlier conversation. "You told me your car was in a ditch."

"Yes, I think it is."

"But you didn't drive it here."

"Didn't I?" She furrowed her brow.

"It's not outside and it's not anywhere around the neighborhood." As Will had driven into the suburban/rural area, he'd kept an eye out for any sign of her white Chevy Impala.

"Oh, I think Noreen took it."

"Where is Noreen?" Will demanded.

"She dropped me off and took the car to the shop."

As if on cue, Will's cell phone rang and he saw the Caller ID was from the woman in question. "Where are you?" he barked into the phone, ignoring the niceties.

"I had to get the car in," Noreen responded, sounding surprised and a little hurt by his tone. "Your mom backed it out of the driveway into the ditch. Did she tell you? I'm getting a rental to drive her in and will be back to pick her up, probably within the hour."

"I wasn't home when you dropped my mother off," he said through his teeth.

"You didn't get your mom's call?"

"She called me from inside my house."

Noreen made a strangled sound, directed at herself. "She said she'd talked to you and you were home! I was going to walk her inside, but she waved me off and I wanted to get the car in . . . oh, golly . . . is everything okay?"

"She's here. I'm here. Everything's fine. We'll see you when you get here."

He snapped his phone shut, half mad at Noreen, half at himself. He didn't know what to do about his mother. There were no easy answers.

She was staring at him, picking up on his controlled anger if not the reason for it. "Was that Dylan?" she asked, and Will just stared at her, flummoxed all over again.

"Mom, Dylan's dead. He's been gone a long time."

"Oh? I thought I just talked to him."

Will could practically count the seconds elapsing inside his head. He told himself to get over it. There was no need to rush. Noreen would return and then he could be on his way.

His mom took another jaw-breaking bite of the cookie. He winced at the sound of her teeth clacking and grinding.

"Do you want me to make dinner?" she asked, as if the idea had just popped into her head.

She hadn't made a meal in a decade.

"Why don't you sit down at the table," Will suggested, forcing himself to be patient. He pulled out a chair for her. "I'll make . . . peanut butter sandwiches."

She beamed at him. "That sounds wonderful."

He slapped peanut butter on bread in a controlled fury as his mother sat down at the table and began babbling on about Dylan. He closed his eyes. His brother was more real to her than the son who'd survived. Damn disease. It had robbed him of her. Robbed him of his only living relative, as his father had died when Will was just a child, from heart problems.

His anger hadn't abated by the time Noreen arrived to collect his mother. She apologized profusely and Will nodded in curt response. Her negligence would not likely be repeated and that, at least, was something.

As he drove toward Gemma's house, he tried to put his anger aside but it just kept growing, morphing, aiming itself at Gemma herself. She'd run down Edward Letton, and though the prick deserved to die, in Will's biased opinion, it was not her choice to make. Vigilantism was a crime. Killing was a *crime.* She'd come back to the hospital with the intention of killing Letton and only hadn't because . . . she'd seen he was on his last legs and there was no need.

Her intention was what mattered. She'd *intended* to end Letton's life. He wouldn't be the last. Maybe he wasn't even the first . . .

That thought gave him pause. Will made a mental note to check other pedophile deaths in the area.

But in any case, it didn't matter how attractive she was. And it didn't matter that he understood, and even sympathized with, her motives, she had to be stopped.

Will set his jaw and his resolve.

Gemma tore through the books in her bedroom but there was no diary to be found. She wandered down to the den but knew she would never have left the journal where it could be discovered by her mother. She glanced at all the books on the shelves but the only red ones she saw were paperbacks, and her journal was leather.

She thought she heard something on her porch and she flew to the front door and flung it open. The darkening evening sky met her, along with a breeze that skittered shriveled leaves across the wood flooring and sent them piling into the corners.

No mysterious message. No one seeing into her soul.

Returning to the kitchen, she fixed herself a meal of cheese, crackers, and apple slices and asked herself if she was ever going to purchase any groceries. She'd enjoyed Sally Van Kamp's chicken casserole, and now had to return the dish—a face-to-face she wasn't looking forward to—but she really needed to stock her shelves. The trouble was, shopping wasn't high on her priority list and she only thought about it when she returned home alone, and by then she had no interest in going out again.

She was munching her last cracker when she was struck by a thought. Dusting off her hands, she climbed the stairs to the attic, which was filled with dust-covered boxes and cobwebs. After surveying the piles of stuff, she hauled open several boxes and found household paraphernalia—old knickknacks, vases, pictures—the kind of various and sundry items that fill garage sales every weekend, but no journal.

She returned downstairs and retreated to Jean's—now her—office. Lost in thought, she didn't immediately notice the two messages on her voice mail, but finally she saw them. The first was an imperious message from Davinia Noack demanding to have a reading; the second was from someone who merely breathed hard into the phone. She listened to them both again. The breather didn't terrorize her, if that's what it was meant to do. Instead, it sounded like someone was just trying to get up the courage to say something.

"Little Tim," she said aloud. That was probably it. She didn't want to think it might be whoever had left the note on her front porch.

Pushing that thought aside, she glanced at the bookshelves again. No red journals. Her eyes traveled over the spines of the volumes as her mind tripped down its own path. This room had been her office for months, now. Why wouldn't she keep her journal here? If she still possessed it, she *would* put it here, wouldn't she? Pull it out from its hiding place and put it on the shelves? She was sure she would.

So, where was it?

The answer was so obvious her gaze was stuck on the journal itself long before she jumped up to pull it down. Its spine was black and there was no writing on it. She pulled it out and saw that the book's front and back leather was blood red.

Thoughts swarmed and her heart pounded as she flipped back the cover. In a child's scrawl she read: Gemma Jean LaPorte. Her mother had bestowed her own name on her as a middle name. Originally, she'd wanted to change Gemma's first name to Jean, but Gemma hadn't responded well to the change, so Jean had become the middle one.

Rifling gently through the pages, Gemma sat down in the squeaking desk chair. With the journal in her hands, it felt as if she'd always possessed it. Apparently she had, as it was on the shelf big as you please. She just hadn't remembered.

Catching some passages, her memories flooded back as if someone had lifted a gate. She suspected Dr. Rainfield was right, that the accident had done the most damage to her memory. Whatever problems she'd possessed since she was a child weren't as bad as she'd feared. As she read blocks of text she remembered everything fully.

And it gave her back her past.

Thank you, Dr. Rainfield, for making me keep this.

The journal started when Gemma was about six, with Gemma drawing pictures and writing their names below the images: CAT, DOG, HORSE, CAMPFIRE, MASK. She examined the picture of the mask. It looked like a square with strings. Not much of a Halloween mask, if that's what it was supposed to be.

Going further, she breezed over the years until high school, then remembered, with enough embarrassment to feel heat enter her cheeks, that she'd had a horrible crush on one of the Dunleavy boys. Jerome. Everyone called him Rome. But he'd been completely oblivious to Gemma's feelings, thank God. He'd gone to work with his older brother Kevin, and they shared a business interest in the PickAxe, Quarry's local bar and tavern. Kevin also shared his parents' resentment of Gemma's family over property rights. Though the property lines had been long established, the Dunleavys seemed to feel they'd been gypped in the final decision of who owned what and how much. Jean had ignored them, and Peter, quiet and reserved as he was most of the time, had warned Gemma to stay away from the lot of them. He felt they were small-minded, mean-spirited, and always felt slighted. Gemma had listened to this with half an ear because she knew Rome Dunleavy wasn't like that at all.

Rome was engaged, she realized suddenly. To a woman Gemma didn't know. They were planning to build on the other side of the Quarry and would, in effect, be Gemma's neighbors.

Gemma flipped a few more pages and encountered Nate Dorrell. Now, with the clarity of hindsight, she saw that she'd jumped to Nate from her hero-worship of Rome Dunleavy. She'd graduated from high school and taken off with Nate as he joined the army. She'd lived in a one-room apartment just off base, and just barely made ends meet working at another diner. Now she closed her eyes and remembered the smells and sounds: the dull surf, the constant stream of traffic, the exhaust, the briny fog, the tolling bell that rang the dinner hour at a nearby halfway house for sometime criminals.

She recalled sex with Nate. Hard, fast, selfish. It wasn't long before she was rethinking how much she wanted to have sex at all, but it didn't matter. If he wanted it, it was on. For a long time she told herself she loved him and that was enough to keep the myth going. Eventually, she grew strong enough to say no.

Here her memory jumped. She couldn't quite recall the events of their breakup, but it hadn't been pretty. It might have even been physical.

Gemma thumbed to the end of the journal. She'd made a couple of last entries concerning her feelings about reading the future for Jean's clients. Her final entry was a question: *When are you going to take matters into your own hands?*

Her blood chilled. Maybe she already had.

Bang, bang, bang!

The journal flew from her fingers, the noise surprised her so much. Gemma scrambled to pick it up, her pulse fluttering. Someone was at the front door. Someone impatient.

She set the journal on the desk, drew a calming breath, then headed for the door, unlatching it and swinging it open.

Detective Will Tanninger waited on the other side.

"Detective," she murmured, feeling her anxiety ratchet up another notch or two.

"Ms. LaPorte."

His voice was cool. Cold. Gemma felt a tingle of fear skitter down her spine. Something had happened. Something had changed.

"What is it?" she asked, as she stood back and he entered the room.

"You went to the hospital yesterday."

Her eyes widened. "No . . . I was in Quarry."

"You went to Letton's room. You talked my guard into leaving and then you entered the room intending to kill him."

The detective looked hard as granite. His face was sharp planes and thin lips. He was angry. Angry at her. It was such a change from the quiet, if intense, man she'd met earlier that she hardly knew what to do or say. "I don't think so."

"You don't think so?" he pounced, as if she'd just made an admission of guilt.

"Yesterday, I talked to you in the morning."

"And you went to the hospital in the afternoon," he said tautly.

"I would remember," she answered, but they both knew that could be a lie.

"He saw your bruised face."

Gemma's hand flew to her cheek as if it had a will of its own.

"You tried to cover it with makeup, like now, but it's still bruised."

Her head felt cottony, her pulse fluttered. "I was home," she insisted, as if from a long way away.

"All afternoon and evening?"

"I took a nap."

"You're going to tell me you don't remember anything at all."

Gemma stared at him. She could see a pulse jumping in his jaw, could feel his controlled fury.

And Gemma had a flash of someone else. Another man, whose angry eyes reached her before his fist did.

That brought her back with a bang and also snuffed out her fear. "Is this the way the sheriff's department works?" she demanded. "Intimidation. Is this your bad cop role? Because it's doing the trick. You're scaring me. Actually, no. You're pissing me off."

"You wanted to kill him. You meant to do it. What stopped you?"

"You have all the answers. You tell me."

"You knew he was going to die anyway, so you walked away."

Gemma recoiled. "He's dying? From his injuries?"

"His wife's been called. No one thinks he'll make it through the night."

Gemma searched her feelings. She would have expected to feel something but her senses were deadened. She thought about responding but couldn't think of anything to say.

Will leaned toward her, waiting. "Nothing?"

Gemma's lips tightened. "You obviously think I'm going to break down and confess to something. I'm not. I don't remember much about the day Edward Letton was run down. You don't have anything on me. No car. No connection. Nothing other than the fact I was in an accident around the same time. So, if your reason for being here is pure harassment, get the hell off my property."

Two bright spots of color burned in her cheeks and her hazel eyes glittered green. Will couldn't decide if he was still angry or falling in lust. Maybe a little of both.

Will had interviewed innumerable suspects, witnesses, family members, and friends. He did it as part of the job, never thinking whether he enjoyed or disliked it. But now he could feel adrenaline running through his veins. He gazed at her hard. He wanted to push her, force her into a slipup. "You ran him down because you knew he was going to kidnap one of the soccer girls. You knew it ahead of time. You followed him to the fields. And you took him out before he could."

Gemma said carefully, "I'm not sorry that girl is safe."

He was fascinated by the way her lips moved, as if she were rounding every syllable just for him. "That's not the issue."

"It's the only issue."

"You can't go around killing people."

"So far I've only been accused of trying to kill one person," she reminded him.

"So far," he shot back.

Gemma sucked in a breath and glared at him. "I am sick and tired of being bullied. If you aren't here to arrest me, then get out of my house!"

"I'm going to find out the truth."

"Then get at it, detective!" She thrust a finger at the door, her own adrenaline singing through her.

Before Will could do anything his cell phone rang. He pulled it from his pocket and looked at the Caller ID. He suddenly knew what it was, knew what he would hear.

"Is it Letton?" he snapped to the caller.

Barb said, "He's gone. Died about a half hour ago. His wife's wailing all over the place. Wants you to nail the bitch that brought him down or she's suing the department."

"Let her sue." He ended the call and shoved the phone in his pocket.

"What?" Gemma asked, her eyes glued to his face, her body tense, expectant.

"Letton's dead."

Chapter Eleven

Gemma was breathing hard, her shoulders sinking as if a puppeteer had let go of her strings. "He's dead," she repeated. The color seeped from her face and she moved woodenly to the couch, sinking like a stone into its cushions. "Oh, my God," she murmured. "My God."

Will, too, felt drained. And angry.

"I didn't kill him."

"Somebody did."

"What do you want to hear?" she said with a return of spunk.

"That it's not your fault," Will threw back. "I want you to tell me anything! Anything at all. I want to hear that you saw what he was planning and your foot hit the accelerator before you knew what you were doing. I want to believe it was an accident."

She regarded him cautiously. "I don't remember."

"Oh, come on!"

"Well, that's your problem, then." She thought about what she'd learned from Macie and Charlotte. That she'd charged out of the diner after someone. She could almost remember that. She could feel the heat of fury and rage that had fueled her flight. She remembered getting behind the wheel of a car. She remembered wanting to kill the bastard.

But that was it. A jumble of feelings and impressions and nothing more.

She *had* wanted to kill someone, however. That was fact.

Had she followed Letton to the soccer field and lain in wait? That felt wrong somehow, as if pieces were missing.

Had the scene in the diner been something else? Something outside the careful planning that had set up Letton's death?

Tanninger's cell phone rang again and he made a sound of impatience before yanking it from his pocket. He seemed torn as to whether he was going to answer it. Finally he turned a shoulder and said, "Noreen. What?"

She watched him carefully. There was something mercurial about him today. As if his control had slipped a little. She felt it in a primal way that touched into her feminine core, which thrilled her a little and pissed her off a lot more.

"I'll pay for it when I pick it up," he told her. "Keep the rental car for now."

"What was that?" Gemma asked when he clicked off.

"Nothing." He seemed to come back to himself. An ironic lift to his lips. "My mother put her car in a ditch."

"Oh."

My mother put her car in a ditch.

Will shrugged and shook his head, as if physically shoving aside his personal problems, and went right back to the issue at hand. "You're right. Letton's death is my problem."

"I'm not sorry he's dead," she said with feeling.

"Neither am I."

"I hope I didn't kill him."

"I thought you said you didn't."

They stared at each other.

Will wanted to kiss her; she could feel it. Her body responded with a surge of expectation that she hoped like hell didn't show on her face. She wanted to kiss him, too. Wanted to grab hold of him and run her hands up his muscled back. Wanted to fit herself to him. It was irrational and so potent that she felt herself lean toward him just as he took a step backward, closed his eyes and clenched his fists.

When he opened them again they were both more in control.

Then he stated flatly, a warning she couldn't miss, "Now it's a homicide."

The delivery girl drove a gray-and-brown truck that trundled down the road at a fast clip. The wolf kept behind her, several cars back. He'd picked her up outside the lane from the house across the field from his. He'd been waiting in his truck at a seaside lookout, the kind of place tourists pulled into to snap pictures. It wasn't far from where he lived and was in sight of the farmhouse's long, narrow drive, so when her truck reappeared on 101, he waited just long enough for it to disappear around a corner where the highway cut through a wall of granite, then he pulled out behind her.

She made a number of stops; he had to drive past her more than a few times to keep from being spotted, but she was walking to the back of the truck and never noticed. He was invisible. Nonexistent.

The thought burned through him. He'd always been invisible to the witch. She'd only seen his brother. Jealousy had raged bright inside him, a flame that seared through his veins. He could hear them through the thin walls night after night. Her moans. His short shouts of ecstasy. The floor shook and he secretively pleasured himself to the sounds of their desire.

One evening he saw her looking out the window, her back

to him, her long hair a curtain to her waist. He was young, but old enough. So he came up behind her, his cock rigid, and pressed himself into her, his head resting on her shoulder. He could feel the starchiness of her dress and hear it crinkle. She whipped around as if he'd hit her with an electric shock and slapped him across the face, screaming.

"Bastard! What are you doing?" she shrieked and slapped him again.

He was too stunned and too humiliated to react.

Her face was contorted with revulsion. "Ever do that again and I'll cut it off, understand?"

She shoved him in the chest and he staggered backward. She pressed him to the wall, her green eyes full of simmering fury. "I'm a witch. Don't forget. I have powers and I will castrate you, you fucker."

"You're my mother," he said weakly.

Her hand cracked across his face again, so hard that his head slammed into the cabinet and his ears rang. "I am not!" she raged.

"What's going on?"

His older brother was framed in the doorway. He looked huge. His gaze slid to the dark-haired woman and back to the wolf. She turned toward him and stated, "I was teaching your brother a lesson. He came up behind me and shoved his cock against my ass."

His brother glared at him with hot eyes. The wolf shook his head. He needed to tell his brother that all he wanted to do was share. That was all. He wasn't trying to steal their mother from him.

"The witch is mine," he whispered to Wolf.

She moved to his brother, her mouth slack and soft. "Oh, baby. C'mere, baby," she crooned, her hands running over his neck and shoulders, her cheek pressed to his as her gaze continued to sear into the wolf's.

The wolf had lost. He'd bowed his head and nodded. He would never come after the witch again, though he thought about it often. All the time. Incessantly.

He'd lost his chance to have her. That day. But in the end she'd been his.

He hoped she was burning in hell.

But there were other witches. And one of them. The One. Had killed his brother.

Witches had to burn. They had to pay. They had to be stopped.

He surfaced slowly, realizing he had followed the delivery girl to her company's home base in Seaside. She was pulling through the chain link fence that surrounded the building, getting ready to turn in her truck.

Soon, she would be heading home.

All he had to do was wait.

In the middle of the night Gemma awoke from a restless sleep, a scream clawing its way from her throat.

My mother put her car in a ditch.

A ditch.

That's what she'd done, too.

She'd run her mother's car off the road and into a ditch.

By mistake.

An accident.

Fumbling for the lamp switch, Gemma was half-blinded when the light suddenly flashed on.

The dream fell away into insubstantial vestiges of itself, as if blown apart. But it wasn't a dream. It was a memory. She could recall the fear, the rush of the road, the twist of the wheel. Highway 26. Toward the coast. Somewhere between here and Seaside. Or Cannon Beach. Or another place . . .

Had someone been chasing her?

Or, was she just tearing away after running Letton down?

And why had she raced past Quarry? Where was she going?

She touched her tender face. She'd slammed it into the steering wheel, or possibly the side window. The impact had been fierce.

She could almost remember. Almost. It was *right there*! Just out of reach.

Why couldn't she grab it?

Maybe you don't want to remember.

That sounded so much like the truth that she flung back the covers and clambered downstairs, desperate to get away from her own thoughts. The journal had only helped her so far.

The recent past was still a mystery. One she was less certain she wanted to unravel.

Wolf sat outside the witch's apartment building. The siding was gray and wind-battered and looked like it could use a good caulking. The outdoor stairway rail had been recently shored up with a criss-cross wood brace that had yet to be painted. She was on the second floor and there was the one stairway up, and another probably at the back of the wrap-around balcony.

He rolled his window down and cold air rushed in the cab, heavy with the scent of seawater. He realized, as if from a long, long way away, that he should be at work. He could fix things. He was good with his hands. He'd taken a job at his brother's place of employment, but it was a loose arrangement. At work they all thought he was a little slow, and he let them. His brother had told his co-workers to knock it off, but they hadn't listened. And now his brother was gone. Gone. But not to hell like the witches. His brother had looked out for him. In the end he'd turned against the mother-witch, too. Her death had bonded them.

He closed his eyes and tucked his chin into his chest. He could still draw the mother-witch to him if he tried. Could bring her close. He wanted to see the terror in her eyes. He wanted to clamp off her screams with the grip of his hands around her neck. He wanted to thrust himself inside her again and again. Bitch. Whore.

He was getting hard thinking about her. He pushed his mind further. A few more minutes. Then he would go after this witch.

She was there. Her green eyes glowing. Taunting him. "Bastard," she whispered, grinning. "I am not your mother. I am a witch."

In a red fog, the wolf climbed from the cab. He was dressed all in black except for a yellow baseball cap that advertised a trucking company. He walked around the back of the building, up the rear stairs. This witch's door was in the center of the front of the building, too obvious. But there was a window on the side. Her bedroom, he guessed. He had a small tool in his hand, a jimmy. It wouldn't take much to pop the window, but she would hear his efforts. He had to think, think . . . but the red fog was expanding and he was filled with mounting desire, like a thundering of approaching hoof beats.

He was about to rip out the window casing and deal with the problems therein when suddenly her front door opened and slammed shut. He heard her coming from the apartment to the back stairs. Before he could move she'd turned the corner to take the back stairs. He stepped back, head bent, stuffing the jimmy into the rear pocket of his pants. If she recognized him it was over. He would have to leave.

She nearly ran into him, then stopped short. "Oh! Sorry. I didn't know you were there."

"S'okay," he mumbled, and moved past her as if he were going the opposite direction.

He could feel her gaze on him as he lurched around the corner she'd just come from, probably wondering which apartment he was heading to. He, in turn, wondered where she was going in her short, white skirt and hooker heels. Her Ford Focus was parked in the front lot.

He pretended to knock on the door one over from her apartment. If anyone answered, he would have to give up his mission entirely. He couldn't afford to be seen. Couldn't afford someone remembering the man with the hunched shoulders and uneven gait. The thought made his pulse beat in his temple; a building rage.

Luckily, no one responded to his knock, and by the time she whizzed around the back of the building in a different vehicle, a black Corvette, no less, he pretended to half turn away in disappointment. He didn't think she even looked back. He'd been forgotten.

He went back to the window and jimmied the casing loose. The creaking and gentle pounding didn't arouse suspicion. Now breaking glass, that was another matter. Everyone knew what that was and responded to it. But a bit of banging could be anything.

He slid the pane out with ease, then reached in and unlocked the window. After pushing aside the curtain and taking a hard look inside, he replaced the glass and went back to his truck. In her hot second car she'd gone to go fuck someone. She would put her feminine spell on him and pump away on his dick and he would think it was about the best sex he'd ever had.

But when the whore returned the wolf would burn her. He had cigarettes and matches in his pocket. He remembered the way the mother-witch blew smoke through her nostrils and opened her mouth to let it spill out in a lazy cloud. She would laugh and laugh at his naked desire.

He ached with need but he wouldn't touch himself. This exquisite torture was for her.

And then his mind drifted . . . to the diner . . . to the one still living that he sought . . .

She'd walked in as big as life. The one he'd been looking for! Right there! Shoulder-length, light brown hair, several strands of which were stuck against her cheek. Her breath held as she reached up and brushed them away. Then the diner's owner hooted and hollered about how glad she was to see her. Someone else had held up a red uniform and she'd seemed momentarily entranced by the color, but then she'd taken a seat at a booth at the end of the row. He could look her square in the face but he'd grabbed a menu and hidden behind it, heart thundering, knees trembling.

She was right there. *Right there!* He'd been hunting her but had lost her in Seaside. She'd disappeared and he'd cursed the fates that had suddenly taken her from him. It had taken a long time to find her. Weeks . . . months . . . years . . .

He'd worked his way east from the coast. Haphazardly. He knew she was a waitress, so he'd stopped at every eatery along Highway 26. He believed he could pick up her scent. She was a witch and they smelled a certain way. When she'd been with his brother he could always tell when she was near.

But he'd about given up.

And then one early morning there she was! Just like that. Not working, just coming in for a bite. He was so excited he nearly missed the fact that she had her eyes on a man in the booth across from him. She tried to disguise it, but she was tuned in to the guy in the baseball cap in a way that infuriated the wolf. He wanted to stand up and roar that the fucking witch had killed his brother. That she had to *burn*.

But the man she was watching had other things on his mind, too. He casually dropped money on the table and headed out the door. A girl on a bike was just arriving and he and the girl exchanged glances. Wolf read it like it was a newspaper. Sex steamed between them.

And then his witch jumped up and flew out of the diner on the man's heels. Wolf had to scramble to leave money on the table for the coffee and danish that hadn't even arrived yet.

He followed her out. The man she was after climbed in a van and moved away. The witch followed in a silver car. Wolf hurried after them as best he could without calling too much attention to himself. As he passed by the girl on the bike she assessed him with sharp eyes. He purposely averted his face and climbed in the truck and nearly spun gravel in his haste to catch up with the witch.

He knew what she wanted with the man. What her kind always wanted. And though the guy's desire for young girls pulled at him, the witch would win. She would take him down. She would tie him up with invisible threads and when he was naked and vulnerable she would finish him off.

Wolf pictured himself riding her, strangling her, burning her. But then the witch in the white skirt and hooker heels came into his fantasy, and she was laughing. Laughing at him. He ripped at her clothes and they turned into brown shorts and a shirt, which made her laugh harder.

He suddenly came to and realized night had fallen in earnest. He'd been in the truck for hours. For a moment he thought maybe she'd come home and he'd missed her, but as if his brain had awakened for just this moment, he saw the black Corvette's headlights pull into the lot and turn toward the back lot.

His mouth turned into a cruel smile. Soon . . . soon . . .

But he'd misjudged. He stared in fury as she appeared from the back stairs, hanging on a young man whose mouth was all over her neck and hair. The witch was giggling. Wolf's rage boiled upward and a growl ripped from his throat.

They didn't hear. They were struggling with each other at the door. Fumbling. Squealing. The bastard actually gave her a few humps against the door, which sent her into new peals of laughter.

Oh, she was filthy.

He clenched his fists. The man wouldn't be leaving. He had no car.

The wolf pondered what this meant.

He thought about it for nearly an hour before he climbed out of the truck and flipped open the GemTop. Leaning in over the tailgate, he popped up the lid to his tool box, fumbling until his hand closed over the wrench. Holding it close to his body, he bent his head, moved to the back of the building, then climbed up the rear stairs. He stepped noiselessly to the window, listening hard. He could hear nothing. He suspected they were both long passed out.

Carefully, he eased the window upward, aware that the pane was just sitting in the casing and could slide out and fall to the ground if he wasn't careful. But he was extremely careful. The sudden exposure to the night air sent the curtains shivering inward and he caught a glimpse of them on the bed. The man was on his stomach, out cold. The witch was lying beside him on her back, completely naked. Her mouth was open but her eyes were closed. The stench of alcohol nearly overpowered him; the wolf was sensitive to scents.

Her hooker heels were tossed on the floor. Her white skirt

bunched and tossed aside. Her bra and panties mixed in the pile. Her uniform part of the overall mess.

The wolf carefully took out the window pane and put it on the deck outside the window, then he pushed the casing up farther and dropped himself inside the room. He landed with a loud thud but neither of them noticed.

This wasn't right. He wanted her to fight. To *know*! The power of the wolf was complete. She was going to die by his hand. Die because she deserved to go back to hell.

And then the man turned over and lifted his head, gazing blearily at the wolf. "Whad da fuck?" he murmured, reaching a leg over the bed.

The wolf moved quickly and slammed the man's head with the wrench. His body tumbled to the floor, going down hard. Wolf felt for a pulse at his neck. It was there. Good. He didn't want to kill him. He was a victim of the witch, too.

And now the witch was his. Wolf climbed atop her and rubbed himself over her. When that didn't wake her up he licked the side of her face but she tasted like sweat. Evil. Sick. Rotting. He slapped her lightly across the face and she moaned but didn't wake up.

"Witch," he whispered. "Whore."

Slowly she opened her eyes. "Phil?" she said.

The wolf suddenly remembered the dead eyes of his brother. In a fury, he clapped his hand over her mouth and pinned her hard to the bed.

"Die," he ordered. His hands circled her throat.

Feebly she reached upward, trying to fight him off. Her body stiffened as she came fully awake but the alcohol still made her dull. Her fingers clawed against the bandage at his neck, ripping it loose.

Wolf's erection failed him and for that he threw back his head and roared. He squeezed her throat. Squeezed and squeezed.

"Witch. Witch! You killed my brother!"

Her eyes rolled upward but he heard her laughter. Another witch's laughter. Inside his head. Louder and louder and louder!

When he came to it was a long time later. Or maybe it was just minutes. But the man was still in the room, lying beside the bed, out cold but breathing heavily. The witch was staring in silent death at the ceiling.

Hurriedly he pulled out his matches and cigarettes. He couldn't take her with him to burn. He couldn't risk it. Things hadn't gone as planned.

But he could sear her flesh. Purify her.

He lit the match and stared at the flame a long moment before touching it to the end of the cigarette.

Chapter Twelve

The diner was bustling as Gemma ripped an order from her notepad and clipped it to the circular stainless-steel drum for Milo. She picked up the plates for table seven, two burger specials, which meant they were complete with fries and "Macie's secret sauce," a form of thousand island dressing. Depositing the burgers, she turned to the booth that had just been occupied, but the elderly couple were still settling themselves down and were a good five minutes away from even picking up the menus.

Gemma had a moment to stare out the front window, which Macie and Charlotte had strung with little jack o'lantern lights—tiny plastic pumpkins surrounding string lights. Outside a stiff breeze was rounding up curled leaves and whirling them into frenzied eddies. The sky was gray, rain looming, but as yet still waiting in the clouds.

The lunchtime crowd was winding down. Gemma had worked half a week and was getting used to the tiredness in her arms and legs. She made a face, grimacing hugely, testing the muscles in her face. Tingly pain and soreness, but the bruising was all but gone. If you didn't look at her too closely, for all intents and purposes, apart from the pinkish tinge of blood in one eye, she looked almost normal.

She hadn't needed to call Dr. Tremaine Rainfield, as it turned out. His father had told him about Gemma and the younger Dr. Rainfield had called her. Reluctantly, because she didn't know if this was the right plan of attack or not, Gemma had agreed to see him. Her appointment was tomorrow, her day off.

For the better part of the week she'd been thinking about her mother's car and trying to figure out which ditch it had landed in. If it were on the side of Highway 26, which was the road she was almost certain she'd been driving, then why hadn't anyone found it? If the license plate had been reported as an abandoned car, word would have reached Detective Tanninger by now. And if he had that information he would have reappeared on Gemma's doorstep.

So, where was it?

As Gemma pondered, she saw Little Tim come loping toward LuLu's front door. She greeted him and showed him to a booth, inwardly sighing at the way his eyes moved over her body. It didn't take a mind reader to know what was going on in his head and Gemma wished like mad that he would get over this sexual attraction because it was damn uncomfortable. She liked Tim and would have liked to be his friend, but things were just too awkward between them.

"You came for the peach cobbler," she said.

"I wanna go to the quarry with you," he insisted.

"I know, Tim, but I told you I have a boyfriend."

"You're just saying that."

"I'll get your peach cobbler." He stared down at the table's faux wood Formica tabletop.

"I don't have money."

"I'm buying it for you. As a friend," she told him, then went to retrieve a piece of the dessert.

She caught Macie's eye and Macie sauntered over to the table as Gemma served Tim. "The peach cobbler," Macie said. "You know, it's put us on the map, Tim. People driving back and forth to the coast stop at Quarry just to have my peach cobbler. It was my Granny Gert's recipe. We're like a must-do tourist stop ever since we were on morning TV. You know that?"

"Uh-uh." He gazed at her, wide-eyed.

"Yep. All summer long. I'm having to go with canned peaches now, but it's still darn good."

Tim pulled his gaze from Macie and attacked the cobbler with his fork. He shoved a massive bite in his mouth. "Ish good," he mumbled.

"You say hi to your mama for me," Macie said, pulling Gemma away. "He's got a real thing for you, hon. It's kinda sweet and kind of a problem."

"Maybe he's the one who left the note on my porch."

Macie squinted at her. "Y'think?"

"I don't know. Maybe. Why?"

"Wha'd it say again?"

"*I see into your soul.*"

"Just doesn't sound like Little Tim, y'know?"

Gemma had to agree.

"Have you gotten any more notes?" Macie asked.

"Just the one. That's why I thought it might be Tim, since I don't feel . . . under siege. If I had a real stalker, someone intent on harming me, I think it would be different."

"I hope you're right. Did you tell that detective about it?"

"Hell, no."

Her firm denial brought a smile to Macie's face. "You got a problem with your law enforcement friend, hon?"

"I just don't want him anywhere near me."

Macie's heavily shadowed and mascaraed eyes twinkled with merriment. "Now, why do I think that has nothing to do with that hit-and-run case he's been dogging after. You're a little taken with him, aren't ya?"

"I don't want him to send me to prison," Gemma answered tightly.

"What do you want him to do?"

Her insinuations scraped along Gemma's nerves. She deliberately changed the subject. "Davinia Noack keeps calling. I don't know how many ways I can say no and still not get through."

"Oh, give her a reading. You sure turned off Sally Van Kamp. That woman has nothing nice to say about your abilities anymore. You know that. She was in here yesterday and just was being so loud and spiteful."

"She left a casserole dish with me," Gemma said glumly.

"Better get it back to her before she adds that to your list of transgressions."

"If I give her any encouragement at all, she'll be right back at my door."

"Well, aren't you the cocky one."

"I read minds, remember?"

Macie laughed. "Oh, give 'em what they want. What's it gonna hurt? And take their money, too. You got a gift, use it."

"You're a lot of help."

"I just don't know what you're fighting, hon. You were given this ability for a reason. Just go with it."

Gemma had no intention of doing as Macie suggested, but she was done talking about it. Pulling off her apron, she said, "Think I'll take off now." She'd been working since the crack of dawn and her shift was over.

"See you tomorrow," Macie said over her shoulder.

"I've got an appointment in the early afternoon," Gemma reminded. "Have to leave a little bit early. Have you got someone to fill in?"

"Oh, Heather should be able to get a ride by then," Macie snorted. "Don't you worry."

On her way home Gemma yawned like she'd been up for days. She yanked on the truck's emergency brake and let herself in the back door. She hadn't been sleeping all that well and it had really caught up with her. Kicking off her shoes, she flopped onto the living room couch and was instantly asleep.

It was the longest English class in the history of English classes, Charlotte determined as her teacher, Mrs. Ondine, rambled on about the story they were to write. Three paragraphs minimum. Subject being something to do with Halloween. And remember the topic sentence at the beginning of each paragraph.

Charlotte stared at her blank sheet of paper, then looked up at the clock, then around the room at her other classmates. Halloween was a time for candy and spooky costumes and fake blood. It shouldn't be an *assignment*, she thought scornfully. Way to smash the fun right out of it.

She quickly wrote a topic sentence: *Halloween is the funnest holiday of the year.* Well, that wasn't exactly true. Christmas was good, too, although Thanksgiving was just about eating a big meal, and though turkey was okay, Charlotte wasn't convinced pumpkin pie was all that great. There was no way Thanksgiving could even compete with Christmas or Halloween.

She erased the sentence and went the other way: *Halloween is a holiday where bad things happen. Candy, for bad toothaches. Scary costumes for scaring the shit out of little kids.* As soon as she wrote it down, Charlotte erased *shit*. That wouldn't work. Mrs. Ondine would call her mother and blah, blah, blah, more trouble would start.

She twiddled her pencil, thinking, thinking, thinking. This paper was too hard.

She glanced at the clock. Ten minutes to the bell, but then another class.

Charlotte looked up and saw that Mrs. Ondine was staring her down in that teachery way that said she was way ahead of her. Bending her head to her task, Charlotte decided she would look busy as a bee. But when the bell rang, she was outta here.

Damn, she wished she had her bike.

Lucky drove down the road in a daydream. She was in a truck, lost to memories, most of them uncomfortable. It was late afternoon and shadows were crawling over the road. The sun had dipped behind the Coast Range and she was somewhat aimlessly traveling down roads, lanes really, that crisscrossed this large, flat, open area of land that led into Laurelton, Hillsboro, Beaverton, and Portland beyond.

A sign appeared on her right: WELCOME TO WOODBINE. POPULATION 3,002.

Who were the extra two? she wondered.

Letton was dead. Gone. Kaput. The whole world knew now because Channel Five with the evening news had interviewed the girl Lucky had saved. Carol Pellter had given an interview, saying she was sorry somebody had to die but he'd been a pretty bad man. Someone else had suggested that God worked in mysterious ways, but Carol hadn't been interested in sharing the spotlight with anyone, even God, so she'd tartly reminded that if it weren't for her nameless friend—a good Samaritan, her father inserted self-consciously—then Carol would be checked out by now and it wouldn't be pretty, gosh darn it.

Letton's nutty wife, Mandy, had tearfully proclaimed that the sheriff's department wasn't doing its job. No one cared that her husband had been murdered! No one cared that the woman in the hospital who'd run her poor husband down had been given a pass!

The news channel's announcer had taken over then, reminding the station's viewers that the Winslow County Sheriff's Department was indeed still looking into Edward Letton's death, and any information regarding the "avenger" who'd run him down in a silver car would be greatly appreciated. (They wouldn't go so far as to label Lucky a good Samaritan.) They'd been continually interviewing persons of interest but no arrests had been made.

The woman in the hospital . . .

Lucky's brows knit together. She wondered if that little slip on local TV had been purposeful. A clue. A way to direct the attention of the public toward what local law enforcement wanted.

Bastards.

She drove through the main street of Woodbine: a grocery market, a lumber store, and a building with office space for lease around a tired-looking flooring shop where the carpet samples in the window looked like they'd been there since the fifties.

The woman in the hospital.

She turned the truck around and drove through Woodbine again. There was something breathless and dead about the place. One of those forgotten half-towns that seemed to be locked in another era.

Ten minutes later she was driving through Quarry, population 5,577. It was like moving through a memory. Her senses were both heightened and dulled. She'd experienced this sensation many times, ever since she could start remembering.

Surprisingly, she wasn't feeling as satisfied as she'd hoped. Yes, she was glad Letton was dead. But there were others. Sometimes, when she was just walking through a store she sensed them, like she had Letton. Other times they seemed to come to her as she was just sitting in her car, like now, although she only had a strange, insubstantial feeling.

She drove on and saw a girl walking down the road toward her. As she passed, the girl lifted a hand and waved and Lucky waved back.

Now, what was that about?

Lucky watched her in the rearview mirror and the girl looked back at her. A cold feeling slipped down her spine.

That girl knows me.

How?

Sheriff Nunce's office was packed with personnel. Will and Barb were there, as was the noxious Burl Jernstadt, naturally. Nunce's forehead was a series of furrows, like a child's depiction of ocean waves.

"I'm not saying I'm forgetting about the woman who killed Letton, Burl," Nunce said with weary patience. "I'm saying we've got another case that's in the forefront."

"Laurelton PD's jurisdiction," Burl argued.

"We're working it together," Nunce reminded.

Burl waved a hand, as if swatting a fly. "But that psycho LaPorte woman killed him, that's what I'm saying. She's batty and unpredictable. She'll go after somebody else."

"I heard someone leaked her name to the press," Nunce said.

Will turned toward Burl. Barb, smiling faintly, followed suit. Jimbo stopped in the office doorway and snorted. "The LaPorte woman should get a medal."

"She's a killer," Burl retorted. "Don't care how much you and Tanninger want to get in her pants."

"Shut up, Burl," Will said.

"Shut up, yourself." He was offended.

Jimbo moved off, the tail of his plaid shirt billowing behind him. It wasn't a closed meeting; that wasn't Nunce's style. But Will would have given a lot to get Burl ousted once and for all.

Nunce raised a finger, as if schooling two errant boys. "Burl, you're here because I'm letting you be. Will, bring us up-to-date on the Selbourne case."

"I talked to McNally. They're tracing Selbourne's movements on the last few days of her life, canvassing Portland bars. I got the name of a friend of hers from the hospital, someone she partied with, DeeAnna Brush. Maybe we'll get some answers soon.

"This morning we got a call from Don Enders at the Clatsop County Sheriff's Department. Another woman's body was found, strangled and burned with cigarettes. A lot like the Selbourne case but she wasn't taken to a separate site after he killed her. Jamie Markum's body was left in her apartment."

"Think it's the same killer?" Nunce asked.

"Could be," Barb answered before Will could respond. "Clatsop County is sending over pictures. Apparently, there was a man with her when she was attacked."

"A man? What do you mean?" Burl frowned hard at Barb as if he thought she was lying.

"Enders says the guy was her date," Will said. "Went back to her apartment with her. They had sex. Seems to have been an ongoing thing between them. She goes to a certain bar in Seaside. He's already there. She pretends she's a hooker even though she's a delivery person for To You Today. He acts like a big wheel, though by day he's a grocery clerk."

"Role playing," Barb said.

"The two of them pass out on the bed, but when he wakes up he's on the floor with a killer headache and a goose-egg on the side of his head the size of a baseball. She's lying on the bed naked. Dead. Burned with a cigarette."

Barb said, "Like Inga Selbourne."

"A serial killer over several counties. The feds'll get involved," Nunce said.

"We're not just giving up on this," Will said.

"Hell, no," Barb said. "Let's check the pictures." She hooked a thumb back to the main room. "Probably on Will's computer by now."

They all walked together toward Will's desk and he accessed the photos Clatsop County had e-mailed him. Jamie Markum's body had been photographed, the lens close to sections of skin. There was a cluster of burn marks just below the belly button.

"Just like Selbourne," Nunce observed.

"So, it is a serial murderer," Burl said, sounding oddly pleased.

"And rapist," Barb said coldly.

"More cigarette burns," Will said. "Inga had two. This looks like three."

Nunce frowned. "What's the significance?"

Will shrugged. "Third kill?"

"If so, that means we've missed one," Barb said.

"Well, he killed in Laurelton. Which is Washington County. Left the body in Winslow."

"Because he was trying to burn it, and chose the airstrip," Barb said.

Will nodded. "Now, he's in Clatsop, Seaside. Maybe there's another one in another county?"

"Different MO. He didn't take this body and try to burn it," Nunce observed.

"He accessed through the window." Will punched a few buttons and called up pictures of the crime scene. "The front of the building is open to view but the bedroom window is on the side. Maybe it was just too difficult to haul out a dead body."

"Then why'd he choose her?" Nunce posed.

"Why did he choose either one of them?" Will responded. "There's gotta be some reason. Maybe the length of their hair. Who knows."

"Jamie's hair was cut short. Kinda boyish, actually." Barb flicked back to the pictures of her body. "See."

"Maybe he likes boys," Burl leered.

"Then he'd probably be targeting them instead of girls." Will's patience was razor thin.

"Send out this information with Selbourne's and see if there's another death that could be related," Nunce said, turning away.

"You want to take that, Burl?" Will asked. "You can use my desk, computer, phone . . . have at it."

But Burl hurriedly followed after Nunce. Real work was anathema.

"Jackass," Barb said. "Why in God's name does the sheriff put up with him?"

Will shrugged. Nunce was heading for retirement and Jernstadt, pain in the butt that he was, enjoyed holding a fishing rod. Any one of them in the sheriff's office could kick up a fuss about Burl's involvement, but nobody was inclined to do it.

As soon as Charlotte got out of English class she made a beeline for the outside door. She almost ran into Robbie Bereth, who was sporting a big black eye and also trying to leave school early, as he was unlocking his bike and gazing around cautiously to see if anyone was looking.

Charlotte was the only one around. She stared at his black eye and said, "I thought your dad was gone."

"Nope," he bit out.

"You get in the way again? I thought he just hit your mom," she said, which earned her a really mean look from Robbie as he jumped on his bike and tore away. Charlotte was envious. He could up and leave *and* on a bike, while she had to walk.

She stomped down the road, kicking up dirt on the side of the asphalt every couple of steps. She would walk right by the Bereth house and she had a vague idea about heading up toward the door and telling off old man Bereth, though she wasn't sure exactly what he looked like. There were a bunch of the logging-truck dads around Quarry, and Charlotte hadn't paid much attention to just who belonged to who. Her own dad was a mystery and her mom always groaned when Charlotte asked about him. "He just drank every dime, hon," she said as the answer to everything. "He did one good thing in his life. He gave you to me."

Almost to the Bereth property, Charlotte saw Gemma drive by in her dad's truck. She raised a hand, her heart leaping as she saw she might get a ride. But Gemma just waved and kept right on going. Charlotte looked back and Gemma did, too, but the truck never turned around.

It was enough to nearly send Charlotte into tears, which shocked her to the soles of her feet. She never cried. Never. That was for babies! But sometimes it seemed like she didn't have a friend in the world and that's how it felt when Gemma just drove on by. She could feel her eyeballs burn and with all her strength she set her jaw and headed up the driveway toward the Bereth house. Robbie's bike was tossed on its side, which pissed Charlotte off. She would never treat her bike that way.

She headed up the rickety front-porch stairs, her steps slowing as she neared the top. Maybe it wasn't such a good idea to approach Robbie's dad all by herself. She was only a girl. One tough, super-bad girl, sure. But . . .

Robbie suddenly burst through the door, nearly barreling Charlotte over. He stopped short in dismay. "What're you doin' here?" he demanded.

"I don't know. I thought we could maybe play, or something."

"With a girl?" he sneered.

She felt like popping Robbie one herself. "Afraid your dad'll see you with a girl?" she sneered right back.

"My dad's at work. You'd know that, if you had a dad."

As soon as the words were out, Robbie looked like he knew he'd gone too far. Charlotte turned around and stomped back down the stairs. She didn't know exactly why she did it. Mainly because he'd really *pissed her off*. But she grabbed up his bike and jumped on it as he screeched and screamed behind her. He lunged for the back of her but she was gone, riding like the wind.

The phone was ringing somewhere far, far away. Gemma swam upward out of sleep, but it was a long way to the surface. It took another few rings before she even recognized that it was her telephone.

She was lying on the living room couch, just where she'd plopped herself after returning from work. But now it was early evening.

And she was completely naked.

Covering herself with her hands, she searched for her clothes. She found her yellow uniform in the hamper in the laundry room. She looked out the back door and saw the truck, parked in its same spot.

Hurriedly Gemma headed up to her bedroom, grabbed some underclothes and slipped into a pair of jeans and a blue denim shirt. She buttoned it up the front and rolled up the sleeves. She grabbed a pair of socks and her sneakers and was sitting on the bottom step, putting them on, when the phone began ringing again.

How many times had it rung before?

Who was calling her?

Dropping her shoes, she lunged for the kitchen phone, hoping to catch it before it went to voice mail. "Hello?" she said a bit breathlessly. "Hello?"

"Is Mizz Gemma LaPorte there?" a gravelly male voice asked.

"Speaking," she responded cautiously.

"Ma'am, you don't know me, but your car's here, on my property?"

Gemma's eyes opened wide. "Oh. Yes. I'm sorry, who are you?"

There was a strained pause. "My name's Patrick Johnson. People call me Johnny. I have a farm off Highway 26, past Woodbine, close to Elsie. You ran your car into a ditch near here. You remember?"

Gemma's hand felt sweaty on the receiver. "Umm . . . I'm sorry. I don't remember much. Do you know where my car is now?"

"Yes, ma'am, it's still here."

"In the ditch?"

"No, ma'am. We winched it to the truck and dragged it to our barn."

"Did you drive me to the hospital?"

"Yessum."

"Thank you," Gemma said, hardly knowing how to react. "You saw the accident?"

"No, ma'am. We found you and took care of things."

"Do you mean you and your wife?"

He hesitated. She had the feeling he was holding something back but she scarcely cared what it was. She was elated she'd found her car before Detective Tanninger. "I mean my grandson," he finally admitted.

"Could you give me directions? I'd like to come see the car and figure out what to do. Doesn't sound like I could drive it, right?"

"No, ma'am." He gave her the address, then slowly related how she could find his place, finishing with, "There's a coupla big rhodies at the end of the gravel drive, and a sign, kinda hidden by 'em, for Johnny's Farm."

"I guess you found me by my address."

"No, ma'am, I used your cell phone directory and called the number you had labeled 'Home.' Was hoping you were outta the hospital and I'd get you. Shoulda called earlier, mebbe." He didn't say why he hadn't and Gemma didn't care.

"You have my cell phone, and my purse, then?"

"Yessum."

"Hallelujah," she breathed. She was just overjoyed. "Well, that's great. Really great. I—um—can I come by now?"

"Surely."

"I'll be there in half an hour, or so. Could you give me your phone number, too, in case I have trouble?"

He did and Gemma was thanking him and hanging up while the last digit still hung in the air.

Chapter Thirteen

The dying rays of the sun illuminated the rhododendrons that flanked Johnny's Farm's driveway as Gemma sped right on by. Out of the corner of her eye she spied the wooden sign, so she turned around in the next available place, a private road nearly a quarter mile west, then she worked her way back. As she approached, she realized the sign had all but been swallowed by the rhododendrons, which were a good eight-feet high with impressive trunks the size of a lumberjack's arms. Their thick, evergreen leaves left JOHNNY'S FARM looking like JOHNNY'S FA and the wood had grayed, the paint faded. Beyond the rhodies was a long, gravel track. As Gemma turned in she could see the roof of a barn over a small rise and a chimney that was probably connected to the farmhouse. A stand of firs stood to the west side of the property, and behind, atop another rise, she could just make out the line of a fence, also out of grayed wood.

She drove up the lane cautiously, her truck rattling through trough-like potholes, making her sway in the driver's seat. Pulling up in front of the farmhouse, which looked similar in age and style to her own, she yanked on the brake and stepped out. A stack of pumpkins sat on the sagging steps of the front porch, ready for carving, and a sharp breeze grabbed her hair, bringing with it a slap of rain. She moved quickly up the porch steps and pressed the bell. Hearing nothing, she made a fist and rapped her knuckles on the front door panel. Eventually she heard someone making their way to the door.

It opened slowly and Gemma guessed this was Patrick Johnson. He hovered somewhere in his late seventies or early eighties, nodding as he opened the door. "You look good, girl. I was worried about you. C'mon in."

Gemma smiled faintly as she entered the house. She could smell the remnants of bacon and fried onions.

"Would you like somethin' to drink?" he asked politely.

"I'd better not. I'm kind of—confused, I guess. You have my cell phone?"

"Yessum." He gestured limply toward the couch in the front room and headed toward the back of the house. Gemma perched uncomfortably and looked around. The cabbage rose wallpaper appeared to be original. Whereas her own home had faced numerous facelifts of one kind or another—paint, carpeting, reroofing, repaving—the Johnson farmhouse felt as if it were sinking under the weight of deferred maintenance.

She inhaled a breath when he returned with her purse and cell phone, each in one hand. She was so grateful she hardly knew what to do. "Can I pay you, a reward? It sounds like if you hadn't gotten me to the hospital, that I might have been far worse off."

"Ah, no." He rubbed his jaw slowly, then looked over his shoulder. "You want to see the car?"

"Yes. Please."

He led the way through the kitchen and out the back toward the barn, moving slowly and deliberately. There was just something about it that stirred a memory inside her brain. This was not the man who'd driven her to the hospital. That person had been much younger.

All thoughts were knocked from her head when she spied her mother's car. If it was her mother's car. Mostly it looked like silver tin foil crumpled from every angle. Gemma was speechless and humbled that the worst she'd gotten from the wreck was her bruised and battered head.

"Wow."

"Lot of damage," Johnson agreed.

"How did you get me out?"

"My grand—" He cut himself off and cleared his throat. "Door just opened up and freed you. Damnedest thing."

"Your grandson helped you," Gemma finished for him. "He's the one who drove me to the hospital."

The old man eyed her as if she'd abused him, head down, eyes turned up, waiting for another blow.

"Why don't you want me to know?"

He sighed and rubbed his face with a gnarled hand. " 'Cause my grandson had been drinking some when he found you. Didn't want to deal with the police, so he drove you to the hospital himself. Came back and told me what he'd done. He wasn't drunk, mind you, but you know how those things go . . ." His lips pursed and Gemma could see he didn't agree with his grandson's choices.

Gemma said, "Is that why you waited so long to get in touch with me?"

"I didn't know we had your purse until today. It was in the car, but we didn't see it when we moved it."

Gemma could see Patrick Johnson had left a lot unsaid about his feelings about his grandson, but she didn't much care. She was just grateful that they'd contacted her first.

She insisted on paying him for his trouble, however, and wrote him a check, which he reluctantly accepted.

"What do you want to do about the car?" he asked.

"Can I leave it for now? I'll have it towed later, if that's okay."

They were walking back to the main house and he just nodded and waved vaguely in her direction. "There's no hurry."

"Thank you," she said gratefully.

"Just glad you're okay, miss. That was a nasty accident. You were settin' there awhile. Musta happened sometime in the morning or early afternoon. Car was down on an angle. Couldn't be seen from the road too well, and my grandson only saw you 'cause he nearly took that corner too fast himself. Overcorrected and almost followed right in after you."

"Where was this?" Gemma asked after a moment of sober reflection.

"One of the side roads off twenty-six." He gestured toward the west.

"I don't remember," she admitted.

"You said you were chasing a child molester."

Gemma stared at him. "I did?"

"That's what my grandson said. You said it over and over again on the way to the hospital."

"Did I . . . mention his name?"

He shook his head.

"Or, whether I caught him . . . ?"

"You could ask my grandson, Andy. But I don't think so. He woulda said so. He'll be home from the mill later on."

"Lumber mill?"

"Yessum."

"I think I'm okay," she said, turning away. "Thank you for everything."

He nodded and shifted away and Gemma walked to her truck. Heading back toward the highway, her head was full of new questions. Had she been chasing Letton? It didn't feel like it. If so, what was she doing so far west from the soccer fields, so far west from Quarry? In the foothills of the Coast Range?

And if she hadn't been chasing Letton, who was the man she'd blasted out after from LuLu's? What had happened to him?

"And who was following you?" she asked aloud. The hunched man who'd creeped out Charlotte.

She really wished her on-again/off-again brain would just get to "on" and stay there.

Charlotte sat on the stool near the kitchen and tried to control her rising panic. She'd stolen Robbie Bereth's bike. Stolen it! Committed a crime. Her heart felt like it was going to gallop right out of her chest. Why had she done that? It was like a bad Charlotte had taken over the good one and there was nothing she could do but pump her legs as fast as she could and race to the diner. As soon as she'd arrived she'd jumped off the bike and pushed it into the shed behind the restaurant. There'd barely been enough room because of all the supplies. Now, she didn't know what to do.

Chewing at her fingernails she felt slightly light-headed. Robbie knew who'd taken it. It wasn't like she could lie and pretend it never happened. And now it was the dinner hour and she still had no idea what to do next.

"Shit," she whispered, then looked over at Milo, who was busy frying burgers and looked to be in his own world.

She could tell her mother, but she cringed from the look she knew she would see in Macie's eyes. This was way worse than cutting out of school early. This was like . . . what you went to jail for.

Maybe she should just get back on the bike and ride it back to Robbie's. Tell him it was a joke. Ha, ha, ha. It kinda was a joke, really. She'd never intended to steal it. She just wanted to . . . have it for a while. It was gonna be dark real soon, so if she decided to ride back it would be dangerous and her mother would wonder where she went.

And anyway, what would happen if she did take it back? She pictured Robbie's mother, who always looked kinda worn down and tired. And Robbie's dad was back, according to Robbie, so what would he be like? He was a bad, bad dude. Maybe he would hit her and knock out a permanent tooth.

Charlotte whimpered, then wanted to slap her own self silly. She'd done this, and she had to take care of it. But how?

Gemma. Gemma would help her.

She eased off the stool and snuck around the corner to the back room and the wall phone. There was a list of numbers written on a notepad affixed above the phone but Charlotte scornfully ignored it. She knew Gemma's number from memory. Dialing quickly, she listened to it ring and ring on the other end. When the voice mail answered, she cleared her throat and said, "Gemma? It's Charlotte. Could you call me at LuLu's? Thanks."

She sat back down on the stool, feeling slightly better. She hoped Gemma would call soon, though, because her mom might decide to leave early to take her home, and home was over five miles away. There would be no way she could take the bike back.

Tearing off a bit of thumbnail with her teeth, she glowered at the customers in the booth at the end of the row. Teenagers. With cell phones.

How am I going to get one of those? she wondered, enviously watching them texting their friends like mad.

It was completely dark by the time Gemma returned to the house, heading in the back door, tossing the truck's keys on the counter. She walked into the living room, remembered she'd woken up naked there, wondered what that was all about, then decided she didn't want to know. If she'd been having a dream she couldn't recall it now.

Although she did think it might have been about Detective Tanninger.

Walking into the den, she threw herself into the chair, then stared up at the ceiling. She didn't know what the hell was happening to her but she felt completely, utterly exhausted.

The voice mail light was blinking on the phone. She almost left it. Probably Davinia Noack or Sally Van Kamp or Allie Bolt. Or Little Tim. She had her cell phone back now, so after she charged it she could pretty much rely on it completely and forget the would-be customers who knew Jean's phone number.

Still . . .

She punched in the code and accessed her messages. There was only one. "Gemma? It's Charlotte. Could you call me at LuLu's? Thanks."

Gemma instantly dialed the diner. Charlotte answered on the second ring. "LuLu's," she said breathlessly.

"Charlotte, it's Gemma."

"Oh, Gemma . . ." Her voice was heavy with dread. In a whispered tone, she quickly told her of her exploits with Robbie Bereth's bike.

"You need to tell your mother," Gemma said.

"Would you take me back there? Please? I just want to get the bike back to him and apologize. Mom's busy. That Heather never showed up today, so she can't leave yet."

"I'll take you, but you have to tell Macie what we're doing," Gemma said. "I'll be there in ten minutes."

By the time Gemma pulled the truck to a stop outside the diner Charlotte was standing beside her, the exterior lights a halo behind her head. She pointed in the direction of the shed, then ran to it. Gemma half-followed, losing Charlotte in the darkness. Then she heard the creak of a door and soon Charlotte was pushing the bike toward the truck. Gemma helped her stow it in the back, slamming the tailgate shut.

"Did you tell Macie?" Gemma asked as Charlotte hopped in beside her.

"Ye-e-s-s-s."

"What did you tell her?" Gemma asked suspiciously.

"I told her I was going to your place for a few minutes, and that I would be right back. She's real busy. I didn't have time to explain everything. Please, Gemma. I'll do it when we get back. Please?"

Gemma shot her a hard look. "We'll talk to her together," she warned.

"Fine." Charlotte sat back in the seat, relieved.

She guided Gemma toward Robbie's house, which was set off the road behind some bushes about halfway to the school. They pulled into the yard. A yellow light shone from above the porch and through the front window there was a strip of illumination between heavy curtains. A head peeked through the slit. A young boy's.

"That's Robbie," Charlotte murmured as they both climbed out of the truck's cab.

A brighter light snapped on and the door opened and the boy sprang out. Behind him a woman trudged out, and she stood on the porch smoking a cigarette as he shot toward where Gemma was hauling out the bike.

"I should smack you!" he declared.

"Robbie," the woman warned wearily.

"I wasn't stealing it," Charlotte said. "I'm sorry. I just wanted it for a while."

"You were stealing it!" he insisted. "I was gonna call the cops!"

"I brought it back," Charlotte said stubbornly, her lack of repentance very clear.

Gemma said sternly, "Charlotte is very glad you didn't

turn her into the authorities. She feels very bad that she caused so much trouble."

"Are you her mom?" Robbie asked suspiciously.

Charlotte snapped, "She's my friend."

"It's all right," the woman on the porch said to Gemma. "Thank you for bringing it back."

Robbie's brows drew into a scowl and he blasted his mom. "You should have let me call the police. They would have thrown her in the drunk tank! She deserves it!"

"No, they wouldn't have, Robbie," the woman said. "Now, get back in here. Thank you for the bike," she added with more energy. "I was going to call Macie tomorrow and get it straightened out." She snapped her fingers at Robbie, who grabbed his bike and threw it alongside the porch, then stamped up the stairs and preceded his mom back into the house. As she turned Gemma saw the bruises along her cheekbone.

"I would never treat my bike that way," Charlotte sniffed as they climbed back in the truck.

"Where is your bike?"

"At my house. Mom won't let me ride it because . . ."

"It makes it easy for you to skip school?"

"I treat my bike way better." A few minutes later, she said in a worried voice, "She knows my mom."

"This is the woman you told me about whose husband beats her," Gemma said.

Charlotte didn't deny it. "I thought he was gone, but he's back."

"How do you know?"

"Robbie said so. I just got so mad at him." She looked out the window into the night.

"Why?"

"Because I just did." They drove on for a few more minutes and then she asked, "What's a drunk tank?"

Gemma pulled into LuLu's parking lot. "Sounds like somewhere Robbie's dad spends a bit of time."

"Why didn't you pick me up today?" Charlotte asked suddenly.

"I just did." She yanked on the emergency brake.

"I mean when I was walking. I waved at you and you waved back, but you didn't stop."

"I don't know what you're talking about."

Charlotte leaned forward and gazed at her hard, searching for something in Gemma's face in the gloom of the cab. "On the road in front of Robbie's house. I saw you!"

Gemma regarded her blankly and shook her head.

"It was you," Charlotte said stubbornly.

"No, Charlotte. I was working today at the diner. I left and went home and I was there until this evening."

"I know it was you!" she declared. "You musta forgot. Did you go to the store or something?"

"No, I took a nap."

And woke up naked.

"Maybe you were sleepwalking. Sleep driving," Charlotte corrected.

"I see Macie in the window," Gemma deflected, not liking the way this conversation was going. "Let's go talk to her."

By the time Gemma returned to the farmhouse she felt like it had been the longest day in history. She yanked the truck to a halt and headed inside. She poured herself a glass of tap water and drank it standing at the kitchen sink, gazing at her own reflection in the window, her image backdropped by the kitchen cabinets and hanging lights. She couldn't see into the black night beyond.

Macie had been understandably upset with Charlotte. She'd sunk into one of the booths and said, "What am I going to do with you?" so Charlotte pointed out that if she'd had access to her bike none of this would have happened. Macie turned eyes covered in parrot-green shadow to Gemma for help. Gemma hadn't had any answers.

She thought about her mother's mangled Camry. It could either be her salvation or her downfall. If she told Tanninger about it, the car would be tested and if there was even the most microscopic evidence that it had made contact with Edward Letton then she would be arrested for vehicular homicide, or manslaughter, or some other equally serious crime that would send her to prison.

If it couldn't be proven that it had made contact with Letton, then she would be off the hook. So, if she hadn't actually rammed the bastard, she was home free.

The question was: was she innocent?

And why had Charlotte thought she'd seen her this afternoon? What did that mean?

She trudged upstairs, dug out the charger for her cell phone, plugged it in, then as it fed the battery she checked the last numbers that she'd dialed. Her home phone. LuLu's. A couple of numbers she didn't recognize which she tried calling now. The first was to a movie theater, which reminded her she'd called about show times. When she punched in the second she was connected to the Noack residence. Luckily an answering machine picked up and Gemma hung up quickly. Hopefully Davinia didn't have her cell number.

Next she checked to see if she had any messages on her cell voice mail. Nothing. Nothing at all. Gemma sighed. She had this depressing sense that she'd been living life in a vacuum, insulated from the real world. She'd made Nate Dorrell her whole world and since being back home had simply been going through the motions of a life.

Putting aside the phone, she dumped the contents of her purse onto the bed. Lipstick. Pens. A comb and brush. Her wallet. She unsnapped the wallet and examined the old bank card and a credit card, which she'd cancelled. There were a couple small pictures tucked behind a checkbook. One of her with Jean and Peter, a number of years earlier. Another of Charlotte. Another of her with Macie and Charlotte in front of LuLu's.

In the checkbook register she saw the listings of utility bills, credit card payments, and deposits from the various clients she'd still been seeing. So she had taken money for her services. Maybe Macie was right and she should just "go with it," but she found the idea distasteful.

Closing the wallet, she went to the drawer that held old credit card statements. She'd run across them earlier and had paid little attention. Now she examined her last few purchases. No surprise she was a steady customer at LuLu's. She also purchased groceries and gas and occasionally went to a department store. She even had a bill or two from the Pick-Axe.

Back down in the kitchen, she looked at her reflection in the window again.

"You need to tell Tanninger about the car," she said aloud.

She slowly picked up the receiver, stood undecided for several minutes, then replaced it just as slowly.

Maybe tomorrow.

Will stripped naked and ran through the shower. For reasons he didn't want to look at too closely he couldn't get Gemma LaPorte out of his head. And it didn't help that he was in the shower with warm water cascading over his head, thinking about Gemma in a thoroughly non-professional way.

A couple more minutes of that and he switched the hot water to cold and stood under the spray as long as he could stand it. He finally yiped and slammed off the spigot. Jesus, that was freezing.

But it did the trick. All he could think about now was

warmth as he grabbed a towel and rubbed his shaking body briskly.

He threw on a pair of sweats and a Georgia Bulldogs jersey, not that he was necessarily a fan but it was something he'd had awhile and it was available. Dressing for success wasn't on his top ten list.

Checking the time, he saw that the news was on and as he clicked on the remote his cell phone rang. He snatched it up from the kitchen counter. Caller ID said: Mom.

"Hi, Mom," he answered, his gaze on his forty-two-inch LCD screen. For the little amount of time he had to watch TV it sometimes caught him up short that he'd splurged for this toy. Not that he didn't enjoy it when he did watch. It just seemed excessive for his lifestyle. The weatherman was predicting a windstorm coupled with driving rain.

"Dylan?" she asked in confusion.

"It's Will, Mom. Dylan's been gone for years."

"Oh." There was a pause and Will used the time to grab a beer from the refrigerator. There was absolutely no food inside and he determined he would head to a nearby tavern that made a decent pastrami, jack cheese, and red onion sandwich. He sometimes asked for them to add a lettuce leaf, just to make himself believe he was eating healthy.

"Do you know where I am?" she asked at length.

"You're at home. At your house. Is Noreen there?"

"Noreen? Oh. No. She went to the grocery store."

"Okay."

This was where it got hard. The struggle to come up with conversation. He'd watched other people with their loved ones just chatter away about nothing. But Will didn't possess the knack. He wanted a meaningful conversation, or he wanted out. He couldn't do small talk. Couldn't fake that he couldn't do it.

"Are you still seeing that girl? What's her name?"

Will instantly had a vision of Gemma. Naked. Hair down. Hazel eyes hit by sunlight so they gazed like glittering emeralds. Skin taut. Breasts round and smooth, and he could visualize his hands moving toward them. He made a sound of frustration, wondering if another cold shower was in order.

But he knew his mother meant Shari, Dylan's ex.

"No, Mom. That was over years ago."

"She was a nice girl." She waxed rhapsodic about Shari for a few disjointed minutes, which made Will want to jump in and deny everything. Shari hadn't been nice. She'd been needy and emotionally manipulative. Why Will had gotten involved was a mystery to him now. Maybe it was because he went for a type. Shari and Gemma shared a passing resemblance, although when he thought of Shari he mostly remembered her complaining.

"I was thinking about her," she went on, her voice turning to a smile.

But Will couldn't hear her anymore. His attention snapped to the television as Mandy Letton appeared in a brief interview.

"The police know who ran him down," she was saying tightly. "They just won't do anything about it!" She'd stuffed herself in a low-cut, tight black dress that pushed her breasts up alarmingly. Will half-expected them to spill onto the screen. Her hair was scraped back from her face and her eyes, her best feature, were huge and wide, full of innocence and disbelief. "She was in the hospital while my husband was . . . suffering." Crocodile tears slid from the corners of those big eyes. "She actually confronted me and called me names. I know people are saying terrible things about Edward, but she *killed* him. Why won't the police arrest her? They know she did it."

"Goddammit," Will muttered harshly.

"Will?" his mother said uncertainly.

"Mom, I have to go. Are you all right? You need anything?"

"I don't want to be alone."

"I'll stay on the phone till Noreen gets back," he said shortly. Now the reporter was asking Mandy if she'd spoken to someone at the police department.

"The sheriff's department," she confirmed. "They're not very cooperative. One of their detectives tried to shut me up and hustle me away. They know I know what they're doing and they're trying to cover up."

"Noreen? She's coming here?"

"Yes, Mom. That's what you said." Will grabbed the remote and hit the volume.

The woman reporter turned to the screen and said that no one from the Winslow County Sheriff's Department had been willing to talk to them. However, a retired detective, Mr. Burl Jernstadt, had allowed a statement. Burl Jernstadt had been a respected member of the department and Sheriff Nunce still engaged his expertise upon occasion.

Will made a strangled sound.

"Are you choking?" his mother asked anxiously.

"Mom, I'll call you right back." He needed to hear what Burl had to say.

"The department has several cases that it's deeply involved with." Burl spoke seriously. His hair was combed and slicked down, and it looked like he'd actually trimmed his ear hair for this interview. His coat was too small, however, making his belly spill forward. He looked like the yahoo he was.

"You want me to call 911? If you're choking I should call 911."

"I'm not choking! Don't call 911!" He heard his tension and knew he was scaring her. "Okay, okay. Just hold on. Okay?" He dropped the phone and scrambled for the DVR. He needed to record this.

"Don't say it, Burl. Don't do it," he warned through his teeth.

"The Letton case isn't as high priority as others," Burl said in a tone that suggested the sheriff's department wasn't playing fair.

"Isn't this vehicular homicide?" the reporter asked. "Mrs. Letton says the authorities know who's behind the vicious attack on her husband."

Burl nodded. "There are several persons of interest."

"One in particular? The woman who was at the hospital when Mr. Letton was?"

Burl struggled. He so wanted to nail Gemma.

Will squeezed his hands into fists, willing Burl not to say it, though he knew the interview had been taped earlier.

"I am not at liberty to say," he stated primly.

The reporter came around it another way, saying a woman who'd shown up with bruises consistent with an automobile accident had actually been one floor below Edward Letton at the same hospital. She'd been released and the authorities had seemingly moved on to other possibilities.

Will swept up his cell phone. "Mom?" Dead air. "Mom?" Nothing. He clicked off, relieved that the segment was over and the news people had moved on to something else.

His phone rang and he checked the number. Barb. Probably as apoplectic as he was.

"Did you see Channel Nine?" she asked, barely reining in her fury.

"Just caught it."

"I'm going to rip him a new one! What a moron. What a complete, utter moron."

"Maybe it's just what we need," Will said.

"How so?" Barb sounded angry that he could even think that way.

"Maybe this'll finally cook Jernstadt's goose."

Barb snorted and rolled that around in her head. “God, I hope so. You going to Clatsop to look at that body?”

Will made a face. “It’d be great to have a first-hand look, but I’ve got to take care of a few things here.”

“Something you’re not telling me about the Letton case?”

“No, I’ve got to call 911 dispatch and make sure they haven’t sent someone to my house to make sure I’m not choking.”

Chapter Fourteen

The offices of Dr. Tremaine Rainfield were in a four-story brick building in Portland's warehouse district, which had been gentrified into condominiums and shops, and a big chunk of it was now known as the trendy Pearl District. Gemma struggled to find parking, finally settling on the highway robbery of a parking structure. She took a ticket from the machine and rattled her truck to the nearest spot, which she had to squeeze into.

It occurred to her as she was locking the vehicle that she should have asked Charlotte what she was driving when she supposedly spotted her.

She took an elevator to the ground level and exited through a glass revolving door to the street. The building she sought was four blocks away and she moved through an overcast day that seemed to bear down on her oppressively.

Rainfield's office building sported dark gray carpet and wood paneled elevator doors. Gemma punched the button for the fourth floor and rode up in silence, her arrival announced by a soft, respectful *ping.* She turned toward a set of glass doors etched with *dr. tremain rainfield* in gold, lowercase letters.

The receptionist gave her a careful smile of greeting.

"Gemma LaPorte to see Dr. Rainfield."

The receptionist gave her a nod and Gemma took a seat in the waiting room. Ten minutes passed before the inner door opened and a woman in scrubs admitted her to a short hallway that led to an office in the back. So there was a clinic somewhere, Gemma deduced.

Tremaine Rainfield's office itself was a study in brown tone-on-tone, with carved wooden statues of quasi-African origin and hammered pewter bowls and plates. Someone had designed it to look more like an upscale law office than a psychologist's place of business. The one softer touch was a glass bowl filled with floating red candles cut into the shape of some spiny-leafed flower.

"Gemma," the doctor said, getting up from his chair and coming around the desk to take her hand. "I haven't seen you in years. Do you remember me?"

He was grinning and she had a flash of the boy he'd been, hanging around his dad's offices. "I do," she said, which pleased him enormously.

Had he known that what she remembered was how he'd scowled and whined when he hadn't gotten his way, his greeting might not have been as warm. He was older than Gemma by four or five years and had exhibited all the signs of extreme jealousy whenever he'd come across her with his father. Bernard Rainfield had always treated Gemma with fatherly kindness and his son, Tremaine, hadn't liked it one bit.

Tremaine's brown hair was cut close and turning silver at his temples. His brown eyes were like his father's, except Gemma didn't detect the inherent kindness she'd found in Bernard's.

"I've been anxious to meet with you," he said. "I've always thought you were my father's most interesting patient."

"You talked about me with your father?"

"More like I listened at doors when we were young. And your mother, Jean, was a colorful character. She was very worried about you. Do you still take the medication my father prescribed?"

He said it casually, but it sent alarm bells ringing in the back of Gemma's head. "I haven't gotten a new prescription in years." She didn't tell him she still had some of the pills and only used them sporadically.

"It was Atavan, mostly. Anti-anxiety. You don't feel the need of them anymore?"

"No." Gemma was careful.

"I understood they inhibited your psychic abilities." Responding to her look of consternation, he said, "That's what Jean believed."

"I don't have psychic abilities."

Tremaine smiled. "I know. That's just what your mother wanted to believe. But I also know you lose time. You told Jean that."

"Well . . . not exactly . . ." Gemma swallowed. It sounded like he knew more about her than she did herself. "I never told my mother I lost time."

"Didn't you?" He cocked his head.

"I'm missing pieces of my life but the journal I wrote helped a lot."

"Good. How far back does it go?"

"Well, to when I started seeing your father. He had me start the journal."

"So, you don't know anything about your past before that point."

"I know I was found on a ferry."

"But you were told that," he stressed. "It's not a memory.

Have you thought about accessing your memories? Regression hypnosis therapy? It might explain a lot of what's been a mystery to you far too long. We might even get to the root of this," he added lightly.

As if the words had actually passed his tongue, she heard his thoughts: *It's DID, and it's a godsend! All I have to do is step carefully. Don't want to scare her.*

She said, "What's DID?"

His body jerked and his eyes widened. "You think you have DID? I didn't know you knew . . . that . . . that's amazing. That you have that awareness. When did you come to that? How? Did something happen?"

His questions came thick and fast. Gemma was growing less and less interested in talking with him. "I asked you what it was. That's all."

"Dissociative Identity Disorder. What was once termed multiple personality disorder. Another self. One that lives outside of your awareness, generally."

"Oh. Okay."

"You don't believe it," Tremaine said, getting all professional again. "Hmmm. Why?"

"I don't even think it exists," Gemma said, staring at the red floating candles. She could see water on their fake petals.

"Oh, it does. It does." His smile was faint.

"I may have some memory problems, but I'm not doing things that I'm not aware of." As Gemma said the words she thought about Charlotte seeing her on the road, and of Letton being run down by a car. Still, she was not going to indulge Tremaine Rainfield just so he could make a name for himself.

"Let me ask you this: what do you think it is?"

"I don't know. Plain old memory lapses."

"There are no plain old memory lapses. They have root causes. Some physical, some psychological. Yours started before you were adopted, by what I've learned. That's why I'm suggesting hypnosis. Repressed memories could become recovered memories."

When she didn't answer, he added, "Wouldn't you like to know whether you're responsible for Edward Letton's death?"

Gemma stared in shock.

"Last night's six o'clock news," he explained. "The widow Letton said a woman who'd been hospitalized the same time as her husband was responsible. And someone from the sheriff's office intimated the authorities weren't doing their job by not arresting her." He slid her a look. "I gather the police don't have enough evidence."

"I'm not responsible for his death," Gemma stated firmly.

"But you don't know for certain, do you?"

"I know."

"Not for certain," he said again.

Gemma's jaw was tight. No, not for certain. Not completely. But it just didn't fit with everything else, and with the healing of her bruises came the conviction that she was innocent of killing Edward Letton.

Still . . . there were questions. Anomalies. Coincidences.

No, not for certain.

Rainfield kept after her to sign up for hypnosis but Gemma demurred, having basically checked out. She didn't know what she wanted other than she didn't want to be Dr. Tremaine Rainfield's show pony. Or guinea pig. Or test case.

But he'd helped her learn a couple of things about herself that she hadn't expected to from this meeting, things Dr. Rainfield never meant to teach. One, she wasn't going to live in fear anymore. If she did run Edward Letton down with her car it could be proved, and as time went on she felt it was a pretty big "if". She found it more and more likely that someone else, someone who looked like her and shared her disgust of anyone who preyed on children—maybe even surpassed it, if that were possible—had been the woman behind the wheel. So, she was going to call Will Tanninger and give him the location of her mother's silver Camry. And she believed—well, hoped—that she would be exonerated.

Secondly, though she'd denied having any psychic ability to the self-serving doctor, she'd finally realized that she may indeed. And though she shied away from the label itself—weren't all would-be psychics a little crazy themselves?—by just being with Tremaine Rainfield she had realized something more about her particular ability. What she could do, to an amazing level, was read the most powerful thoughts inside a person's head. What was uppermost on their mind. Their strongest desires, needs, fears. Dr. Tremaine Rainfield wanted to use Gemma to further his career. Milo was worried about his pregnant girlfriend, Shirl. Sally Van Kamp had wanted news on her son when she was really worried that he was an addict, no matter what she sputtered to the contrary.

Whoever Gemma had chased out of the diner was a pedophile in his mind, if not yet in action.

And somehow she was fairly certain she'd been chasing someone other than Edward Letton. Not *certain*, no. But fairly certain. Certain enough to trust the information to Will Tanninger.

Before she left the parking garage she scrolled through her cell phone where she'd stored the detective's number. Before she could stop herself, she punched in the call and then headed out through the garage gates to the street.

Sheriff Nunce ducked his head inside the door and said to Will, "Can you come into my office?"

Will looked up from his notes. Barb was on the phone but her eyes shot from Will to Nunce and back, her brows lifting. It had to be about Burl.

"Sure." Will followed after the older man and stood inside the office as Nunce closed his door, an action out of the ordinary in itself. Will waited, half-knowing what was to come.

"You know I'm planning to retire, and because of it I've been—loose with some of the protocol." He grimaced, and with an effort Will kept his countenance merely interested. Loose with protocol was an understatement. "Haven't wanted to fight all the little battles that flare up. I've let Burl overstep his bounds and it hasn't been right. I called him this morning and reminded him that he no longer works here. I also told Dot not to admit him past the gate."

Will inclined his head. "I expected something after last night's TV showing, but wow."

"Burl's a good man," the sheriff defended.

Not hardly, Will thought, but wisely kept silent.

"But . . ." Nunce walked around his desk and sank into the chair, absently picking up a rubber band and rotating it like a wheel with the help of his two pointer fingers. "He overstepped his bounds with that damn interview. And he's too personally involved in the case. Keeps blabbering on about his friendship with the Dunleavys and how the LaPortes are crazy, and all. Unprofessional, but then he's no longer a part of this office."

Will nodded. *And hasn't been for a long time.*

"I called you in here because I'm afraid you're going to get the brunt of it. Burl thinks you're soft on the LaPorte woman. He blames you for not arresting her, when he knows full well we don't have the evidence."

Will's smile was cold. "I can take it."

Nunce nodded shortly. "Good."

Thinking the interview was over, Will headed toward the door. Before he could open it, Nunce said, "Do you still consider her a suspect?"

"A person of interest," Will clarified.

"Anything new that would link her to the crime?"

"No."

"I just didn't want it forgotten, with this psycho-burner out there."

"I think about it all the time," Will told him.

"Okay."

Once in the hall Will almost ran into Barb. "Listening at keyholes?" he asked her.

"If I have to. What did Nunce want?"

"To make sure we haven't given up on the Letton case, and to let me know that Burl is *persona non grata* around here, based on his connection with the Dunleavys, the LaPortes' neighbors."

"Oh, really." Barb's brows lifted.

"One less headache," Will said.

"What about the Letton case, though. It's stalled."

Will's cell buzzed and he pulled it from his pocket. The number looked somewhat familiar but it didn't immediately click in his head. God, if it was about his mother again . . . "Tanninger."

"Detective? This is Gemma LaPorte."

Will's steps slowed automatically, and Barb, who was keeping stride with him, slowed down as well, looking askance. He tried to wave her off but she stubbornly stood pat. "Hello," he greeted Gemma a bit more cautiously than he would have if he were alone.

"You told me to call you if I remembered anything."

"Yeah?" His interest quickened.

"I'd like to talk to you in person. Would it be all right if I stopped by the department after work tomorrow?"

"Um . . . Why don't I come your way."

"I'm at LuLu's diner tomorrow."

"Peach cobbler," he said. "I remember."

He thought he could almost hear her smile. "See you then, detective."

As he hung up, Barb said suspiciously, "Peach cobbler?"

"Yep." He headed toward the staff room and the locker that held his coat.

"Damn it, Tanninger, you're going to see that LaPorte woman!"

"I'm going home," he said.

"You're going to that diner where she works!"

"Not tonight."

"Tomorrow?" When he didn't answer, she accused, "You're not the choir boy you let everyone believe."

He found himself smiling inside, his thoughts turning to Gemma. It was foolish and dangerous, but he couldn't help himself. But Barb was bristling beside him, so he made his most angelic, choir-boy face and started in on "Ave Maria" in an off-key, warbling baritone which made Barb make a retching sound and shoot him the middle finger.

"Hilarious," she said, turning away from him.

He thought so and was laughing out loud as he gave Dot the high sign and she buzzed him outside to the late afternoon shadows.

Lucky woke with a lurch to find herself slouched behind the wheel of her truck. It was night, she was on a country road, and clouds covered the moon and stars, leaving her staring into almost pure blackness. She squeezed her eyes closed and opened them slowly. It was still night. Her last memory was of late afternoon.

Carefully, feeling needles and pins in her right leg as she stirred, she peered hard through the windshield, trying to make shapes out of the darkness. She determined she was on that same road where she'd seen the girl who'd waved at her. She'd been obsessed by thoughts of the girl. Who was she? Why did it feel so important? Was she in danger? Lucky had incredible antennae when it came to sensing pending trouble.

Turning on her lights, she pulled onto the road, heading in the direction of the town of Quarry. She had an aversion to the place, which she'd recognized subconsciously, but only now fully realized that she'd been avoiding it. Wrinkling her nose, she decided maybe it was time to face whatever was bothering her about the place. With a kind of dread she didn't understand, she pressed the accelerator a bit, feeling like she was heading toward an unknown doom.

A darkish van rattled out of a driveway without stopping and Lucky jammed on her brakes. "Hey!" she yelled, but the van driver couldn't hear her as it sped ahead of her toward Quarry.

Lucky immediately felt the affront of a driver who'd damn near been sideswiped. She touched her toe to the accelerator again, her earlier misgivings buried under a righteous indignation. Who the hell was this yo-yo?

The van swept into Quarry ten miles over the speed limit. Lucky slowed down. She didn't want to draw any attention to herself. She got the heebie-jeebies as she passed the Pick-Axe tavern and shivered in spite of herself. The van turned in almost directly across from the tavern into LuLu's diner.

Alarm bells rang inside Lucky's head. LuLu's . . . A hand-printed sign advertising homemade peach cobbler had been tacked onto the permanent free-standing wooden one with LuLu's Diner written in script. Lucky tucked her truck between two others in the back lot just as the van driver slammed out, his vehicle jolting to a stop under the electrical pole. She caught a glimpse of his hardened face in the sodium vapor light. Shivers raced along her spine. She knew him. Could feel the blast-furnace fury he was consumed with.

She leapt out of her vehicle and, hiding between the cars, watched him approach the front of the diner. Something stopped him. Some latent remnant of good sense or self-preservation. Whatever his issue he couldn't just crash inside and take it out on his target with the whole damn restaurant as his witness.

Lucky's eyes zeroed in on the man as she crouched behind a newer Dodge Ram truck and gazed at him across the hood.

And then *she* came out of the restaurant. The girl. Saying something over her shoulder, a backpack carelessly looped over one shoulder. Unaware that disaster was waiting for her.

The angry man took a step toward her. Lucky moved to the front of the truck, poised on the balls of her feet.

"You fucking little thief," he spat at the girl who stopped in her tracks, stunned. "You think you can just take my son's bike and get away with it?"

"I brought it back," the girl said in a strangled voice.

"You *stole* it!" he roared.

The girl tried to be brave but she was shaking. "I said I was sorry."

It took all of the man's strength to keep a grip on his temper. He stared at the girl whose face had contorted into a frown. There was something here. Something Lucky could feel. Her heart began a slow, painful tattoo. She knew that look in the man's eyes, could sense his changing emotions, from rage to driving lust. She'd suffered through it enough times. He stared at the girl with hot eyes and Lucky's fists clenched. She wanted to slam the bastard's head in the ground, strangle him, cut off his balls. He wanted the girl. *Wanted* her. Like Edward Letton had wanted the soccer player.

Red fury filled Lucky's head, nearly blinding her. She would go after him bare-handed if he made one move on the girl.

The front door of the diner slammed open, the screen flapping back on itself as a man in a cap stepped up. "He botherin' you, Charlotte?" the newcomer demanded.

The girl hesitated and the angry man spat on the ground and turned away. "It's okay, Captain," she said quietly. But she couldn't take her gaze away from the man who was now striding to his gray van.

Lucky eased back out of sight, backing up toward her own vehicle, her eyes glued to the man's vehicle. When he slammed his door shut she bolted for her truck, twisting the handle as he threw his van into drive. It rattled out of the lot and turned west.

Moments later Lucky moved out behind him. She had no plan of action. Nothing but her wits.

But she was bound and determined to kill the bastard. Take him out. Make the world a better place. There was no right or wrong.

There was simply now.

Charlotte headed back inside the diner, shaking, the Captain at her heels. Macie was in the kitchen. Charlotte had left a few minutes early. Had planned to wait in the car and turn the radio on. Now she hesitated before telling her mom what had just taken place.

"Jesus, Joseph, and Mary," Charlotte murmured to herself.

The Captain's eyes snapped fire. "What'd that man say to you?"

"Uh . . . nothing much."

"He was swearing at you. Who was he?" The Captain was full of repressed rage.

"I don't know."

Macie came out of the kitchen, wiping her hands on a towel. "What is it?" she asked sharply, seeing her daughter's pinched face. She looked at the Captain.

"Man in a van was swearing at her," he said.

"What did you do?" her mother asked.

"Nothing!" Charlotte declared resentfully. "I was just walking to the car."

"You must have said something, or done something. He wouldn't just swear at you."

"Well, he did." Charlotte clomped to one of the booths and sank into it, tucking her chin on her crossed arms. She had to think. Think. She felt scared and weirded-out at the same time. That man was Robbie Bereth's father!

"What happened?" her mother asked in a calmer voice. She sank into the seat opposite Charlotte's.

Charlotte looked into Macie's thickly mascaraed eyes. The only person who would really understand was Gemma. She was the one Charlotte needed to talk to. "I need to call Gemma," she said.

"Oh, no. Leave her be. She's got things she's working through. She'll be here tomorrow."

"But I'll be at school!"

"Oh, good. You actually plan to go."

"I need to tell her something!"

"Well, tell me, and I'll tell her tomorrow."

Charlotte glowered and buried her face into her arms again. Okay. Tomorrow. She would tell Gemma after school. Of course, she would have to leave early again to make sure she got to the diner before Gemma's shift was over, but that just meant staying up a little later tonight and getting ahead on a few more assignments.

"What?" Macie cocked an ear her way as Charlotte mumbled into her arms.

"I said okay."

"Good. Well, come on. We're done here. Denise and Milo will close up." She slid out of the booth and Charlotte reluctantly followed.

* * *

At first the van appeared to be heading back to the house from which it had come, but the driver suddenly must have guessed she was on his tail because he circled around and wound back to Highway 26. His tactics confirmed that she was behind him, but there was nothing for it now but to stay on his taillights.

He was heading toward the coast, but then he veered off, onto a private logging road. Cool-headed, Lucky turned in behind him, hearing gravel crunch beneath her tires. These roads wound for miles and she was unfamiliar with this one, but she was on a path and intended to stay there.

Abruptly the man pulled over. Lucky slowed and pulled in behind him, her headlights illuminating his van. Reaching over, she unlatched the glove box and grabbed her .22. Small as it was, it felt heavy in her hands. Her heart beat hard and fast.

He rolled down his window and she did the same. "Who the fuck are you?" he yelled from inside.

Lucky didn't respond. She waited, counting slowly in her head. A minute passed. Two. All around them were stately Douglas firs except for the gravel line where the logging road aimed into darkness.

Suddenly his door flew open and he jumped into her headlights. She saw the crowbar in his hand.

Her spit dried in her mouth. She'd set this in motion. He was a dangerous beast.

"Come on, bastard," she whispered.

He glared at her, head thrust forward. Lifted the crowbar high. With a yell he ran forward and flailed at her headlights. *Smash.* Splintering glass tinkled in the aftermath.

Her right beam still held steady.

"Get out of here!" he screamed, advancing on her.

Lucky threw open her driver's side door and jumped to the ground. He slammed it shut, nearly on her, breathing hard.

"Who are you?" he demanded. His eyes fell on the gun, leveled at his chest.

"One more step and I'll shoot you," she said through gritted teeth.

His mouth curved into a humorless smile. "Oh, will you?"

"Watch me."

He turned instead and headed for her other headlight. Lucky followed him and aimed.

Blam.

He shrieked to high heaven and grabbed backward, stumbling. She'd hit him in the ass. He fell down and crawled forward, flipping onto his back and staring up at her through the uncertain light, his expression incredulous. "Why? Why?"

"Because you like little girls, you fucker."

"I'll kill you!" he screamed.

"I don't think so."

They were frozen. Staring at each other. "I know you," he said in disbelief. "You followed me before. You put your damn car in the ditch." He was breathing heavily.

"You wanted that girl at the diner. How many have you molested already?"

"That girl stole my boy's bike! She needed to be taught a lesson. That's all I was gonna do."

"Liar."

Lucky raised the gun and the bastard just stared at her through wide, horror-filled eyes. She wanted to shoot him dead. Leave him like so much road kill. Let his rotted corpse be found by someone else.

But—she—couldn't—do—it.

She ground her teeth together. She'd suspected this. Suspected she couldn't kill in cold blood.

It infuriated her.

Sensing her indecision, he scrambled backwards, moaning at the bullet lodged in his butt. He was lucky she didn't have a more powerful weapon or the bullet would have passed right through him and left one hell of an exit wound.

She let him go. Let him explain how he'd got shot in the ass.

Feeling incredibly weary, she watched him climb back into his van, switch on the lights, turn around and leave the way they'd come in. Lucky got back in her truck, laid her head on the steering wheel and fell into a storm of tears she didn't understand. She cried for all the terrible things she'd done. All that she'd lived through. All the innocent children who endured horrible torture at the hands of self-serving, arrogant, sick adults.

She turned the truck around and followed in the wake of the van, whose taillights vanished as it turned east onto the highway toward Quarry. She decided to head back to Seaside and so when she reached the highway she went west.

She'd barely gone a mile when she saw headlights behind her, closing fast. He's coming after me, she marveled. She sped up. Not far ahead was a passing lane. She moved to the right side lane and slowed down. He came on her hard, his headlights bearing down.

Bam. He rammed into her, but it was more a tap as she'd pressed her foot to the accelerator as he approached. But the steering wheel jumped in her hands and she scrambled to hold it firm before slamming on her brakes, bracing herself.

Hit me, you bastard, she thought furiously.

At the last second he swerved around her. The side window was down and he was shouting obscenities.

He had to be losing blood. Had to be running on adrenaline.

He was ahead of her and she hit the pedal, the truck jumping ahead with a spurt.

But he was weaving. Bad.

Across their two lanes and into oncoming traffic, and back.

Catastrophe loomed.

Distantly, around a corner, she could see the beams of an oncoming vehicle. An innocent victim.

She screamed.

The gray van lurched from the oncoming lanes back, skimming in front of her. Lucky stood on her brakes and her truck shimmied, tires shrieking, as the van slid by as if on ice and right off the edge of the road, tumbling into a ravine.

Yanking the wheel as hard as she could, Lucky straightened out her truck. She saw brake lights from the oncoming car as it came to a stop to help.

Lucky didn't wait. She tore forward and headed straight to the coast, worried only one headlight and a damaged rear end were a dead giveaway to anyone looking for her.

Chapter Fifteen

Gemma tried to stifle a yawn as she poured coffee into the cups of the middle-aged foursome in the back booth. As soon as one yawn ended another began.

"Too much partying for you," the man with the horseshoe-shaped balding dome announced.

"I went to bed early," Gemma denied.

"Uh-huh." He waggled his brows at her as if they were in on the joke together.

When Gemma returned to the kitchen she fought back another yawn.

Macie said, "Just how late did you make it to bed?"

"Not really sure." Gemma shook her head. She'd woken up on the couch in the wee hours of the morning, but she couldn't really remember falling asleep. At least this time she'd had her clothes on.

"Heather's going to actually make it in today," Macie said, "and Denise is here, so if you need to go on home, go ahead."

"Thanks. I might."

"Did anything happen?" she asked in concern, giving Gemma a searching look.

"No. I'm fine, really. Just tired. Maybe this is a reaction to seeing Tremaine Rainfield yesterday. I kinda had a realization."

"What do you mean?"

"I've been running away from the truth and I don't want to anymore. Okay, so I can't remember everything. I've got most of it. So, if there's bad stuff I haven't learned yet, bring it on." She paused. "And I quit taking any medication awhile back. It was hit or miss anyway, and I just want to start fresh."

"Sounds like a good plan."

"I asked Detective Tanninger to meet me here this morning," Gemma admitted.

"Yeah?"

"I have some things I want to talk over." Gemma thought about the demolished car in Patrick Johnson's outbuilding. A part of her still wanted to keep that information to herself.

Macie put a hand in her apron to check for her notepad and started to head to one of the booths to take an order when she turned back suddenly. "Which reminds me, Charlotte wants to talk to you. She was all insistent last night, but I told her to leave you alone."

"Know what it was about?"

"Haven't a clue. She got in some kind of pissing match in the parking lot with some jackass who was swearing at her, at least that's what the Captain said, if you can believe him. Half the time he just likes to make a fuss. But Charlotte was upset. I couldn't get her to tell me what it was about."

"Maybe I'll stick around and wait for her to get home from school."

"That should be about noon," she said darkly.

Gemma grinned. She knew she should probably care

more that Charlotte was such a truant, but since no one denied she wasn't getting her work done—in fact she was excelling in it—it was tough to be a hard-ass.

"Don't worry about sticking around just to see Charlotte. She asked me about home schooling her, can you imagine?" Macie said in horror.

Gemma laughed, an honest to goodness *har, har, har*.

Macie cocked her head and smiled. "That's a sound I haven't heard in a long time."

"I'm unburdening myself," Gemma said. "It's—freeing."

"Just don't let that detective railroad you into admitting something you didn't do."

"Won't happen."

"Okay, then. If you need me, just say so and I'll send him outta here so fast it'll make your head spin."

The door opened and a woman in her sixties with coiffed silver hair strutted in, chin lifted defiantly. She pinned Gemma with a sharp look from pale blue eyes. Davinia Noack, Gemma realized, greeting the woman with a remote smile as if she didn't recognize her, and indicating an empty booth.

Davinia was having none of it. "Gemma LaPorte," she said accusingly, firmly rooted to the floor just inside the door. "I heard you were working here. I heard you were avoiding me, but I couldn't believe it. What are you doing, my dear? When God bestowed such a talent on you. Why do you spurn His gift?"

Gemma grabbed some menus. "The booth in the corner's open," she said, determinedly leading the way.

Davinia followed on her heels. "Why are you being like this?"

"I'm . . . not my mother," she said, handing Davinia a menu.

Immediately Davinia dropped it as if it burned her. "I'm

not dining," she stated flatly. "I came here to reason with you. And to give you some information that you sorely need."

"Okay." Gemma made a high-sign to the table of four. She was pretty sure they needed coffee refills.

"You know my Carl, sometimes he goes to the PickAxe." Her lips puckered as if the word tasted sour. "Well, he was there when Kevin Dunleavy and his brother Jerome were having a heated discussion about you." Gemma had been moving away but now she glanced back. Davinia's eyes glowed with triumph at gaining her attention. "That's right. They were very nasty about Jean and you. Poor Carl didn't know whether to say something in your defense or not. I told him he should have!"

"What exactly were they saying?"

"They said both of you were freaks and that you were a killer." Her face flushed. "They've always been very nasty boys!"

Gemma instantly wanted to defend Rome, but she held herself back. So, he'd been a school crush. What did she really know about him? "Well, sticks and stones, Davinia," Gemma said, though the Dunleavys' continual condemnation of her family was really pissing her off.

"Will you really not give me a reading?" she asked, her imperious demeanor slipping a bit.

Gemma lifted a hand as she headed for the foursome. "Call me. I'll call you back, I promise, and we'll make an appointment."

"Bless you, child!"

Macie looked over at Gemma with amusement. Gemma just shook her head, called herself ten kinds of a fool, then glanced at the clock. Nine-thirty. She wondered when Will Tanninger planned on showing up.

* * *

". . . Thanks, Mac," Will said into his cell phone. He swiveled his desk chair and saw Barb give him a *what gives?* look. He'd been scribbling on a pad and she came around to look over his shoulder as she cruised by. "Doesn't sound like any of 'em is our guy, but I'll pass the information on to Enders." He hung up and said to Barb, "Mac canvassed the bars where Inga Selbourne liked to party. She hooked up with a few different guys, but wasn't really attached to any of them. Apparently the last one she was interested in was a real estate guy named Daniel Sommers. He's since moved on to another party girl who's alive and well, and no one knows anything."

"Maybe he's lying. Could be a great cover."

"Mac doesn't think so. Our doer seems more antisocial. This group parties together."

"He could fit himself in," Barb said stubbornly. "Act like he's one of them." She loved playing devil's advocate.

"I don't think he could fit himself in," Will disagreed. "He's leaving his DNA all over the place like he doesn't know or care. He's got some major cuts he needs to hide, courtesy of Inga. He's compelled to burn the bodies and mark them with cigarettes. And it seems like he's escalating. If he burned a first one that we haven't found yet, that one was awhile ago. These two, Selbourne and Markum, were killed in the space of a couple weeks."

"If there is a first one," Barb repeated.

"We've sent out enough information that if she exists, we could get a hit," Will said.

"The cigarette burns could be random."

"Could be."

She finally acknowledged, "But they're so deliberate they look like he's doing it on purpose. You think it's a message for us?" Then, pissed: "Not us. The feds. They're taking all our information and giving us nothing."

"Their case. Doesn't mean we can't have our own theories."

Barb asked, "What're yours?"

"Our guy doesn't seem like the kind who wants to dance the dance. He doesn't care about publicity, or that we're all trying to find him. He only seems interested in finding his targets and killing them."

"Burning them," Barb said. "Maybe he just hasn't gotten around to dancing the dance."

"Does it feel that way to you?" he asked. "Like he's engaging us in a game?"

"No," she admitted. "But I'm no expert."

"There's some reason he's targeting his victims. Something cues him to his next one. And it doesn't seem like he has a check-off list. He's not methodically marking them off. His victims are all over the place, as if they cross his path somehow and he tags 'em."

"His path is from Laurelton to outside Seaside and maybe beyond."

"Serial killers can cover a lot of distance. Bundy went from Washington to Florida and back with lots of places in between."

Barb said, "This guy's no Bundy."

Will nodded. "He's too local."

"Why do you say that?"

"Laurelton airstrip. You gotta know how many people work there and that you can get away with leaving a body there. That's not something you're going to just run across. He's been around the area enough to know that."

"You think he's from Laurelton?"

Will shook his head. "Maybe he was just at the hospital. Maybe that's how he found Inga. I think he's from the coast somewhere. He found Jamie Markum by some means. Maybe he was at the bar, but then wouldn't he have seen her with the guy?"

"Phil . . ." Barb glanced down at some of her notes. "Herrington."

"I don't think he followed her from the bar."

"So, where'd he pick her up?"

"Her route? She works for To You Today."

Barb smiled. "You gonna share that with the feds?"

"They've probably already thought of it."

"I'll take that as a no."

Will said, "I'm going to call Don Enders at Clatsop County and talk some more. Jamie's homicide is in his jurisdiction."

"So, what about victim one, if she exists? Where's she?"

"Somewhere between here and Seaside, or along the coast? Not toward Portland and denser population. Our guy's more small town."

"A lot of theory without a lot of fact," Barb observed, but she wasn't trying to criticize him. As Will shut down his computer, then shoved his chair back from his desk, she asked, "Where are you going?"

"To Quarry to talk to Gemma LaPorte."

Her brows arched. "Business or pleasure?"

"Pleasure."

She'd been about to needle him with another question, but his answer stopped her short.

"She promised me a piece of peach cobbler from the diner where she works."

"Oh, right. Bet that's not all she promised."

"So far, that's it."

"Watch yourself, Tanninger."

"I'll take it under advisement."

"I mean it. There's something about her that you like, but she's a mystery. She's hiding something."

"You're starting to sound a little like Burl," he said as he headed out the door. It was too bad their working relationship seemed to always spiral down to this.

"Better than being a sucker," she called after him.

Charlotte tried to think of a way to escape, but she could feel the teachers and administration staring at her, like they'd all banded together to keep her on the school grounds. She was never alone with just kids. There was always some adult hanging around, looking kind of stupid and out of place. She knew it was because of her. They were all focused on keeping her at school.

Shit.

And Robbie Bereth, who wasn't in any of her classes, thank the Lord, was a real pain in the butt. Glaring at her across the playground. Talking with his friends, one of whom was a big, fat bully and who'd yelled something at Charlotte she hadn't really understood. One of those bad words that you only hear on HBO or Showtime or in the movies.

Didn't matter. They could say what they wanted. Charlotte had something on Robbie, something really big. Too big to fall into a pissing match over. In fact, she felt sorry for him and that had kept her temper in check when he acted like such a moron with his buddies.

What she had was that Robbie's dad was the guy Gemma had chased from the diner. The one who'd looked at Charlotte all strange and icky-like. She had the distinct feeling he'd be the kind who would try to lure you into his car with one of those lies, like he was looking for a lost puppy and could she help him. He was a bad dude, for sure.

"Ass-wipe," she muttered aloud.

Mrs. Ondine gazed at her fiercely. "What did you say, Charlotte?"

"She said ass-wipe," Davey Corulo piped up, the traitor.

The teacher held a finger up to Davey, annoyed with him but still fixed on Charlotte. "Should I send you to the principal's office?"

Are you asking me? Charlotte almost said, but lowered her eyes and shook her head. Sometimes you just had to act like you were beaten.

"Have you finished your Halloween story?"

Charlotte nodded. She didn't trust herself to speak.

"You haven't turned it in."

Charlotte flipped open her notebook and handed over the paper to Mrs. Ondine, who glanced at it and frowned. For a moment, Charlotte worried that she'd forgotten to remove "shit" from her final draft, but then Mrs. Ondine said, "Did you get help with this?"

Charlotte was outraged. More because other kids got all kinds of help from their parents and she hardly ever asked Macie to step in. "No," she stated flatly.

"In my experience, most kids don't hate Halloween," she said. "Just the opposite."

"I don't hate Halloween. I was picking the other side. You said there are two sides to every issue."

Mrs. Ondine inhaled noisily through her nose. She wasn't completely old. She maybe was younger than Mom, but she had this way of being that made her seem *ancient.* "Not sure you really developed an ending," she said, turning away.

Charlotte could tell that there was an issue developing between them and they were going to be on opposite sides. Inwardly sighing, she wondered how—*how*—she was going to get out of here and find Gemma.

She felt Davey's eyes on her and slid him a cold glare.

Don't mess with me, ass-wipe, she thought, but she didn't say it.

* * *

When Will Tanninger walked into LuLu's, heads turned. He was with the sheriff's department. He was tall and broad-shouldered. His hair was a tad longish and added a rakish touch to his chiseled face, and the wind that had kicked up outside had tossed a brown lock nearly into one eye. Gemma felt heat rush through her as she watched him brush it back. She pretended to not even notice him as she snapped an order up and pushed the wheel around so the page was in front of Milo's nose.

Macie was finishing an order and she glanced over, her brows lifting, and Denise automatically reached a hand up to smooth her own wild, brown curls. Gemma called herself an idiot for caring, noticing, wanting something she couldn't have. Yes, she knew he wasn't immune to her; he'd said he didn't want her to be guilty. But that could mean anything. Didn't count for anything in the man/woman arena.

Will had spied Gemma, so there was no hiding from him. She stepped briskly up as Denise asked, "Would you like a table?"

"I'm actually here to see Ms. LaPorte," he said, greeting Gemma with a faint smile.

"Oh." Denise gave Gemma a long look before she turned away.

"Would you like a table?" Gemma repeated.

"Although I definitely want to try the peach cobbler, I've got some other appointments, so I'd better pass." His gaze traveled down her lemon yellow uniform. "Can we talk somewhere?"

Gemma turned back and caught Macie's eye. Macie sidled up, giving Will the elevator eyes. "You can leave right now, hon. We've got it covered. Heather swears she'll be in at one, but even if she flakes on me again, we've still got it covered."

"Sure?"

"Uh-huh."

Gemma grabbed her coat from the back room, then Will held the front door and they walked onto LuLu's porch. The wind snatched at her hair and felt cold against the fingers that held her coat closed at her throat. Rain blew fitfully, a sideways flurry. Also cold. "Hello, winter," Gemma murmured.

"I didn't mean to take you from work," he said.

"No, I know. I've been tired all day, so Macie told me to leave. I'm just filling in while I figure things out."

"You want to go to my car?" He glanced around dubiously. There was nowhere to be safe from the elements outside, and nowhere to be free from eavesdroppers inside.

"Sure."

Together they hurried, heads bent, through the fitful, wind-driven slaps of rain. Will quickly unlocked the door to his department-issued vehicle, a tan-and-brown sedan with *Sheriff's Department* slanted in letters across the doors. Gemma got in the passenger side and slammed the door, and as Will climbed in the driver's side she caught a whiff of spicy men's cologne, understated. Not too much, just enough to make her want to inhale deep into her lungs.

He looked at her and she looked at him. She said, "You want to kiss me."

Surprised, he yanked his gaze away. "What makes you say that?"

"Because it's true."

"You called me with some information?" he reminded her, seeking to get the conversation back on track.

Gemma nodded. "I want to tell you something about myself first. I can read people's emotions. I mean, really read them, sometimes. It helps if I can see the color red at the same time, but it's not mandatory."

Will half-smiled. "What?"

"I know what it sounds like, but I'm not crazy. No matter what the Dunleavys say."

"You know about them?"

It was her turn to look surprised. "How do you?"

"The feud between your family and the Dunleavys was brought up by a retired deputy who lives in Woodbine," Will explained. "A friend of the Dunleavys."

"And he told you they think I'm crazy?"

"All LaPortes are crazy," he said, straight-faced.

"Damn, I'm sick of this small town. I don't know why I came back!" Gemma declared. Then she held up her hand. "Yes, I do."

Will said, "Don't worry. He hasn't tainted my view of you."

"But hearing that I can read minds, how's that working for you?"

"I thought you said you read emotions."

"Okay." Gemma inhaled a deep breath. "Let me start over. Reading emotions is like reading minds. I feel the emotion and know why it's there. Simple in some cases. Not as obvious in others."

"You can read my emotions?"

She shot him a sideways look. She was close enough to see that his eyes weren't as dark brown as she'd initially thought. There were striations of gray in the irises. "Yes."

"Okay."

"You don't want to ask me what you're feeling?"

"I know what I'm feeling. Frustration."

"You wanted to kiss me the other night. You still want to."

He broke eye contact, glanced away, then met her gaze again blandly. "What if I said you're wrong."

"You'd be a liar."

"I want you to be straight with me, and I want you to be innocent of all charges. That's what I want."

"I'm not trying to put you on the spot, detective. I'm just proving a point."

"Okay."

There was silence for a moment, then Gemma said, "I went to see a psychologist yesterday, Dr. Tremaine Rainfield. I thought he could help me, but now I'm not so sure. He wants me to go under hypnosis to recover some of my repressed memories. But not about what happened with Edward Letton's accident; that's secondary. He wants me to go way back to my childhood, to those pieces of my past that are a complete washout, memory-wise.

"But what he really wants is for me to be his test case. He wants to make a name for himself by using my case. He's known me for years, peripherally, because I used to see his father, Dr. Bernard Rainfield, throughout my childhood. Apparently I've had memory lapses for years."

"So, he's going to cure you and hold you up as an example?"

"Do you know what DID is, detective?"

"I've heard of it before—"

"It's Dissociative Identity Disorder. Which means Tremaine thinks I have multiple personalities." She shook her head. "I don't even know where he gets that. Something in my past maybe . . . I didn't ask. But that's not what my memory lapses are about. That's not it."

"Okay."

"Okay?" she repeated suspiciously.

"I'm waiting to see where this is going. I don't have your ability to read minds."

She made a sound of frustration, then stated flatly, "I know where my mother's car is."

That got his attention. "Where?"

"I got a call from a farmer near Elsie. His grandson was the one who found my car. In a ditch with me in it. The Camry's in their barn. Wrecked pretty badly. It was the grandson who took me to the hospital."

"It—wasn't the car that brought you to the hospital."

"Nope."

Will could tell he'd really pissed her off, but what had she expected? He didn't believe for a minute that she had extra abilities. And it really chafed him that she thought she could read him so well. Even if she was right. "When did you get the call?"

A pause. "A couple of days ago."

"So, okay. Let's go see it."

"I already have."

"Then let's go see it again," he said. "That's why you called me, isn't it?"

Gemma said, "After it's examined you'll be able to tell if it ran down Letton, won't you?"

He nodded. "If there's forensic evidence."

"I didn't do it," she said. "I would know if I had."

"See . . ." He exhaled slowly. "It's that kind of comment that leaves me wondering. *I would know if I had* isn't the same as *I know I didn't*." When she didn't respond, he twisted the key in the ignition and asked, "What's the address?"

Gemma told him, then added, "I went to see it for myself. As soon as Patrick Johnson called. His grandson, Andy, works at a lumber mill but he's off work by three. He's not around in the evenings much, but we could catch him this afternoon, I suppose."

Will saw his trip to Clatsop County and a meeting with Detective Don Enders disappearing. The burn psycho wasn't really his case anyway. He'd just wanted to meet with Phil Herrington personally, to get a feel for what had happened the night Jamie Markum was killed. But if he went, Will's actions would undoubtedly rile up the feds, and though a part of him kind of liked the idea of poking a stick at them, another part knew it wouldn't do anything to progress the case.

Better to just do his own thinking and see what cropped up.

And besides, the revelation of the car took precedence.

And he was scared of what those results might end up being.

He glanced over at Gemma, who'd gone quiet, the frown on her face revealing she might be regretting being so frank with him.

When he switched off the ignition, she asked, "What are you doing?"

"We've got time to kill before the grandson gets off work. Looks like I'm gonna get that peach cobbler after all."

The wolf slowly, deliberately removed the spare tire from the ten-year-old Volvo wagon and slowly, deliberately replaced it with the original tire, which he'd patched after removing a bolt from the center of its tread. Construction sites were dropping stuff everywhere and drivers were picking it up.

"Hey, dummy!"

He didn't look up from his task, just rolled the tire to the rear of the vehicle and flipped up the rear hatch. The spare fit under a section in the floor of the wagon.

"You got a problem with your hearing? Just because Easy wanted you to have 'gainful employment,'" Rich said in a sing-song voice, "doesn't mean you can just show up whenever you like. Seth's gunnin' for you, buddy. You were supposed to be here two days ago. What happened?"

Wolf didn't respond. He'd shown up at the garage today and gotten to work. Seth had been on the phone and had waved him in the general direction of the cars, and Wolf had taken it from there.

But now Seth was gone somewhere and Rich always got mean when Seth left him in charge.

"My brother talked to Seth but he didn't get me the job. I got the job."

"Bullshit, moron. Seth liked Easy and so he took you on. But your brother's gone now, isn't he? Dead, dead, dead." Rich mimed throwing a noose around his neck and jerking the rope tight, his eyes rolling back and his tongue hanging out.

Wolf's blood boiled but he didn't change expression. He wouldn't mind killing Rich but that wasn't his mission.

"Wha'd you and him do to your old lady?" Lachey asked now, and Wolf felt both fear and rage. He knew about that? *How?*

As if hearing the words inside the wolf's head, Rich went on, "Easy told me about how you wanted to stick your dick into her wet pussy. But she didn't want you 'cause you were too stupid. But Easy . . . he had a way with women, huh. Even dear old Mom. Said she was a witch. Said she was an Injun witch."

Wolf went completely still except for his beating heart. He could feel it galloping in his chest like a wild animal. He and his brother had had a pact. His brother would never tell. Never! Wolf was stunned to realize that he had.

Lachey was leaning against the wall, watching him, goading him. The wolf could not let himself be goaded. It was not his mission. But against his will he thought of the mother-witch. Her swelling breasts. Her freshly laundered dress. Her smoky breath. Her black hair.

His head felt like it was about to explode. He needed the One witch. The one he'd followed. He needed her bad.

"You gettin' a boner, there, *Wolf*?" he sneered. "Thinking about fuckin' your honey-hot mama. Easy talked about how good she was. Mmmhmmm." He moved his crotch around in a circle, grinning. "Wha'd you do to her, huh? Where is she? She dead like your brother?"

"Fuck you," Wolf stated flatly.

Rich started laughing and he changed his circular motion to hip thrusts. "Your brother take her against a wall like this?" he asked, turning toward the line of car parts hanging on the walls. He started moaning and jerking and pretending, his head turned Wolf's way, his mean eyes filled with the devil's mischief. "You hear her moanin', wished it were your dick inside instead of Easy's. Huh? That why you killed her?"

"I didn't kill her," he said.

"Yeah? That's not what Easy said."

"My brother wouldn't lie."

"He wasn't lying. And neither was Ani."

The wolf saw red. A curtain of red covered his eyes. He turned toward Rich, stumbled forward. Lachey yanked a piece of pipe from the wall and waited for the attack.

"Come on, fucker," he whispered.

"Rich!"

Seth's voice boomed across the garage. He wasn't a big man, but he had a tense way about him that the wolf, and Rich, too, eyed with a certain amount of respect.

Rich kept an eye on Wolf, who'd stopped in his tracks. He hung the piece of pipe back on the wall. "I was just funnin' with him," he said, unperturbed, and sauntered away.

Seth frowned at Wolf and gestured for him to follow him into his office. Wolf complied and as soon as they were inside, Seth started in: "Your brother wanted me to take you on and I did. He's been gone a long while and you've been out to lunch. *Out to lunch.* You don't show up. You don't call in.

You don't act like you even want a job. What the hell's going on with you?"

"I just work on special projects," Wolf said.

"That's what your brother said. That's how he talked me into hiring you and you sure as hell know your way around a car or truck, that's for sure. That's why I haven't kicked your sorry butt to the curb. But I am now. I've been thinking about it all day. I had some work that needed to be done, and you weren't anywhere. No phone. What the hell happened to that? You forget to pay the bill, or don't you care? Maybe you don't want people calling you. You're a goddamn hermit. But I need somebody who I can *get a hold of*."

Wolf just stared at him. Seth had fired him. That's what he'd heard.

"Your attitude just brings the Rich Lacheys of the world on you like a pack of jackals." Seth glared at him. He was mad, but he was also unhappy. "Damn it," he said. "I'm going to have to let you go." With that he punched open the cash drawer and pulled out a wad of bills. "About three hundred," he said. "For work already done. That's it."

Wolf took the cash and turned toward the door. He was almost relieved. He wanted to kill Lachey, but if he could get away and never come back then he would get over it.

"Wait!"

The wolf stopped but didn't turn around. He heard the cash drawer open and shut again.

"For the car washing," Seth said, and pressed another group of twenties in his hand. "I don't know how many you did, but I don't want to cheat you. You've taken good care of them."

Wolf wondered when the last time was that Seth looked at the cars, but it wasn't his problem anymore. He counted up how much cash he had at home and how much this was, but the numbers escaped him. He would figure it out later. He could get another job. He wasn't worried.

And besides, he needed time to plan his next hunt. For her. He knew where she haunted.

His head wanted to explode. He could feel the need building.

Seth had given him time. And he was going to use it.

Chapter Sixteen

What had she been thinking?

Gemma groaned internally as she watched Will work his way through his dessert. She was hovering by the kitchen even though she'd been officially relieved of duty for the day.

Macie gazed at her indulgently. "He's real cute."

"I told him I read his mind."

"How'd that go for you?"

She made a strangled sound. "He thinks I'm a nut case. And now we're going to go look at Jean's car." Quickly she filled Macie in on the call from Patrick Johnson and her trip to his farm. "Why did I call him?" she asked, staring at Will. "If I'd kept it to myself, maybe he would have never known."

"Oh, you know yourself better than that. If you can't remember, that's one thing. But purposely hiding that information? Just not like you, hon."

An hour later she was in Will's car again and they were on their way. In her head Gemma had tried out about fifty different openings to explain herself, but none of them seemed like they would work.

Her nerves were drawn tight. As they approached the lane to Johnny's Farm, she actually pulled back in her seat, afraid of what he would find.

Will flicked her a look, his own thoughts spinning fifteen different ways. It was silly, maybe, but he was having a damn hard time holding on to his emotions, keeping them packed away under lock and key. He didn't want any of that "I can feel your emotions" to be even marginally true. She'd known he wanted to kiss her before he'd really admitted it to himself. No big mystery. Some people were just better at picking up those kinds of vibes, women especially..

But still . . . he felt a little out of control and it wasn't a comfortable feeling.

Gemma pointed out the lane to turn onto and Will bumped the cruiser along a pothole filled quarter-mile of leanly graveled track. The rain was coming down in shivering fits and the wipers were slapping quickly back and forth to clear the windshield.

As he pulled up to a farmhouse a wiry, older man wearing a fedora stepped off the porch and introduced himself as Patrick Johnson. His gaze flicked over Will's uniform as he and Gemma climbed out of the car and hurried to the protection of the porch. Will shot a glance at Gemma, whose face was unnaturally white.

"You okay?" he asked her. She'd been pretty quiet in the car.

She brushed hair away from her face and the wind tossed it back in front of her eyes. "Jean's car's in the barn," she said, pointing to the building opposite the house.

"C'mon, then," Johnson said, leading the way, bending his head against the elements. He threw open the sliding door with surprising strength and they all scurried inside. Johnson left the door open and rain smacked against the back of Will's jacket as he stared at the beat-up silver Camry taking center stage. Above was a hayloft and leaks in the roof were tossing down streams of water.

One look at the license plate and Will knew that this was indeed Jean LaPorte's car. He'd read the plate numbers enough times to have memorized them.

And it was wrecked front, back, and center. He, too, shot a look at Gemma and she caught it and understood.

"I'm lucky to be alive," she said.

"From the looks of it. Yeah." He turned to Johnson. "Your grandson drove Gemma to the hospital?"

"That's right."

"In what car?"

"He has a gray Japanese one, too."

"A Camry?"

Johnson shook his head. "He'll be home soon. You can talk to him."

"You and your grandson pulled the car from the ditch together?"

Will bent down in front of the vehicle, paying deep attention to the front bumper. When he straightened he realized Gemma was shifting her weight guiltily from one foot to the other and Johnson's frown had deepened as he clearly considered the ramifications of his actions and what the authorities might make of them.

Will said, "I'm going to have the car impounded." He punched a number into his cell phone and talked to someone who would take care of it.

As Will hung up, Johnson looked around as if he were trapped. "We weren't trying to hide nothing."

"You probably saved my life," Gemma said quickly, absolving him of any wrongdoing.

They headed back outside and across to the farmhouse porch.

"My grandson, Andy . . ." Johnson spurted out, then stopped himself when a well-used, older model silver Acura bumped toward them up the drive. Billy Mendes got it wrong, Will realized as he watched the car pull to a stop. It had just seemed like Gemma's savior had been driving her mother's car, but in reality Gemma's savior, Andy Johnson, had simply possessed a car that was similar in style and color.

Andy stepped out and stopped short at the sight of the three of them. He looked ready to bolt, but Patrick waved him over. Reluctantly he bent his head to the rain and wind, his head and shoulders getting soaked in those few seconds as he crossed to where they stood, a scowl across his face. "Yeah?"

Patrick explained that Gemma had called the sheriff's department and the Camry was going to be impounded. "Why?" Andy demanded belligerently. "She just went in the ditch."

Will didn't bother to address that. Instead, he said, "Why didn't you see Gemma into the hospital? Why drive her there and drop her off at the door?"

"Are you accusing me of something?"

"No, son," Patrick said. "They're just taking the car and going."

"I was afraid for her, okay? She was bleeding." Andy gestured backwards toward the Acura. "All over my car! And she said she was fine. Said it over and over again."

"Could you show me where you found the car in the ditch?"

Will could feel the reluctance and hostility coming off the younger man in waves. Will had met his type many times. Guys who resented authority figures, especially cops. Andy Johnson had been up to something the night he brought Gemma to the hospital, some smaller crime, Will would bet. Smoking dope with some buddies. Shooting off pistols in their backyards after having a few drinks. Stealing gas from some neighbor's car. He didn't really care what it was, he just wanted as much information as he could get.

Eventually, Andy drove him and Gemma to the crash site. They pulled to a stop and all three got out of the car. Gemma held her hand to her forehead to fight off the fits of rain, and Will bent forward to view the ditch. Broken Scotch-broom limbs and deep ruts in the field grass told the story. Will could see the tire marks where Johnson's truck had backed in and winched the Camry from where it landed.

He didn't say much as they returned to the ranch, and he said less as he and Gemma climbed back into his vehicle and headed back toward Quarry. Gemma was as remote as a distant moon. There were still hours of daylight left but you'd never know it with the black clouds making everything appear as if night had already fallen. As they neared Quarry, passing by residences, Gemma looked out the passenger window and stared at the jack o'lanterns grinning back at her, as if they knew all her secrets.

"Hard to believe Halloween's in just a couple of days," she remarked.

"You sure you're all right?" he asked as they pulled into LuLu's parking lot. He stopped next to her truck, the engine idling.

"I'm just tired," she said. "I've been tired all day." She opened the door, then took a moment before heading into the wind and rain. "I don't know why I told you all that about me. I probably do sound half nuts. I guess we'll know more after forensics goes over the car." She tried to make her voice light but she could hear her own fears coming through. He couldn't miss it.

"I'll call you later," he said.

"Thanks."

She didn't know exactly what that meant but it made her feel better. Climbing behind the wheel of her father's truck, she followed his car out of the lot. All she wanted was a bath and bed and maybe not to wake up till tomorrow, except when he called her.

* * *

Charlotte had to wait until the last bell and then she tore from the school. She veered by the buses. If she rode, it would take her home, not to the diner, but she wanted to go to neither. She wanted to go to Gemma's house, which the diner was closer to than her own home.

But what if Gemma wasn't there? What if she stayed late at the diner, or just went somewhere else?

She needed to talk to her. Needed to. Maybe she should go to the diner. But that meant a different bus and the darn bus drivers knew her and wouldn't let her off where she demanded just because she said so. Something about liability.

So, that meant walking, but walking meant going right in front of Robbie Bereth's house and the idea gave her a crawly feeling all over her arms and legs. If his dad was there . . . ?

The wind shot a gust at her hard enough to make her take a step back. Charlotte thought about it for a few seconds more then raced to her bus and waved at the driver, who'd shut the door but now opened it, a glower on her face at the extra effort. Like it was so-o-o-o hard.

Shivering, Charlotte climbed on. She would call Gemma at home from her house.

Leaves danced and spun down the street in a mini-cyclone. Lucky watched them, the sides of the street seeming to loom closer to each other at the far end, a natural perspective that made her feel claustrophobic. On her near right, LuLu's diner reminded her of all the diners she'd worked in, the way she'd scratched out a living in the real world like the rest of the working stiffs, while she existed in her own world, where the rules were what she made them.

To her left was a rough-hewn pine-sided tavern with small, mean windows and a big door with an iron pickaxe handle large enough for Paul Bunyan's hand. Smoke drifted from a river-rock chimney, to be snatched away by the wind and thrown onto the street. She could smell the acrid scent while she held her jacket down with her fists inside her pockets. Her hair flew around her face and she let it as she absorbed this moment. She was meant to be here.

She walked slowly up the street halfway, then back to the bar, aptly named the PickAxe. There was no one out in the wind. Through the windows at LuLu's, she could make out a few customers in booths, each booth lit by a triangular lamp. They were eating diner food the same the world over: meat loaf, hamburgers, BLTs, iceberg lettuce and crouton salads with an occasional tomato thrown on top, root beer floats, and Cokes with ice.

It was with a sense of inevitability that she grabbed the iron handle and pulled open the heavy door to the PickAxe. Her eyes had to adjust to the gloom. It was just what she would have expected, almost like she'd been there before. Beaten-up fir floors, scarred tables tossed haphazardly around the room; the fireplace with crackling fir smoking up the place; a river-rock hearth meant for sitting; dull brass overhead chandeliers that had seen better days and offered minimal illumination; a couple of prized straight-backed wooden booths along one wall; a big-screen television with silent, flickering images; a highly-polished curved bar with bottles of liquor clinking gently against a background mirror, as someone had opened one of the mean, little windows and brought in the late October weather.

A man and a woman stood behind the bar, the man leaning over its expanse, reading a paper, the woman balanced against the counter with the bottles, arms wrapped under her breasts. Both of them looked at Lucky as she entered, but it was the man near the TV who barreled past the few customers at the tables and came right up to Lucky, leering with big, uneven teeth that caught her attention.

"Crazy bitch," he said. "What are you doin' here?"

She gazed at him curiously. He was a bully and he was scared of her. Terrified right down to his center. She sensed, too, that he would love to do her physical harm and was surprised. She'd had her share of men try to take advantage of her but not nearly so fast.

"Hey, c'mon, Kev." The man at the bar had lifted his head from his paper and he gazed over at them, worried. The woman moved protectively to his side and Lucky saw they were together. Man and wife, by the rings on their hands.

Kev's lips pulled back. "I know all the LaPortes, Gemma," he spit out. "All you fuckin' crazies." He waved his fingers in front of her face. "Do some of your voodoo shit. Read my future."

"Voodoo shit," Lucky repeated.

"Kev." The other man stepped from behind the bar and wifey charged after him, grabbing his arm as they came to where Lucky stood.

"Fuck you, Rome," Kev said without heat. "This is between me and the LaPortes." He pointed a finger at Lucky's nose. "They're all thieves. Stole our land. Got it by lying on their backs. Those county records are a fucking lie! I know about your mom and Judge Lafferty, don't think I don't!"

"Well, then, you're the only one," Lucky said. She was getting pretty fed up with this yahoo.

"Oh, that's right, you can't remember. Ha, ha, ha." He clapped his hands and moved one step back to encompass the few other people in the bar. "Here's Gemma LaPorte, our resident psychotic, but she never remembers nothin' important. Convenient."

Rome put a hand on Kev's arm, but Kev shook him off and shot him a deadly look.

Lucky suddenly felt a wave of something from Rome. Appreciation? Apology? Maybe a grain or two of lust? The wife clearly wanted Lucky to go back out the door and evaporate. She was having trouble hanging on to her husband.

"He's not cheating on you," Lucky said to her. "Yet."

She reared back and turned big eyes on Rome. The look of horror that crossed his face as he gazed at Lucky was almost comical.

"See!" Kev crowed. "What do you want to say about me, bitch? What about me?" He slapped his chest with his palms.

"I see you in a straight jacket in a rubber room," Lucky improvised. "Drooling. Playing with yourself, which is the only sex you've had since your daddy showed you how. And you thought the LaPortes were crazy . . ."

Kev's slitty eyes grew huge. Lucky took a step back, waiting for the explosion. She was pretty sure the top of his head was going to blast off. "Jean screwed all the people who count," he said in a harsh whisper. "People in power. And she got the records changed, but that's gonna change back. The Dunleavys are getting their land back. And the LaPortes can just go fuck themselves!"

"You would know," Lucky said blandly.

"Gemma, don't," Rome moaned.

"You should leave," his wife said shakily.

Kev reached out as if to grab her arm. "Touch me and you die," she hissed. He blinked, stopped himself, taken aback.

Lucky chose that moment for her retreat. She hadn't meant to create a scene, but then she hadn't known about this Gemma person and her "crazy family."

She had a memory of another man, an older man, her father maybe? A doctor. Shivering, she clutched at her hip and the injury there. The door she kept shut on her past blasted open and with sudden clarity she remembered the nights he bullied her, the nights he snuck into her bedroom and forced himself on her. She was young. Too young. He never had the courage to approach her unless he'd been drinking, and then he was too big and determined for her to push him away. She remembered the sour smell of alcohol on his breath.

Renewed rage filled her. He was the first man she'd murdered. When she was older. When she could take care of things the way they should be. She'd lured him onto the jetty one storm-filled afternoon and sent him spinning over the edge of the cliff into the sea. An accident, most said. Suicide, some whispered.

Not near enough payback, Lucky thought, but it was all she could get.

"You took her *with* you?" Barb practically screeched into the phone. "You couldn't just get the address and have the car impounded? You had to take her there with you?"

Will was almost back to the department when Barb reached him. She'd called to find out how his trip to Clatsop County was going and Will had filled her in on the turn of events.

Now he wished he hadn't.

"Evidence is evidence," he stated flatly.

"You think she's a damsel in distress," Barb accused. "You're trying to save her."

"Hear anything back on a possible first victim?" Will tried to divert her. "From any other county?"

"Nothing that's even close. So, where is she now? Did you take her home? Maybe I should ask where *you* are?"

"I'm in the damn parking lot outside. I'll be in in a minute. Anything else going on?"

"Traffic fatality on twenty-six last night. Guy's van was over a ridge and nobody found it till today. Motorist called 911 last night and said they thought they'd witnessed an accident. She got routed to Clatsop County. Took awhile to find the vehicle as it was just over the Winslow County line and went way down over the hill. They're getting the driver out now."

"No one else in the car?"

"Just the driver, as far as I know."

Will made a sound of agreement. He didn't really give a damn, but it was a relief to have Barb off his neck.

"The witness thought there was some kind of game going on between the van and a truck with one headlight. The truck sped off after the van went over the edge. The witness got a partial license plate number."

"What kind of game?"

"Moving in and out at each other. Sounds like stupid kids, if you ask me. Driver of the truck got scared and headed west."

"What kind of truck?"

"Tan or dirty white."

"Make?"

"Sorry. Our witness says it happened fast and it was dark."

Traffic fatalities didn't make Will's desk, generally, unless they had an intentional cause. This one straddled the line between accident and vehicular homicide.

"Is there enough of the partial plate, coupled with the truck, to narrow it to a particular vehicle?"

"Ralph's working on it."

Smithson. Will grunted. Good luck getting him to offer up any real information to Will. "You're going to have to handle this one," he told Barb.

"Smithson thinks he's the detective instead of the traffic cop," Barb said with a snort. "I'll have to sit on him hard."

Will had walked to the door and hurried inside, shaking rain from his hair. Dot smiled and mimed, "Tsk-tsk," behind the glass and buzzed him through. He headed toward the staff room lockers and hung his coat up.

Barb appeared in the doorway. "So, what did she say about the car?"

"What do you mean?"

"She called you up and told you where it was. She's not worried we'll find incriminating evidence?"

"She didn't know where the car was. When she learned, she called."

"You believe that?"

"Yes."

"You believe she's innocent?" she asked, arching a skeptical brow.

"That car was damn near crushed. The fact that she's walking around is a miracle."

"She could have run down Letton, then put the car in the ditch on purpose, to wipe off any evidence."

"Pretty drastic, when bleach and a scrub brush would do a better job."

"She panicked," Barb proposed. "Did the deed and then just panicked."

Will met her snapping dark eyes. "Let's go on the assumption that she had a simple accident."

"Simple accident," she repeated.

Ignoring her, Will said, "That she didn't run Letton down. If she didn't, then who did?"

"Nobody, Will. That's the problem. Gemma LaPorte's the killer. And everyone's faced that fact but you."

Gemma awoke slowly, aware that a phone was ringing in some distant place. She also realized she was in the bathtub and the water had grown cold.

She climbed from the tub and started shivering. Outside the wind had escalated to an out-and-out howl and the rain was a rushing roar against her roof. Wild weather.

Her robe was hanging on a hook on the back of the bathroom door. She grabbed it, wrapped it around herself, and did a fast race walk to the nearest telephone, but it stopped ringing just as she snatched up the receiver. Her pulse beat hard as she considered it might be Will. She wanted it to be him. She *willed* it to be him.

The phone beeped once at her, declaring she had an unheard voice-mail message. Quickly she dialed in her code and a few moments later the electronic voice said, "You have three new messages."

Three?

"Gemma. It's Charlotte," came the somewhat tremulous voice on the first message. Didn't sound like Charlotte at all.

Gemma flicked a glance at the time. Six o'clock p.m. A lot of hours since she'd left Will.

"I'm at home. Please call me. *Please!*"

She listened to the next message. "Gemma, when you get home, call me immediately. It's Charlotte. I'm at home."

And the third message: "Gemma, it's Charlotte. I have something to tell you but I don't want Mom to overhear. She's still at the diner. Call me back. Please. I'm at home." She rattled off the number.

Gemma punched in the numbers and the phone barely rang before it was snatched up. "Hello?" Charlotte's voice said nervously.

"Charlotte, it's Gemma."

"Oh, my God. Thank God! I've been calling and calling. Mom's on her way home so I can't talk long. But *I saw the guy*!" Before Gemma could ask, "What guy?" Charlotte declared, "It's Robbie Bereth's dad! He came by the diner to tell me off about stealing the bike. But he's the guy, Gemma. The one you chased out of the diner that day!" Her voice dropped. "Oh, crap. Mom's here. He's the guy, Gemma. He's the guy!"

"When . . . when did he come by the diner?"

"Yesterday. I wanted to call you but I couldn't. He's creepy. Just all cold and starey. Screamed at me, but then made me feel like . . . yech . . ."

"He's the guy I was chasing that day? You're sure?"

"Yes."

"But Charlotte, I want to get this right. Remember you

thought you saw me a couple of days ago and I didn't stop to pick you up?"

"I've gotta go. I don't want Mom to know. Not yet!"

"What was I driving?"

"You still can't remember?" Charlotte sounded really upset. "Really?"

Gemma didn't know how to say it wasn't her. "Was I in a—car?"

"You were in your truck! Your dirty white truck!"

She slammed the phone down and the connection was lost.

Gemma replaced the receiver and stared into space.

A prickly sensation ran up her arms. She could almost remember.

Almost.

But almost is only good in horse shoes and hand grenades.

Why couldn't she remember seeing Charlotte?

Chapter Seventeen

By the time Will left the department the wind and rain had turned into a full-fledged storm, the kind normally reserved for late November. Fir trees bent and swayed overhead like they were nodding to their partners in some scripted dance. Will's wipers were snapping back and forth and still the water was thick as honey.

He swore beneath his breath. If he had any sense he'd just go home, slosh some scotch into a glass and sip it slowly in front of the television. If the power went out, he'd sip it in the dark.

Normally this scenario would have been pleasing, but his brain just wouldn't stop. It kept traveling a well-used track, and it came back time and again to Gemma LaPorte.

He couldn't get a bead on her. Couldn't decide whether she was being straight with him or involved in some elaborate fantasy, maybe one she didn't even know she'd created.

He didn't believe she'd run down Edward Letton, but he didn't believe she was completely innocent, either. If forensics came up with some kind of evidence that her car had hit

Letton he would still have trouble believing it. Maybe she wasn't completely in her right mind. Maybe she was sleep-walking, or in a walking coma. Maybe she was lying, making up fantastic stories to obfuscate the truth.

Maybe she couldn't remember because she didn't do it.

Gemma LaPorte's the killer. And everyone's faced that fact but you.

He yanked the wheel and turned in the direction of Gemma's farmhouse. The decision was made without conscious thought.

He wanted to be with her.

Gemma put the teakettle on the stove with unsteady hands. After adding a tea bag to her mug, she watched the electric burner coil heat up to a glowing orange and cinched her robe tighter around her waist.

The man she'd been chasing was Robbie Bereth's father?

Could Charlotte be right on that? Normally Gemma would have said so, absolutely. But the fact that Charlotte insisted she'd seen her driving her truck—that she'd actually waved at Charlotte!—gave her pause. Why would Charlotte say that? She clearly believed it, but it just wasn't true.

Unless . . .

Unless it was possible that she'd been driving and simply couldn't remember?

"Driving," she said aloud.

She shivered. She'd heard of people driving in an alcoholic blackout and ending up somewhere with no memory of how they got there. Was that it? Some kind of chemical imbalance that had her leading a life she couldn't recall?

"It's not DID," she said.

The teakettle shrieked and she jumped, though she was staring right at it. Her nerves were clearly shot. Grabbing her mug, she filled it halfway, then added sugar and milk. She took a swallow and felt the heat of it run down her esophagus. Good. She was cold from the inside out and that gleefully howling wind and slashing rain weren't helping matters.

Faintly, as if from far away, she heard her doorbell ring. In this storm? Feeling overly paranoid and melodramatic, she grabbed the poker from the fireplace before answering the door. Snapping on the light, she threw the door open, the weapon tight in her right hand.

"Gemma!" Little Tim protested, his eyes turning to the poker in consternation. Rain dripped from his soaked head as he stood under the porch light.

In his hand was a white envelope, almost translucent from the rain.

"Oh, Tim," Gemma said above the wind's roar, her right arm relaxing. Dropping the poker, she clutched the robe tightly to her throat. It felt like she'd run a marathon.

He was slightly embarrassed as he handed her the envelope. "I have another one," he said.

Gemma accepted it and realized one mystery was solved. "You left the note that said, 'I see into your soul.'"

He said shyly, "From a book. They're romance."

The paper nearly disintegrated in her hand as she pulled out the note: *We are one heart.*

"Tim, I told you I have a boyfriend."

"No, no. I'm your boyfriend."

"No, Tim."

"Yes! Yes, Gemma! We need to go to the quarry. Lover's Lane. I've got to show you something!"

He grabbed her arm as if to drag her after him and Gemma resisted. "No, Tim," she said sternly.

"We need to kiss!"

"*No*, Tim!"

He moved in to kiss her, smacking his mouth hard to hers. Gemma's robe loosened and she felt herself instinctively tense, ready to shove her knee hard into his groin. She just managed to stop herself. This was Little Tim. He was a problem, not a threat.

Twin yellow beams from an approaching vehicle bumped toward them, cutting through the sheeting rain. Gemma jerked back sharply from Tim's embrace. He gazed at her in hurt and she yanked her robe to her neck even tighter.

"You must come!"

Gemma looked past him and, as it came close to the house, she recognized Will's patrol car. Relief flooded her. "That's my boyfriend," she said.

"Noooooo!" Tim threw back his head and wailed. "I love you! I love you!"

Will's tires sloshed through deep, rain-filled ruts. He stopped the car and cut the lights, opening the door. Tim got a clear view of him. With a loud wail into the wind, Tim took off on a lurching run, past Will's vehicle in the direction of the main road, his cries deep and heart-wrenching.

Will seemed about to go after him, but Gemma ran into the rain to meet him. She sloshed barefoot through mud puddles, squinting against the driving rain. "Will . . . Will . . ."

"What's wrong? Who's that?" He craned his neck to where Tim had disappeared.

It seemed the most natural thing to throw herself into his arms. If he was surprised he hid it well, holding her close. "That's Little Tim. We need to take him home. I know where he lives. Let me get some clothes . . ."

She hurried back inside, leaving muddy footprints across the wood floor and up the stairs. Quickly she threw on her jeans and a long-sleeved black T-shirt. She grabbed her boots and socks, where she'd thrown them before her bath, and raced back downstairs. At the bottom step she yanked the socks and boots on, then met Will, who was standing just inside the front door.

"What about a jacket?" he asked.

"I'm okay. C'mon. We've got to find him!"

She locked the door and they raced to Will's car, climbing inside together. Will turned around and they headed down the driveway to the main road but Tim was nowhere to be found.

"He's cutting across the fields," Gemma said.

"In this weather?"

"It's what he does," she said helplessly. "He knows the area."

"You want me to go after him?"

He meant on foot but Gemma shook her head. "No. You won't find him." She thought a moment. "He might go to the ridge above the quarry. He wanted me to go with him."

"Tonight?" Will looked through the windshield at the sheer force of the weather.

"Until I told him you were my boyfriend," Gemma admitted. She was shivering. Quickly she brought Will up to speed on her relationship with Tim Weatherford and explained about the two notes he'd brought to her door. "Let's go to his house," Gemma finished. "He lives with his mother."

On the way to the Weatherfords' home, Will said, "Why didn't you tell me you got a note? It could have been sent by a stalker, someone who meant you real harm."

"But it wasn't."

"But you didn't know that till tonight."

"It doesn't matter now."

"It sure as hell does," Will argued.

"I didn't know whether you were friend or foe, okay?" Gemma burst out. Her shivering intensified, so Will started shrugging out of his jacket, his eyes on the road.

"Here," he said without looking at her.

"I'm fine."

"Bullshit."

Reluctantly she slipped it on, smelling his scent, feeling his residual body heat.

At the Weatherfords', Tim's mother Vera simply shook

her head. "Timmy'll come home when he's ready," she said. "He always does."

"We could go to the ridge," Gemma began, but Vera would hear none of it.

"If you find him and bring him back before he's ready, he'll just go back there."

"But it's miserable out!"

"Doesn't matter to him." Vera was soft-spoken but firm. "Go home. Get out of your wet clothes. Thank you for caring, but he'll come home."

"You're sure?" Will asked her.

"Yes, sir."

They got back in the car and drove through the dark night. Everything was close and dark. Inside the car was a warm mustiness, their own heat cocooning them inside together.

At Gemma's, Will followed her back inside the front room. He locked the door behind them and they both stood a moment, the porch light coming through the side windows, the rest of the room in darkness.

"Here," Gemma said, pulling off his jacket. "Thank you."

"Should I hang it up, or am I leaving?"

"Um . . ." She put the coat in the front closet, feeling a little off-balance.

Her hair was wet and her eyes looked exceptionally dark in the dimmed room. Will had an almost irresistible desire to pull her into his arms. She looked luscious and innocent and he wondered if he were going slightly mad. Good old, dependable Will. Wanting to ravish this woman where she stood.

"You said you told Tim I was your boyfriend," he reminded her.

"Yes, well . . . yes. Sorry. I just thought it was better to lie." She heard herself and how that sounded, adding lamely, "Well, in this case, anyway."

"Lying sometimes has its place."

"Wow. There's a turnaround. You've been all about me

telling you the truth, like I've been purposely lying to you. I haven't been."

He nodded.

"Was there a reason you stopped by? Sorry I pulled you into action. But . . . I thought you were going to call? Oh, God. Do you already have some news?"

"I don't know anything more about your car, if that's what you mean," he said. "It's way too early for results, even for a rush job."

"So, I've got a reprieve for at least a few more hours." Gemma gazed into his serious eyes. There was something going on inside him and she automatically tried to read his feelings. He was making it difficult, she realized. On purpose. Keeping himself as shut down as he could. "If I'm charged with a crime, I guess I'll be prosecuted. But I'm not guilty."

"You don't think you are."

"I don't think I am," she agreed, inclining her head. Then, "Have you eaten? I don't think I have." She headed for the kitchen and Will followed her. Both of them were still dripping rain from their clothes and leaving tracks across the floor. She caught him looking down at the mess and waved it away.

"You don't know whether you've eaten?"

"I fell asleep in the bathtub. Got up and made myself some tea and then Tim showed up on the porch. Pretty sure I missed dinner."

"How long were you asleep?"

"I have no idea."

"Was it minutes . . . or hours . . . ?"

"Minutes, probably."

"Probably."

She was standing in the center of the kitchen. Now she turned to meet his gaze directly. "Sometimes things are hazy. That's all."

"Periods of time are missing."

She shrugged.

"You can read minds, and you're missing blocks of time. Some psychologist thinks you're a case of multiple personality."

"DID," she corrected tonelessly. "And I read emotions."

"Like you read mine today."

"I wasn't wrong, was I?" she asked, lifting her gaze to meet his.

He found himself focusing on the curve of her mouth and the bones in her neck, exposed by the black T-shirt's v-neck. It was like she was a magnet for his eyes. He'd never been so entranced, and he could almost believe she possessed special powers because he was powerless to look away. "No," he said, his voice a rasp.

Her eyes closed. "Thank you." Her lips shook and he could tell she was the one fighting emotion now. He believed her, and it mattered.

Will crossed to her as if pulled by a cord. He lightly placed his hands at her shoulders, as if expecting her to collapse in front of him. She looked like she could collapse.

"I do read emotions," she said, her eyes still closed. "I know what people are feeling. My mother had these clients who would come to her because they wanted to know their futures. Jean was a flim-flam artist, though she wasn't despicable. She half-believed she had 'the gift.' But she depended on me because I could . . . come through. I could feel what was uppermost on their minds. Their strongest emotion. Fear. Desire."

Now, she opened her eyes. More green than hazel in the harsh overhead kitchen light. Outside the wind slammed against the house, rattling the panes. Inside Will remembered his dream of Gemma stepping naked from the shower.

He rubbed the pad of his thumb over the curve of her jaw, watching his hand's progress, his blood thickening, heating. "What am I feeling?" he asked.

Her lips quivered into a smile. "Too easy."

"What are you feeling?"

"Well, I'm not hungry—for food." Her gaze fastened on his lips, and to his disbelief she stretched on her tiptoes to feather a kiss lightly over them.

Will's pulse leapt. He leaned down and captured her in his arms, his mouth hungrily finding hers, feeling her lips mold and respond to his.

And in that moment a gale slammed into the house and the lights went out.

It stopped them for a moment. Locked them in a kiss. Then Gemma half-laughed, and Will intensified the kiss and they were backing up to the cabinets. Gemma felt her hips collide with the counter and the strength of Will's body, fitting itself to hers. Her head swam. She hadn't made love to a man since Nate. She could scarcely remember what it was like.

Except she could recall the *want*. The *need*. Her hands yanked at his shirt impatiently. Her fingers undid buttons and pulled. She felt his own hands slide beneath her shirt and move upward to her bra, his palm cupping and kneading her breasts.

"I want you," he murmured. "You were right."

She kissed him harder and he yanked her shirt over her head. Her bra followed, unsnapped deftly and tossed aside.

And then the rest of her clothes were coming off and she was tugging at his. She started laughing, then swept in her breath when his head bent to her breast, his mouth covering one nipple and sucking hard. "Will," she murmured tremulously, her hands in his hair, holding him to her. She was sliding down the cabinet. Her knees were water. She wanted to throw back her head and writhe against him.

And then they were on the floor, grappling for each other. "This is insane," he muttered, his voice thick with both passion and amusement.

"Upstairs," she gasped, and he pulled her to her feet.

Half-dressed, they stumbled together through the dark, still laughing. Gemma felt free and out of control. She led Will up the steps to her bedroom and they tumbled onto the bed. The blinds were open but there was sheer blackness outside the window.

Gemma didn't waste time. She pushed his shirt from his shoulders. There wasn't the faintest bit of illumination; everything was done by touch. Will's hands swept over her body as he pulled off the rest of her clothes. Her stomach sucked in as his hands kneaded her flesh, his hard, naked body coming down atop hers on the bed.

She ran her hands through his hair and kissed him with abandon. *So long*, she thought. *So long since anyone had loved her.*

His tongue rimmed her ear and her whole body shuddered. It was excruciating, the time he took. She wanted to grab him and pull him inside her, and with that thought in mind her hand closed over him, stroking him as he murmured something unintelligible in her ear. Her heart pounded in her ears and her blood ran hot. *I want you!* she thought, or maybe she screamed it.

And then he thrust himself inside her, claiming her, and Gemma's hands raked over his back. He moved rhythmically and she met each crest. Her throat arched and she felt herself reaching, reaching, desperately wanting. She tried to say something. Let him know what she needed, but he was pushing her to the brink. Thrusting, touching, his breath in her ears harsh with desire.

One hand dragged across her breast and her nipple hardened. He bent down and captured it with his mouth, sucking hard. Gemma moaned and twisted, her hands dragging his head to her breast. Quickly he shifted position, turning her atop him so she was straddling him. She moved against him and he held her hips in place, thrusting hard until she was writhing. Faster and faster, to a dark, sensual place.

And then the wave hit her and she cried out, moving frantically. She held one of his hands to her breast as she moved on him, her body finding a rhythm of its own. He arched suddenly and groaned, holding her hard, one hand at her hip, anchoring her down to him as if she were about to fly away.

Then she collapsed against him, gasping. Beneath her breasts his heart was thundering. She fought to get her breath under control and the effort was wasted. She nuzzled his cheek with her lips and he turned and kissed her. Then his lips curved beneath hers.

"What?" she whispered against his skin.

A limb slammed against her window, making them both jump. The rustle of leaves and wind sounded furious.

"The gods are angry," he said.

"Are they?"

"Maybe just jealous."

She wrapped her arms around him as tightly as she could. She felt so possessive of him. Didn't want to let him go. Didn't want time to pass and take her from him. She hadn't realized how alone she felt, completely alone, until this moment.

"What am I feeling?" he teased.

Gemma's emotions were raw and though she wanted to banter with him, she didn't trust herself to be that strong. "You're thinking that you want a repeat," she said.

"Maybe you are psychic," he murmured, then wrapped his hand in her hair and pulled her mouth to his again.

Chapter Eighteen

Kevin Dunleavy thought of himself as a good guy. He only drank as much liquor as he could hold, which was quite a bit 'cause he had a large frame, large bones. He never beat his ex-wife, except for those times she'd really, really deserved it, and that had only been about three times, maybe four. He didn't cheat at cards, much, and though people thought he had a mean mouth he really was just kidding when he said those kinds of things. As his buddy Burl liked to say, *Pardon my French.*

So, it was with a feeling of persecution and injustice that he listened to his brother Rome's wife, Patsy, whine about how he'd treated the LaPorte whore. "You don't want her cryin' all over town about how bad you were to her," Patsy was saying in that nasal twang that just about sent him out of his mind. "Bad for business. We can't afford to lose more customers. You gotta be nicer, Kev. You just gotta."

Shut the fuck up, Patsy.

Through a fixed smile, he said, "I don't think your name's

on the loan, cupcake. This ain't your place. It's mine and Rome's. So mind your own beeswax."

He walked away before he could say something else, something Rome wouldn't approve of. Sometimes his brother was such a tight-ass.

He weaved around tables in the candlelit room, heading toward the bar. The storm had knocked out the power and they weren't even really open, so he figured he might as well drink. Dragging out a bottle of so-so scotch, he poured himself a hefty dose and found Patsy at his elbow, disapproving as ever.

"Get away from me," he growled. Women were a pain in the ass. Always. Kids were a pain in the ass most times. He should know. He and Amy had popped out Brant and he was weak and asthmatic and teary when he should have been strong and healthy. Sometimes Kevin wondered if Amy hadn't done the bangity-bang with some other schlump. He just knew that kid couldn't be his.

"Maybe we should close the doors," Patsy said, nervously looking around.

"Where's Rome?"

"Upstairs."

Upstairs was a sharply sloped attic used for storage, but both Rome and Kevin sometimes headed there for a bit of well-deserved peace and quiet. But it truly churned his guts that his brother had retreated there tonight and left him with his pain-in-the-ass wife.

Kevin stomped up the stairs, groping in the dark, swearing, his eyes narrowing on the faint candlelight emanating from above. As his head popped up and he looked around the attic space he saw Rome sitting in the chair in a circle of light from one of the cheap votive candles they put out on the tables, a bottle of expensive scotch beside him on the table, sipping away.

"You fucker," Kevin growled. "You can't drink the good stuff."

"You gonna stop me?"

Kevin tossed back the drink in his hand and poured himself a hefty dose from Rome's bottle. He glared down at his brother, whose hair was still thick while his was marching toward the back of his head.

Rome said dreamily, "I'd sure like to give Gemma what she's looking for. Did you see her? She's just dying for it."

"Only if you give her more of our property," Kevin sneered. "LaPortes don't want somethin' for nothin'."

"She does," Rome said positively. "I've been thinking about going over there. Knock on her door. Talk to her nice and get her to let me in. Then we'd go at it hard. Down on the floor. Buckin' away." He smacked his lips several times and thrust his hips.

Kevin was infuriated. He had no interest in fucking any LaPorte whore ever. What they needed was to have their mouths slapped and their heads banged into the walls 'till their skulls cracked.

"You're sick," he told his brother.

Rome gazed at him blearily. He'd had a lot of scotch. "She liked me. Had a real thing for me. Still does, I'll bet."

The thought of his brother having sex with Gemma LaPorte made Kevin want to slam his fist into the attic wall. It couldn't happen. He wouldn't let it. He had to stop it before Rome did anything to try and get in her pants because Rome was an idiot. He would fall for her! It was just like him. And then she would look at Kevin and laugh triumphantly.

Touch me and you die.

She'd threatened him, the reckless bitch. And she was going to pay for that.

He'd never killed anyone, though he'd put a few fellows in the hospital, assholes who really deserved it. But the only good LaPorte was a dead LaPorte, and Kevin Dunleavy was just the man for the job.

Grabbing the bottle, he drained the last inch into his glass, then threw it back, feeling its burn sear his throat.

Gemma LaPorte had to die. He just had to figure out how to make it look like an accident . . . or maybe his brother's fault.

Just before morning the lights shot on. Gemma awoke to the overhead lamp shining cold and bright down on her, illuminating the red walls, and then she heard the furnace kick on. It was after that she remembered the male body beside her in bed. For half a beat she was embarrassed, but then, as she watched Will's eyes open, she said somewhat shyly, "We've got power again."

His hair was tousled and she could see the smooth muscles of his chest. "It's Halloween."

"You're right. It is."

"And the storm's over."

Gemma would have liked to turn off the light but wasn't sure she wanted to jump naked out of bed. Will saw her dilemma and grinned. "I'll get it," he said, then slid out of bed, unembarrassed, and walked to the light, switching it off, plunging them into darkness once more.

"The lights are on downstairs," Gemma realized, seeing a strip of illumination below her bedroom door as Will slid into bed beside her once more, his warmth enveloping her.

"Mmmm," he said, his hand traveling over her skin, bringing goosebumps to her flesh. His face pressed into her neck and she felt her senses swim a bit. When his hand moved more possessively, dipping between her legs, she melted open, her tongue caressing the edge of his jawline.

He climbed atop her, his hands on her hips, his body fitting itself between them. His right hand smoothed the scar that ran down her hip and leg, noticed the missing flare of bone. "What happened?" he asked into her mouth.

Her nerve endings tingled. She pulled his hand away and shivered. "I've always had it."

"Sensitive?"

"Very."

"How about here?" he asked gruffly, and his hands found the cleft between her legs.

Gemma sucked in a breath and smiled, and Will's lips crashed down on hers, also smiling. "Yes," she whispered, and they both chuckled until other emotions took over.

Charlotte scowled through the school bus window, watching the sun send weak rays through the clouds. The roadside was littered with branches and dirt and leaves and the asphalt looked like someone had laid a carpet of fir needles. The bus managed to travel right over most of it.

Why couldn't the storm have lasted longer? Maybe take a power pole or two down. She'd been gleeful all night until she fell asleep, certain that Halloween would be a holiday.

But then the power came on and her mother got up and started getting ready to go to the diner. Charlotte had taken that as a bad sign. "There's no school today," she'd declared.

"Turn on the TV," Macie answered with a yawn. "Only school closed is North Creekside and that's because the furnace went out."

"That's not fair!"

Her mother had ignored her and here she was, on her way to school, her Halloween story still missing a good ending, forced to go to school on the best holiday of the year.

Well, at least the weather looked okay for trick-or-treating, she determined, but a day off from school would have been way better.

* * *

Will's cell phone rang as he and Gemma were in the shower. They both heard it and Will kissed Gemma hard, then stepped out, grabbed a towel and walked quickly to where the phone had landed: Gemma's bedroom floor.

"Tanninger," he said.

"It's nine-thirty," Barb said. "Where are you?"

"Taking a shower."

"I've got some kind of odd information for you. You know that gray van that went over the ridge? The dead guy's name is Spencer Bereth."

"Spencer Bereth supposed to mean anything to me?" Will had tucked the towel around his waist and now sensed Gemma coming in the room behind him. He reached his free hand back for her and she took it, her own hand surprisingly cold.

"Only that he's from Quarry. Been picked up a few times for suspected abuse, but the wife won't admit he beats her, or her kids."

"I take it you think his history has something to do with the accident." Gemma released his hand and headed toward her closet. He could hear her rooting around inside and looked over to see her grab some clothes and head back toward the bathroom. A sudden wave of modesty?

"He was playing duck and weave with another driver. Possibly a woman. The witness doesn't know. But I wrestled Ralph for the partial license plate. He's crying like a baby to Nunce, but I'm checking on it."

"Okay." He heard Gemma shut the bathroom door with surprising finality.

"And get this. Spencer Bereth? Somewhere along the way, he got in a tussle with a gun. He was shot in the ass with a .22."

"Shot?"

"I think this woman driver is our avenger, that's what I

think." Barb's voice grew sterner. "She shot Bereth but he got away, so she ran him down."

"That's a leap."

"Same MO."

"Not the gun," Will said.

"And doesn't the LaPorte woman drive a truck? White, or whitish? That's the description we've got. Fits for me."

"Witness said there was only one headlight."

"She coulda had it fixed by now."

Will felt himself tighten up. "We don't even know for sure the driver was a woman."

"It will be. When we chase down the license plate."

"What's that number?" Will grated. He wanted to shout at her that it wasn't Gemma, but he managed to keep himself in check.

"I'll give it to you when you show up here. You just can't bear to believe your damsel in distress could be a killer," Barb declared, thoroughly pissed. "Fine. I'll work the case without you." She hung up with a sharp click.

Will quickly grabbed his clothes and dressed, as pissed at Barb as she was at him. Maybe he was working too hard to absolve Gemma, defending her at every turn, but Barb was working just as hard to nail her. Hell, she really was getting as bad as Burl.

He was just about to rap on the bathroom door when it opened and Gemma stood in the aperture. Her hair was wet and combed away from her face. Her cheeks were pink from the heat of the shower, but she looked pale in a pair of jeans and a loose, tan sweatshirt.

"I've got to go to work. See you later?" he asked.

She nodded. "I'm going to check with Macie and see if she needs some help this afternoon. I'm not on, but it's Halloween and people might want off early."

"I guess we know what our costumes are: a cop and a waitress."

As he headed for the door she came halfway down the stairs, then hesitated. "Will?"

He turned back. "Yeah?"

"Why did you mention Spencer Bereth?"

It felt like Will's blood slowed inside him. "You know him?"

"If he's who I think he is, I may have met his family."

"Tell me what you know about him," he said flatly.

"Why? What's happened to him?"

Will's emotions were at war inside him. He shouldn't talk to her about Bereth. Barb thought she was a suspect in his death. But then, this was his opportunity to learn what she knew. "He was the victim of a fatal accident."

She seemed to lose all strength, collapsing on the step, her hands still on the stairway rail. "Macie's daughter, Charlotte, is classmates with Robbie Bereth. She and I—returned—Robbie's bike, and I met the mother. Charlotte seems to think Robbie's father beats her. I never heard his name."

"So you've never met him," Will said slowly.

She shook her head, but wouldn't meet his eyes. "Not that I know of. When . . . when was this accident? Last night?" She lifted hopeful eyes.

"The night before. His van went over a ridge. He was the only occupant and he'd been dead for hours before he was found."

She could feel him watching her closely, almost with fascination, as she would watch a poisonous snake. She'd been home the night before. Home alone. It shouldn't matter. She had nothing to do with Spencer Bereth. It was Charlotte who'd had a run-in with him.

"It was a single-car accident?" Gemma asked.

"A witness saw another vehicle. A truck. But when Bereth's van went over the ridge the truck sped off west."

"Did the truck driver know the van went over the ridge?"

"We haven't found the driver of the white truck yet."

"White truck?" The color drained from her face.

It was damning. Will had said it deliberately but he didn't like her response.

But I have a partial license number, Will reminded himself. And now finding out whom it belonged to had just jumped to the top of his to-do list.

The wolf knew where to find her. He'd been there, seen her there before. But he'd been too eager. She'd chased out of the diner and he'd chased after her and he'd gotten too close and she'd ended up in the ditch. There was a car approaching the opposite direction so he'd had to drive away. His frustration had made him throw back his head and howl. He'd tried several other times to go back for her but there had been too much traffic, too much activity. Drivers flying by, unaware there was anyone inside the mangled silver car.

And then a young man had finally stopped and realized she was there. Wolf had cruised slowly along and then, when her savior had gotten her safely into his car, Wolf had followed them to the hospital. She'd stepped out of the vehicle, teetering, and the man had driven away. There'd been a moment when Wolf could have grabbed her. Almost. But her unsteady steps were faster than he'd reckoned on, and she made it inside the building.

These thoughts ran clearly through Wolf's mind. They were a relief, because things had been getting kind of wavy. Sometimes he wasn't sure what day it was. Sometimes his dreams were more real than what he knew to be reality. Sometimes the mother-witch was *right there*!

But this one—the One—had killed his brother and he had to make her pay. Had to burn her and send her back to the fires of hell. He was going to throw himself on her and listen to her scream. And then burn her. Burn her bad.

His head was pounding, a hammer slamming against an anvil. *Slam. Slam. Slam.*

He was here. In Quarry. Could he risk going back to the diner? There were witches there. Many witches. Maybe he could have a taste of one of them . . . just a taste . . . before he got the One. The murderess.

He pulled the truck into the lot and stepped out. A baseball cap was tilted low over his eyes. He was in jeans and a red-and-black hunter's jacket, the collar pulled up over the healing wounds on his neck. Ducking his head, he entered the diner and then stopped short, his heart seizing.

The witches were all dressed like witches in cartoons. Black gowns. Pointed hats. In disbelief, he stared until his eyeballs felt dry in their sockets. One of the witches sidled toward him, a stack of menus cradled in one arm. She had long, black hair. Like the mother-witch. And green eyes. And a smoky flavor that expelled from her mouth when she said, "Hi, I'm Heather. Let me show you to a booth."

And she sashayed ahead of him in a black skirt with silvery stars on it. Wolf moved after her, dreamlike.

He sat down where she indicated, and when she handed him the menu, his hand brushed her fingers. Electricity. Desire.

"Happy Halloween!" she said, bending over to relight the candle on his table. He caught a glimpse of curved breast.

> *You can't touch, little fucker,* the mother-witch said in his head. And she laughed and laughed in her harsh, smoky voice. Cackled. His hands circled her throat and he choked her and choked her. He threw her on the floor and fucked her over and over and still she laughed. On and on. Filling his head. Until finally she was still. It was October. Under a full moon. And then he dragged her outside and set her, and the fields behind his house, on fire. It had been a brilliant orange, smoke-filled in-

ferno. Hell on earth. He'd just managed to drag her charred body away from the scorching blaze before the volunteer fire department saw fit to arrive and finally put it out. While they toiled he shoved her body into the basement closet and screamed and ranted at her until his brother came home to chaos.

"What happened?" EZ demanded, racing from Wolf to the window to outside. He was EZ to Wolf, not Easy like the dumb fucks like Lachey had labeled him because he screwed around a lot.

"I killed her," Wolf said. "Burned her."

EZ's eyes had glowed like mirrors in the firelight. "What?"

"I fucked her and killed her and burned her."

"She's out there?" He threw an arm in the direction of the fire, his face contorted with revulsion and fury.

The wolf had nodded. Recognized that his brother didn't understand. Better to let him think she burned.

"They'll find her body," EZ said.

"No."

"They will."

But Wolf just shook his head and of course they never did. The days were blurred and unseparated. EZ moved out of the house to an apartment. He pretended everything was the same. He helped get Wolf the job. But he was distant. He'd gone somewhere else. Away from Wolf. Away from the mother-witch. Wolf hadn't known for a while that it was because of her, the One. Ani. EZ had been crazy nuts about her. That's what he said. Crazy nuts. But she'd used him up and killed him.

Wolf had been lost at that time. In a dark place. A hell of his own. He buried the mother-witch's body behind the house under the charred earth, under a full moon. Now the land was green again, but his brother had never come back and he never would.

The wolf had slowly realized his mission. He had to kill witches. All witches. He had to kill Ani. Find her. Shove his cock inside her while she thrashed and wailed. Then burn her.

He gazed at the flickering flame in the votive. His eyes traveled past the other customers to Heather. She was giggling and tossing back her hair. As if sensing his eyes on her, she flounced over to take his order.

Wolf couldn't remember the last time he'd eaten. Food disinterested him. He said, "Do you wear other costumes?"

"Huh?"

"On other days?" His eyes traveled past her to the only waitress who wasn't dressed in Halloween garb. She had an orange button on her breast that lit up and flashed Boo To You! on and off.

"You mean our uniforms? Sure. Mine's powder blue. Know what you want?"

Wolf's gaze blurred. The mother-witch's garb was blue.

"Grilled cheese," he blurted. "Water."

"Okay, then." Off she went, her hips swaying.

The wolf's fingers wrapped around the edge of the table and he tried to slow the heavy beating of his heart, tried to pull himself back from the abyss, tried to gain control.

But all he wanted to do was screw this young witch-whore and burn her. Send her back to the fires of which she was born.

Heather Yates thought Halloween was a fun holiday, though working at the diner today was lame, lame, lame. The diner job was just to keep her old man happy, since he was paying for her classes at Portland Community College and expected her to invest in her education, too. Not that he'd had to fork over much so far. He was just a cheap bastard.

She guessed she loved him. He was her father, duh. But he could be such a *ginormous* pain in the ass. So she got a C on her accounting test. So what? Jesus. It was his idea that she take business classes and she just wasn't into it. Now, fashion designer—she could do that. But these classes made her feel like her head was stuffed with cotton and her eyes were crossing.

Working her way through school was just a time-waster, really, until Barry asked her to marry him. He was real close, now. She could tell. She'd been hinting about a ring and thought Christmas was too far away. Wouldn't it just be the coolest if he bought it for her for Halloween!

She wanted to squeal with delight at the thought. It was all she could do to keep her excitement contained. But the thought of him giving her a little velvet box while they were making out at Lover's Lane tonight was enough to give her a little thrill right down *there*!

She wriggled her hips and shivered, glancing around the diner. The only person who seemed to notice was that creepy cretin in the baseball cap. He thought the diner uniforms were costumes? "What planet are you from, psycho?" she whispered beneath her breath, but then the door opened and a cute older couple in matching clown noses walked in.

She laughed and said, "Hi, I'm Heather. Let me show you to a booth. You both are *soooo* cute!"

Chapter Nineteen

"No need, hon," Macie said into the phone. "Denise and Heather are here and the Halloween crowd is thinning out. Everybody's getting ready to go home and take their kids trick-or-treating. You just stay put and take it easy. I gotta keep reminding myself that you're a part-timer. I could get way too used to having you every day, and that just won't work."

"I'll be there tomorrow," Gemma promised.

"No way. You're not on Saturday's schedule. I'm counting on you on Sunday."

"I could be there both Saturday and Sunday."

"To hell with that. Get a life, girl!" she snorted, then said over her shoulder, "Milo, for God sakes, what is wrong with you? The orders are piling up. I gotta go," she said into the phone, then clicked off before Gemma could say another word.

Gemma hung up, thought briefly, wildly, about calling Will on his cell phone, then forced herself to go sit in her office. Macie was right. She was marking time and it was time to move on. Get out of the diner business and find what she wanted to do, what she was good at.

She just didn't want it to be psychic readings.

She wanted Will. Wanted him right now. In her bed. Wrapped around her like a vine. Wanted to make love for hours.

She made a sound of disgust and shook her head at herself.

Think about something else, she told herself, forcing thoughts of Will aside.

Immediately the name *Spencer Bereth* ran across the screen of her mind in big, black letters.

Someone had run him off the road. Someone had shot him. Someone had killed him.

Charlotte's voice: *It's Robbie Bereth's dad! He came by the diner to tell me off about stealing the bike. But he's the guy, Gemma. The one you chased out of the diner that day!*

"But I didn't kill him," she said aloud.

Will said it was two days ago, right?

"I was home. Or at Tremaine Rainfield's office."

But yesterday you were really tired. Like you'd been awake all night when you were sure you'd slept like the dead.

And a few days ago you woke up naked on the couch with no memory of taking your clothes off.

"But I didn't kill him," she said again, in a voice that sounded less convinced.

Will looked down at his desk, then over at Barb's empty seat. He was wondering where she was when she came down the hall with Sheriff Nunce. "I've decided to retire," the sheriff said as he entered the room. "For real. You should run for the job," he told Will.

Will smiled faintly. His mind had been on the way Gemma's hips moved when she walked, the way her hair swung around her chin, and her lips curved, and her breasts felt, warm and firm and luscious. What would the sheriff think if he knew his number-one choice for his position was sleeping with a suspect in a homicide?

"What's with you?" Barb asked as she rolled back her chair and perched on it.

Nunce was talking amiably with Jimbo, whom he'd met in the hall. Will watched them walk off together.

"Have you got that partial plate number?"

"Yeah. But I'm not giving it to you."

"Okay. Why?"

"Because you've been sleeping with the enemy."

Will had been in the process of looking over the notes on his desk. Now he deliberately didn't react. She couldn't know. It was just a figure of speech. Still, his heart rate jumped. "I'm assuming you mean Gemma LaPorte."

"I don't know what the fascination is for her but you've got it bad."

He picked up his cell phone and placed a call. Barb gave him the *Who?* frown and he said, "My mother. I want to know how she rode out the storm." Then, "Hi, Mom, it's Will." And he turned a shoulder to Barb, more to collect himself than worry that his conversation was overheard. His mother gave him an earful about what she thought of the noise of the storm and Will let her ramble. Barb kept her eyes on him for a while, then finally dug into her own work.

When Will said good-bye and hung up, Barb reached over and handed him a paper. He glanced at it. It was the partial license plate. "I've got about four possibles for a white or tan truck."

Will's heart beat hard. He gazed down at the numbers. They weren't even close to Gemma's father's truck's license. It hadn't been her vehicle.

His relief was so intense he sat frozen for several moments.

Then he came back to the sixty-four-thousand-dollar question: whose was it? Who was doing this?

It almost seemed like someone wanted Gemma to be the prime suspect.

Halloween night was clear though scudding clouds shut out the moon and stars. Wolf sat in his truck and turned the cigarette pack over and over in one hand. He thought of the mother-witch and how she would light up, aware he was watching her, how she would slide him a sideways look, almost like she wanted him. But she was waiting for his brother. She let smoke drift lazily from an open mouth, enjoying that he couldn't take his eyes off her.

Tonight he'd parked above the quarry but out of sight in between scrub oak and sumac. He'd come here because that's where she'd come—the witch girl. To a ridge high above the quarry. He'd waited patiently for her outside the diner, idling the time watching little children trick-or-treating with their parents, and older kids running in packs, whooping and hollering and carrying loaded bags of candy.

He'd followed this one in her witch's garb to a slightly run-down, two-story house. She'd been greeted by an older man, whom Wolf now knew was her father. She treated him with disinterest, almost disdain. Wolf could hear the old man demanding to know where she was going. He didn't much like that she was leaving with "that no-good Halberton boy." Wolf had parked on the road in front of the house, his truck wedged between two other vehicles, a beat-up Ford Explorer and an old black, now gray, Dodge Monaco. His truck and GemTop fit right in.

That "no-good Halberton boy" had showed up driving a souped-up green Camaro with no muffler. He got out of the car, his jeans so loose they about fell off his hips. He had a scrubby goatee and a buzz cut that had grown out about an inch. The wolf saw a tattoo of some kind on the back of his neck, just visible above the collar of his brown leather jacket.

There was something about him that reminded him of his brother. He could almost hear Ezekiel's voice.

"Call me EZ," he said. "Like nice and easy. I'm a lover, not a hater."

"But you're always yelling," the wolf said, wanting to understand, desperate to learn from him.

"When am I yelling?"

"When you fuck our mother."

"Shut your stinking mouth!" EZ had grabbed him by the throat, surprising him. "We don't fuck, okay. She's a witch. A witch! She has powers and she needs me."

"She's a witch . . ." he had repeated.

"She comes from those people," EZ whispered. "Those women who live alone. One of them fucked an Injun and that's where she came from. They killed that Injun boy. Smashed his head in with a rock. She told me. And they left her with his tribe but the tribe didn't want her 'cause she was a witch. So they left her on a large, smooth rock and they went away."

"Where?" Wolf asked.

He waved vaguely. "South. They were tired of their young men mixing with the witches, so they left. But she's not the only one. There are more."

The wolf had absorbed the lore.

"She uses me," EZ said. "I can't stop. I won't." But the look on his face was full of torture.

"Why won't she take me instead?" the wolf asked.

"Because you're not smart," EZ had stated. "Whoever your daddy was was a moron, not like mine. Mine was a doctor. He was supposed to treat her, but he fell under her spell."

"Then I'll kill her," the wolf said soberly.

"Don't be a damn idiot." EZ snorted. "She can't be killed. She sucks out your life force."

But the wolf knew he could kill her. From that day forward he determined she would die. He would fuck her himself and then send her to hell. And he would find those other witches and take them, too.

But one of them had gotten to EZ first. He was close to finding her but these other ones had to go, too. He had a sense of time running out. Of being unable to fulfill his destiny, of ridding the world of them. But he would take this one, and his brother's murderer. That he could do.

She came out of the house in new clothes. A short black skirt which flashed bare legs above shiny black boots and a red jacket. She'd scrubbed herself clean of the hag makeup and now she looked like a little whore.

She kissed the scraggly-bearded boy and jumped in the passenger side of his Camaro. The wolf let them get ahead of him and then followed them to the ridge. He stayed well back. He saw them park and the whore-witch jumped on top of that no good Halberton boy and they were wrestling in the front seat, ripping at each other's clothes. The wolf now understood they'd chosen this spot above the quarry on purpose. That this was a prime spot for sex.

He felt himself go hard. He didn't want them to have sex. He wanted to stop them now. But there was still some traffic. Still some Halloween activity, although the whore-witch and her boy didn't care. Another car drove by and cat-called at them.

He had to let them go at it.

It didn't matter.

She would be his.

He saw her in his mind in her pale blue uniform. The same color as the mother-witch's.

He turned the cigarette pack over and over, tapping it against his thigh.

The phone rang and Gemma's eyes snapped open. She'd fallen asleep fully clothed on her bed, reading about DID. And then she'd been dreaming about Will Tanninger and the images that crossed her mind brought on a slow blush as she shook off the remnants of sleep. Glancing out the window she saw that night had fallen while she'd indulged in her fantasy. At that same moment, her doorbell rang and she hurried downstairs, grabbing up the phone as she headed to the front porch.

"Hello," she said into the receiver. Through the side windows she thought she saw trick-or-treaters. Some black material floated on a breezy upsurge.

"Gemma? It's Vera Weatherford. I know I said Tim always comes home but he didn't last night. I was wondering if I could call that detective you were with?"

Gemma snapped to attention. "I'll call him. Do you have any idea where Tim might have gone?"

"Um . . . maybe the quarry?"

Back to Lover's Lane. Gemma wondered if he'd tried to coerce a different woman besides herself to join him there. "I'll call Detective Tanninger and we'll go look for him," Gemma promised.

"Bless you," Vera said.

Gemma was distracted as she opened the door. For a moment she stared at the young visitor in the Batman suit. "Charlotte?" she said.

"Batman," Charlotte said from behind the mask, her voice faintly distorted. "Although some people think I'm Bruce Wayne."

The headlights of the car parked at the end of her drive,

where the clearing gave way to her house, flashed at her twice. Macie. "Well . . . just a minute, Bruce."

"Batman," she corrected.

"I've got to get some bat food. You can step inside, if you like. It's in the kitchen."

Gemma hurried to a cupboard where she'd purchased one bag of tiny Snickers bars. She'd done it on a whim because she seldom received trick-or-treaters. Snagging it open, she grabbed a couple of bars and handed them to Charlotte who put them in a black Hefty bag. "Planning to make a haul?" Gemma observed dryly.

"Did you tell that detective about Mr. Bereth?" she asked urgently.

"Charlotte, Mr. Bereth was in a bad accident."

"What?" she asked, sounding dazed. Then, "He's dead, isn't he? Robbie wasn't at school today cuz his dad's dead." Alarmed, she asked, "Did he die on Halloween?"

"No, earlier."

"Oh." She processed that, then said, "He was a bad dad."

Gemma forced herself not to check the time. She wanted to call Will and head out to find Tim.

Macie tapped the horn and Charlotte slowly turned back to the door. "I gotta go," she said reluctantly. "Will you tell me more about Robbie's dad? I think he was like that other guy. I think that's why you were chasing him."

"That other guy?"

"The one who was trying to kidnap that soccer girl."

Gemma, who'd been distracted, gave Charlotte her full attention. "I didn't run Mr. Bereth off the road," she assured her.

"Okay."

"You believe me?"

She gazed at her through the Batman mask. "I believe you mean what you say," she said cryptically, then she hurried down the steps and ran to her mom's car.

Disturbed, Gemma placed a call to Will, surprised and thrilled when she got through immediately.

"I'm just leaving work," he said. "Climbing into my Jeep. Was thinking about coming your way . . ."

There was a world of information left out that Gemma picked up on. "Can't wait," she said with a smile in her voice, then, "But I have a task for us, first." Quickly she explained about Little Tim and Will offered to help before she could even ask.

Thirty minutes later a black Jeep pulled up to the house. Gemma had never seen his personal vehicle and she was also surprised to see him in jeans, a brown corduroy shirt, and a windbreaker. She stepped onto the porch to greet him and he pulled a pig mask from his pocket and put it on.

"I guess we aren't in uniform for Halloween after all," Gemma said.

"Maybe you're not. Cops are pigs, you know."

She laughed and he pulled off the mask and swooped her near, planting a kiss on her mouth, pushing her back through the open doorway at the same time. They kissed and fumbled and stroked each other with more fun than desire, and only when things started turning serious did Gemma reluctantly pull back from his embrace.

"Duty first," he said, his lips slightly swollen from her kisses.

She kissed him one more time, gently biting his lower lip and pulling on it, reluctantly releasing it. "Duty first," she repeated on a sigh.

Will had put off following up on the partial license plate for the vehicle that had run Spencer Bereth's van off the road. He could chase down the possibles on Saturday. Today, tonight, he wanted to spend with Gemma.

They took his Jeep to the quarry, approaching on a pothole-riddled access road that led up to the ridge. When they reached Lover's Lane, Will let the Jeep idle, its headlights cutting through the empty darkness above the quarry, twin beams that only emphasized the fact that the space below held no definition from this height.

There were two other vehicles parked on the headland. Both were dark and seemed abandoned. Will and Gemma climbed from the Jeep and Will swept his light over the nearest one. A head popped up, eyes blinking in annoyance.

"You're not going to bust them, are you?" Gemma asked.

"Hell, no," Will said. "I'm not that much of a pig. And I'm off-duty."

"Sort of," Gemma said, her gaze sweeping over the quarry. A faint drift of fog hung close to the ground far below. "Tim doesn't appear to be here."

Will's flashlight ran over the other vehicle but no affronted heads appeared. "Any kind of trail down?"

"Used to be," Gemma said. "There's a road closer to my house, over that way." She gestured to the southeast.

Will next swept the beam of his light over the ground. There were lots of muddy ruts from would-be lovers' tires and the faint outline of a rocky track through the underbrush. The engine of the car nearest to them fired, and it backed out with mud splattering everywhere, hitting Will's pant legs as it peeled away. "Maybe I was too nice to them," he muttered and Gemma chuckled softly.

It was all he could do to keep from pulling her close again and engaging in some minor lovemaking.

"C'mon," he said, and they held hands and started down the trail.

The wolf had bided his time. It had taken every scrap of self-control he possessed not to drag the witch-whore from the green Camaro by her hair before her boy could fuck her. He needed the commotion to die down, to have them to himself. His nerves were stretched raw and he felt like it was never going to happen but suddenly it was just him and the Camaro's steamed-up windows.

They'd locked the car, so the wolf had to be strong and fast. He carried his heaviest wrench, rounded the vehicle to the driver's side, which was pressed against an overgrown laurel, and smashed in the rear driver's-side window. The whore-witch shrieked and grabbed for her top but Wolf saw the bouncing globes of her breasts. The boy beneath her was struggling for breath. Wolf knew he was still inside her. He took the wrench and smacked him near his ear. He stopped moving instantly.

"Stop! Stop!" the whore was screaming. "You killed him. Oh, God! You killed him!"

She was crying, screeching, scrabbling for the door, trying to escape, trying to get out the passenger side. He let her and when she tumbled out, buck-ass naked except for the tiny shirt she was holding to her chest like a shield, he grabbed her by her hair. She wheeled and shrieked like a banshee. Wolf slapped her hard and she fell down. He wanted to take her right there. In the mud. Where she deserved to lie. He jumped on her and wrapped his hands around her neck, strangling. Her fingers clawed at his and she gasped for air. Her body thumped and thrashed beneath him, stirring his need.

"Witch," he ground out.

Her eyes bugged. She recognized him but couldn't speak.

And then the sound of an approaching car.

Wolf jumped to his feet, dragging her with him. He slammed shut the open door of the Camaro and then pulled his still struggling victim to the undergrowth. She was making sounds so he was forced to press her windpipe harder until all that was left was a last soft *whoosh* from her emptying lungs.

The couple in the newly arrived car got right at it. The

wolf could see their shadows and silhouettes from the interior lights they didn't immediately turn off. His lips pulled back in a sneer. But the woman wasn't wearing a disguise. She didn't try to hide her identity. She was not a witch.

He watched for several moments, then he pulled her further, deeper, away from the cars and the quarry, which was where he would dearly have loved to take her. That should be her final resting ground. Her and the One.

Alone with the whore-witch, deep in a copse of trees and high, overgrown bushes, he pulled the cigarettes from his pocket. He couldn't have her. She was already dead. But he could burn her.

Carefully, he lit a match, touching the flame to the end of the cigarette, puffing just enough to make certain it was lit. He'd been so careful with the other two. He'd been so needful, marking his conquests. Labeling them. Marking them with their numbers. But now that was over. His hand shook a little as he seared the burning tip into her flesh. Once. Twice. Three times. Then a frenzy of burning.

Burn. Burn. Burn, whore!

The scent of searing human flesh woke him to the moment. They would smell her.

Suddenly afraid, he extinguished the cigarette and slung her limp form over his shoulders, stealing through the woods, oblivious to slapping wet branches and sharp limbs that drew harsh lines on the skin of his face.

He worked his way back to his brother's truck, breathing hard, sweating, his sweat mixing with a lightly falling rain. Opening the GemTop, he threw her in the back. She was a tangle of legs, arms, hair, and breasts. For a moment he wanted to lick those breasts but she was dead. He would have to wait for the one he sought.

He would make sure he had time with her.

She was the witch who'd taken his brother from him.

He would drive into her till she screamed on her way back to hell.

Turning the ignition, he put the truck in gear and rumbled away from the quarry.

But he would be back.

Gemma slipped down the rocky trail to the base of the quarry. It was damper at the bottom. The air was thick with pent-up rain. The fog lay damp and soggy against her face and turned her hair to limp strands.

She shivered and looked over her shoulder, feeling a sudden malevolence she couldn't understand but that felt decidedly real.

Will was ahead of her. She reached for his sleeve, afraid to get too far from his warmth and security. They worked their way to the bottom, then Will picked his way, with Gemma at his left shoulder, through the broken rocks and scraggly plants along the quarry's ravine.

"Tim!" Gemma called. She'd been calling his name sporadically on the way down. "Tim! It's Gemma."

There was no answer. Just a soft soughing of the wind, high above. Will twisted around and looked up but the fog obscured his Jeep and the abandoned vehicle at the crest of the ridge. "Tim!" he called out.

They both waited. "What do you think?" Gemma asked at length as they traversed the quarry. She looked east toward her own property, and north to the Dunleavys. The gray fog deadened everything.

"Why does he come to the quarry?" Will asked.

"I don't know."

"Maybe it's more about Lover's Lane," he theorized. "That's where he wanted to take you."

"Maybe he's still up on the ridge," Gemma agreed. Then a moment later, "Maybe he watches the lovers who come here?"

Will grunted. “He’s a Peeping Tom?”

“He doesn’t really understand what’s okay behavior and what isn’t.”

They called Tim’s name several more times, then slowly hiked back up to the top. Another car had appeared but when Gemma and Will showed up in their headlights they shouted some obscenities and reversed out in a hurry.

There was no sign of Tim.

Will shone his flashlight on the abandoned car. Again nothing moved. He stepped closer and noticed the seat belt was hanging outside the closed passenger door. The windows were fogged.

Something felt off so Will moved closer. It looked like the rear driver’s-side window had been smashed in. With the end of his flashlight, he knocked against the passenger door window pane. Then he tried the handle. It opened easily.

And an arm and head flopped down, hanging outside.

Gemma screamed, then cut herself off abruptly, a hand at her throat.

Will bent down to the man. “He’s alive,” he said.

Quickly he called 911 while Gemma just stared. He seemed familiar. “I think he’s been to the diner,” she said in an unsteady voice.

“Can you help me lay him down?”

They carefully pulled the man’s body from the car, supporting his neck, keeping his back as straight as possible. Will’s flashlight revealed the blow to his temple where a stream of blood from a gash ran down his neck.

And then they heard the whimpering. Will whipped around, his beam catching Little Tim in its illumination. His face was contorted. He had a girlie magazine folded in one tight fist. “He burned her,” he said. “I could smell it. I thought he wanted to love her, but he burned her.”

“Who?” Will demanded. “Where?”

Tim ran to Gemma and nearly knocked her over. He was

sobbing and shaking. He pointed with the magazine in the direction of the woods. "But he's gone now. He took her." He looked up and saw the unconscious form of the man on the ground. "Is he dead?" he wailed.

"No," Gemma said. "No, he's alive."

"He took her!" he cried again. "Burned her and took her. It smelled so bad!"

"You saw him?" Will asked.

Tim nodded. He waved in the general direction they'd come on the access road. "He took her away."

"Who?" Will asked again.

Little Tim looked at him fearfully from the comfort of Gemma's embrace. "The cigarette man."

"The cigarette man?" Will repeated, a cold finger drawing a line down his spine.

"I saw the cigarette tip," he said, pointing toward a grouping of trees. "It was orange. And then I smelled it. And then he carried her away."

Will met Gemma's eyes. "I need to wait for the paramedics."

"We're okay," she said. "Right, Tim? We're okay for now."

He sniffed and gathered her closer. "We're at Lover's Lane," he said shyly.

"Yes, we are."

It seemed like forever before they heard the sirens. Will checked the Camaro's registration then got on his cell phone to his partner. As the ambulance arrived, lights flashing, Tim finally let go of Gemma to observe, his eyes wide. The EMTs jumped out and Gemma pulled Tim back to give them room. They worked over the unconscious man and loaded him into the back of the van.

Will said, "I'm going to take you and Tim home and then head to the hospital."

"You think the guy who did this is the . . . ?"

"Yeah." Will was terse.

"What guy?" Tim asked.

"Not a nice one," Gemma answered.

"No." Tim shook his head dolefully, then cast a worried glance in the direction of the copse of trees.

Fifteen minutes later they were on their way, following the ambulance from the site. Will said quietly, "We're going to search the area, but Tim, did you see the vehicle that left? The one the cigarette man was driving?"

"Noooooo. I heard it leave."

"Taillights? The back, red lights? Did you see them?"

"Noooooo." He gazed at Will with worried eyes.

"It's all right," he told him.

They drove to the Weatherford home. Vera had the lights on, and she hugged her big son when he lumbered up the front porch steps and into her waiting arms. "He was a mean man," Tim said when Gemma and Will turned to leave. Then, a little desperately, "I see into your soul, Gemma!"

"It's okay, Tim," Gemma assured him.

They climbed into the Jeep and drove back to her farmhouse. "Are you going to come back after?" she asked him as he dropped her off.

He wanted to more than anything, but he knew how things were shaping up. "I doubt I'll be able to. If this guy's our psycho, the shit's really going to hit the fan."

"Whose car was it? Can you tell me?"

"It's registered to Barry Halberton."

Gemma shook her head. "He seemed familiar but I don't know . . ."

"I'll call you tomorrow," Will promised, then lifted a hand and turned the Jeep around as Gemma let herself into her house. She'd left more Snickers bars in a bowl outside the door but they looked untouched. Charlotte had been her only trick-or-treater.

Nevertheless, she moved cautiously through the house, testing every window and door. She felt almost violated; the events of the night filled her head with emotions she didn't want to examine.

She checked her phone messages and heard Tremaine Rainfield ask her to call him. He said that though the next day was Saturday, he would really like to see her again.

Gemma thought about her ability to read emotions as she walked into her red room. She suddenly wanted to know more about herself. If Tremaine could help . . . ? Before she could change her mind, she called his number and left a message saying she would be happy to meet with him the next morning. The walls were pressing in and she needed tools to keep them from crushing her.

Barry Halberton woke up in Laurelton General's ER. His head throbbed and his vision was slightly blurry. He was undressed under a sheet and suddenly he remembered taking his pants off and having Heather on top of him.

"Heather!" he called, shooting to a sitting position. Immediately a team of nurses gently pushed him back down. One of them, a young, pretty one, said, "Sir, you need to lie down. You've been in an accident."

"An accident?"

And then the serious-eyed face of a man in a black jacket and jeans gazed down at him. "Are you Barry Halberton?"

"Yeah. Where's Heather?"

"What's Heather's last name?"

"Uh . . . Yates . . . Is she okay?" he asked, panicked. Then, "Oh, my God! He broke into our car. Smashed the window! Where's Heather! I need to see her."

"Mr. Halberton, stay down," the nurse ordered, her hands on his arms.

"Heather's missing," the man said. "We're trying to find her."

"What?" Barry was beside himself. "He took her. He's going to kill her."

"Can you tell us what he looked like?" the man asked calmly.

Barry moaned and closed his eyes. He saw the looming head come toward them in the front seat. "Like an ape. Big head and shoulders. Oh, God . . ." He leaned over the gurney and vomited.

"Sir, you need to leave," the nurse said sternly to Will.

Will flipped out his badge but it held no sway. He was forced to take a few steps away but Barry yelled, "Find Heather. She works at the diner."

"Which diner?" Will asked.

The nurse glared at him and then at Barry.

"LuLu's."

Chapter Twenty

Gemma awoke as if from a bad dream. Faint illumination was filtering through her bedroom blinds, and when she pulled them up she saw that the sun was fighting its way out from between two large, dark gray clouds.

She checked the time. Nine-thirty. Glancing around the room, she let her mind shy away from the events of the night before, yet she couldn't forget that a woman was missing.

Shuddering, she quickly went through her morning ablutions: shower, change of clothes, makeup. Macie had said she didn't need her help today, and Gemma, although she felt drawn to the safety and routine of the diner, was determined to start new.

With Will.

She thought about calling him. She knew he'd gone to the hospital and she could imagine the craziness at the sheriff's department today in the wake of the abduction. Though the feds had been careful not to let too much out about the two other murdered women, a decision that had been helped by the fact they'd been found in different counties, this third victim, if that's what it turned out to be, was bound to blow the case wide open to the press. The "burn" psycho would be front-page news.

If Tim was right, which she kinda thought he was.

Her phone rang and she glanced at the Caller ID, didn't recognize the number, so she answered cautiously, "Hello."

"Gemma? It's Tremaine Rainfield. I got your message. You sounded like you might be interested in going under hypnosis."

"What I want is to move on," she told him clearly. "I feel like I've been carrying around a lot of stuff I need to just let go of. That's why I'll do it."

"Great." He clearly didn't care about her reasons, just was happy to get on with it. "This morning or afternoon? At my offices?"

"Let's make it early afternoon."

"See you then."

Outside the PickAxe the street was filled with Halloween debris: rafts of Silly String in neon colors. A smashed bag which had been filled with candy, candy that was spread all over in sticky, mud-covered piles. A broken Lone Ranger mask, its elastic back torn. Dots, spilled from their ripped, shredded box, were dissolving gummily in standing water. A pirate's sword which was really light cardboard covered with aluminum foil.

Kevin Dunleavy frowned down at the mess and kicked aside some of the Dots. He'd opened the front door to gaze across at LuLu's, glaring at its raft of customers. He resented the diner's booming business. He just about hated that Macie woman and her nosy bitch of a daughter. That girl was always watching, like she was taking notes, or something.

And the LaPortes owned the building. Gemma LaPorte. He'd like to smash his fist in her face and his boot in her hot little crotch before he killed her.

"Psychic, my fuckin' ass," he muttered, slamming back inside to the semidarkness. There'd been a Halloween party of sorts the night before and the black-and-orange streamers that hung limply around the windows and from the brass lights, just plain pissed him off. He tore down a streamer and stomped it into the floor.

Patsy appeared, her face wan as she walked in from the back door.

"What're you doin' here?" Kevin growled.

"I'm getting ready for lunch."

"They're all over at the diner, stupid bitch. That's where they go. Pancakes and eggs sunny-side up and club sandwiches and hamburgers . . . when's the last time we sold a burger, huh? When?"

"Last night." Her words were clipped. He could almost hear the *asshole* she didn't have the nerve to tack on at the end.

Fury licked through his veins. With an effort he charged through to the bar, his eye on the bottle of expensive scotch. He'd forced himself to keep to just four drinks the night before. Had to keep the damned partiers happy and buying. It wasn't that long ago that he'd gotten in a fight with one of their big spenders and he'd been crawling on his belly and begging ever since. The dumb fuck just loved to see good ol' Kev squirm.

Jesus. What a life.

The door opened, letting in weak sunshine and a blast of cold air. Burl Jernstadt's bulky form entered and Kev grunted a hello at him. Here was someone who understood his frustration. A compadre. A drinking pal.

"What a fuckin' mess out there," Burl said. "Pardon my French."

"Ready for a scotch? God, don't tell me you think it's too early."

"I don't have a job no more, courtesy of Detective Will Tanninger, so pour it neat and make it tall."

Kev snorted and filled Burl's order and a glass for himself as well. He gave Burl the cheap stuff and his hand hovered over the expensive bottle, debating. Oh, hell. He deserved something good. He broke open the seal on the expensive scotch and filled himself one hefty dose.

Burl didn't notice. He was already bitchin' and moanin' and whiny-whinin' about Tanninger some more. Truth to tell, Kev was sick of it. The man's constant crying made him want to puke.

"He's been getting into that nutso Gemma LaPorte's pants. I overheard Barb on her cell phone letting him know what she thought about it. She's been all over him like white on rice, but nope, he likes the crazies."

Kev's fury resurfaced when he thought about Gemma LaPorte. *Touch me and you die.* Who did she think she was, threatening him? She was the one who was going to die, all right.

Burl worked his way through his drink, and kept on and on about Tanninger. Kev sipped more slowly and made a gross face at Patsy, who hovered around like a bad smell. He could tell she was gonna rat on him to Rome. Well let her.

"We shoulda played a trick on her last night," Burl said suddenly. "Soaped her windows. Disabled her car."

"On Gemma?" Kev was beginning to have a tad bit of trouble keeping interested, what with Burl's monotone.

"Yeah, for fun. Something. Scare her shitless. Watch Tanninger run around like he's got a hot poker up his ass, trying to figure out who's after her."

Kev liked that idea. It warmed him inside. But he didn't want Burl involved in any way. He wanted to sneak up on Gemma LaPorte and scare her till she wet her pants. He had a sudden vision of throwing her down on the ground and sticking his dick inside her dirty little pussy. Take that, whore. And again. And again.

"I gotta go," he said, tossing back the remains of his second drink. The cheap scotch. Not the good stuff. Not necessary after the first drink.

"Where ya off to?" Burl demanded, but Kev was out the back door, lurching toward his '66 El Camino, his pride and joy. White. Beautiful. Shouldn't be driving it drunk.

But hell, he wasn't drunk.

And it was high time he taught Gemma LaPorte a lesson she wouldn't forget.

Lucky had the distinct feeling she was supposed to be somewhere, but she was poised in her newly borrowed Hunk O'Junk brownish Chrysler sedan, parked on Quarry's main street. She'd opened the door to her past and let little, jagged-sharp pieces of memory escape, memories she mostly refused to acknowledge. Now she thought of her father. Or the man who claimed to be her father, as he'd adopted her when she was too young to remember.

The day she'd walked him onto the jetty was dark and threatening. Everyone knew you shouldn't walk on the jetty with a storm coming in. She'd been young, but strong, lithe and agile and she'd taken care of herself from the time she could remember. The doctor liked his pills and he liked to make it an evening at home with her as much as he could. Pills and his little girl. She'd grown up feeling first ashamed, then increasingly angry. Then she'd started recognizing the signs of what was to come: his stupid amorous talk, his lurching drunkenness.

She learned from others in town that they suspected what had been going on but had turned a blind eye.

So she took him out on the jetty. Begged him to take her,

though he tried to back out. Said she'd be such a good little girl for him. Helped him with his pills.

And as they stumbled along, holding hands, she continued to coax even though the clouds grew black and the wind whistled and the waves swept upward, glorious in their force.

She tripped him. So simple. And right at that moment a wave crashed onto the jetty and knocked her down, sweeping dear old dad into the sea. He screamed and she saw the "O" of his mouth as he realized he was going in the ocean. She had to hang on with all the strength she possessed or be swept in with him and she did, head down, a grim smile of satisfaction on her face. She was found by a man who'd witnessed the whole thing, who rained scared accusations down on her about "idiots who walked on the jetty in a storm." He blamed the doctor, not Lucky, though he'd seen that she'd been the one instigating the walk, because the doctor should have known better.

The doctor's brother was brought in to take her. There was talk of giving her back to her real mother, but she was crazy. So, Lucky slipped away. No one was going to take her. Ever again. Without her consent.

Now Lucky gnawed on the back of one knuckle. That was the truth, wasn't it? That was her history. It wasn't a made-up story. That's how she'd come to this point.

As she considered, she saw a vintage El Camino rattle past, its frame dent-free, its grillwork shining even if the engine sounded a little rough.

The bastard from the PickAxe was at the wheel. Bent over the wheel. Swerving a bit as he hauled ass down the main street.

Lucky read his emotions as he passed by as if they were written against the sky. He wanted to rape and kill someone.

She said simply, "No," to the empty bench seat of her car, and she pulled out behind him.

He drove to a long lane that was bordered by shrubs and

looked to Lucky like it could be a trap. She parked her Chrysler about fifty feet away, in a turnaround that bordered the property but was screened from the main road by Scotch broom and scrub pine. She then worked her way back to the drive and walked down it carefully, ready to dart into the underbrush if he suddenly came back the way he'd gone in.

She reached the end of the lane and the back of the El Camino at the same moment. He was striding up to the front porch of a farmhouse, not bothering to hide his approach. He was drunk as a skunk, too, she realized, which probably accounted for his poor judgment. If he really wanted to attack whoever lived here then he would have been wise to be more discreet.

He pounded on the front door, pressed a hand against the bell half a dozen times. When nothing happened, he screamed, "LaPorte, you fucking bitch! Answer the goddamned door!"

LaPorte? So was this the home of the well-hated Gemma?

A few moments later Kev turned around, slipped on some leaves on the porch, swore pungently, then staggered back to the El Camino. Lucky eased into the surrounding shrubbery, squatting down, making herself small.

He turned the vehicle around, throwing mud from beneath spinning tires, then headed back the way he'd come. Lucky stood up and stepped from her hiding spot, her gaze on the farmhouse. A strange frisson of awareness came over her. She felt caught in a tractor beam, dragged by forces other than her own will toward some nameless and unwelcome truth.

The sound of an approaching car broke the spell. Lucky jumped back toward her hiding spot, scrambling behind a clump of Scotch broom. A county law enforcement vehicle entered the drive and pulled up to the house. As she watched, a tall, somewhat familiar dark-haired man stepped from the car and walked toward the house.

Lucky was hit with a wave of desire so strong it made her

inhale sharply. It broke over her head and left her heart pounding, her thighs weak. She almost sat right down in the mud because she had the most powerful feeling that she'd made love to him. Recently. Her legs wrapped around him, his hips grinding deliciously into hers.

Who is he?

Will knocked on Gemma's door and waited for nearly a minute. He knocked a second time, louder, then stood back and squinted up at the place. Maybe she wasn't here. He called her home phone, and when he got her voice mail he tried her cell, which sent him to its voice mail immediately.

Frustrated, he drove by the diner, but neither her truck nor Gemma herself appeared to be at LuLu's. Sensing how disappointed he was, he swore under his breath. He needed to forget about her for a while. He was inordinately bad about picking women, and he didn't want whatever this was with Gemma to be another mistake. He wanted it to work.

The whole area was being searched for Heather's body. Will had gone to visit Heather's parents, whom she still lived with, and had broken the news that their daughter was missing. Their panicked gazes were embedded in his inner vision. He'd planned to go from their place directly to join the hunt, but between the feds and the rest of the sheriff's department, the search was well in hand. He was debating heading on into LuLu's and explaining Heather's disappearance to Macie, but decided against it. If the girl wasn't supposed to work today, it would just be fanning the flames of gossip and worry. If she was, the Yateses had probably already called and informed Macie of Heather's possible abduction.

And he wanted to tell Gemma who the missing girl was first.

Jesus, what a mess. He prayed to God he was wrong

about what had happened to Heather, but he suspected she was either dead already, or dying at the hands of their psycho flesh burner.

His cell rang and he glanced at the Caller ID. Barb. "What's up?" he answered.

"Where are you?"

"In Quarry, but I'm thinking about following up on that partial license plate number unless the search team wants me."

She snorted. "The feds have made it clear they've got it in hand. And anyway, if it's our guy, the feeling is that he took the girl with him. Like he took Inga Selbourne. We'll probably discover her barbequed in a few days."

Will winced at the terminology. "They said that?"

"Just quoting Burl. He was outside the offices, trying to talk Dot into letting him inside. I came out and said he was wasting his time and he went off on you."

Will made a noncommittal sound.

"I told him his banishment was directly from Nunce but he won't believe it. He's an asshole. We all know it."

Will decided to change that subject. "I've got four possible trucks. Two in Portland, one in The Dalles, and one in Seaside, that could match the partial."

"And you're going to Seaside," Barb guessed. "Who owns that one?"

"Carl's Automotive Repair and Car Rental."

"Think our girl rented the truck to do her deed?"

"Maybe."

"I've got a call into Cecelia Bereth," Barb informed him. "Spencer Bereth's widow. She hasn't called back, so I might go over there and see what I can find out. I talked to some people at Laurelton General. Cecelia's shown up twice at the ER with a fractured arm. They have two boys, one's thirteen and already been written up for a minor in possession of marijuana. The younger one's been at the ER for contusions."

"Prince of a guy," Will observed coldly.

"One of the neighbors called me. She says she saw them fighting one day in the grocery store parking lot. Apparently good old Spence smacked Cecelia with the back of his hand because she accused him of looking lustfully at the female bagger's chest."

"I don't want to sound like I'm giving good old Spence any kind of break, but a lot of guys look lustfully."

"Yeah? Well, apparently this cashier hasn't got any breasts yet. Daughter of the store owner and she's about twelve and was just helping out for the afternoon. The neighbor was yucked out and so am I."

Will, who was driving his own Jeep rather than a patrol car, had turned onto Highway 26 and was heading west. Barb's words brought up a mental image of the interior of Edward Letton's van. "He a pedophile?"

"Seems to like little girls," Barb said. "I'm going to check with the store people, too. See if any of them remember the incident. Maybe this has something to do with his death, maybe not."

"All right. I'll follow up on the truck."

"You know, if it was your friend, Gemma, who ran him off the road, she's been doing the world a favor," Barb said.

Will had no answer to that. "Keep me informed on the psycho-burner."

"Will do. What do you think about him taking Heather Yates from Lover's Lane on Halloween? Pretty bold."

"Like I said, he's escalating. And maybe losing his grip."

"Think he saw her at the diner?"

Will realized he'd made a concentrated effort not to think about that case. It wasn't his, and he didn't like its proximity to Gemma. But Barb's words forced his mind to run through the events of the night before, whether he wanted to or not. "I don't know, and I don't know what his criteria is. The feds probably have an idea but they're not telling us." Something niggled in his head and for a moment he thought he had it, but then it flew away and he was unable to grab it.

"What do you think's going on there?" she asked, but he could tell she was just ruminating as well.

"Nothing good." Will hung up. He should have been glad, he supposed, that with everything else going on Barb had stopped attacking Gemma, at least for the moment. Instead all he felt was worry and a cold, growing certainty in his gut that, when this all shook down, he wasn't going to like what he found.

Lucky followed the sheriff's department man's black Jeep Cherokee from a safe distance. He was heading toward the Coast Range, which made her stomach jump and her heart squeeze. Where was he going? Did it have anything to do with her? She felt anonymous in her boosted Chrysler sedan, but vulnerable for reasons she couldn't quite explain.

The man from the sheriff's department kept right on going. Lucky let cars get in between them, so she fell further and further behind. As they crested the last pass, she pressed her toe to the accelerator and pushed past them until she had a clear two-lane road in front of her, even if it twisted and turned and gave only short stretches of visibility.

But as she entered the long, flat section just before 26 intersected with 101, she saw her quarry's car up ahead. It was late afternoon. Early evening, really. She could just make the Jeep out, as the cloud cover had given the day a gray cloak. She moved up a bit on him but stayed far enough back not to gain attention.

What was he doing?

A few minutes later, he slowed to make a turn. Lucky gasped.

He was turning into Carl's Hunk O'Junks.

She drove past, careful not to swivel her head or give him any reason to look in her direction.

What was he doing?

Could he possibly *know*?

Carl's Automotive Repair and Car Rental had another sign posted toward the side of the garage: Carl's Hunk O'Junks. Beyond that were about thirty vehicles in varying stages of disrepair. Mostly they needed new paint jobs. It was hard to say whether their interior guts were reliable.

Will entered the garage and heard the low rumble of a compressor and the *fzzz-fzzz* sound he associated with someone removing lugnuts. Sure enough, as he rounded the rear bumper of a lifted blue SUV, he saw a man bent over the task of replacing the vehicle's front tire.

"Hey," Will said, and the man whipped around, air gun in hand. He was a tough, lean man with a long face, just under six feet. "Detective Will Tanninger, Winslow County Sheriff's Department," he introduced.

"Holy Jesus, man! Don't sneak up on me." His eyes examined Will's uniform critically. "What do you want?"

"I'd like to speak to the owner. Carl?"

"Seth. He's Carl's son. Carl died of the cancer a few years back." The man set down the air gun, wiped his hand on his overalls, held it out to Will. As Will shook it, he said, "Rich Lachey. Seth's not here today, so I'm holding down the fort all by my lonesome. Something I can help you with?"

Will considered Lachey. The man looked like the kind of mean son of a bitch who tore the wings off flies. But looks could be deceiving and all Will needed was to check on the license plate of one of Hunk O'Junks trucks. He explained as much to Lachey who glanced over his shoulder where, if he had X-ray vision, he could have looked through the garage wall to where the rentals were parked.

"You wanna go look at 'em, have at it."

"Do you have the vehicles' corresponding plate numbers?"

"Well, sure. They're in the file. But I don't think I can show you nothin' without Seth's consent. I gotta job here I'd like to keep, if you know what I mean."

"Why don't I start with the cars?" Will suggested, and Rich swept an arm in the general direction and went back to his task.

It started to drizzle as Will stepped outside. The break in the rain was over for now. Hatless, as ever, he bent his head and stepped cautiously around mud puddles that had started to dry and now would fill up again. Muck along their edges sucked at the soles of his shoes.

Will worked his way around the cars, ignoring them, focusing on the trucks. There was a white truck, two tan trucks and two light gray ones. He realized the gray ones only had license plates on one end and he stepped in a puddle that went halfway up his shoe as he walked around them. Their license plates weren't even close to the one he sought. Muttering under his breath, he passed them and moved further through the vehicles, aiming for the white one which had a fine layer of grime all over its paint job. Its license plate didn't match, either, so he moved on to the tan ones. Will examined them carefully. Neither of them matched either.

Huh.

But one of the tan trucks had a broken headlight, like the vehicle had glanced off something. Skin tingling, Will bent down and examined the crunched metal. There was a scrape of tannish paint, close to, if not exactly, the shade of Spencer Bereth's wrecked van. He walked toward the back where there was a scrape and the bumper was twisted.

Maybe Gemma traded the plates.

The thought occurred to him but he rejected it outright.

He knew the plate numbers of her father's truck and Jean's car. This wasn't close.

But then here . . . here was a whole plethora of license plates.

Slowly, methodically, Will examined the rest of the Hunk O'Junks. Most of them were ten-plus years old. Not quite vintage. Definitely not close to approaching new. Halfway through the job his breath stopped, his heart started pumping hard. There was a silver Honda Accord parked to the far rear of the lot, and it had a deep dent in the hood. Will stared at it hard, afraid to touch it. He looked through the driver's side window and examined the steering wheel and the windshield. No obvious signs of blood. Whoever had driven this car may not have sustained any injuries, but whoever it was, it wasn't Gemma. Her car—Jean's car—was accounted for.

He went back to the front and noticed faint threads caught in the crumpled front bumper.

Will swallowed. He would bet his badge that this was the car that had run down Edward Letton.

That meant Gemma was safe. She couldn't have been driving this car, and her mother's.

But there were a lot of hours between the time of Gemma's accident and when Andy Johnson found her, he reminded himself.

But two cars? Two *silver* cars?

Too much of a coincidence. There weren't those kinds of coincidences in nature. Two women who looked like Gemma driving two silver cars on the same day.

Will closed his eyes. It just didn't make sense. Yet . . . yet . . . this car . . .

Carefully, he examined the license plate of the vehicle, his pulse racing light and fast. He didn't recognize it.

Straightening, Will walked carefully around every car in the lot and then suddenly there it was: the partial license number. On a red '94 Volvo wagon.

He sloshed back to the garage, now heedless of the rain and mud. Rich Lachey was just stepping outside. "Hey, Seth's back!" he hollered. "I was just comin' to getcha."

Will walked across the garage's concrete slab, leaving muddy footprints in his wake. He went to the office door, wiped his feet on a mat, found Seth inside. The man had just hung up his coat and was turning toward his desk when he saw Will, taking in his rain-dampened shoulders, wet hair and muddy feet. "Rich said you were out looking at the cars."

"I need to know the license numbers and which vehicle they are assigned to. I think someone's moved them around."

"What? Nah."

"I'm assuming they're left outside, ungated."

"But no one would . . ." He shook his head. "No point to it."

When Seth realized Will wasn't about to be put off, he lifted his palms. "Well, fine then." He walked to a file cabinet and yanked open a drawer. "They're all in these files," he said. "You can look 'em up yourself. I got things to do."

"I'd like to know who rented one of your tan trucks recently. Will that information be in these files?"

"Nope. But I can tell ya who off the top of my head."

Will had taken the two steps toward the file drawer and now he glanced back at Seth. "Who?"

"Nobody. Not a human being. We ain't actually been real busy around the rental business lately," he said in disgust. "Last time we rented out was in August, and it was the minivan. Came back with a big scratch the bastard swore was there in the beginning, though I always check. Got in a wrangle, we did. He threw fifty bucks at me and I let it go."

"Well, someone's been driving one of the tan trucks and they broke a headlight and put some rear end damage on it."

"Uh-uh. No way."

"And the silver Accord has a big dent on the hood and a smashed bumper. Was that there before?"

Seth swore violently and yanked open the back door to his office. "Show me," he bit out and Will was forced away from the files to lead Hunk O'Junks' owner to the damaged vehicles. Seth looked ready to explode.

"Woulda been nice if somebody told me," he declared furiously when they went back inside. He threw the accusation toward the garage, in Lachey's general vicinity.

Lachey took instant offense. "I ain't in charge of the rentals. Never was."

"Who is?" Will asked.

"I am." Seth threw himself into the chair, which reared back like it was going to break a spring. But Seth knew how much stress the spring could take and he popped back upward, his expression dark.

Will ran through the files until he found the tan truck. Its license number corresponded to the partial in his possession. "Bingo," he said thoughtfully. He glanced over at Seth. "I believe the tan truck that is supposed to have this license number was involved in an accident a couple of nights ago. I'm going to call the Clatsop County Sheriff's Department and have them impound it."

"The hell you will. That truck's been sitting out there for six months or more!"

"Someone stole it and ran another vehicle off the road. That driver's dead. Vehicular homicide. You want to fight about that?" Will asked blandly.

Seth looked poleaxed.

"And the other car. The silver Accord. We'll be taking that one, too."

"Another homicide?" he asked with a sneer.

"As a matter of fact, yes." Will watched the color drain

from the other man's face. "Got any idea who could be taking your cars? Maybe a woman?"

Seth laughed shortly. "Women don't much like my Hunk O'Junks, detective. They want remote locks and leather interiors and GPS and fifteen cup holders for their morning lattes. Any woman wants one of these is way down on her luck."

Lucky sat in her car, hands white-knuckled around the steering wheel of the sedan. She was parked on a rutted, two-lane drive on the property adjacent to Carl's, a service road for an industrial park that was only about half-filled. Lucky had her binoculars fixed on Carl's place and saw the man walking among the rentals, then a few moments later Seth and the man reappeared and looked hard at some cars. The tan truck *and* the silver Accord.

"Oh, God," she murmured.

Her head buzzed. She felt like she might pass out. Did he know she'd had one of the trucks? Did he? Did he know she'd traded in her last one after running that bastard off the road? Did he?

Dimly she was aware that a large truck was backing from one of the bays of the building nearest to the road where she was parked. She had to leave. To move. To keep from being discovered.

Easing her car into drive, she pulled forward, to the end of the lane where her view of Carl's was obstructed. She turned into a parking spot whose yellow lines were all but obliterated. The building next to it was dark and empty, its business long defunct.

The large truck rumbled away, toward the road. Quickly Lucky turned her car around and parked on the edge of the drive. It was growing dark. The shorter days lost light quickly. After about fifteen minutes the sheriff's man's Jeep drove away from Carl's and turned east, away from the coast. She followed a few moments later.

He drove all the way to Quarry and Lucky stayed behind him, letting cars in between them, then moving ahead of them in the passing lanes that dotted this stretch of 26 when it felt like she was getting too far behind. She thought he might go back to that same house, but instead he kept steadily on until he got to the outskirts of Laurelton. There he turned in to a residential area, which forced her to fall back.

It was early evening but black as midnight as his taillights pulled into a driveway and he parked the Jeep outside the garage. She watched the headlights flick off as she drove on past and onto a side street. By the time she'd gotten herself turned around and dared drive in front of his three-bedroom ranch, he'd turned on the lights in the dining room and through the bare windows she saw him walking down the hall.

So, this was his home.

Parking catty-corner from his house, she adjusted her rearview to keep an eye on him. Then suddenly his garage door went up and he walked back outside to the Jeep.

Quickly, she ducked down and prayed he would go the other way. She didn't want his lights to wash over her car, possibly catching her in his headlights.

Her wish was granted and he turned down a separate street. Fast as she could, Lucky fired her engine, jammed the car into drive, turned in a neighbor's drive and followed after him again. The Jeep was nowhere in sight when she reached the street and she momentarily panicked.

Then two cars ahead, she saw the black Cherokee drive beneath a street light. He was turning back toward Quarry.

Lucky eased in after him, glad for the protection of her medium-brown Chrysler. Her heart did a flip-flop. Had Carl realized she'd taken it? Maybe that's what his trip outside with the sheriff's man meant.

Examining her gas gage, she realized she needed to fill up and fast. She couldn't afford to be stranded. That spelled disaster. Lucky followed the man into Quarry then drove past him to a fill-up station. When the young male attendant came out to help her, she asked for ten dollars' worth, reaching inside her purse for the money.

He smiled at her as if they were friends, which kind of spooked her out. When he finished the fill-up and took her money, he said, "You ever gonna give Aunt Davinia a reading, Gemma?"

"Excuse me?"

"She said you would. I was just wondering when. My girl kinda wants one, too. She believes in all that stuff."

Gemma. That bastard Kev from the PickAxe had called her that, too. *Gemma LaPorte. The woman who lived at the farmhouse.*

Lucky stared at the attendant. She was pretty sure she didn't know him. And she sure as hell didn't know what he was talking about. She was afraid to ask too many questions, afraid he might realize he wasn't talking to this Gemma person.

The name sent a shiver across her skin. She could feel gooseflesh rise. It sounded familiar but her association with it wasn't positive.

She had to get out of Quarry. She suddenly knew it as if someone had whispered the warning on the wind.

She was thinking of heading back to the west, but, as if it were meant to be, she suddenly saw Kev pull out of the PickAxe and barrel down the road in his El Camino as if the devil were on his tail. She followed.

It came as no serious surprise that he headed back to the house he'd cruised around before, turning off his lights as he entered the long driveway. The bastard. He meant someone serious harm. This Gemma person, most likely. She didn't dare pull down the drive, so she went back to her turnaround, parked, then walked along the edge of the lane again, careful to keep close to the brush on the eastern side in case she needed to dive for cover. Her night vision wasn't bad, and as long as she wasn't surprised by a car she could keep on the trail of good old Kev without him knowing.

Kev's vehicle was parked in the gloom at the end of the drive, far enough back from the house that the home's occupants might not know he was there. No ringing the bell and yelling this time. He was sneaking up. Stealing around the shrubs that bordered the western end of the house, spindly, deciduous azaleas, their stalks bending forward as if reaching for this man bent on murder.

She wished, suddenly, fervently, that she'd brought her gun with her. She'd taken it from her last Hunk O'Junks' glove box and, after replacing the bullets, stuffed it in the Chrysler's, where it was sitting right now, out of reach.

Kev slipped around the back of the house. Hugging the edges of the Scotch broom, Lucky bent down and moved stealthily after him. She had no weapon, but the urge to take him down was a living thing inside her. She could sense what was in his soul. Blackness. Hate. Sadism.

He was crouching near the back porch, waiting. Lucky rose on the balls of her feet. She wouldn't hesitate this time. She would hurtle herself on him, jab her knee into his crotch. Grab the man by the scrotum and yank with all her strength.

She hoped she killed him.

Before she could move, the door opened and a woman stood on the back porch. She held a poker in her right hand. In the soft yellow light streaming from the kitchen window, Lucky saw her profile.

She felt her muscles go weak.

Who?

"Get the hell off my property, Dunleavy," the woman said coolly. "I've already called 911."

Lucky pressed the back of her hand to her mouth. This woman . . . ! She looked just like her. *Just* like her. And she sounded like her, too.

Good God . . . this woman . . . this Gemma was her *twin*!

Chapter Twenty-One

Gemma fought back her tiredness with everything she had. Earlier Tremaine Rainfield had told her in his most doctor-y voice that her fatigue was because she was accessing deep and painful memories and it took a whopping amount of energy—something nobody really talked about much in the psychology-biz apparently, until their patients felt like they'd been hit by a sledgehammer. To Gemma this felt more like the exhaustion of physical exercise.

She'd met with the younger Dr. Rainfield and he'd run her through his hypnosis exercises. She'd allowed him to try to put her under, truly believing she would be a poor subject. But then she'd suddenly woken up, her eyes flying open, sitting in the same deep, leather chair he'd pointed out for her to take.

Only it felt like a year had passed. Not forty minutes.

And Tremaine was gazing down at her with an expression she couldn't read. So with the little energy she had left, she fought to tap into his emotions. It didn't take much. What she sensed was a well of disappointment. His disappointment. Apparently things had not gone well.

Understanding, she said, "Not DID," the first words out of her mouth after she awakened.

He looked away. "Well, it was never a certainty anyway," he said.

Yeah, but you were counting on it.

"What happened?" she asked, then memory came back hard and fast, a fist to her solar plexus. She damn near doubled over.

Red. Blood. Searing pain. A looming figure with a mask. A medical mask, she recalled. Screaming.

"You grabbed your hip," Tremaine said, his voice breaking into her nightmare.

She touched it again. The missing part of her hip bone felt like it was on fire.

Red. Bright red blood.

She remembered her grandmother. Or maybe just an older woman she'd assumed was her grandmother. Native American. Steeped in the old ways. While her children and their families lived in modern houses and shopped at grocery stores, Totu stayed in a one-room hut with Gemma, whom she'd taken in at the behest of . . .

Fuzziness. Gemma's mother, maybe? Gemma couldn't remember back that far. It was difficult enough to recall the old woman.

"I called her Totu," Gemma said.

"She did the surgery?" Tremaine asked.

"Surgery?"

He pointed to Gemma's hip. "May I look? From what you said I think you suffered some major trauma. An accident of some kind."

Gemma had wanted to deny him. It felt like some secret side of herself was being violated, but she also wanted answers. She half-undressed and Tremaine examined her hip meticulously. When he ran his finger over the scar she shivered from the inside out.

"Was Totu Native American?" he asked.

"Yes. How . . . ?"

"You called her Injun."

"I did?" Gemma said, embarrassed.

"With affection. So, she must have allowed or encouraged you. Can you tell me more about her? She cut out a pretty large piece of your bone."

"I don't remember anything else about her," Gemma murmured. That was the truth. She had no recollection of being put on the ferry and left by a woman who had taken her in, taken care of her.

She didn't tell him about remembering the medical mask. That didn't seem in keeping with Totu and she wanted to examine these new revelations away from Dr. Rainfield.

"Why are you convinced it's not DID now?" she asked him, when he'd finished asking more questions of her, and she'd asked more of him until they'd exhausted the subject of her recollections.

"No alternate personality emerged. No guilt. Nothing." He gazed at her thoughtfully. "Other than the fact that you think you can read minds."

Emotions, she thought, but didn't say it.

"Your repressed memories appear to be rooted in trauma. The pieces missing all your life may simply be your coping device. Nothing really more than your strong need not to remember past pain."

Gemma should have felt relief but mostly she experienced a sense of letdown. Nothing had changed in her life.

He went on to explain about the tiredness being related to her working through her problems, and Gemma, though she questioned that diagnosis, admitted she'd woken up recently after some deep, deep sleep that felt almost like a coma. She'd even woken up naked, which he'd found perfectly normal.

Maybe he was right. It did feel like things were coming to some kind of conclusion. Maybe that's what her feeling of a future Armageddon had meant. Not a violent end as much as a finale of her old life. Maybe her new life was with Will.

She left his offices, headed home, her thoughts on the events of the evening before. At home she'd thought she might toil over them, waiting for Will's call, but she went directly to sleep. Dreamless. Her subconscious working through the new memories, keeping most of them still under wraps, allowing only a little peek now and then. It angered her that she couldn't access them all, even under hypnosis. But she'd gotten a lot of them. Enough to knock her out for most of the afternoon and evening.

She'd awoken to darkness. The red of her bedroom walls was shrouded in shadow. Good. She was going to change the color immediately. She wasn't tiptoeing around her abilities anymore, whether they be good or bad. She was done with that. She just wanted to be normal.

The noise came from the back porch.

The hair on the back of her neck rose. Her heart started pumping hard.

Little Tim?

No. Something else. Some*one* else.

She tiptoed down the stairs in the dark and grabbed the poker. The kitchen light was on, spilling through the window to the back porch. One look and she saw who it was.

In a kind of cool, controlled fury she stepped onto the back porch and said, "Get the hell off my property, Dunleavy. I've already called 911."

* * *

Lucky melted back into the shrubbery, her hands to her head, her stomach clenching. She had a twin. A twin. A *twin*! No wonder people confused her with Gemma. She could still see through the thin stalks. She couldn't take her eyes off the woman with the poker.

A shudder went through her from the soles of her feet to the top of her head.

And almost as if this duplicate of herself could feel her, she watched Gemma turn her way and gaze directly at the spot where she squatted, her muscles and skin quivering.

"Did you hear me?" Gemma demanded. Dunleavy stood like a gaping moron.

She felt something, then. A whisper across her flesh. She glanced away, briefly, toward the underbrush.

And that's when Dunleavy lurched toward her.

She swung the poker up like a golf club at the top of its arc. They glared at each other and Gemma sensed that he intended to do her real harm.

"Fuckin' whore," he muttered.

"One half-step closer and I'm calling the sheriff's department myself."

He reached out one leg and jiggled a toe, staggering a bit. She realized he was half drunk. "You're a whore just like your mother. I know about her getting on her back for the judge. That's how you got the land."

"It's my land." Her voice was cold. "At least you got that right."

He seemed to finally realize she meant business because he slapped the air at her and turned away. "Cunt," he slurred out, clomping back to his El Camino.

Gemma damn near threw the poker at him. She was sick of listening to his filth, sick of his insinuations, sick of him.

But as sick of him as she was, she still didn't feel the same revolting fury and need for retribution that she did when she'd learned about Spencer Bereth. Him she'd wanted to kill.

Maybe she had.

But no. It hadn't come out in her session with Tremaine Rainfield. No repressed guilt.

Unless she was even better at hiding it than she knew.

Dunleavy climbed in his vehicle and gunned the engine. Gemma looked past him, to the waving branches of Scotch broom. For a moment her breath caught. It looked as if someone were crouching there. Someone watching her. Then the image disappeared.

Feeling like she was being overrun by the heebie-jeebies, she slammed back inside the house, locked the back door, then systematically checked every other door and window.

Cunt. The word rolled around in Lucky's head like a pinball, too awful to settle. She'd been called a lot of things. That being one of them. But whoever leveled the epithet at her generally found she wasn't going to take it.

It was easier for her to concentrate on her own growing hatred for Kev than think about the woman who was her twin. She could feel a whole host of memories kicking around inside her brain, trying to escape, like cats inside a burlap bag. She refused to open that sack. Didn't know what it meant. Was scared of what might be inside.

Instead she followed Kev away from Gemma LaPorte's. She expected him to head back to the PickAxe but instead he drove to a 1970s split-entry with peeling gray-painted siding and sagging concrete steps that led to a door with a gold plastic sidelight. Lucky had stayed in her share of rundown places but she was faintly surprised Kev wasn't doing any better, since he owned the tavern.

The answer drove right up to them. An older BMW, still looking pretty nice, screeched to a halt and a blonde woman stepped out. Lucky ambled the Chrysler past, rolling down her window and twisting her rearview to get a better look at what was transpiring with Kev and his angry wife/ex-wife/girlfriend/ex-girlfriend. The blonde started yelling immediately, the gist being unpaid child support.

Lucky drove to the end of the street and turned around in the driveway of another split-entry that was dark inside and out. By the time she returned to Kev's he and his lady friend were just going inside the house. Before the door shut Lucky saw him backhand the woman so hard her head snapped around and she stumbled.

Lucky pulled the car to the curb across from Kev's house and cut the engine. She sat in the Chrysler, immobilized by memories and a cold rage that was seeping into her thoughts. She pulled her .22 from the glove box. Memories swirled. The back of a man's hand against her jaw. The doctor. The bastard her mother *gave her to.*

Gemma had escaped that fate. Her mother had given her to the old woman with the gray braids, she recalled. An Indian. It had been some kind of offering, from one crazy old bat to another. Before she'd killed the doctor she'd learned the truth, had extracted the information as best she could when the bastard was kind to her, which was seldom. Lecherous devil.

Her mother had walked away, though in time Lucky had known where to find her. She'd wanted her to pay for what she'd done, but had learned to her chagrin that the woman who'd borne her lived in her own inner world. She was pathetic and had maybe even felt like she was doing the right thing by giving up her girls for others to raise. Unfortunately, the doctor had been the wrong person. A secretive man with twisted, sexual needs that he visited on his young daughter. Ani. She'd wanted anonymity and had basically achieved it over time, leaving one part-time job for another as she moved up and down the coast, working mostly as a waitress. Picking up the odd skill here and there, like carjacking. Learning to survive on her wits.

But Gemma . . . she'd been raised by someone who loved her, hadn't she? Kev resented her, but Kev was a sadistic worm. Ani didn't know what to think about Gemma. Her sister. She would think about that later.

But she knew what to do about Kev.

Her emotions in check, she entered the unlocked front door and followed the screaming and ranting up a short flight of steps to the living room. Kev had his lover by the dark roots of her bleached hair. They both looked up in shock when she appeared.

"Gemma?" The woman's voice trembled. Her chest was heaving from exertion.

Gemma. The sound of her sister's name stopped her again. In that second Kev dropped his woman and came at her, one hammy fist brushing her jaw. Ani staggered back and lifted the gun.

"I'll kill you."

"Get the fuck outta here!" he yelled.

"Stop." She aimed for his broad gut.

"Kevin! Kevin!" the woman howled. She stumbled toward them and Kevin pushed her hard, sending her flying. She crashed into a wall and slid down into a heap, moaning. Then he charged at Ani and she fired point blank. Three times. His body jerked with each hit and he looked stunned. "You shot me," he said, thumping down to his knees.

Ani stared down at the man whose upper torso was starting to fall forward. A bubble of blood appeared at the corner of his mouth.

Quick as a cat, she slipped around him, down the stairs and out the front door.

* * *

Will rubbed his temples and snatched up his coat, heading for the door. He'd been grilled by the feds, who seemed to think his trip to Carl's Automotive was suspicious. Earlier, he'd stopped at his house just long enough to get a call from his mom, who was confused about all the Halloween costumes the day before, no matter how Will explained about the holiday. "I know about Halloween," she said, though clearly this was a missing piece. "But one was dressed like she worked for the Red Cross. All white uniform with little cap—"

"Mom, I've got to go." Will had cut her off when his cell phone started ringing. The call was from Barb and he suspected, which later turned out to be the truth, that he was being called in. "Is Noreen there?"

"She's always here," she'd said, sounding slightly put-out at the thought. "When are you coming to see me?"

"Soon."

"Bring that girlfriend of yours."

He eased off the phone. Damn disease. His mother was way too young to be suffering from it. If she couldn't even remember Halloween, what was next?

He had called Barb back and then headed to the department. All the while he was grilled by Agent Sadowski, a particularly persistent federal agent whose suspicious manner rubbed Will the wrong way, his mind had followed paths of its own. Thinking. Testing. Adding pieces together. That niggling thought that was just out of reach.

And when the answer had come to him it was so obvious that he didn't understand what had taken him so long.

"They all wear uniforms," he'd said aloud, ignoring whatever last question the agent had asked him. "Inga Selbourne was a nurse, Jamie Markum was probably wearing the To You Today uniform when he ran across her, and Heather worked in a diner."

The agent frowned.

But Barb was there and with him instantly. "You said Barry picked her up at her house and took her to Lover's Lane . . . in her diner uniform? I'm not saying I don't like your theory, but . . ."

"He knew she worked at the diner," Will said. "He saw her there."

"He's a customer?" Barb's brows lifted.

"We know she worked at the diner," the agent said dampeningly, trying to keep control of what he considered his interview.

"Maybe," Will had answered, and would have left right then except for the annoying Sadowski, who got all officious and demanded that Will finish telling him all about the events of the night before, even though he'd already reported everything to Nunce that very morning.

Now, he was just happy to be able to leave. He called Gemma on her cell from his car and finally she picked up. "There you are," he said, relieved.

"I'm at the diner. You didn't tell me it was Heather." She sounded upset rather than accusatory.

"I know. I've been trying to call you."

"What does it mean? Why Heather? Whoever's doing this feels so close. First the nurse from the hospital, now *Heather*?"

He could have reminded her that Jamie Markum had been a victim as well, and she had lived and worked around Seaside. He could have told her his theory about the burn-psycho's targets wearing uniforms. He could have tried to dissuade her a lot of different ways, but he understood what she meant all too well. It did feel close.

"Any news?" she asked.

"They're still searching."

She shivered. "Oh, God, I hope we're wrong and she's okay."

Will didn't answer because he couldn't make himself offer platitudes he didn't feel.

"I went to see Tremaine Rainfield this morning," she said. "Regression hypnosis."

"Learn anything?" Will asked, surprised. He thought she'd rejected the idea of helping out the younger Dr. Rainfield.

"Yes and no. Look, I'm kind of in the middle of talking to Macie. Can I call you back?"

"Sure. I'm headed home. But I'll meet you at your place?"

"Okay . . ." She sounded a bit distracted. "Later."

He hung up and drove the rest of the way to his house. He wanted to take a shower and change just to try to get the stink of the day off him. He wanted to see Gemma and explain everything to her. He wanted to make love to her.

He'd just stepped out of the shower when his doorbell rang. He had a moment of worry, thinking maybe his mother had found the keys again.

But when he opened the door Gemma was standing on the porch, in a black jacket and jeans, a wry smile curving the corner of her mouth, a bulky black leather purse he'd never seen before hitched over one arm. Her hair was down and seemed longer than he remembered.

"Hi, there," she said.

He gazed at her, nonplussed. "I thought we were meeting at your place."

She cocked her head. "Thought I'd surprise you. Was I wrong?"

He slowly shook his head. He'd expected her to blast him with questions about Heather and the burn-psycho, and he planned to tell her his progress on Spencer Bereth's killer, but since she seemed to have put it all on hold he just reached out an arm and pulled her inside. She laughed at his bold move and then wriggled madly, like she wanted to get away. But when her eyes, wide and hazel, met his, whatever she read in his smoldering gaze brought an answering look in her suddenly sober expression. Her lips parted and she slipped her arms around his neck. "Let's make love," she said huskily.

"I don't remember telling you my address. Did you read my mind or something?"

"Or something," she said, giving him a quick smile. "I'm going to take you away from here. We'll go somewhere where no one can find us."

"I wish," he said with feeling.

"We can combine work and pleasure. Let's go to the beach. Stop by and look at that car again."

"What car?"

"The one you think was involved in Edward Letton's death?"

Will's pulse was thundering, emotion and desire racing through his bloodstream. "I haven't had a chance to tell you that," he said slowly, thickly. Her hands had moved from around his neck and were sliding down his torso.

"I'm scaring you." Her hands slid into his crotch, cupping him through his jeans and she sank to her knees, drawing down his zipper.

This was a new Gemma. He hardly knew what to think. "I thought you only read emotions," he managed to get out.

She looked up at him as if surprised, then glanced away, oddly thoughtful. "I see a whole lot more than I want to," she admitted. With that, she stepped back, gently dropped her purse to the ground, then slid her arms out of her jacket and stood before him in a black, long-sleeved, body-hugging T-shirt. Slowly, she pulled it over her head, posed before him in only a bra.

"So, are you just going to stand there?" she breathed.

Danger, Will Tanninger. Danger. Danger.

He heard the voice inside his head. He sensed there was something very wrong with Gemma. Maybe this was the alternative personality Rainfield had believed she possessed. Maybe she existed after all. Maybe that hypnosis session had released her. He needed to think clearly, keep her at arm's length.

"You're not acting like yourself," he said.

With a flick of the back clasp, her bra was dispensed with. She slipped out of it, dropped it to the floor, then moved toward him, crushing the globes of her breasts against his chest, wrapping a leg around his. "I don't feel like myself," she admitted. "I want you. Now. Don't say no . . ."

Her mouth captured his and her tongue flicked inside his mouth.

Will tried to keep a handle on his emotions, but she'd consumed his thoughts ever since they'd made love. He wanted her and damn the consequences.

They moved to the bedroom as one, his arm clamped around her, their mouths together. She stripped off his boots and jeans and shirt and everything else, then pushed him onto the bed. He lay there, mesmerized, as she unsnapped her jeans and did a slow wriggle, letting the denim slide down her hips and long thighs. He saw the scar on her hip, the indent from the missing hipbone. She kicked off her shoes, stepped out of her jeans and pulled the wispy panties down with extended fingers, watching him.

"My God," he murmured.

"You're mine," she said.

"You got that right," he admitted and she slid on the bed atop him, sliding herself over him, along the length of his shaft, but lightly.

"We're going to take our time," she breathed into his mouth. Then she suddenly moved from the bed and dug through his pockets till she found his cell phone.

"You can't turn that off," he said as she pushed the End button.

"Yes. I can."

With a flick of her wrist she tossed the phone toward the doorway. Then she slid down his body and wrapped her mouth around him and began to suck with ever increasing pressure.

Barb Gillette was sick of manning the desk. She wasn't exactly Will's partner. That's not how the sheriff's department worked. It was more of an understood thing, but somehow she'd become relegated to the "stay at home wife" while he was out in the field. And she was tired of being control central.

Punching in his cell number, she was sent straight to voice mail. Her brow furrowed. Odd. Will never turned off his phone. She tried again and the same thing happened.

"Barb, can you come here?"

It was the sheriff, and though she generally was eager to be summoned, she was also sick and tired of the federal agents who acted like the sheriff's department was somehow under their employ. She should have left with Will. She should have.

"Sadowski has been telling me Will's theory about the vics all wearing uniforms," Nunce said, indicating the agent. "You think that's right?"

Barb nodded. "We always knew he was targeting them somehow."

"So, he's got some problems with authority?"

"Women in authority," Barb said. "I've been trying to reach Will without a lot of success. He's on the Bereth murder, too."

"I need to talk to him," Sadowski said presumptuously.

Barb stood on one foot and then the other. She had a

sense of time ticking by. "I'll try to find him. Was there anything else?"

"Does Will think the perp lives around here?" Nunce asked. "Since two of the abductions took place in Laurelton and Quarry."

"We'll know more when we find Heather." Barb knew Nunce was just throwing out these comments to keep Agent Sadowski happy. It didn't help her need to get moving, however.

"Sit down, Detective Gillette," Sadowski barked. "You're making me nervous."

"With all due respect, I need to get back to my job."

"I need some information," he retorted.

"Call 411," she said, and left the room in three long strides, knowing she would be reprimanded and not caring a whit.

Will lay on his back as long as he could stand it, then he flipped Gemma over and drove into her, feeling a little like he was living someone else's life. She threw back her head and moaned, her hands clasping the covers. She moved with him like an animal and when his heavy-lidded eyes searched for hers, he was faintly surprised to see her gazing at him in a predatory manner.

Danger . . .

But then her mouth opened and her throat arched and her body thrashed. "Uh . . . uh . . . come on . . . oh, come on . . ."

Will exploded inside her, his body stiffening as his thoughts skittered away, lost in sensation. He collapsed against her as her own orgasm went on and on, her fingers raking down his back till he was certain she'd drawn blood.

He lay on her, both of them gasping for air as if they'd run a marathon. Finally, he pulled away from her, his gaze studying her face as his emotions came back under control and he was able to think more clearly. He didn't know this Gemma and frankly, though he was physically excited by her, he wasn't sure he wanted to know this Gemma much better.

He rolled off the bed, intending to get his phone, but quick as lightning she jumped up and beat him to it. "No, no, no," she said. "Not yet."

"Gemma, I have to turn it on."

"You've been down less than half an hour. Wait a sec." She put a finger to her lips and stepped out of the room.

He started to follow her but she said, "Uh, uh. I'm coming right back."

Will grabbed up his boxers and jeans and pulled them on, catching sight of himself in the mirror. He lifted a hand and ran it through his own tousled hair and froze in the act. It was his right hand. He dropped it and did the same action with his left hand, watching himself. Left. Right. Left . . .

Realization dawned. He could see it in the reflection of his own stunned eyes.

Her scar. Gemma's scar. It had seemed slightly different to him but now he realized it was *on the wrong side.* Gemma's scar was on her right hip. Whomever he'd just made love to—correction, *had sex with*—had a scar on her left hip.

They weren't the same woman.

They were twins.

The scars were from some kind of surgery.

Separated twins.

Siamese twins.

This woman was not Gemma.

She reappeared in the doorway with silken ropes . . . and a .22 pointed directly at his heart.

"I'm sorry," she said. "I'm not this Gemma person and I knew you'd figure it out."

"You're her conjoined twin." His voice was dry, arid as the Sahara.

He saw the blood drain from her face, then quickly return, suffusing her cheeks with color. "Yes," she said, and he saw she'd realized it for the first time. "That's what the doctor did. That's why I was a gift."

"A gift?"

Her lip curled. "To a man who found me attractive at a—young—age."

Will's hands were up. "I'm not going to hurt you," he said, staring down at the gun.

"Yes, well, that remains to be seen."

"Gemma needs to know about you."

"She's not the only one who reads minds, you know. Emotions. You're trying to distract me so you can get away. You've figured out that I was the one who took care of Letton. And Bereth. And Kev."

"Kev?"

"Nobody should have to go through what I did. Nobody. They all deserved to die," she said tautly, then hitched her chin toward the bed. "You need to lie down."

"I can't." He kept his gaze trained steadily on her.

"I will shoot you," she said conversationally. "I don't want to hurt you, but I will. I can't have you going to find Gemma. I need some time to think."

"I'm not going to lie down."

To Will's shock she pulled the trigger.

Blam!

A bullet whizzed past his ear, nearly deafening him.

"Lie down," she said.

She meant what she said. She was a killer. Gemma's sister . . . "What's your name?"

She took a step toward him, the gun at his breast bone. "Lie down." Then she laid her palm on his chest and gave him a push. He sank to the bed. "I won't hurt her, and I don't want to hurt you. But I've got to figure this out."

He believed her. He also suspected that Barb was trying

to get hold of him, that if she didn't reach him soon she would come looking for him, that the first place she would start was his house.

He lay back and wondered if he could take the chance to overpower her. But there might be collateral damage. A stray bullet could kill either one of them, and he sensed she was telling the truth about just needing some time.

"Take this rope and tie your right wrist to the bedpost," she directed. Her eyes, so clear and wide, were like Gemma's and yet he knew he would be able to tell them apart from now on.

If there was a from now on.

Be smart, he told himself. *Rely on Barb.*

"Who are you thinking about?" she asked sharply. "Who is this woman? Not Gemma?"

"I'm thinking about staying still," he said as he clumsily looped the silken rope around his right wrist and tied it to the bedpost. The gun waggled around dangerously in front of him.

She tied his left wrist herself, tugging on the ropes hard, then checked and further tightened his right wrist. Will's circulation was constricted but the rope fabric was slick. He was certain he would be able to free himself in time.

It was the amount of time that mattered.

"If you hurt Gemma . . ." He couldn't finish the thought.

"I won't kill her as long as you stay here."

"I won't leave."

"Liar."

To his surprise she leaned into him, examining him closely. "You love her," she said, running a finger along his jaw. She then licked the line her finger had trailblazed. Will pulled back and she suddenly straddled him.

"I've just got to figure out what to do about you . . ." she whispered. "I haven't wanted a man in a long, long time, but I want you. You."

As if he were the mind reader, Will realized he'd underestimated the danger to Gemma. He hadn't counted on being the prize. Though this woman swore she just needed time to think, she was emotionally unstable and she could easily change her mind.

"Stay with me," he whispered.

"Nice try." She gave him a quick smile. "I'll be back."

And then she was gone.

Chapter Twenty-Two

Gemma walked out of the diner to her truck and Charlotte came flying at her heels. Her face was fraught with worry. "Who took Heather?" she demanded.

"Will's looking into it. And the FBI. We should know something soon."

"Is this because of Mr. Bereth?"

Gemma, who'd been thinking about Will and Tim and Heather and the diner, finally gave Charlotte all her attention. "No, of course not. This is something else."

"But you were following him. And that other guy was following you. Is that who this is?"

All the hairs on Gemma's arms felt like they were standing at attention at once. "Oh, no. That was . . ."

"Was what?" Charlotte demanded when Gemma trailed off into silence.

"It's two separate cases. And we don't know for certain where Heather is."

"Yeah?" Charlotte was skeptical.

"The authorities are on it. We just have to wait."

Gemma left with Charlotte staring after her, a line drawn between her brows. She picked up her cell to call Will when it rang in her hand. Not recognizing the number, she said cautiously, "Hello."

"Gemma LaPorte. This is Detective Gillette with the Winslow County Sheriff's Department. I'm looking for Detective Tanninger."

His partner. Barb. "Uh . . . he's not with me," she said. "I was going to call his cell phone."

"He's either out of range or it's turned off or the battery's dead. He's unreachable."

"I don't know what to tell you."

"Have you talked to him this afternoon?"

Her accusatory tone bothered Gemma a bit. "We're supposed to meet back at my house later."

"Where are you now?"

"In my truck. Leaving LuLu's," she answered coolly.

"Are you wearing a waitress uniform?"

The question came out of left field and Gemma couldn't miss the alarm in her voice. "No, I wasn't working today. Why?"

Detective Gillette made a strangled sound on her end of the wire. "Never mind. I'm letting the case infect me. Please have Will call me. Agent Sadowski wants to talk to him some more."

Gemma heard the click of the ended call.

What had she meant about the uniform?

Her cell phone rang in her hand and Gemma breathed a sigh of relief when she recognized Will's number. "You know your partner's trying to get hold of you?" she greeted him in exasperation. "She thought you'd run out of battery or something. Where are you?"

"I know where you live," a woman's voice responded. "If you want to see your lover again, you'll meet me there."

Gemma's lips parted. Who? The woman's voice. It was

like a razor, shearing through the walls she'd erected around her own memories.

Blood . . . surgery . . . and someone else. A doctor. Her mother. Totu.

"Who are you?" Gemma demanded, blocking her ears to the quaking in her own voice.

"Ani," the woman answered.

Gemma and Ani. Gemma-ani. Gemini.

She could hear her real mother sing-songing, telling her that she would be safe with her father's family. That Totu would care for her and that Ani would be in good hands with the doctor.

"My sister," Gemma said.

But the phone was dead. Will's phone. Her sister. Her twin sister had him under her power.

The showdown—the Armageddon—Gemma always knew was coming was with her own sister.

The wolf threw the dry sticks in the back of the truck on top of the witch-girl's dead body. They reached to the roof of the GemTop and filled the entire bed. He'd already packed up a few meager belongings, all that he could take with him. He had to leave this place, this graveyard. Today he would find Ani—the murderer—and tonight he would make his pyre and burn her and the witch-girl.

Then it would be done.

As much as he would be able to do.

A sharp breeze was blowing off the coast, cutting through his wool coat, blasting his cheeks. He tugged on his watch-cap, bringing it down further over his ears.

As Wolf slammed the back of the truck shut he heard the sound of tires crunching on gravel. Approaching tires. He froze and his face grew grim. He had no time for anything but his mission. He needed to leave the foothills near Deception Bay and head back over the Coast Range to Quarry.

He didn't want to turn around and even look at whoever had driven up his lane by mistake. Whoever it was wasn't looking for him.

So, it was with shock that he heard, "Bart!" from the driver of the older model Taurus wagon.

Slowly, he swiveled around, staring as Seth Bellarosso slammed out of the Taurus and headed his way, blowing on his fingers. Then Wolf was in motion. Quickly he strode to meet him. He couldn't have Seth getting too near his brother's truck, maybe catching a peek beneath the GemTop.

"What are you doing here?" Wolf demanded.

"You been taking my cars?" Seth fired right back. "A detective from the Winslow County Sheriff's Department showed up and they're impounding two of the vehicles. Said they thought a woman stole them and used them in crimes, but I got to thinking that maybe it was you."

"No."

"Easy vouched for you but Easy's dead."

"Ani killed him."

"I know, I know. And Easy said you killed your mother. Everybody's a murderer." Seth threw up his hands in disgust. "All I know is someone's been boosting my cars. And now the brown Chrysler's gone." He glanced around and waved an arm toward the truck. "Is Easy's truck the only vehicle here, Bart? Or will I find another one parked behind the house?"

"Go look," the wolf invited. It bugged him that Seth wouldn't call him Wolf. Bartholomew Haines had died about the same time as his brother Ezekiel.

But Seth was staring at him as if he'd said something important. Wolf ran his last words through his mind but there was nothing that made any sense.

"It's Ani," Seth said suddenly. "She took the cars. Your brother taught her how to be a car thief, didn't he? And the bitch took *my* cars."

A whiff of the witch-girl rose on the air. Wolf smelled it but pretended not to. His pulse beat slow and hard.

Seth grimaced. "Something dead around here."

"Yeah."

"You know where Ani is?" he demanded.

"No."

"I'm gonna call that detective and tell him who to look for. She's somewhere around the coast. Always turns up like a bad penny."

Seth slammed back into his Taurus and reversed with a roar down Wolf's driveway.

Ani wasn't at the coast. Ani was in Quarry. He'd found her at the diner but she'd followed that guy, drove her car into the ditch and wound up at the hospital. Then he'd lost her again when he'd killed the nurse-witch, but she was still there.

And she was driving a Chrysler sedan. He knew the car well.

If Quarry was where she lived, then Quarry was where she would die. The One. The true witch. In her little crisp dress with its white collar and her long, smooth legs and her ways of mewing and moaning to EZ. She'd strangled him with the lamp cord. He'd known it from the beginning. But she'd been elusive—had fooled the police—and he hadn't been ready to send her back to hell at that time anyway. He hadn't understood his mission completely then. He'd had to think. Remember. Listen to the witch-mother's harsh laughter as he lay on the bed and saw her face above him. *I only want your brother,* she said, smoke drifting from her curved lips.

Seth was after Ani.

Now Wolf bolted for his truck. Time to leave. Time to find

the witch who'd seduced his brother. Kill her. Kill her like he'd killed the mother-witch. Lash her to the burning pyre.

At the base of the quarry.

Barb called Will's cell for about the twentieth time. Finally it started ringing instead of going straight to voice mail. "Jesus, about time," she muttered. "Come on, come on."

The phone was answered. She could hear the connection. But no one spoke. "Will?" she asked. A moment later she was listening to dead air.

She grabbed up her purse, holstered her gun, put on her jacket. Her expression was grim when the sheriff suddenly popped his head in the door. She straightened, ready to take the heat for her earlier insubordination. "Amy Dunleavy called 911. Some woman came into their home and now Kevin Dunleavy's dead."

"How? Who?"

Nunce shook his head. "Shot with a small caliber."

Barb froze. "A .22? Like Spencer Bereth?"

"Maybe."

Fuckin' A, she thought. Gemma LaPorte. Gemma La Porte had killed Letton, Bereth, and now Kevin Dunleavy.

"She's a killer, sheriff," she said unsteadily. "And I can't get hold of Will."

A harsh line cleaved Nunce's forehead. "He's with her?"

"She said she was meeting him at her house. She could have been lying." Barb was in motion. "Maybe she's already there." She was almost out the door, but then she stopped herself. "Wait. I'll call her again. Will was at least smart enough to give over her phone numbers." With shaking fingers Barb tried the home phone first but it just rang and rang. She then pressed the buttons for Gemma's cell and was nearly bowled over when she answered again.

"Hello," Gemma said cautiously, her voice strained.

"Where are you?" Barb demanded, then quickly added, "This is Detective Gillette."

"Oh . . . I'm . . . going back to the diner."

"I thought you were meeting Will at your house."

"I don't know where he is," she blurted out fearfully. "Can you find him?"

Barb's eyes narrowed. "What happened?"

"I got a call on his cell . . . from a woman . . . I think she may be the one you're looking for . . . I think she has Will!"

Her delivery was halted. Like she was making it up. Barb couldn't tell what kind of game she was playing. "I'll meet you at the diner," she said.

A hesitation. "Okay."

Gemma was lying. She was heading to her house as fast as she could, the truck's engine roaring though the damn thing barely crested forty-five miles per hour. She didn't know what she expected from Ani, but she didn't want Will's partner in the way. She knew that wasn't going to work. She had to face Ani head on and hope she could reason with her.

If not . . . she wondered if she could kill her.

To save Will.

Will worked his wrists against the ropes, pulling hard, succeeding only in feeling them tighten. He set his jaw. What he really needed to do was release the pressure. Let the ties relax. If he could just slip his wrist down gently . . .

He closed his eyes and gently moved his left wrist. His captor had been so intent on making sure that the wrist he'd tied—the right one—was tightened down that his left had just been given more cursory attention. He tugged lightly. The silken rope edged up his thumb pad a tiny bit.

In time . . . in time . . .

But there was no time.

Relax. Be calm.

Get free . . .

Barb reviewed what Gemma had told her on her way to Quarry. She felt she was being manipulated. The last time she'd talked to Will he'd been on his way home. Gemma had told her they were meeting at her place, then those plans had changed.

Or had they?

Maybe Will was already there.

Or maybe Will was at his own home.

Or maybe Gemma had told the truth about going to the diner.

Eenie, meanie, miney, mo . . .

Barb chose Gemma LaPorte's home.

It was with a feeling of coming home that Ani drove the Chrysler into her hiding spot and walked down the long drive to the farmhouse where Gemma LaPorte lived. Gemma, who'd been saved by their Indian grandmother and then adopted out to the LaPortes. Her sister Gemma, who'd been loved and nurtured while Ani had been forced to forge a different path.

But they were the same. The detective—Will, as the voice on the phone had called him—said Gemma read minds—emotions—and Ani could as well. That's how she'd first sensed Letton's intentions. That's how she'd learned to avoid the doctor when he was getting in a "mood."

She resented the fact that Gemma had been loved. Still, they were sisters. Ani just wasn't sure what to expect from her.

Wouldn't it be great if they could just trade places? But

that would never happen while Gemma was alive. And Ani could never have Will for the same reason.

And Ani realized, also, that the gig was up. She couldn't go back to Seaside, or Deception Bay, where it all began. She would have to leave. Go far away after this. Will knew what she'd done. She'd told him. It was only a matter of time.

But if she was gone, then this would all fall on Gemma. Will could say there were two of them all he wanted, but no one would believe him. Why should they?

Or maybe they would. She wasn't sure.

But she knew if she was gone, then she wasn't with Will. She couldn't kidnap him forever. He would escape.

He and Gemma both might have to die, she thought with a pang.

But maybe she could keep Will for a while.

Just a little while.

Before she had to kill him, too.

Gemma slammed the truck up the lane, bumping along. The damn thing shimmied and shook like it was in its death throes, and the action brought her driver's window down about halfway on its own. A second later it fell in to the door and shattered as cold air reached in and lifted Gemma's hair. She shivered at the frigid air against her neck.

There was no other vehicle in sight. Gemma wondered if she was walking into some kind of trap. She was furious, her earlier fear crystallizing into anger. How dare this Ani kidnap Will. How dare she play with their lives like she'd been doing this past month! All the fears about her own culpability . . . all the energy wasted . . . she wanted to strangle this *sister.*

She slammed out of the truck and hurried up the back porch, letting herself inside cautiously, locking it behind her. The poker was back in its wrought-iron holder and she hurried to the living room and snatched it up. Her weapon of choice, she thought with a twinge of self-awareness. She hadn't run anyone down with a car. She hadn't shot anyone. She'd chased Bereth but had ended up in a ditch.

She toured the upstairs, holding the poker like a club. There was no one in the house as far as she could tell. Cautiously, she went back down the stairs. Glancing toward the front door she nearly fainted. A woman was looking inside.

Her own face.

The poker nearly fell from her nerveless fingers and she had to catch herself. Her head buzzed. She realized she was going to faint.

The woman outside rattled the door, pointing angrily for Gemma to open it. The fact that she wasn't some specter, that she really existed and wanted Gemma to let her in, added an odd normalcy that kept Gemma from passing out.

Wondering if she was opening Pandora's box, Gemma unlatched the door and stepped back.

And Ani walked through.

They stood in the living room silently, gauging each other. Gemma felt weird, but she thought she'd feel weirder. It was surreal, yet it was the showdown she'd been waiting for.

"Where's Will?" Gemma asked. "What have you done with him?"

"He's lying in bed where I left him." A corner of her mouth lifted. "Tied to the bedposts."

Her voice . . . it was slightly deeper than Gemma's. Smokier. "You kidnapped him."

"He invited me in. Thought I was you, of course. He was ripping off my clothes before I could introduce myself."

Gemma wanted to believe she was lying, but she could read Ani clearly. The picture that came to her mind made her slam the door on her thoughts. She couldn't breathe.

"Put that thing down," Ani said calmly.

Gemma didn't hear her. Didn't respond. She barely noticed that Ani was carrying a small handgun that was hanging at her side, held by loose fingers.

"You killed them all, didn't you?" She was surprised at how only mildly curious she sounded.

"I had to. I didn't really get that you were around. It kind of came to me later, like a bolt out of the blue. Was it like that for you?"

"When you called."

She nodded. "I like Will. I could fall in love with him. I didn't think I could love someone, but I don't know . . . maybe . . ." She took a deep breath and exhaled slowly. "Do you remember our mother?" she asked suddenly.

"No. Our real mother, you mean?" Gemma shook her head.

"She's crazy. Lives in Deception Bay. A psychic." Seeing Gemma's reaction, she said, "You do know her."

"No, it's just . . . my adoptive mother thought she was a psychic."

"Thought?" She frowned. "Oh, I see. She used you as her conduit. Huh. Maybe she wasn't as perfect a mother as I thought."

"She wasn't perfect," Gemma responded.

"She wasn't a child molester, though, was she?"

"No. . . ."

"My adoptive daddy was."

"Dr. Loman?" Gemma said without thinking.

"You know."

Gemma gazed at her helplessly. "Only through hypnosis. Only today."

"I just learned about you today." She gestured to Gemma's hip. "We were stuck together and our mother thought we were from the devil. She gave me to Loman and you to our grandmother, I think."

"Totu."

"That was her name?"

"It's what I called her. But she left me on a ferry and I was found and adopted out. I think . . ." Gemma said, delving back into the deepest recesses of her mind. "I think she wanted to keep with the old ways. Out of step with her family. And I scared them because I could predict things and they would happen."

"Mind reading." Ani leaned in close. "And maybe a bit more?"

Gemma gulped. "Maybe," she said, admitting it to herself for the first time.

There was a sound on the porch and they both whipped around. A woman stood there. In jacket and slacks. She peered through the window at the two of them and her mouth dropped open.

"Detective Gillette," Gemma realized aloud.

At that moment the detective pushed open the door, gun raised.

As if she'd expected it all along, Ani simply lifted her handgun and shot her.

Chapter Twenty-Three

Wolf kept a window rolled down even though the air felt like it was full of ice crystals. The witch-girl smelled. One day and she already gave off her evil odor. Proof that she needed to be sent back to hell and soon. Tonight.

He drove down the rutted track that led to the bottom of the quarry. Twice he had to get out and remove debris from the road. No one had been down this route in a long time. Good.

As soon as he reached the bottom, he feverishly pulled out all the sticks and the witch's body. He flung her into the bushes then began building his pyre. There were logs. Many of them, and he had a hatchet to cut them. He worked methodically and quickly and by the time night was drawing its curtain he was satisfied that it was good enough. He would come back when he had Ani. Then he would burn them both, but only one of them would be dead first.

Climbing back in his truck he sniffed the interior. Dead smell, but not as strong. Good. He threw it into gear and headed back up the track. Ani was in Quarry. He knew it.

All he had to do was cruise around for the brown Chrysler and she would be his.

"You shot her," Gemma gasped.

The detective lay unconscious on the floor, still breathing, but unevenly.

Ani looked stunned herself. "I didn't think I could do it. But she had a gun."

"You shot her!" Gemma repeated.

"It's all right. It's a .22. Just a little hole. She'll be fine."

Ani didn't sound sure, and in a wild moment Gemma dropped the poker with a clatter and jumped her. "Where's Will?" she shrieked. "Where's Will? Did you shoot him, too?"

Ani wasn't ready for Gemma's assault. The gun flew from her hand, skittered across the floor. She grabbed Gemma's hair and Gemma grabbed hers right back. They flung together as one against a wall. A picture turned crazily, the edge of the frame hitting Gemma just above the eye.

Then they were on the ground, rolling, huffing, screaming. Gemma had never fought anyone in her life but she was *furious.* She wanted to strangle her. Shake the truth from her. *Kill* her.

Ani kicked and thrashed and tried to throw a leg over her. Gemma parried with a knee to Ani's gut. She heard a satisfying, "Ooof!" but then Ani's hand was at her throat, squeezing till she couldn't breathe, couldn't get a thread of air.

"Stop," the detective's voice rasped.

Surprised, Ani's grip loosened and Gemma rolled away. Her hand encountered the gun. She scrambled for it as Ani jumped on her again, knocking her flat on her back. But Gemma had the gun. She held it between them as Ani straddled her, pushed it to Ani's gut.

"Don't . . ." Ani said.

They stared at each other, breathing heavily. A trickle of blood ran down Gemma's face from the wound at her hairline. Ani stared at her twin. Stared and stared. Slowly she raised her hands in surrender then rose to her feet.

Gemma's finger was on the trigger. Her hand was shaking like she had the palsy. This woman had killed Edward Letton and Spencer Bereth and God knew how many others. Had let Gemma nearly take the blame for it, whether by accident or design. She was a murderess. Her heart as cold as a snake's.

Yet . . .

She couldn't do it. She couldn't pull the trigger. She *couldn't*.

As Ani walked out the door Gemma reached for her cell phone, dialed 911, then knelt beside the woman on the floor whose eyes were open and full of pain. She kept her gaze away from the spreading pool of maroon blood.

Will, sweating, worked his thumb down under the rope. He contorted his arm and got a loop nearly over his finger.

"C'mon, c'mon, c'mon . . ."

And suddenly the hand slipped through as if it had been greased. Hurriedly, he yanked at the other rope, taking twice as much time freeing himself as he should. He was swearing like a truck driver. How long? How long?

An hour. Tops. Since she left. Maybe an hour and ten.

He yanked on a shirt and jacket, grabbed his keys and ran through a bitterly cold evening to his Jeep.

Ani climbed in the Chrysler, lost in memory and emotion and now a feeling of sheer discombobulation. Her mother—their mother—had given them up because they were the devil's seed, joined at the hip, touched by Satan. The doctor had muttered this story aloud when Ani was very young.

She wanted to lay her head down on a feather pillow and sleep for a millennium. Her mind raced uncomfortably. She didn't want to think back. Didn't want to remember. She was half-furious with Gemma that she'd forced her to.

The doctor had surgically separated them. Ani could vaguely remember the scent of some noxious odor. Ether, maybe. She could see the green mask and his eyes. And heard someone screaming. Gemma. Or maybe herself.

Recovery. And the sense of loss. No Gemma, she realized now.

And after all this time they'd been reunited but it was too late. Too late.

She was barely away from Quarry, headed west, toward the coast, though she shouldn't. They knew her there. They knew her in Seaside and even more so in Deception Bay. She hadn't been back to the small town where she was born since she'd killed the doctor. She hadn't wanted any foster homes. She'd wanted freedom.

She felt something on her face and reached up. Wetness. Dragging her hand away, she expected to find blood. She'd been hurt.

But it wasn't blood. It was tears.

Disturbed, she pulled over at the next pull-out. She left the car running, its lights on, and simply lay her arms over the steering wheel, pressing her forehead into it, squeezing her eyes closed. She had to think, and thinking felt impossible. She hoped to hell she hadn't seriously injured that woman detective. That wasn't part of her plan.

Rap, rap.

She nearly jumped out of her skin at the sound of someone tapping on her window. Her heart leapt. A cop?

But she thought the face behind the glass looked familiar. Rolling down the window, she asked, "Bart? What are you doing here?"

A meaty fist slammed into her face and she saw stars.

"I am the wolf," he growled.

Ani felt herself being dragged from the car. She saw the waiting truck. Ezekiel's truck? She wanted to ask him why he had his brother's vehicle but couldn't form the words.

A gale of wintry wind off the back of the mountains smacked her in the face, clearing her head. He had her by her feet, pulling her hard as sticks and rocks crawled under her jacket and scratched her skin.

Then his face was suddenly in front of hers. Nose to nose. Crazy, hate-filled eyes.

"You killed him!" he roared, nearly deafening her.

She prayed for traffic. Any car. If she could keep him from getting her in his truck someone would eventually come. Someone would see.

As if reading her thoughts, he threw her over his shoulder. She kicked and flailed and he tossed her as if she were a rag doll into the back of the truck, then grabbed her flailing wrists and lashed them together with electrical cord. That caught her attention just long enough for Bart to finish the job and slam the GemTop shut. It was dark, cold, and rank. She sniffed. There was fir and pine but something else. Something human.

Ani scrambled to the back of the GemTop as he threw the truck in gear and lurched forward. Her forehead smacked into metal. The impact, on top of the crushing blow from his fist, sent her down to the bed of the truck. Feebly she tried to twist her wrists against the electrical cords. She saw the depth of Bart's feelings now. She'd strangled EZ with the lamp's cord. She'd fooled the authorities but not EZ's brother. Bart wanted payback. She'd just never felt him mentally capable enough to harbor such resentment. Her mistake. And now she was paying for it.

She tried to reach for the latch to open the back of the truck. She couldn't find it. If she could just get it down. If she could just open it up.

But they were barreling fast. The movement banged her head up and down. She knew she was going to get sick and she turned her head and retched.

Where was he taking her?

Will drove up the drive to Gemma's, heedless of water-filled potholes and the waving arms of Scotch broom. He heard branches scrape his paint job. He saw only a mental image of Gemma and her sister.

If he was too late . . . if it was his fault for getting caught . . . for not escaping soon enough . . . for losing his cell phone . . .

"God, help me," he bit out through clenched teeth.

He stood on the brakes and slid the Jeep to a shuddering halt. A moment later he heard sirens. Approaching sirens. He waited a half-second then bolted for the front door. Those sirens were coming here. For Gemma!

He practically slammed the door off its hinges, barreling through. To his shock he saw Gemma on the floor, kneeling beside a prone Barbara Gillette, holding a pillow beneath Barb's head. Gemma looked his way and Barb's eyes swiveled dully.

"Will!" Gemma cried. Tears sprang to her eyes at the sight of him.

"Your sister did this?" he demanded.

"Ani."

"Ani? That's her name?"

Barb's eyes had closed. White and red lights and the wail of the siren overcame everything. Will touched Barb's forehead and her mouth twitched. He then looked at Gemma whose white face pronounced her worry.

The EMTs bustled inside. In quick order they lifted Barb onto a gurney and carried her to their van. "It's just my shoulder," she said weakly.

"I'll meet you at the hospital," Will told her.

She didn't seem to hear.

"We'll take good care of her," a familiar male voice told him as his partner slammed the van's doors.

Will looked up and met Billy Mendes's eyes. He nodded. Mendes jumped into the driver's side and they headed down the lane, sirens *woo-wooing,* lights strobing. Will and Gemma stood in relative silence until the ambulance was well away.

"She found you," Gemma said. "She went to your house?"

"She knew where I lived."

"You thought she was me." Will's dark eyes gazed deeply into Gemma's and she added, "She said you made love to each other."

Will's jaw worked. "I made love to you," he rasped.

Gemma nodded, tried not to care. She turned away but he caught her close and held her. She felt the sob that racked her body and she tried to hold it in but couldn't. She simply cried and let him hold her.

"I didn't kill anyone," she said on a sniff. "I told you so."

"I'm sorry I didn't know it wasn't you," he whispered. "I knew something was wrong, but—"

"No, don't. You couldn't have known."

"How did Barb get here?"

Gemma sighed and gave him a blow-by-blow of the events since Ani had left him and come to Gemma's. "She just came in the door and Ani shot her," Gemma finished, her voice hiccuping a bit.

"Do you know where Ani was going? What she was doing?"

"She said she thought she was falling in love with you. Maybe she went back to your place to be with you."

"Maybe." Reluctantly he released her from his embrace. "I've gotta get to the hospital."

"I'm coming with you."

He should have argued with her, he supposed, but he didn't know where Ani was and he didn't trust Gemma to be safe without him. With a nod, he led the way through the blustery night to his waiting, mud-splattered Cherokee.

Wolf thumped and bumped down the access road to the quarry. He was determined to get there before Ani could free herself from the back of the truck. And each time the wheels flew over some rock or limb he hoped that it caused her pain. He listened hard to hear if she cried or yelped or pleaded but apart from the sound of her body tossing around, she'd been eerily silent.

Witch.

At the base of the quarry he yanked the vehicle to a halt, jamming on the brake for maximum recoil. Her body slammed against the cab and Wolf smiled with satisfaction. But when he threw open the GemTop she was suddenly on him, clawing with hands lashed together. One fingernail hooked onto his eye and scraped.

Blinded, furious, he crushed her shoulders with his big hands and yanked her out, throwing her down like so much trash. She was kicking. Wouldn't quit. He saw her slim, jean-clad legs and narrow hips and threw himself on her. He would take her here. Fuck her like the whore she was. And then burn her at the stake.

Like he'd done to the mother-witch.

Feeling him upon her she suddenly went limp, her arms over her head. He gazed into her eyes, expecting fear. Instead he saw a glimmering seduction and it surprised and revolted him.

Then her arms came down together and pain exploded in his head. She had a rock and she was beating him. He wrested the rock from her and slammed it against her temple. She went instantly still.

Briefly he worried he'd killed her but when he leaned down, he caught the sounds of her shallow breathing.

After a moment he got up and began adding more limbs to the pyre. Dry ones that he'd pilfered from a woodpile under a shed roof of a home along the highway before he'd found Ani. Easily stolen. Needed to make his pyre grow to over ten feet. Everything was coming together beautifully. As if it had been planned by something bigger than himself. God, maybe.

He was on the right path.

Feeling self-satisfied, he grabbed up the witch-girl's body from where he'd flung it, wrinkling his nose at the stench. He lashed the body to the pyre with wire that he wrapped around the whole circumference for stabilization.

Then he added more and more wood while the whore who'd killed his brother lay in a crumpled heap on the ground. He thought about taking her right then but somewhere a voice entered his head.

"You've done good, Bart," it said. "Witches have to be burned. You had to kill the mother-witch and now you have to kill Ani. She deserves to die for what she did to me. Burn her, Bartholomew. *Burn her.* Then I'll have peace."

The wolf grabbed up armloads of branches, his strength renewed as he feverishly added to the pyre.

The ER waiting room was empty this night. Too early for the Saturday night accidents. Will paced outside the doors to the examining rooms where they were working on Barb. Gemma stood by the windows, staring into the parking lot where lights shined on the painted surfaces of vehicles and left fuzzy pools of illumination on the asphalt.

Nunce had shown up, looking rather disheveled for him. He kept smoothing a hand over the back of his head, but it was his wrinkled shirt and cockeyed collar that told the story of his hasty dressing. Will wanted to continually ask the hospital staff if Barb was going to be all right, but Nunce had taken over that job, so he was relegated to pacing.

Finally an ER doctor came through the doors and glanced around, focusing on both Will and Nunce. "She's in surgery," he said without preamble. "Bullet went into her shoulder and didn't exit. We're taking it out."

"She going to be all right?" Nunce asked.

"She's stable and strong. Nothing vital was hit. You can see her tomorrow." And then he stiff-armed his way back inside the closed doors.

"She's going to be all right," Will said, relieved.

Gemma, hearing the doctor's report, came to his side. "I'm so glad," she said on a hard swallow.

Nunce gave her a long look. He'd been told that Gemma's twin sister had shot Barb, but he seemed to still be having trouble believing Gemma was innocent of all charges.

"I'm going to take Gemma home," Will said. "Then I'm coming back to the hospital."

Nunce nodded. "Nothing to do till morning, but don't think either of us would sleep."

"You got that right."

Ani's head was crashing like waves pounding onto a shore. She felt strangely weightless. She couldn't move. Couldn't even open her eyes. With a tremendous effort, she lifted her lids to slits. It was dark. Night. Outdoors. And she was so uncomfortable.

Vaguely she realized she was strapped down. Onto something. She could smell damp wood and the stench of decay. Carefully, she moved her eyeballs to the right and she saw she was strapped onto a pile of wood. There was something there. Just to the right of her vision. A woman's arm. Someone else.

Understanding ran through her like a cold stream. This wood was going to be burned. She and the other woman were going to be burned.

Urgently she struggled against her bonds but she was held down fast. Her hands were strapped to her sides. Her torso and legs fastened tight to the hard limbs that dug into her back. Her head was free but it didn't help her.

She saw that electrical cord held her hands. A stretch of chicken wire covered her torso and legs. If she could get her hands free she might be able to wriggle out from underneath the wire. It was tight, but the branches behind her back, though hard, could be moved around a bit if she pressed on them with her body.

"There you are."

Her eyes shot to the man in front of her. They were eyeball to eyeball. Ani strapped to the pile of wood; Bart standing in his boots.

"What are you doing, Bart?" she asked him, pretending ignorance. "What are you doing?"

"You killed my brother."

"No."

He got in her face, his eyes black in the shadows and screamed, "You killed him! You took him, whore! I followed you. I found you at the hospital!"

"What?"

"I waited for you but . . ." He turned away, as if a thought had just struck him. "There was another witch. I burned her."

"I wasn't at a hospital," Ani said. She had to keep him talking. Had to. If he decided to touch a flame to this . . . pyre . . . she would be gone.

"Fucking liar!" he roared. "You followed that man. That unlucky man. And ran him off the road and you drove right into the ditch. I found you."

"I didn't drive in the ditch. I went to Carl's. Traded cars."

He jumped on her, wrapping his hands around her neck

until tears came to her eyes. Her head pounded. She was concussed. She was certain he was going to kill her right now.

"You filled EZ's head with all kinds of lies about how you were the same. Grew up near each other. Had bad experiences. He told me, and that's when I knew you had to die. You weren't the same. You're a witch."

"Like your mother," Ani said. "Ezekiel told me about you."

"You killed him!"

"He tried to rape me!" she spat. "So, I fought back. Strangled him to defend myself!"

The wolf threw himself away from her and screamed, slamming his hands over his ears. "Lies! Witch lies!"

Ani glanced at the other woman, wondering if she was listening, if she would help distract him. She pulled at her tethered hands.

And then she realized the other woman was dead.

Her heart filled with ice. This was going to be her funeral pyre.

Will turned the Cherokee into Gemma's drive. They'd hardly said ten words to each other on the drive back. There was too much to process. Too many jigsaw pieces that needed to be turned around and turned around until they fit into the entire puzzle.

And underneath it all Will couldn't escape the guilt he felt about sleeping with Ani. It was a small piece of the whole; he knew that. But it was vital. And though logic dictated he was innocent of betrayal, it didn't mean Gemma would understand emotionally. He wasn't even sure he did.

"I should have known," he said as they pulled up to the house.

"You couldn't have." Gemma didn't try to misunderstand. Her thoughts were obviously on the same path.

"I should have anyway."

"I blame her, not you."

Gemma threw open the passenger door and stepped out, closing her eyes and turning her face to the rustling wind. Faintly she smelled smoke.

"Will," she said urgently, eyes flying open.

He was still inside, getting ready to turn the vehicle around and head back to the hospital. "What?"

"Fire."

He practically leapt from the Jeep. The wind tossed the scent toward them. "Where's it coming from?" he demanded.

"West. But there's nothing there. Scrub brush. Until you get past the quarry to the woods."

"Past the quarry to Lover's Lane, then the woods," Will corrected.

"It's closer than that," Gemma said. She turned north, in the direction of the Dunleavys' property, thinking perhaps she was wrong. But there was nothing there.

"The quarry," Gemma said.

Will turned to frown at her. She could see his expression in the light from the headlamps. "Why?"

She was helpless to answer, to explain. Sometimes she just knew things.

"Get back in," Will commanded, and Gemma jumped into the passenger seat, slamming the door behind her as Will made a three-point-turn and blasted back up the drive and then ground gears, picking up speed on the highway.

"Wait. It's right here. The access road," Gemma declared. "Somewhere soon."

Will's headlights caught the spot between scrub brush. New tracks cut through the mud at the entry. Will turned in and bumped along, his headlights rocking in front of them.

But as bad as the road was, it was obvious someone had cleared off the worst of the debris to make it passable.

They saw the orange glow and smelled the hot smoke long before they got to the base of the quarry. Gemma gasped as they came into the clearing and there, in front of them, was a dark, cone-like mound that stretched to the sky, eager flames working from the bottom, a gleeful, building roar.

"Oh, my God," she murmured, a catch in her throat.

"There," Will said harshly, pointing. Ahead of them, an ape-like figure in a dark coat and watchcap barreled away from their headlights. A white truck with an opened Gem-Top and tailgate sat to one side.

Will cut the engine, grabbed his gun and leapt from the Cherokee, running as soon as he hit the ground. Gemma scrambled outside. "Stop!" Will yelled to the man, slowing down and lifting the gun with both hands. To Gemma's shock the man zigzagged and came back on Will, hitting him at the knees before Will could aim and fire. There was an *ooof* as they hit together. The man turned on him, slamming an elbow in Will's ribs and they tumbled forward and thrashed together on the ground.

The gun, Gemma thought. *Get the gun.*

"Help me!" came a thin cry above the growing, dull roar of the fire.

Desperately, Gemma whipped around. Who? Where?

The smell of burning flesh caught her up short.

Someone was being burned alive!

She screamed and ran toward the fire, eyes stinging with smoke. Out of the corner of her eye Will was still rolling around on the ground with the heavier man. She half-turned toward them, then saw the back side of the pyre and Ani lashed to the burning sticks. There was another body partially engulfed in flames. Burning. Searing. The cooked smell making Gemma's stomach revolt.

But Ani . . .

She charged forward, scrabbling at the thin cords tied around Ani's wrists. Electrical wire? She yanked and yanked. Heard wood crack above the sizzle and the dull rush of the fire. Then she was overcome by smoke. Her head swam and she staggered back, coughing, hacking, down on all fours.

She had to help Ani . . . Will . . . her sister . . . her lover . . .

The wind roared down in a spiral, sending sparks and smoke upward in a funnel. Gemma tried to get to her feet but couldn't breathe. Couldn't see. On all fours she crawled toward the pyre but the heat was intense.

"Ani," she shrieked, but a gale blew the words back into her throat along with ash and smoke. She turned away, coughing, forced backwards on hands and knees.

She thought she heard someone calling her name. "Will," she croaked. "Will!"

The inferno grew wilder and hotter. She remembered her cell phone and dragged it from her pocket. Dialed 911. Couldn't answer the dispatcher.

"Help. A fire," she tried, but the wind snatched her words, her voice.

And then hands were helping her to her feet. Male hands. Will's hands. She stumbled toward him and though she tried to walk he half-dragged her away. She buried her face in his coat. She was blind. Hot.

"Gemma," he murmured. "Gemma. God, are you all right? Gemma!"

She tried to nod. They were outside of the core of fire, thirty feet away before she could look up to give him assurance. She glanced around for the man Will had been wrestling with. The psycho-burner.

"He got away. Ran toward the fire." Will was shouting above the flames' roar.

"Ani . . . I tried . . ."

Suddenly the man was raging toward them, charging like

a bull, head down. Will pushed Gemma behind him. She screamed but no sound erupted. The man threw himself at Will hard and they hit the ground in a heap. "She's a witch!" he bellowed. "A witch. She killed him and he can't be saved until she *dies*!"

"Ani," Gemma whispered, turning toward the pyre. She couldn't see her sister from this angle. She could smell the searing flesh.

The man punched at Will, again and again, connecting with Will's arm, head, torso, as Will sought a stranglehold on him.

But the man in the watchcap was strong and determined. He smacked Will hard and clambered to his feet, turning his face to the sky, roaring like a wounded animal. "All witches must die! Die by fire. Sent back to the fires of hell!"

Gemma shrank back but he turned to her, his eyes mirroring the flames.

Then he charged straight for her, a beast backdropped by the unholy orange light of the inferno.

Chapter Twenty-Four

"Stop, or I'll shoot!" Will yelled harshly.

Her attacker didn't hear him. Didn't pay attention. Wild-eyed, he went after Gemma.

"You?" he muttered. "You!"

Gemma took an automatic step back. He charged her, grabbed her by the neck.

Blam. Blam.

She heard the shots, felt the man's body react. But he didn't stop. Grabbed her neck. Squeezing the life from her.

Blam.

Will was yelling. Yelling and yelling. Gemma saw spots in front of her eyes. Her fingers pried at his strong hands. Behind them the pyre was raging, and heat and smoke billowed out. Then Will was there, yanking the man back, warning him as he staggered away, sighting him down the gun which he held steadily between both hands.

"I'll kill you. I'll kill you. I'll kill you." The words were pouring from Will's mouth as he followed the man with his gun.

Gemma's hand was at her throat as she gulped air. She put out a hand—to what? Stop Will? Tell him to save Ani?

The staggering man went straight for the fire. To Gemma's horror, he threw himself on the hellish inferno. Will ran forward but the heat was intense. He struggled, bent his head against the onslaught of heat, but could not move forward and was forced to retreat.

Then he was back with Gemma, his arms surrounding her. She buried her face in his smoke-saturated jacket. Instantly, she pulled herself free. "Ani," she said. "She was on the pyre. Over there!"

She pointed a finger to the opposite side of the raging pyre but as she did, it collapsed backward. There was no missing the smell of roasted flesh. Gagging, she stumbled away and vomited into the underbrush over and over again.

When she tried to go back again to save her sister, Will held her tightly. "She's gone," he told her. "She's gone."

Gemma dug her hands into her own hair. "He killed her! He thought she was me. I was the one who worked at the diner. I was the one with the uniform."

"We don't know that."

"That's why he kills them," she cried.

"Gemma . . ."

"It's my fault," she said.

"You know that's not true." And then he held her close while she clung to him, her eyes burning from smoke and heat, her insides feeling sheared and torn.

She was still gripping him like a lifesaver when Will's calls for backup and to the fire department were answered and emergency vehicles came screaming into the quarry. It was becoming a much too familiar sight.

Gemma watched through dull eyes as water from tanks atop the fire truck was shot in frothy arcs onto the pyre. For all the searing heat and roaring destruction, it took only minutes to put the fire out because the flames, fed only by the scattered limbs of the pyre, had not jumped to the wetter surrounding flora. The fire's fuel was gone. Charred branches and small logs and ashes were left. And bone and flesh.

The fireman in charge came over to Will. "There appears to be two bodies."

Will nodded, but Gemma said, "No, there should be three. A man's and two women's."

"There's a man's body and a woman's," he said, then walked back to the other workers.

"Who's the third?" Will asked Gemma.

"There was a woman's body tied next to Ani's. A dead body, before the fire."

Will grimaced. "Ah. Heather Yates."

"So, where's Ani?"

They looked at each other. "Could she have gotten free?" Will asked her.

"I pulled on her wrists. They were tied with electrical cord. I might have gotten her hand free . . . maybe . . . But it was so hot!"

A car came barreling down the road, a latecomer. Will looked over, expecting backup. But the man charging their way brought a string of epithets to his lips. "Damn. He still has access. Musta picked it up on a scanner."

Gemma looked around, confused.

"Get outta here, Burl," Will said, striding to meet him.

The newcomer pointed a furious finger at Gemma, stabbing the air. "She killed Kevin! Shot him like a dog. Fuckin' crazies. Fuckin', fuckin' crazies!"

"It wasn't her," Will said. He placed both palms on Burl's chest and the older man shoved him aside, enraged.

"You don't have me fooled!" he screamed at Gemma, his stabbing finger nearly poking her nose. "You did it. And you've cast your spell over stupid Tanninger here. But I *know*!"

"So help me, Burl," Will warned tightly, "if you don't back off, I'll arrest you."

He whirled on Will. "Bastard."

"Bring it." Will's fists came up like a pugilist. "Bring it."

The man warred with his own cowardice. Gemma read him easily. In the end, he threw Will the finger and swore violently and stomped off.

"Pardon your French," Will yelled after him.

"What does that mean?" Gemma asked when he came back to her.

"Nothing. Come on. Let's get out of here. I gotta check on Barb and then I want a hot shower and some sleep."

"At my place?"

"If that's okay with you . . . ?"

She smiled and grabbed his soot-covered hand with her own.

Ani moved as if she were an old woman. She trekked back to the highway, forced to dodge into the underbrush at each new, approaching vehicle, crying out at the pain. The flesh on her back was burned. Her head felt like an aching stone on her neck. She hurt like she'd never hurt before.

When she reached the highway she was startled when a man suddenly appeared before her and she let out a short, stifled scream.

"Gemma," he said. "What happened to you?"

"Who are you?" she asked dully.

"It's me. Little Tim! You need some help? Let Tim help you."

Little Tim was not all that little, and he didn't seem like the brightest bulb, either. But salvation sometimes came in the oddest forms. "Can you help me get to my car? It's up the highway a ways."

"I don't drive. But my mom does."

"She has a car?"

"Uh-huh. You know she does."

"If you could get me the keys . . ."

"She wouldn't like that. She'll help you. She likes you. Not like me, though." He gave her a sly, sideways look. "I see into your soul."

Despite the fact she was almost passing out, Ani could see into his soul as well. He was feeling a kind of puppy-love mixed with sexual attraction toward Gemma. Well, she could work that for all it was worth. "Get me the keys and I'll kiss you like a man," she said.

His eyes got huge. "Come on!"

"How far is it?"

He pointed. "Just over there."

She didn't know if she could make it.

She had to make it.

Had to.

With everything she possessed she gritted her teeth and walked along the road, diving into the shrubbery when a car passed, which Tim thought was a great game, before marching steadily toward his home.

Two days later Will watched them wheel Barb toward him in the hospital lobby. She was pale and looked like she'd lost ten pounds, but there was a tautness to her jaw that read like someone was going to get one hell of a piece of her mind. She looked past Will and said, "So, where's your Siamese twin girlfriend? You sure as hell'll come up with a whopping fish story to clear her name."

The corner of his mouth lifted. "She's working at the diner."

"Really."

"And the politically correct term is conjoined twins."

"Of which the bad one got away."

Will shrugged.

"I wish I'd been there to see you take on Burl," she grumbled. "And I wish you'd knocked him flat."

"Me, too."

"How're you gonna find her?"

"Ani? I don't know."

At the hospital exit Barb climbed out of the wheelchair and got to her feet. "Nunce was hanging around like he thought he was getting an award."

"He was worried about you."

"Yeah? He spent all the time talking about you. How you should run for election. How the department needs you, blah, blah, blah." She gave him a look as he held the door for her, then sneered at his proffered hand. "I'm not an invalid. Any chance you'll go after that job?"

"I don't know what the hell I'm doing."

"Falling in lust. That's what you're doing, you bastard," she said without heat.

He laughed and Barb's lips quirked.

"So, who's the psycho-burner. Bartholomew what?"

"Bartholomew Haines," Will told her. They'd tracked down the license number of the truck and learned it belonged to a deceased man named Ezekiel Haines, who'd been employed at Carl's Automotive. A follow-up phone interview with Seth Bellarosso had given him an earful on both the brothers. Now he filled Barb in briefly on the relationship between Bart, Ezekiel, and Ani as far as Seth knew it. He finished with, "He thinks Bart was schizophrenic. Dimestore psychology, but something was way off with the guy. Rumor is, he killed their mother, a sometime prostitute around the town of Deception Bay. Tillamook County's digging up the land around her house. He called her a witch. His relationship with her seemed to set the stage for the rest. He carted the dead bodies around in his truck before he found where he wanted to . . . burn them."

"How long ago did the mom die?"

"About five years. I'm going to do a little research on my own. See if I can learn anything else."

"She wear a uniform, the mom?"

"She worked as a waitress some." He tried to help Barb into his Jeep but she slapped his hands away. Then her face drained of color and she had to hang on to the door. Will gave her his arm to lean on and she reluctantly accepted it.

Once they were both inside and Will had guided the Cherokee out of the parking lot, she said, "Too bad he's dead. He might've been able to give you some answers about himself and this Ani twin of Gemma's."

"I talked to one of the mechanics at Carl's, Rich Lachey. He had a lot to say about Bart, most of it just a bunch of badmouthing and supposition. But he said Bart's brother used to imply that he had a sexual relationship with the mother, and that Bart had killed her because of it. Also, Ani may or may not have been responsible for Ezekiel's death, but it looks like Bart blamed her either way."

"So, he focused on Ani but somehow got her confused with Gemma?"

Will had a flash of remembrance of Ani atop his body. Confused. Yes. Making love to Gemma the past few days had buried the images but they were still there, lurking, like a disease in remission.

"There was a lot of confusion," Will said. "Gemma followed Spencer Bereth out of LuLu's and ended up putting her mother's car in a ditch. Gemma's friend, Macie, who owns LuLu's, has a daughter who saw Bart then follow Gemma out of the diner at that same time. Looks like Bart thought

Gemma was Ani and he tracked her to the hospital, but then got sidetracked by Inga Selbourne."

"The uniform."

"He was unraveling. Have you heard Dr. Tremaine Rainfield's take on him?"

Barb snorted. "I didn't know he'd gotten involved. Publicity-monger."

"He's still pushing that multiple personality theory. Says Bart may have suffered from several personalities. Called himself Wolf, according to Lachey. Like that proves anything."

"Well, he was fixated on his mother."

"That's an Oedipal complex, not DID, or whatever the hell it's called now." Will made a sound of disgust. "Rainfield got his face on TV this morning, theorizing about Haines."

"Guess everybody got what they wanted." She looked out the passenger window. "So, are you going to the diner after you drop me off?"

"I'd invite you, but you look like death warmed over."

"If I felt better I'd kick your ass."

Will laughed and Barb chuckled, too. He threw her a glance, thinking that he didn't want the sheriff's job, but he was beginning to like the way things were working out with his partner.

Charlotte ran out of school at the sound of the bell, smack into Robbie Bereth, who was making a beeline for his bike. They both stopped short, staring at each other.

"I'm sorry about your dad," Charlotte blurted.

Robbie turned away. For a moment Charlotte thought he might be mad, but as he flung a leg over his bike she saw his mouth was quivering.

"You need any homework help?" she yelled after him.

"I'm good."

He slowed down, throwing a foot out to drag across the asphalt. Glancing back at her, he said, "I suck at math."

"I got an A plus on the last test."

He thought that over, then asked belligerently, "You gonna make me give you my bike?"

Charlotte glared at him. Boys were so dumb! "I never wanted *your* bike," she declared. "I was just mad. I was going to help you for free!"

"Why?"

"Because I was a butt-hole."

Her terminology brought a smile to his face. "You were a butt-hole," he agreed. Then he flung his leg back over the bike and peddled off, yelling, "Come over later, butt-hole."

Charlotte smiled in satisfaction. She didn't have to like Robbie much, but she could help him and maybe he'd get over the fact that she really had been pretty shitty to him.

"Charlotte?"

She started guiltily. She hoped she hadn't said that word out loud. Turning, she said, "Yes?" cautiously, to Penelope Messerlin's mom. Penelope was looking kind of worried that her mom was even talking to Charlotte.

"Would you like a ride? Penelope and I are going to LuLu's for some cobbler and ice cream."

Penelope's thin face looked pinched, like she was going to cry.

"I would love it," Charlotte said with a big grin. "Thank you very much!"

Gemma untied her apron and hung it up, glancing over at Milo, who tended to slide his gaze away ever since she'd predicted Shirl's pregnancy. She pressed her lips together. She was going to have to make some decisions about embracing her talents, or at least learning to accept them.

"You going home?" Macie asked. Today the eye shadow was an odd mauve color. Her face looked years older since the news about Heather had come through. They were all suffering a kind of depression that wouldn't lift.

"After Will stops by."

"I know what you're thinking," she said. "Sometimes I got the gift, too, y'know."

"Okay." Gemma smiled faintly.

"You're going to that little town on the coast and learning about your sister and you. And you want to find your momma. Your real one."

"Actually, I was deciding whether to see Davinia Noack and Allie Bolt. They've been hounding me."

"Same thing," Macie said. "Gotta figure out the past before you can face the future."

"Good thing you're not giving any readings."

Macie just waved her off. Gemma glanced over the heads of the few customers in the restaurant to the parking lot outside. The clouds were steel gray, threatening precipitation. She saw Will's Jeep Cherokee pull in and she waited for him to come in the door.

When he did, he brought a swirl of cold air with him and a dash of rain. She said, very clearly, "You're thinking about marrying me even though I'm a strange, psychic nutcase."

"Actually, I was thinking about peach cobbler."

Gemma's brows lifted. "Really."

He laughed. "You got it right the first time."

From the back of the kitchen Milo started laughing like he'd never stop. Macie joined him, the release of tension like a cool welcome breeze.

"The answer is yes, Detective Tanninger. But first . . ."

"A trip to Deception Bay."

Gemma nodded slowly. Maybe she would learn something more. Maybe she wouldn't.

But she had found Will.

And that was more than enough.